WATER SLEEPS

Tor Books by Glen Cook

The
Eighth Chronicle
of the
Black Company

WATER SLEEPS

Glen Cook

BOOK THREE
OF
GLITTERING STONE

A TOM DOHERTY ASSOCIATES BOOK / NEW YORK

WATER SLEEPS

Copyright © 1999 by Glen Cook

Edited by Patrick Nielsen Hayden

A Tor Book
Published by Tom Doherty Associates, Inc.
175 Fifth Avenue
New York, NY 10010

Tor Books on the World Wide Web:
http://www.tor.com

Tor® is a registered trademark of Tom Doherty
Associates, Inc.

Library of Congress Cataloging-in-Publication Data

Cook, Glen.
    Water sleeps / Glen Cook. — 1st ed.
        p.   cm. — (Chronicle of the Black
Company ; 8th) (Book of
    glittering stone ; 3)
    "A Tor book"—T.p. verso.
    ISBN 0-312-85909-0 (acid-free paper)
    I. Title. II. Series: Cook, Glen. Chronicle
of the Black Company; 8th.   III. Series: Cook,
Glen. Book of glittering stone ; 3rd.
    PS3553.05536W38   1999
    813'.54—dc21   T98-43786
                                       CIP

First Edition: March 1999

Printed in the United States of America

0 9 8 7 6 5 4 3 2 1

For John Ferraro
and all the wonderful
Ducklings, all in a row
It was a great
little party

I

In those days the Black Company did not exist. This I know because there were laws and decrees that told me so. But I did not feel entirely insubstantial.

The Company standard, its Captain and Lieutenant, its Standardbearer and all the men who had made the Company so terrible, had passed on, having been buried alive at the heart of a vast desert of stone. "Glittering stone," they whispered in the streets and alleys of Taglios, and "Gone to Khatovar," they proclaimed from on high, the mighty making what they had been so determined to prevent for so long over into a great triumph once the Radisha or Protector or somebody decided that people ought to believe that the Company had fulfilled its destiny.

Anyone old enough to remember the Company knew better. Only fifty people had ventured out onto that plain of glittering stone. Half of those people had not been Company. Only two of those fifty had returned to lie about what had happened. And a third who had come back to retail the truth had been killed in the Kiaulune wars, far away from the capital. But the deceits of Soulcatcher and Willow Swan fooled no one, then or now. People simply pretended to believe them because that was safer.

They might have asked why Mogaba needed five years to conquer a Company that had passed on, squandering thousands of young lives to bring the Kiaulune domains under the Radisha's rule and into the realm of the Protector's twisted truths. They might have mentioned that people claiming to be Black Company had held out in the fortress Overlook for years after that, until the Protector, Soulcatcher, finally became so impatient with their intransigence that she invested her own best sorceries in a two-year project that reduced that huge fortress to white powder, white rubble and white bones. They might have raised these points. But they remained silent instead. They were afraid. With cause, they were afraid.

The Taglian empire under the Protectorate is an empire of fear.

During the years of defiance, one unknown hero won Soulcatcher's eternal hatred by sabotaging the Shadowgate, the sole gateway to the glittering plain. Soulcatcher was the most powerful sorcerer alive. She might have become a Shadowmaster to eclipse those monsters the Company had pulled down during its earlier wars on Taglios' behalf. But with the Shadowgate sealed she could not conjure killer shadows more powerful than the few score she had controlled when she worked her treachery on the Company.

Oh, she *could* open the Shadowgate. One time. She did not know how to close it again, though. Meaning everything inside would be free to wriggle out and begin tormenting the world.

Meaning that for Soulcatcher, party to so few of the secrets, the choice must be all or very little. The end of the world or making do.

For the moment she is making do. And pursuing continuous researches. She is the Protector. Fear of her steeps the empire. There are no challenges to her terror. But even she knows this age of dark concord cannot endure.

Water sleeps.

In their homes, in the shadowed alleyways, in the city's ten thousand temples, nervous whispers never cease. *The Year of the Skulls. The Year of the Skulls.* It is an age when no gods die and those that sleep keep stirring restlessly.

In their homes, in the shadowed alleyways or fields of grain or in the sodden paddies, in the pastures and forests and tributary cities, should a comet be seen in the sky or should an unseasonable storm strew devastation or, particularly, if the earth should shake, they murmur, "Water sleeps." And they are afraid.

2

They call me Sleepy. I was withdrawn as a child, hiding from the horrors of my childhood inside the comfort and emotional safety of daydreams and nightmares. Any time I did not have to work, I went away in there to hide. The evil could not touch me there. I knew no safer place till the Black Company came to Jaicur.

My brothers accused me of sleeping all the time. They resented my ability to get away. They did not understand. They died without ever understanding. I slept on. I did not waken fully till I had been with the Company for several years.

I keep these Annals today. Somebody must and no one else can, though the Annalist title never devolved upon me formally.

There is precedent.

The books must be written. The truth must be recorded even if fate decrees that no man ever reads a word I write. The Annals are the soul of the Black Company. They recall that this is who we are. That this is who we were. That we persevere. And that treachery, as it ever has, failed to suck the last drop of our blood.

We no longer exist. The Protector tells us so. The Radisha swears it. Mogaba, that mighty general with his thousand dark honors, sneers at our memory and spits on our name. People in the streets declare us no more than an evil, haunting memory. But only Soulcatcher does not watch over both shoulders to see what might be gaining ground.

We are stubborn ghosts. We will not lie down. We will not cease to haunt them. We have done nothing for a long time but they remain afraid. Their guilt cannot stop whispering our name.

They *should* be afraid.

Somewhere in Taglios, every day, a message appears upon a wall, written in chalk or paint or even animal blood. Just a gentle reminder: *Water Sleeps.*

Everyone knows what that means. They whisper it, aware that there is an enemy out there more restless than running water. An enemy who will, somehow, someday, lurch forth from the mouth of his grave and come for those who played at betrayal. They know no power that can prevent it. They were warned ten thousand times before they gave in to temptation. No evil can preserve them.

Mogaba is afraid.

Radisha is afraid.

Willow Swan is so afraid he barely functions, like the wizard Smoke before him, whom he indicted and tormented for his cowardice. Swan knew the Company of old, in the north, before anyone here recognized it as more than a dark memory of ancient terror. The years have seen no calluses form on Swan's fear.

Purohita Drupada is afraid.

Inspector-General Gokhale is afraid.

Only the Protector is not afraid. Soulcatcher fears nothing. Soulcatcher does not care. She mocks and defies the demon. She is mad. She will laugh and be entertained while being consumed by fire.

Her lack of fear leaves her henchmen that much more troubled. They know she will drive them before her, into the grinding jaws of destiny.

Occasionally a wall will carry another message, a more personal note: *All Their Days Are Numbered.*

I am in the streets every day, either going to work, going to spy, listening, capturing rumors or launching new ones within the anonymity of *Chor Bagan*, the Thieves' Garden even the Greys have not yet been able to extirpate. I used to disguise myself as a prostitute but that proved to be too dangerous. There are people out there who make the Protector seem a paragon of sanity. It is the world's great good fortune that fate denies them the power to exercise the fullest depth and sweep of their psychoses.

Mostly I go around as a young man, the way I always did. Rootless young men are everywhere since the end of the wars.

The more bizarre the new rumor, the faster it explodes out of Chor Bagan and the more strongly it gnaws the nerves of our enemies. Always, always, Taglios must enjoy a sense of grim premonition. We must provide them their ration of omens, signs and portents.

The Protector hunts us in her more lucid moments but she never remains interested long. She cannot keep her attention fixed on anything. And why should she be concerned? We are dead. We no longer exist. She herself has declared that to be the reality. As Protector, she is the great arbiter of reality for the entire Taglian empire.

But: *Water Sleeps.*

3

In those days the spine of the Company was a woman who never formally joined, the witch Ky Sahra, wife of my predecessor as Annalist, Murgen, the Standardbearer. Ky Sahra was a clever woman with a will like sharp steel. Even Goblin and One-Eye deferred to her. She would not be intimidated, not even by her wicked old Uncle Doj. She feared the Protector, the Radisha and the Greys no more than she feared a cabbage. The malice of evils as great as the deadly cult of Deceivers, their messiah the Daughter of Night and their goddess Kina, intimidated Sahra not at all. She had looked into the heart of darkness. Its secrets inspired in her no dread. Only one thing made Sahra tremble.

Her mother, Ky Gota, was the incarnation of dissatisfaction and complaint. Her lamentations and reproaches were of such amazing potency that it seemed she must be an avatar of some cranky old diety as yet undiscovered by man.

Nobody loves Ky Gota except One-Eye. And even he calls her the Troll behind her back.

Sahra shuddered as her mother limped slowly through a room gone suddenly silent. We were not in power now. We had to use the same few rooms for everything. Only a short while ago this one had been filled with loafers, some Company, most of them employees of Banh Do Trang. We all stared at the old woman, willing her to hurry. Willing her to overlook this opportunity to socialize.

Old Do Trang, who was so feeble he was confined to a wheelchair, rolled over to Ky Gota, evidently hoping a show of concern would keep her moving.

Everyone always wanted Gota to go somewhere else.

This time his sacrifice worked. She had to be in a lot of discomfort, though, not to take time to harangue all who were younger than she.

Silence persisted till the old merchant returned. He owned the place and let us use it as our operational headquarters. He owed us nothing, but nevertheless, shared our danger out of love for Sahra. In all matters his thoughts had to be heard and his wishes had to be honored.

Do Trang was not gone long. He came back rolling wearily. The man behind the liver spots seemed so fragile it had to be a miracle that he could move his chair himself.

Ancient he was, but there was an irrepressible twinkle in his eyes. He nodded. He seldom had anything to say unless someone else said something incredibly stupid. He was a good man.

Sahra told us, "Everything is in place. Every phase and facet has been double-checked. Goblin and One-Eye are sober. It's time the Company speaks up." She glanced around, inviting comments.

I did not think it was time. But I had said my piece when I was planning this. And had been outvoted. I treated myself to a shrug of despair.

There being no new objections, Sahra said, "Start the first phase." She waved at her son. Tobo nodded and slipped out.

He was a skinny, scruffy, furtive youngster. He was Nyueng Bao, which meant he had to be a sneak and a thief. His every move had to be watched. In consequence he was so generally observed that no individual examined in detail what he actually did so long as his hands did not stray toward a dangling purse or some treasure in a vendor's stall. People did not look for what they did not expect to see.

The boy's hands stayed behind his back. While they were there, he was not considered a threat. He could not steal. No one noticed the small, discolored blobs he left on any wall he leaned against.

Gunni children stared. The boy looked so strange in his black pajama clothing. Gunni raise their children polite. Gunni are peaceable folk, in the main. Shadar children, though, are wrought of sterner stuff. They are more bold. Their religion has a warrior philosophy at its root. Some Shadar youths set out to harass the thief.

Of course he was a thief! He was Nyueng Bao. Everyone knew all Nyueng Bao were thieves.

Older Shadar called the youngsters off. The thief would be dealt with by those whose responsibility that was.

The Shadar religion has its streak of bureaucratic rectitude, too.

Even such a small commotion attracted official attention. Three tall, grey-clad, bearded Shadar peacekeepers wearing white turbans advanced through the press. They looked around constantly, intently, oblivious to the fact that they traveled in an island of open space. The streets of Taglios are packed, day and night, yet the masses always find room to shrink away from the Greys. The Greys are all men with hard eyes, seemingly chosen for their lack of patience and compassion.

Tobo drifted away, sliding through the mob like a black snake through swamp reeds. When the Greys inquired about the commotion, no one could describe him as anything but what prejudice led them to presume. A Nyueng Bao thief. And there was a plague of those in Taglios. These days the capital city boasted plenty of every kind of outlander imaginable. Every layabout and lackwit and sharpster from the length and breadth of the empire was migrating to the city. The population had tripled in a generation. But for the cruel efficiencies of the Greys, Taglios would have become a chaotic, murderous sink, a hellfire fueled by poverty and despair.

Poverty and despair existed in plentitude but the Palace did not let any disorder take root. The Palace was good at ferreting out secrets. Criminal careers tended to be short. As did the lives of most who sought to conspire against the Radisha or the Protector. Particularly against the Protector, who did not concern herself deeply with the sanctity of anyone else's skin.

In times past, intrigue and conspiracy had been a miasmatic plague afflicting every life in Taglios. There was little of that anymore. The Protector did not approve. Most Taglians were eager to win the Protector's approval. Even the priesthoods avoided attracting Soulcatcher's evil eye.

At some point the boy's black clothing came off, leaving him in the Gunni-style loincloth he had worn underneath. Now he looked like any other youngster, though with a slightly jaundiced cast of skin. He was safe. He had grown up in Taglios. He had no accent to give him away.

4

It was the waiting time, the stillness, the doing nothing that there is so much of before any serious action. I was out of practice. I could not lean back and play tonk or just watch while One-Eye and Goblin tried to cheat each other. And I had writer's cramp, so could not work on my Annals.

"Tobo!" I called. "You want to go see it happen?"

Tobo was fourteen. He was the youngest of us. He grew up in the Black Company. He had a full measure of youth's exuberance and impatience and overconfidence in his own immortality and divine exemption from retribution. He enjoyed his assignments on behalf of the Company. He was not quite sure he believed in his father. He never knew the man. We tried hard to keep him from becoming any-one's spoiled baby. But Goblin insisted on treating him like a favorite son. He was trying to tutor the boy.

Goblin's command of written Taglian was more limited than he would admit. There are a hundred characters in the everyday vulgate and forty more reserved to the priests, who write in the High Mode, which is almost a second unspoken, formal language. I use a mixture recording these Annals.

Once Tobo could read, "Uncle" Goblin made him do all his read-ing for him, aloud.

"Could I do some more buttons, Sleepy? Mom thinks more would get more attention in the Palace."

I was surprised he talked to her that long. Boys his age are surly at best. He was rude to his mother all the time. He would have been ruder and more defiant still if he had not been blessed with so many "uncles" who would not tolerate that stuff. Naturally, Tobo saw all that as a grand conspiracy of adults. Publicly. In private, he was amenable to reason. Occasionally. When approached delicately by someone who was not his mother.

"Maybe a few. But it's going to get dark soon. And then the show will start."

"What'll we go as? I don't like it when you're a whore."

"We'll be street orphans." Though that had its risks, too. We could get caught by a press gang and forced into Mogaba's army. His soldiers, these days, are little better than slaves, subject to a savage discipline. Many are petty criminals given an option of rough justice or enlistment. The rest are children of poverty with nowhere else to go. Which was the standard of professional armies men like Murgen saw in the far north, long before my time.

"Why do you worry so much about disguises?"

"If we never show the same face twice, our enemies can't possibly know who they're looking for. Don't ever underestimate them. Espe-cially not the Protector. She's outwitted death itself more than once."

Tobo was not prepared to believe that or much else of our exotic history. Though not as bad as most, he was going through that stage where he knew everything worth knowing and nothing his elders said—particularly if it bore any vaguely educational hue—was worth hearing. He could not help that. It went with the age.

And I was my age and could not help saying things I knew would do no good. "It's in the Annals. Your father and the Captain didn't make up stories."

He did not want to believe that, either. I did not pursue it. Each of us must learn to respect the Annals in our own way, in our own time. The Company's diminished circumstance makes it difficult for anyone to grasp tradition. Only two Old Crew brothers both survived Soulcatcher's trap on the stone plain and the Kiaulune wars afterward. Goblin and One-Eye are haplessly inept at transmitting the Company mystique. One-Eye is too lazy and Goblin too inarticulate. And I was still practically an apprentice when the Old Crew ventured onto the plain in the Captain's quest for Khatovar. Which he did not find. Not the Khatovar he was looking for, anyway.

I am amazed. Before long I will be a twenty-year veteran. I was barely fourteen when Bucket took me under his wing. . . . But I was never like Tobo. At fourteen I was already ancient in pain. For years after Bucket rescued me, I grew younger. . . . "What?"

"I asked why you look so angry all of a sudden."

"I was remembering when I was fourteen."

"Girls have it so easy—" He shut up. His face drained. His northern ancestry became apparent. He was an arrogant and spoiled little puke but he did have brains enough to recognize it when he stepped into a nest of poisonous snakes.

I told him what he knew, not what he did not. "When I was fourteen, the Company and Nyueng Bao were trapped in Jaicur. Dejagore, they call it here." The rest does not matter anymore. The rest is safely in the past. "I almost never have nightmares now."

Tobo had heard more than he ever wanted to about Jaicur already. His mother and grandmother and Uncle Doj had been there, too.

"Goblin says we'll be impressed by these buttons," Tobo whispered. "They won't just make spooky lights, they'll prick somebody's conscience."

"That'll be unusual." Conscience was a rare commodity on either side of our dispute.

"You really knew my dad?" Tobo had heard stories all his life but lately wanted to know more. Murgen had begun to matter in a more than lip-service fashion.

I told him what I had told him before. "He was my boss. He taught me to read and write. He was a good man." I laughed weakly. "As good a man as belonging to the Black Company let him be."

Tobo stopped. He took a deep breath. He stared at a point in the dusk somewhere above my left shoulder. "Were you lovers?"

"No, Tobo. No. Friends. Almost. But definitely not that. He didn't know I was a woman till just before he left for the glittering plain. And I didn't know he knew till I read his Annals. Nobody knew. They thought I was a cute runt who just never got any bigger. I let them think that. I felt safer as one of the guys."

"Oh."

His tone was so neutral I had to wonder. "Why did you even ask?" Surely he had no reason to believe I had behaved differently before he knew me.

He shrugged. "I just wondered."

Something must have set him off. Possibly an "I wonder if . . ." from Goblin or One-Eye, say, while they were sampling some of their homemade elephant poison.

"I didn't ask. Did you put the buttons behind the shadow show?"

"That's what I was told to do."

A shadow show uses cutout puppets mounted on sticks. Some of their limbs are manipulated mechanically. A candle behind the puppets casts their shadows on a screen of white cloth. The puppeteer uses a variety of voices to tell his story as he maneuvers his puppets. If he is sufficiently entertaining, his audience will toss him a few coins.

This particular puppeteer had performed in the same place for more than a generation. He slept inside his stage setup. In so doing, he lived better than most of Taglios' floating population.

He was an informer. He was not beloved of the Black Company.

The story he told, as most were, was drawn from the myths. It sprang from the Khadi cycle. It involved a goddess with too many arms who kept devouring demons.

Of course it was the same demon puppet over and over. Kind of like real life, where the same demon comes back again and again.

Just a hint of color hung above the western rooftops.

There was an earsplitting squeal. People stopped to stare at a bright orange light. Glowing orange smoke wobbled up from behind the puppeteer's stand. Its strands wove the well-known emblem of the Black Company, a fanged skull with no lower jaw, exhaling flames. The scarlet fire in its left eye socket seemed to be a pupil that stared right down inside you, searching for the thing that you feared the most.

The smoke thing persisted only a few seconds. It rose about ten feet before it dispersed. It left a frightened silence. The air itself seemed to whisper, "Water sleeps."

Whine and flash. A second skull arose. This one was silver with a slightly bluish tint. It lasted longer and rose a dozen feet higher before it perished. It whispered, "My brother unforgiven."

"Here come the Greys!" exclaimed someone tall enough to see over the crowd. Being short makes it easy for me to disappear in groups but also makes it tough for me to see what is happening outside them.

The Greys are never far away. But they are helpless against this sort of thing. It can happen anywhere, any time, and has to happen before they can react. Our supposed ironclad rule is that perpetrators should never be nearby when the buttons speak. The Greys understand that. They just go through the motions. The Protector must be appeased. The little Shadar have to be fed.

"Now!" Tobo murmured as four Greys arrived. A shriek erupted from behind the puppeteer's stage. The puppeteer himself ran out, spun and leaned toward his stage, mouth wide open. There was a flash less bright but more persistent than its predecessors. The subsequent smoke image was more complex and lasted longer. It appeared to be a monster. The monster focused on the Shadar. One of the Greys mouthed the name "Niassi."

Niassi would be a major demon from Shadar mythology. A similar demon under another form of the name exists in Gunni belief.

Niassi was a chieftain of the inner circle of the most powerful demons. Shadar beliefs, being heretical Vehdna, include a posthumous, punitive Hell but also definitely include the possibility of a

Gunni-like Hell on earth, in life, managed by demons in Niassi's employ, laid on for the particularly wicked. Despite understanding that they were being taunted, the Greys were rocked. This was something new. This was an attack from an unanticipated and sensitive direction. And it came on top of ever more potent rumors associating the Greys with vile rites supposedly practiced by the Protector.

Children disappear. Reason suggests this is inevitable and unavoidable in a city so vast and overcrowded, even if there is not one evil man out there. Babies vanish by wandering off and getting lost. And horrible things do happen to good people. A clever, sick rumor can reassign the numb evil of chance to the premeditated malice of people no one ever trusted anyway.

Memory becomes selective.

We do not mind a bit lying about our enemies.

Tobo yelled something insulting. I started to pull him away, dragging him toward our den. Others began to curse and mock the Greys. Tobo threw a stone that hit a Grey's turban.

It was too dark for them to make out faces. They began to unlimber bamboo wands. The mood of the crowd turned ugly. I could not help but suspect that there was more to the devil display than had met the eye. I knew our tame wizards. And I knew that Taglians do not lose control easily. It takes a great deal of patience and self-control for so many people to live in such unnaturally tight proximity.

I looked around for crows, fluttering bats, or anything else that might be spies for the Protector. After nightfall all our risks soar. We cannot see what might be watching. I held onto Tobo's arm. "You shouldn't have done that. It's dark enough for shadows to be out."

He was not impressed. "Goblin will be happy. He spent a long time on that. And it worked perfectly."

The Greys blew whistles, summoning reinforcements.

A fourth button released its smoke ghost. We missed the show. I dragged Tobo through all the shadow traps between the excitement and our headquarters. He would be explaining to some uncles soon. Those for whom paranoia remains a way of life will be those who will be around to savor the Company's many revenges. Tobo needed more instruction. His behavior could have been exploited by a clever adversary.

5

S ahra summoned me as soon as we arrived, not to chastise me for letting Tobo take stupid risks but to observe as she launched her next move. It might be time Tobo walked into something that would scare some sense into him. Life underground is unforgiving. It seldom gives you more than one chance. Tobo had to understand that in his heart.

After Sahra grilled me about events outside, she made sure Goblin and One-Eye were acquainted with her displeasure, too. Tobo was not there to defend himself.

Goblin and One-Eye were not cowed. No forty-something slip of a lass could overawe those two antiques. Besides, they put Tobo up to half his mischief.

Sahra said, "I'll raise Murgen now." She seemed unsure about that. She had not consulted Murgen much recently. We all wondered why. She and Murgen were a genuine romantic love match straight out of legend, with all the appurtenances seen in the timeless stories, including gods defied, parents disappointed, desperate separations and reunions, intrigues by enemies and so forth. It remained only for one of them to go down into the realm of the dead to rescue the other. And Murgen was tucked away in a nice cold underground hell right now, courtesy of the mad sorceress Soulcatcher. He and all the Captured lived on, in stasis, beneath the plain of glittering stone, in a place and situation known to us only because Sahra could conjure Murgen's spirit.

Could the problem be the stasis? Sahra got a day older every day. Murgen did not. Had she begun to fear she would be older than his mother before we freed the Captured?

Sadly, after years of study, I realize that most history may really pivot on personal considerations like that, not on the pursuit of ideals dark or shining.

Long ago Murgen learned to leave his flesh while he slept. He retained some of that ability but, sadly, it was diminished by the supernatural constraints of his captivity. He could do nothing outside the cavern of the ancients without being summoned forth by Sahra—or, conceivably, chillingly, by any other necromancer who knew how to reach him.

Murgen's ghost was the ultimate spy. Outside our circle none but Soulcatcher could detect his presence. Murgen informed us of our enemies' every plot—those that we suspected strongly enough to ask Sahra to investigate. The process was cumbersome and limited but still, Murgen constituted our most potent weapon. We could not survive without him.

And Sahra was ever more reluctant to call him up.

God knows, it is hard to keep believing. Many of our brothers have lost their faith and have drifted away, vanishing into the chaos of the empire. Some may be rejuvenated once we have had a flashy success or two.

The years have been painful for Sahra. They cost her three children, an agony no loving parent should have to bear. She lost their father as well but suffered little by that deprivation. No one who remembered the man spoke well of him. She suffered with the rest of us during the siege of Jaicur.

Maybe Sahra—and the entire Nyueng Bao people—had angered Ghanghesha. Or maybe the god with the several elephant heads just enjoyed a cruel prank at the expense of his worshippers. Certainly Kina got a chuckle out of pulling lethal practical jokes on her devotees.

Goblin and One-Eye were not usually present when Sahra raised Murgen. She did not need their help. Her powers were narrow but strong, and those two could be a distraction even when they tried to behave.

Those antiques being there told me something unusual was afoot. And old they are, almost beyond reckoning. Their skills sustain them. One-Eye, if the Annals do not lie, is on the downhill side of two hundred. His youthful sidekick lags less than a century behind.

Neither is a big man. Which is being generous. Both are shorter than me. And never were taller, even long before they became dried-up old relics. Which was probably when they were about fifteen. I cannot imagine One-Eye ever having been anything but old. He must have been born old. And wearing the ugliest, filthiest black hat that ever existed.

Maybe One-Eye goes on forever because of the curse of that hat. Maybe the hat uses him as its steed and depends on him for its survival.

That crusty, stinking glob of felt rag will hit the nearest fire before One-Eye's corpse finishes bouncing. Everyone hates it.

Goblin, in particular, loathes that hat. He mentions it whenever he and One-Eye get into a squabble, which is about as often as they see one another.

One-Eye is small and black and wrinkled. Goblin is small and white and wrinkled. He has a face like a dried toad's.

One-Eye mentions that whenever they get into a squabble, which is about as often as there is an audience but nobody to get between them.

They strain to be on their best behavior around Sahra, though. The woman has a gift. She brings out the best in people. Except her mother. Though the Troll is much worse away from her daughter.

Lucky us, we do not see Ky Gota much. Her joints hurt her too bad. Tobo helps care for her, our cynical exploitation of his special immunity from her vitriol. She dotes on the boy—even if his father was foreign slime.

Sahra told me, "These two claim they've found a more effective way to materialize Murgen. So you can communicate directly." Usually Sahra had to talk for Murgen after she raised him up. I do not have a psychic ear.

I said, "If you bring him across strong enough so the rest of us can see and hear him, then Tobo ought to be here, too. He's suddenly got a lot of questions about his father."

Sahra peered at me oddly. I was saying something but she did not get what I meant.

"Boy ought to know his old man," One-Eye rasped. He stared at Goblin, waiting to be contradicted by a man who did not know his. That was their custom. Pick a fight and never mind trivia like facts or common sense. The debate about whether or not they were worth the trouble they caused went back for generations.

This time Goblin abstained. He would make his rebuttal when Sahra was not around to embarrass him with an appeal to reason.

Sahra nodded to One-Eye. "But first we have to see if your scheme really works."

One-Eye began to puff up. Somebody dared suggest that *his* sorcery needed field-testing? Come on! Forget the record! *This* time—

I told him, "Don't start."

Time had caught up with One-Eye. His memory was no longer

reliable. And lately he tended to nod off in the middle of things. Or to forget what had gotten him exercised when he roared off on a rant. Sometimes he ended up contradicting himself.

He was a shadow of the dried-up old relic he was when first I met him, though he got around under his own power still. But halfway through any journey, he was likely to forget where he was bound. Occasionally that was good, him being One-Eye, but mostly it was a pain. Tobo usually got the job of keeping him headed in the right direction when it mattered. One-Eye doted on the kid, too.

The little wizard's increasing fragility did make it easier to keep him inside, away from the temptations of the city. One moment of indiscretion could kill us all. And One-Eye never quite caught on to what it meant to be discreet.

Goblin chuckled as One-Eye subsided. I suggested, "Could you two concentrate on what you're supposed to be doing?" I was haunted by the dread that one day One-Eye would doze off in the midst of a deadly spell and leave us all up to our ears in demons or bloodsucking insects distraught about having been plucked from some swamp a thousand miles away. "This is important."

"It's always important," Goblin grumbled. "Even when it's just 'Goblin, give me a hand here, I'm too lazy to polish the silver myself,' they make it sound like the world's about to end. Always important? Hmmph!"

"I see you're in a good mood tonight."

"Gralk!"

One-Eye heaved himself out of his chair. Leaning on his cane, muttering unflattering remarks about me, he shuffled over to Sahra. He had forgotten I was female. He was less unpleasant when he remembered, though I expect no special treatment because of that unhappy chance of birth.

One-Eye became dangerous in a whole new way the day he adopted that cane. He used it to swat people. Or to trip them. He was always falling asleep between here and there but you never knew for sure if his nap was the real thing. That cane might dart out to tangle your legs if he was pretending.

The dread we all shared was that One-Eye would not last much longer. Without him, our chances to continue avoiding detection would plummet. Goblin would try hard but he was just one small-time wizard. Our situation offered work for more than two in their prime.

"Start, woman," One-Eye rasped. "Goblin, you worthless sack of beetle snot, would you get that stuff over here? I don't want to hang around here all night."

Sahra had had a table set up for them. She used no props herself. At a fixed time she would concentrate on Murgen. She usually made contact quickly. At her time of the month, when her sensitivity went down, she would sing in Nyueng Bao. Unlike some of my Company brothers, I have a poor ear for languages. Nyueng Bao mostly eludes me. Her songs seem to be lullabies. Unless the words have double meanings. Which is entirely possible. Uncle Doj talks in riddles all the time but insists he makes perfect sense if we would just listen.

Uncle Doj is not around much. Thank God. He has his own agenda—though even he does not seem clear on what that is anymore. The world keeps changing on him, not in ways he likes.

Goblin brought a sack of objects without challenging One-Eye's foul manners. He deferred to One-Eye more lately, if only for efficiency's sake. He wasted no time making his opinions known if work was not involved, though.

Even though they were cooperating, laying out their tools, they began bickering about the placement of every instrument. I wanted to paddle them like they were four-year-olds.

Sahra began singing. She had a beautiful voice. It should not have been buried this way. Strictly speaking, she was not employing necromancy. She was not laying an absolute compulsion on Murgen, nor was she conjuring his shade—Murgen was still alive out there. But his spirit could escape his tomb when summoned.

I wished the other Captured could be called up, too. Especially the Captain. We needed inspiration.

A cloud of dust formed slowly between Goblin and One-Eye, who stood on opposite sides of the table. No, it was not dust. Nor was it smoke. I stuck a finger in, tasted. That was a fine, cool, water mist. Goblin told Sahra, "We're ready."

She changed tone. She began to sound almost wheedling. I could pick out even fewer words.

Murgen's head materialized between the wizards, wavering like a reflection on a rippling pond. I was startled, not by the sorcery but by

Murgen's appearance. He looked just like I remembered him, without one new line in his face. None of the rest of us looked the same.

Sahra had begun to look something like her mother had back in Jaicur. Not as heavy. Not with the strange, rolling waddle caused by problems of the joints. But her beauty was going fast. In her, that had been a wonder, stretching on way past the usual early, swift-fading characteristic of Nyueng Bao women. She did not talk about it but it preyed upon her. She had her vanity. And she deserved it.

Time *is* the most wicked of all villains.

Murgen was not happy about being called up. I feared he suffered the malaise afflicting Sahra. He spoke. And I had no trouble hearing him, though his words were an ethereal whisper.

"I was dreaming. There is a place . . ." His irritation faded. Pale horror replaced it. And I knew he had been dreaming in the place of bones he described in his own Annals. "A white crow . . ." We had a problem indeed if he preferred a drift through Kina's dreamscapes to a glimpse of life.

Sahra told him, "We're ready to strike. The Radisha ordered the Privy Council convened just a little while ago. See what they're doing. Make sure Swan is there." Murgen faded from the mist. Sahra looked sad. Goblin and One-Eye began excoriating the Standard-bearer for running away.

"I saw him," I told them. "Perfectly. I heard him, too. Exactly like I always imagined a ghost would talk."

Grinning, Goblin told me, "That's because you hear what you expect to hear. You weren't really listening with your ears, you know."

One-Eye sneered. He never explained anything to anybody. Unless maybe to Gota if she caught him sneaking back in in the middle of the night. Then he would have a story as convoluted as the history of the Company itself.

Sounding like a woman pretending not to be bitter, Sahra said, "You can bring Tobo in. We know there won't be any explosions or fires, and you melted only two holes through the tabletop."

"A base canard!" One-Eye proclaimed. "That happened only because Frogface here—"

Sahra ignored him. "Tobo can record what Murgen has to say. So Sleepy can use it later. It's time for us to turn into other people. Send a messenger if Murgen finds out anything dangerous."

That was the plan. I was even less enthusiastic about it now. I wanted to stay and talk to my old friend. But this thing was bigger than a bull session. Bigger than finding out if Bucket was keeping well.

6

M urgen drifted through the Palace like a ghost. He found that thought vaguely amusing, though nothing made him laugh anymore. A decade and a half in the grave destroyed a man's sense of humor.

The rambling stone pile of the Palace never changed. Well, it got dustier. And it needed repairs ever more desperately. Credit that to Soulcatcher, who did not like having hordes of people underfoot. Most of the original vast professional staff had been dismissed and replaced by occasional casual labor.

The Palace crowned a sizable hill. Each ruler of Taglios, generation after generation, tagged on an addition, not because the room was needed but because that was a memorial tradition. Taglians joked that in another thousand years there would be no city, just endless square miles of Palace. Mostly in ruin.

The Radisha Drah, having accepted that her brother, the Prahbrindrah Drah, had been lost during the Shadowmaster wars, and galvanized by the threat of the Protector's displeasure, had proclaimed herself head of state. Traditionalists in the ecclesiastical community did not want a woman in the role, but the world knew this particular woman had been doing the job practically forever anyway. Her weaknesses existed mainly in the ambitions of her critics. Depending who did the pontificating, she had made one of two great mistakes. Or possibly both. One would be betraying the Black Company when it was a well-known fact that nobody ever profited from such treachery. And the other error, of particular popularity with the senior priests, would be that she had erred in employing the Black Company in the first place. The terror of the Shadowmasters being expunged in the interim, by agency of the Company, did not present a counterargument of any current merit.

Unhappy people shared the meeting chamber with the Radisha.

The eye automatically went to the Protector first. Soulcatcher looked exactly as she always had, slimly androgynous, yet sensual, in black leather, a black mask, a black helmet and black leather gloves. She occupied a seat slightly to the left of and behind the Radisha, within a curtain of shadow. She did not put herself forward but there was no doubt who made the ultimate decisions. Every hour of every day the Radisha found another reason to regret having let this particular camel shove her nose into the tent. The cost of having tried to get around fulfilling an unhappy promise to the Black Company was insupportable already. Surely, keeping her promises could not have been so painful. What possibly could have happened that would be worse than what she suffered now had she and her brother helped the Captain find the way to Khatovar?

At desks to either hand, facing one another from fifteen feet, stood scribes who struggled valiantly to record anything said. One group served the Radisha. The other was in Soulcatcher's employ. Once upon a time there had been disagreements after the fact about decisions made during a Privy Council meeting.

A table twelve feet long and four wide faced the two women. Four men sat behind its inadequate bulwark. Willow Swan was situated at the left end. His once-marvelous golden hair had gone grey and stringy. At higher elevations, it had grown extremely sparse. Swan was a foreigner. Swan was a bundle of nerves. Swan had a job he did not want but could not give up. Swan was riding the tiger.

Willow Swan headed up the Greys. In the public eye. In reality, he was barely a figurehead. If his mouth opened, the words that came out were pure Soulcatcher. Popular hatred deservedly belonging to the Protector settled upon Willow Swan instead.

Seated with Swan were three running-dog senior priests who owed their standing to the Protector's favor. They were small men in large jobs. Their presence at Council meetings was a matter of form. They would not take part in any actual debate, though they might receive instructions. Their function was to agree with and support Soulcatcher if she happened to speak. Significantly, all three represented Gunni cults. Though the Protector used the Greys to enforce her will, the Shadar had no voice in the Council. Neither did the Vehdna. That minority simmered continuously because Soulcatcher arrogated to herself much that properly applied only to God, the

Vehdna being hopelessly monotheistic and stubborn about keeping it that way.

Swan was a good man inside his fear. He spoke for the Shadar when he could.

There were two other men, of more significance, present. They were positioned behind tall desks located back of the table. They perched atop tall stools and peered down at everyone like a pair of lean old vultures. Both antedated the coming of the Protector, who had not yet found a suitable excuse for getting rid of either, though they irritated her frequently.

The right-hand desk belonged to the Inspector-General of the Records, Chandra Gokhale. His was a deceptive title. He was no glorified clerk. He controlled finances and most public works. He was ancient, hairless, lean as a snake and twice as mean. He owed his appointment to the Radisha's father. Until the latter days of the Shadowmaster wars, his office had been a minor one. The wars caused that office's influence and power to expand. And Chandra Gokhale was never shy about snatching at any strand of bureaucratic power that came within reach. He was a staunch supporter of the Radisha and a steadfast enemy of the Black Company. He was also the sort of weasel who would change all that in an instant if he saw sufficient advantage in so doing.

The man behind the desk on the left was more sinister. Arjana Drupada was a priest of Rhavi-Lemna's cult but there was not one ounce of brotherly love in the man. His official title was Purohita, which meant, more or less, that he was the Royal Chaplain. In actuality, he was the true voice of the priesthoods at court. They had forced him upon the Radisha at a time she was making desperate concessions in order to gain support. Like Gokhale, Drupada was more interested in control than he was in doing what was best for Taglios. But he was not an entirely cynical manipulator. His frequent moral bulls got up the Protector's nose more often even than the constant, quibbling financial caveats of the Inspector-General. Physically, Drupada was known for his shock of wild white hair. That clung to his head like a mad haystack, the good offices of a comb being completely unfamiliar.

Only Gokhale and Drupada seemed unaware that their days had to be numbered. The Protector of All the Taglias was not enamored of them at all.

The final member of the Council was absent. Which was not unusual. The Great General, Mogaba, preferred to be in the field, harrying those designated as his enemies. He viewed the infighting in the Palace with revulsion.

None of which mattered at the moment. There had been Incidents. There were Witnesses to be Brought Forward. The Protector was not pleased.

Willow Swan rose. He beckoned a Grey sergeant out of the gloom behind the two old men. "Ghopal Singh." Nobody remarked on the unusual name. Possibly he was a convert. Stranger things were happening. "Singh's patrol watches an area immediately outside the Palace, on the north side. This afternoon one of his patrolmen discovered a prayer wheel mounted on one of the memorial posts in front of the north entrance. Twelve copies of this sutra were attached to the arms of the wheel."

Swan made a show of turning a small paper card so the light would fall upon the writing there. The lettering appeared to be in the ecclesiastical style. Swan failed to appreciate his own ignorance of Taglian letters, though. He was holding the card inverted. He did not, however, make any mistakes when he reported what the prayer card had to say.

"*Rajadharma*. The Duty of Kings. Know you: Kingship is a trust. The King is the most exalted and conscientious servant of the people."

Swan did not recognize the verse. It was so ancient that some scholars attributed it to one or another of the Lords of Light in the time when the gods still handed down laws to the fathers of men. But the Radisha Drah knew it. The Purohita knew it. Someone outside the Palace had leveled a chiding finger.

Soulcatcher understood it, too. Its object, she said, "Only a Bhodi monk would presume to chastise this house. And they are very few." That pacifistic, moralistic cult was young and still very small. And it had suffered during the war years almost as terribly as had the followers of Kina. The Bhodi refused to defend themselves. "I want the man who did this." The voice she used was that of a quarrelsome old man.

"Uh . . ." Swan said. It was not wise to argue with the Protector but that was an assignment beyond the capacities of the Greys.

Among Soulcatcher's more frightening characteristics was her seeming ability to read minds. She could not, really, but never insisted that she could not. In this instance she found it convenient to let people believe what they wanted. She told Swan, "Being Bhodi, he will surrender himself. No search will be necessary."

"Hunh?"

"There is a tree, sometimes called the Bhodi Tree, in the village of Semchi. It is a very old and highly honored tree. The Bhodi Enlightened One made his reputation loafing in the shade of this tree. The Bhodi consider it their most holy shrine. Tell them I will make kindling wood out of the Bhodi Tree unless the man who rigged that prayer wheel reports to me. Soon." Soulcatcher employed the voice of a petty, vindictive old woman.

Murgen made a mental note to send Sahra a suggestion that the guilty man be prevented from reaching the Protector. Destruction of a major holy place would create thousands of new enemies for Soulcatcher.

Willow Swan started to speak but Soulcatcher interrupted.

"I do not care if they hate me, Swan. I care that they do what I tell them to do when I tell them to do it. The Bhodi will not raise a fist against me, anyway. That would put a stain on their kharma."

A cynical woman, the Protector.

"Get on with it, Swan."

Swan sighed. "Several more of those smoke shows appeared tonight. One was much bigger than any seen before. Once again the Black Company sigil was part of all of them." He brought forward another Shadar witness, who told of being stoned by the mob but did not mention the demon Niassi.

The news was no surprise. It was one of the reasons the Council had been convened. With no real passion, the Radisha demanded, "How could that happen? Why can't you stop it? You have men on every street corner. Chandra?" She appealed to the man who knew just how much it cost to put all those Greys out there.

Gokhale inclined his head imperially.

As long as the Radisha did the questioning, Swan's nerve stood up. She could not hurt him in ways he had not been hurt before. Not the way the Protector could. He asked, "Have you been out there? You should disguise yourself and go. Like Saragoz in the fairy tale. Every street is clogged with people. Thousands sleep where others have to walk over them. Breezeways and alleyways are choked with human waste. Sometimes the press is so thick you could murder somebody ten feet from one of my men and never be noticed. The people playing these games aren't stupid. If they're really Company survivors, they're especially not stupid. They've already survived everything ever thrown at them. They're using the crowds for cover exactly the way they'd use the rocks and trees and bushes out in the countryside. They don't wear uniforms. They don't stand out. They're not outlanders anymore. If you really want to nail them, put out a proclamation saying they all have to wear funny red hats." Swan's nerve had peaked high. That was not directed at the Radisha. Soulcatcher, speaking through her, had issued several proclamations memorable for their absurdity. "Being steeped in Company doctrine, they wouldn't be anywhere around when the smoke emblems actually formed. So far, we haven't even figured out where they come from."

Soulcatcher unleashed a deep-throated grunt. It said she doubted that Swan could figure out much of anything. His nerve guttered like a dying lamp. He began to sweat. He knew he walked a tightrope with the madwoman. He was tolerated like a naughty pet for reasons clear only to the sorceress, who sometimes did things for no better reason than a momentary whim. Which could reverse itself an instant later.

He could be replaced. Others had been. Soulcatcher did not care about facts, insurmountable obstacles or mere difficulties. She cared about results.

Swan offered, "On the plus side there's no evidence, even from our most eager informants, that suggests this activity is anything but a low-grade nuisance. Even if Black Company survivors are behind it—and even with tonight's escalation."

Soulcatcher said, "They'll *never* be anything but a nuisance." Her voice was that of a plucky teenage girl. "They're going through the motions. They lost heart when I buried all their leaders." That was all spoken in a powerful male voice, by someone accustomed to unquestioning obedience. But those words amounted to an oblique admission that Company members might, after all, still be alive, and the final few words included in a rising inflection betraying potential uncertainty. There were questions about what had happened on the plain of glittering stone that Soulcatcher herself could not answer. "I'll worry when they call them back from the dead."

She did not know.

In truth, little had gone according to anyone's plan out there. Her escape, with Swan, had been pure luck. But Soulcatcher was the sort who believed Fortune's bright countenance was her born due.

"Probably true. And only marginally significant if I understood your summons."

"There are Other Forces Afoot," Soulcatcher said. This voice was a sybil's, rife with portent.

"The Deceivers have been heard from," the Radisha announced, causing a general startle reaction that included the disembodied spy. "Lately we've had reports from Dejagore, Meldermhai, Ghoja and Danjil about men having been slain in classic Strangler fashion."

Swan had recovered. "In classic Strangler work, only the killers know that it happened. They aren't assassins. The bodies would go through their religious rites and be buried in some holy place."

The Radisha ignored his remarks. "Today there was a strangling here. In Taglios. Perhule Khoji was the victim. He died in a joy house, an institution specializing in young girls. Such places aren't supposed to exist anymore, yet they persist." That was an accusation. The Greys were charged with crushing that sort of exploitation. But the Greys worked for the Protector and the Protector did not care. "I gather that anything you can imagine can still be found for sale."

Some people blamed a national moral collapse on the Black Company. Others blamed the ruling family. A few even blamed the Protector. Fault did not matter, nor did the fact that most of the nastier evils had existed almost since the first mud hut went up alongside the river. Taglios *had* changed. And desperate people will do what they must to survive. Only a fool would expect the results to be pretty.

Swan asked, "Who was this Perhule Khoji?" He glared over his shoulder. He had a scribe of his own recording the meeting back there in the darkness. Plainly, he wondered why the Radisha was familiar with this particular murder when he was not. "Sounds like the guy got something he had coming. You sure it wasn't just his adventure with the little girls gone bad?"

"Quite possibly Khoji did deserve what happened," the Radisha said with bitter sarcasm. "He was Vehdna, so he'll be talking it over with his god about now, I would imagine. His morals don't interest us, Swan. His position does. He was one of the Inspector-General's leading assistants. He collected taxes in the Checca and east water-front areas. His death will cause problems for months. His areas were some of our best revenue producers."

"Maybe somebody who owed—"

"His child companion survived. And he did call for help. The sort of men who handle troublemakers in those places arrived while it was happening. Stranglers did it. It was an initiation killing. The Strangler candidate was inept. Nevertheless, with the help of his arm-holders, he managed to break Khoji's neck."

"So they were captured."

"No. The one they call Daughter of Night was there. Overseeing the initiation."

So the strong-arm guys would have been scared witless once they recognized her. No Gunni or Shadar wanted to believe the Daughter of Night was just a nasty young woman, not a mythic figure. Few Taglians of those religions would find the courage to interfere with her.

"All right," Swan conceded. "That would mean real Stranglers. But how did they recognize the Daughter of Night?"

Exasperated, Soulcatcher snapped, "She told them who she was, you ninny! 'I am the Daughter of Night. I am the Child of Darkness Forthcoming. Come to my mother or become prey for the beasts of devastation in the Year of the Skulls.' Typically portentous stuff." Soulcatcher's voice had become the mid-range monotone of an educated skeptic. "Not to mention that she was vampire-white and a prettier duplicate of my sister as a child."

The Daughter of Night feared no one and nothing. She knew that her spiritual parent, Kina the Destroyer, the Dark Mother, would shelter her—even though that goddess had stirred not at all for more than a decade. Rumors about the Daughter of Night had run through the underside of society for years. A lot of people believed she was what she claimed. Which only added to her power over the popular imagination.

Another rumor, losing currency with time, credited the Black Company with having forestalled Kina's Year of the Skulls back about the time the Taglian state chose to betray its hired protectors.

The Deceivers and Company alike had a psychological strength vastly exceeding their numbers. Being social ghosts made both groups more frightening.

What signified most was that the Daughter of Night had come to Taglios itself. And that she had shown herself publicly. And where the Daughter of Night went, the chieftain of all Deceivers, the living legend, the living saint of the Stranglers, Narayan Singh, surely followed like a faithful jackal and worked his evils, too.

Murgen considered aborting his mission to warn Sahra to call everything off till this news could be assessed. But it would be too late to stop everything now, whatever else was happening.

Narayan Singh was the most hated enemy of the Black Company still standing upright. Not Mogaba, nor even Soulcatcher, who was an old, old adversary, were as eagerly hunted as was Narayan Singh. Nor did Singh harbor any love for the Company. He had gotten himself caught once. And had spent a long time being made uncomfortable by people overburdened with malice. He had debts he would love to collect, should it please his goddess to permit that.

The Privy Council, as was customary, degenerated into nagging and finger-pointing soon afterward, with the Purohita and Inspector-General both maneuvering to get a rung up on one another, and maybe on Swan. The Purohita could count on the backing of the three tame priests—unless Soulcatcher had other ideas. The Inspector-General usually enjoyed the support of the Radisha.

These squabbles were generally prolonged but trivial, more symbol than substance. The Protector would let nothing she disapproved of come out of them.

As Murgen started to leave, his presence never having been detected, two Royal Guards rushed into the chamber. They headed for Willow Swan, though he was not their captain. Perhaps their news was something they did not care to share with the unpredictable Protector, their official commander. Swan listened for a moment, then slammed a fist onto the tabletop. "Damn it! I knew it had to be more than a nuisance." He bulled past the Purohita, giving the man a look of contempt. There was no love lost there.

It has started already, Murgen thought. Back to Do Trang's warehouse, then. He could prevent nothing already in motion, but he could get word to those still at headquarters so they could get after Narayan and the Daughter of Night as soon as possible.

7

Sahra changed faces as easily as an actor swaps masks. Sometimes she was the cruel, cunning, coldly calculating necromancer who conspired with the Captured. Sometimes she was just the near-widow of the Standardbearer and official Annalist of the Company. Sometimes she was just Tobo's doting mother. And whenever she went out into the city, she was Minh Subredil, another being entirely.

Minh Subredil was an outcast, the half-breed by-blow of a priest of Khusa and a Nyueng Bao whore. Minh Subredil knew more about her antecedents than did half the people on the streets of Taglios. She talked to herself about them all the time. She would tell anyone she could trap into listening.

Minh Subredil was a woman so pathetic, so shunned by fortune, that she was an old, bent thing decades before her time. Her signature, which made her recognizable to people who never had encountered her, was the small statue of Ghanghesha she carried everywhere. Ghanghesha, who was the god in charge of good luck in Gunni and some Nyueng Bao belief. Minh Subredil talked to Ghanghesha when there was nobody else who would listen.

Widowed, Minh Subredil supported her one child by doing scut-work day labor at the Palace. Each morning well before dawn she joined the assembly of unfortunates who gathered at the northern servants' postern in hopes of gaining work. Sometimes she was joined by her dead husband's retarded sister Sawa. Sometimes she brought her daughter, though seldom anymore. The girl was getting old enough to be noticed.

Subassistant housekeeper Jaul Barundandi would come out and announce the number of positions available for the day, then would select the people to fill them. Barundandi always chose Minh Subredil because, though she was too ugly to demand sexual favors of, she could be counted upon to kick back a generous percentage of her salary. Minh Subredil was a desperate creature.

Barundandi was amused by Subredil's omnipresent statue. A devout Gunni of the cult of Khusa, he often included in his prayers a petition that he be spared Subredil's sort of luck. He would never admit it to his henchmen but he did favor Subredil some because of her poor choice of a father. Like most villains, he was wicked only most of the time and mainly in small-minded ways.

Subredil, as Ky Sahra, never prayed. Ky Sahra had no use for gods. Unaware of his tiny soft spot, she did have in mind a destiny for Jaul Barundandi. When the time came. The subassistant would have ample opportunity to regret his predations.

There would be many, many regrets, spanning the length and breadth of the Taglian empire. When the time came.

We went out through the maze of confusion and distraction spells Goblin and One-Eye have spent so many years weaving throughout the neighborhood, a thousand layers of gossamer deception so subtle only the Protector herself might notice them. If she was looking. But Soulcatcher does not roam the streets looking for enemy hideouts. She has the Greys and her shadows and bats and crows to do that work. And those are too dim to notice that they are being guided away from or subtly ushered through the area in a manner that left it seeming no more remarkable than any other. The two little wizards spent most of their time maintaining and expanding their maze of confusion. People not trusted no longer got within two hundred yards of our headquarters. Not without being led.

We had no trouble. We wore strands of yarn tied around our left wrists. These enchanted loops softened the confusion spells. They let us see the truth.

Thus we often knew what the Palace intended before plans went into motion. Minh Subredil, or sometimes Sawa, listened in while the plans were being made.

I muttered, "Isn't it awfully early for us to be out?"

"Yes. But there will be others already there when we take our place." There are a lot of desperate people in Taglios. Some will camp as near the Palace as the Greys will allow.

We did reach the Palace area hours earlier than ever before. But there were rounds of the darkness to make, brothers of the Company to visit in their hiding places. In each instance the voice of the witch came out of the wreckage that was Minh Subredil. Sawa tagged along behind and drooled out of the corner of her twisted mouth.

Most of the men did not recognize us. They did not expect to do so. They expected to receive a code word from those in charge that would expose us as messengers. They got that word. Chances were good they were in some disguise themselves. Every Company brother was supposed to create several characters he could assume in public. Some did better than others. The worst were called upon to risk the least.

Subredil glanced at the fragment of moon sneaking a peek through a crack in the clouds. "Minutes to go."

I grunted, nervous. It had been a while since I had been involved in anything directly dangerous. Other than wandering around the Palace or going to the library, of course. But nobody was likely to stick me with sharp objects there.

"Those clouds look like the kind that come right before the rainy season." If they were, that season would be early. Which was not a pleasant thought. During the rainy season that is what it does, in torrents, every day. The weather can be truly ferocious, with dramatic temperature shifts and hailstorms, and thunder like all the gods of the Gunni pantheon are drunk and brawling. But mainly I do not like the heat.

Taglians divide their year into six seasons. Only during the one they call winter is there any sustained relief from the heat.

Subredil asked, "Would Sawa even notice the clouds?" She was a stickler for staying in character. In a city ruled by darkness you never knew what eyes watched from the shadows, what unseen ears were pricked to overhear.

"Uhm." That was about as intelligent a thing as Sawa ever said.

"Come." Subredil took my arm, guiding me, which was what she always did when we went to work at the Palace. We approached the main north entrance, which was only two-score yards from the service postern. A single torch burned there. It was supposed to show the Guards who might be outside. But it was situated so poorly it only helped them see the honest people. As we drew closer, someone who had sneaked in along the foot of the wall jumped up and enveloped the torch in a sack of wet rawhide.

The crude, startled remark of one of the guards carried clearly. Now, would he be incautious enough to come see what had happened?

There was no reason to believe he would not. The Royal Guards had had no trouble for almost a generation.

The sliver of moon vanished behind a cloud. As it went, something moved at the Palace entrance.

Now came the tricky part, making it look like we screwed up a sure thing by going in right at a shift change.

A sound of scuffling. A startled cry. Somebody else demanding what was going on. A rattle and clatter as people rushed the gate. Clang of metal. A scream or two. Whistles. Then within fifteen seconds, answering whistles from several directions. Exactly according to plan. In moments the whistles from the Palace entrance became shrilly desperate.

When first the idea was broached, there had been serious debate about whether or not the attack should be the real thing. It seemed likely taking the entrance would be easy. A strong faction, made up of men tired of waiting, just wanted to bust in and kill everybody. While that might have offered a certain amount of satisfaction, there was little chance Soulcatcher could be destroyed, and such wholesale murder would do nothing to liberate the Captured, which was supposed to be our primary mission.

I had convinced everyone that we needed to launch an old-fashioned, Annals-based game of misdirection. Make the enemy think we were up to one thing when actually we wanted to accomplish something else entirely. Get them running hard to head us off in one direction when we were following a completely different course.

With Goblin and One-Eye now so old, our deceits have to be increasingly intellectual. Those two do not have the strength or stamina to create and maintain massive battlefield illusions. And, though willing to share their secrets, they had not been able to arm Sahra for the struggle. Her talent did not extend in that direction.

The first Greys charged out of the darkness, into the ambushes waiting to receive them. For a while it was a vicious slaughter. But, somehow, a few managed to get through to support the Guards barely hanging on at the Palace entrance.

Subredil and I moved into position against the foot of the wall, between the big entrance and the servants' postern. Subredil hugged her Ghanghesha and whimpered. Sawa clung to Subredil and drooled and made strange little frightened noises.

Though the attackers piled up heaps of Greys, they never quite managed to break through the defense of the entryway. Then help arrived from inside. Willow Swan and a platoon of Royal Guards burst through the gateway. The attackers scattered instantly. So fast, in fact, that Swan screeched, "Hold up! There's something wrong!"

The night lit up. The air filled with hurtling fireballs. Their like had not been seen since the heavy fighting at the end of the Shadowmaster wars. Lady had created those weapons in vast numbers and a few had been husbanded carefully since then. The men employing them had not been involved in the attack on the entrance. They clung to the fire plan, which counted on everyone being able to pick Swan out from amongst the Guards and Greys.

His life depended on it.

Fire fell to the side of the group away from Subredil and me. Willow was afraid. When fire swiftly shifted to fall on the entry and cut him off, he was supposed to retreat toward the service entrance. Past us.

Good old Swan. He must have read my script. As his men were being torn apart by fireballs just yards away, he skittered along, hand against the wall, staying just steps ahead of destruction. Molten stone and chunks of burning flesh flew over his head and ours and I realized that I had underestimated the fury of my weapons, perhaps fatally. It was definitely a mistake to have committed so many.

Swan stumbled over Minh Subredil's ankle. Somehow, when he hit the cobblestones, he found himself face-to-face with a drooling idiot. Who had a dagger's point neatly positioned under his chin. "Don't even breathe," she whispered.

Fireballs hitting the Palace wall melted their way right in. The wooden gateway was on fire. There was plenty of light by which our brothers could see us signal that we had gotten our man. Fire became more accurate. The resistance to the Greys coming to help became less porous. A second apparent attack came forward. A couple of those brothers collected Swan. They kicked and cursed us. And took our weapons with them when they went away, part of a general retreat as the attack wave fled from no evident resistance.

As they disappeared into the darkness, the thing that we had feared most occurred.

Soulcatcher came out on the battlements above to see what was happening. Subredil and I knew because all fighting ceased within seconds once somebody spotted her. Then a storm of fireballs flashed her way.

We were lucky. She was sufficiently unprepared that she could do nothing but duck. Our brothers then did what they were supposed to do. They got the heck out of there. They got downhill and lost amongst the population before the Protector could release her bats and crows.

It was my belief that the activity would have all the nearby part of the city in an uproar within minutes. The men were supposed to help that along by launching absurd rumors. If they remained calm enough.

Subredil and Sawa moved two dozen yards closer to the servants' postern. We had just settled down to drool and be held and whimper while we watched the corpses burn when a frightened voice demanded, "Minh Subredil. What are you doing here?"

Jaul Barundandi. Our boss. I did not look up. And Subredil did not respond until Barundandi stirred her with a toe and asked again, not unkindly. She told him, "We were going to be here early. Sawa needs to work bad." She looked around. "Where are the others?"

There had been others. Four or five even more eager to be first in line. They had fled. That might mean trouble. No telling what they might have seen before they ran. An early stray fireball was supposed to have panicked and scattered them before Swan got to us but I could not recall that having happened.

Subredil turned more toward Barundandi. I held on to her tighter and whimpered. She patted my shoulder and murmured something indistinct. Barundandi seemed to buy it, particularly when Subredil discovered that one of her Ghanghesha's trunks had broken off, and she began to cry and search our surroundings.

Several of Barundandi's associates were out as well, looking around, asking one another what happened. The same thing was going on at the main entrance, where stunned Guards and sleep-fuddled functionaries asked one another what had happened and what they should do and, holy shit! some of those fires burned all the way through the wall and it was six or eight feet thick! Shadar from as far as a mile away were arriving, gathering dead and wounded Greys and also trying to figure out what had happened.

Jaul Barundandi's voice gentled further. He beckoned his assistants. "Help these two inside. Be gentle. The high and the mighty may want to talk to them."

I hoped my start did not give us away. I had counted on getting inside early but it had not occurred to me that anyone might be interested in what two near-untouchables might have seen.

8

I need not have worried. We were interviewed by a seriously distracted Guard sergeant who seemed to be going through the motions mainly as a sop to Jaul Barundandi. The subassistant had evidently suffered an overinspiration of ambition in thinking he could win favor by providing eyewitnesses to the tragedy.

His solicitude began to fade once he had little to gain. A few hours after we were taken inside, while excitement still gripped the Palace and a thousand outrageous rumors circulated, while leading Guardsmen and Greys kept bringing in more and more trusted armed men and sending out more and more spies to watch the regular soldiers in their barracks, just in case they were in on the attack somehow, Minh Subredil and her idiot sister-in-law were already hard at work. Barundandi had them cleaning the chamber where the Privy Council met. A huge mess had been left there. Somebody had lost her temper and had worked out her anger by tearing the place up.

Barundandi told us, "Expect to work very hard today, Minh Subredil. Few workers showed up this morning." He sounded bitter. He would not garner much kickback because of the raid. It did not occur to him to be thankful he was still alive. "Is she all right?" He meant me. Sawa. I was still doing a credible job of shaking.

"She will manage as long as I stay close. It would not be good to put her anyplace where she cannot see me today."

Barundandi grunted. "So be it. There's work enough here. Just don't get in anybody's way."

Minh Subredil bowed slightly. She was good at being unobtrusive. She seated me at a wide table about a dozen feet long, piled up lamps and candlesticks and whatnot that had gotten thrown around. I invoked Sawa's narrow focus and went to work cleaning them. Subredil began cleaning floors and furniture.

People came and went, many of them important. None of them noticed us except the Inspector-General of the Records, Chandra Gokhale, who kicked Subredil irritably because she was scrubbing the floor where he wanted to walk.

Subredil got back onto her knees, bowing and begging pardon. Gokhale ignored her. She began cleaning up spilled water, showing no emotion whatsoever. Minh Subredil took that sort of thing. But I suspect Ky Sahra had just formed a definite opinion about which of our enemies should follow Willow Swan into captivity.

The Radisha appeared. The Protector was with her. They settled into their places. Jaul Barundandi appeared soon afterward, meaning to get us out of there. Sawa seemed to notice nothing. Her focus on a candlestick was too narrow.

A tall Shadar captain bustled in. He announced, "Your High-ness, the preliminary tally shows ninety-eight dead and one hundred twenty-six injured. Some of those will die from their wounds. Min-ister Swan hasn't been found but many of the bodies are burned too badly to identify. Many that were hit by fireballs caught fire and burned like greasy torches." The captain had trouble remaining calm. He was young. Chances were good he had not seen the conse-quences of battle before.

I kept working hard to shove myself way down deep into char-acter. I had not been this close to Soulcatcher since she held me prisoner outside Kiaulune fifteen years ago. Those were not happy memories. I prayed she did not remember me.

I went all the way down into my safe place. I had not been there since my captivity. The hinges on the door were rusty. But I got in-side and got comfortable while remaining Sawa. I had just enough attention left to catch most of what was happening around me.

The Protector suddenly asked, "Who are these women?"

Barundandi fawned. "Pardon, Great Ones. Pardon. My fault. I did not know the chamber was to be used."

"Answer the question, Housekeeper," the Radisha ordered.

"Certainly, Great One." Barundandi kowtowed halfway to the floor. "The woman scrubbing is Minh Subredil, a widow. The other is her idiot sister-in-law, Sawa. They are outside staff employed as part of the Protector's charity program."

Soulcatcher said, "I feel I have seen one or both of them before."

Barundandi bowed deeply again. The attention frightened him. "Minh Subredil has worked here for many years, Protector. Sawa ac-companies her when her mind is clear enough for her to accomplish repetitive tasks."

I felt him trying to decide whether or not to volunteer the news that we had witnessed the morning's attack from up close. I clung to my safe place so hard that I did not catch what happened during the next few minutes.

Barundandi chose not to volunteer us for questioning. Perhaps he reasoned that too intensive an attention paid to us might expose the fact that he was charging us half our feeble salaries for the right to work our hands into raw, aching crabs.

The Radisha finally told him, "Go away, Housekeeper. Let them work. The fate of the empire will not be decided here today."

And Soulcatcher waved a gloved hand, shooing Barundandi out, but then halted him to demand, "What is that the woman has on the floor beside her?" Meaning Subredil, of course, since I was seated at the table.

"Uh? Oh. A Ghanghesha, Great One. The woman never goes anywhere without it. It's an obsession with her. It—"

"Go away now."

So it was that Sahra, at least, sat in on almost two hours of the innermost powers' responses to our assault.

After a while I came forward again, enough to follow most of it. Couriers came and went. A picture of generally upright behavior by the army and people took shape. Which was to be expected. Neither had any real reason to rise up right now. Which was nothing but good news to the Radisha.

Positive intelligence just made the Protector more suspicious, though. The old cynic.

"No prisoners taken," she said. "No corpses left behind. Quite possibly no serious casualties suffered. Nor any great risks endured, if you examine it closely. They fled as soon as there was a chance someone would hit back. What were they up to? What was their real purpose?"

Reasonably, Chandra Gokhale pointed out, "The attack appears to have been sustained with exceptional ferocity till you yourself appeared on the battlements. Only then did they run."

The Shadar captain volunteered, "Several survivors and witnesses report that the bandits argued amongst themselves about your presence, Protector. It seems they expected you to be away from the Palace. Evidently the attack would not have been undertaken had they known you were here."

One of my touches of misdirection. I hoped it did some good.

"That makes no sense. Where would they get that idea?" She did not expect an answer and did not wait for one. "Have you identified any of the burned bodies?"

"Only three, Protector. Most are barely recognizable as human."

The Radisha asked, "Chandra, how bad was the physical damage? Do you have an assessment yet?"

"Yes, Radisha. It was bad. Extremely bad. The wall appears to have suffered some structural damage. The full extent is being determined right now. It's certain to be a weak point for a while. You might consider putting up a wooden curtain-wall in front of what is going to become a construction area. And think hard about bringing in troops."

"Troops?" the Protector demanded. "Why troops?" Her voice, long neutral, became suspicious. When you have no friends at all, paranoia is an even more natural outlook than it is for brothers of the Black Company.

"Because the Palace is too big to defend with the people you have here now. Even if you arm the household staff. An enemy doesn't need to use any of the regular entrances. He could climb the outside wall where no one is watching and attack from inside."

The Radisha said, "If he tried that, he'd need maps to get around. I've never seen anyone but Smoke, who was our court wizard a long time ago, who could get around this place without one. You have to have an instinct."

The Inspector-General observed, "If the attack *was* undertaken by elements descended from the old Black Company—and the employment of fireball weapons would suggest *some* connection, even though we *know* that the Company was exterminated by the Protector—then they *may* have access to hallway maps created when the Liberator and his staff were quartered here."

The Radisha insisted, "You can't chart this place. I know. I've tried."

Thank Goblin and One-Eye for that, Princess. Long, long ago the Captain had those two old men scatter confusion spells liberally, everywhere. There were things he had not wanted the Radisha to find. Things that remained hidden still, among them those ancient volumes of the Annals that supposedly explain the Company's secret beginnings but which have been a complete disappointment so far. Minh Subredil knows how to get to them. Whenever she gets the chance, Minh Subredil tears out a few pages and smuggles them out to me. Then I sneak them into the library and when no one is watching, I translate them a few words at a time, looking for that one phrase that will show us how to open the way for the Captured.

Sawa cleaned brass and silver. Minh Subredil cleaned floor and furniture. The Privy Council and their associates came and went. The level of panic declined as no new attacks developed. Too bad we did not have the numbers to stir them up again every few hours.

Soulcatcher remained uncharacteristically quiet. She had known the Company longer than anyone but the Captain, Goblin and One-Eye, though from the outside. She would accept nothing at face value. Not yet.

I hoped she broke a mental sprocket trying to figure it out, though I feared she had already done so, because she kept wondering about the burned bodies and Willow Swan. Could I have planned so obviously that she was confused only because she kept looking for something beyond the kidnapping?

I finished the last candlestick. I did not look around, did not say anything, just sat there. It was difficult to focus my thinking away from the danger seated across the room when my fingers were not busy. I gave praise to God, silently, as I had learned was proper for a woman when I was little. Equal praise was due Sahra's insistence on staying in character.

Both served me well.

At some point Jaul Barundandi came back. Under the eyes of the Great Ones, he was not an unkind boss. He told Subredil it was time to leave. Subredil bestirred Sawa. As I got to my feet, I made some sounds of distress.

"What is that?" Barundandi asked.

"She's hungry. We haven't eaten all day." Usually the management did provide a few scraps. That was one of the perks. Subredil and Sawa sometimes husbanded some of their share and took it home. That established and sustained the women's habit of carrying things out of the Palace.

The Protector leaned forward. She stared intently. What had we done to tickle her suspicion? Was she just so ancient in her paranoia that she needed no clue stronger than intuition? Or was it possible that she really *could* read minds, just a touch?

Barundandi said, "We'll go to the kitchen, then. The cooks over-prepared badly today."

We shuffled out behind him, each step like leaping another league out of winter toward spring, out of darkness into light. Four or five paces outside the meeting chamber, Barundandi startled us by running a hand through his hair and gasping. He told Subredil, "Oh, it feels good to get out of there. That woman gives me the green willies."

She gave me the green willies, too. And only the fact that I had gone deep into character to deal with them saved me giving myself away. Who would suspect that much humanity in Jaul Barundandi? I got a grip on Subredil's arm and shook.

Subredil responded to Barundandi softly, submissively agreeing that the protector might be a great horror.

The kitchens, normally off limits to casual labor, was a dragon's hoard of edible treasures. With the dragon evicted. Subredil and Sawa ate till they could barely waddle. They loaded themselves with all the plunder they thought they would be allowed to carry off. They collected their few coppers and headed for the servants' postern before anyone could think of something else for them to do, before any of Barundandi's cronies realized that the customary kickbacks had been overlooked.

There were armed guards outside the postern. That was new. They were Greys rather than soldiers. They did not seem particularly interested in people going out. They did not bother with the usual cursory search casuals had to endure so nobody carried off the royal cutlery.

I wish our characters had more curiosity in them. I could have used a closer look at the damage we had done. They were putting up scaffolding and erecting a wooden curtain-wall already. The glimpses I did catch awed me. I had only read about what the later versions of those fireball throwers could do. The face of the Palace looked like a model of dark wax that someone had stuck repeatedly with a white-hot iron rod. Not only had stone melted and run, some had been vaporized.

We had been released much earlier than usual. It was only mid-afternoon. I tried to walk too fast, eager to get away. Subredil refused to be rushed. Ahead of us stood quiet crowds who had come to stare at the Palace. Subredil murmured something about ". . . ten thousand eyes."

9

I erred. That mass of people had not come just to examine our night's work and marvel that the Protector's dead men could be so frisky. They were interested in four Bhodi disciples at the memorial posts that stood a dozen yards in front of the battered entrance, outside the growing curtain-wall. One disciple was mounting a prayer wheel onto one of the posts. Another two were spreading an elaborately embroidered dark red-orange cloth on the cobblestones. The fourth, shaved balder and shinier than a polished apple, stood before a Grey who was sixteen at the oldest. The Bhodi disciple had his arms folded. He looked through the youngster, who seemed to be having trouble getting across the message that these men had to stop doing what they were doing. The Protector forbade it.

This was something that would interest even Minh Subredil. She stopped walking. Sawa clung to her arm with one hand and cocked her head so she could watch, too.

I felt terribly exposed standing out there, a dozen yards from the silent gawkers.

Reinforcements for the young Grey arrived in the person of a grisled Shadar sergeant who seemed to think the Bhodi's problem was deafness. "Clear off!" he shouted. "Or you'll be cleared."

The Bhodi with folded arms said, "The Protector sent for me."

Not having gotten Murgen's report yet, Sahra and I had no idea what this was about.

"Huh?"

The disciple preparing the prayer wheel announced its readiness. The Sergeant growled, swatted it off the post with the back of his hand. The responsible disciple bent, picked it up, began remounting it. They were not violent people, the Bhodi disciples, nor did they resist anything, but they were stubborn.

The two spreading the prayer rug were satisfied with their work. They spoke to the man with folded arms. He bowed his head slightly, then raised his eyes to meet those of the elder Shadar. In a voice loud but so calm it was disturbing, he proclaimed, "*Rajadharma*. The Duty of Kings. Know you: Kingship is a trust. The King is the most exalted and conscientious servant of the people."

Not one witness had any trouble hearing and understanding those words.

The speaker settled himself on the prayer rug. His robes were an almost identical shade. He seemed to fade into a greater whole.

One of the secondary disciples passed him a large jar. He raised that as though in offering to the sky, then dumped its contents over himself. The Shadar sergeant looked as rattled as the youngster. He peered around for help.

The prayer wheel was back in place. The disciple responsible set it spinning, then backed off with the two who had spread the prayer rug.

The disciple on the rug struck flint to steel and vanished in a blast of flame just as I recognized the odor of naphtha. Heat hit me like a blow. I was in character strongly enough to whimper and grab Subredil with both hands. She resumed moving, eyes wide, stunned.

The man inside the flames never cried out, never moved till all life was gone and the charred husk left behind toppled over.

Crows circled above, cursing in their own tongue. So Soulcatcher knew. Or soon would.

We continued moving, into the now-animated crowd and through, heading home. The Bhodi disciples who had helped prepare the ritual suicide had disappeared already, while all eyes were fixed on the burning man.

10

I can't believe he did that!" I said, still climbing out of Sawa's smelly rags and crippled personality. Word had beaten us home. The suicide was all anyone wanted to discuss. Our own nighttime effort had become secondary. That was over and they had survived.

Tobo definitely did not believe it. He mentioned that in passing and insisted on telling us everything his father had seen inside the Palace last night. He referred to notes he had made with Goblin's help. He was thoroughly proud of the job he had done and wanted to rub our noses in it. "But I couldn't really get him to *talk* to me, Mom. Anything I asked seemed to be just an irritation. It was like he just wanted to get it over with so he could go away."

"I know, dear," Sahra said. "I know. He's that way with me, too. Here's some nice bread they let us bring home. Eat something. Goblin. What did they do with Swan? Is he healthy?"

One-Eye cackled. He said, "Healthy as a man with cracked ribs can be. Scared shitless, though." He cackled again.

"Cracked ribs? Explain."

Goblin told her, "Somebody with a grudge against the Greys got overexcited. But don't worry about it. The guy is going to have plenty of opportunity to be sorry he let his feelings get the best of him."

"I'm exhausted," Sahra said. "We spent the whole day in the same room as Soulcatcher. I thought I would burst."

"*You* did? It was all I could do not to run out of there screaming. I concentrated so hard on being Sawa that I missed half of what they said."

"What didn't get said might be more important. Soulcatcher was really suspicious about the attack."

"I told you, go for the throat!" One-Eye barked. "While they still didn't believe in us. Kill them all and you wouldn't have to sneak around trying to figure out how to get the Old Man out. You could make those guys at the library do your research for you."

"We'd've just gotten killed," Sahra said. "Soulcatcher was already looking for trouble. The news about the Daughter of Night did that. Speaking of whom, I want you two looking for her, and Narayan, too."

"Too?" Goblin asked.

"Soulcatcher will hunt them with a great deal of enthusiasm, I expect."

I observed, "Kina must be stirring again. Narayan and the girl wouldn't come to Taglios unless they were confident of her protection. Which means the girl will start copying the Books of the Dead again, too. Sahra, tell Murgen to keep an eye on them." Those terrible, ancient volumes were buried in the same cavern as the Captured. "I had a thought while we were up there—after I ran out of candlesticks and didn't have anything else to do. It's been a long time since I read Murgen's Annals. It didn't seem like they had much bearing on what we're trying to do. Being so modern. But when I was sitting there, just a few feet from Soulcatcher, I got a really creepy feeling that I had missed something. And it's been so long since I studied those things, I can't guess what."

"You should have time. We'll need to lie pretty low for a few days."

"You'll be going to work, won't you?"

"It would be suspicious if I didn't."

"I'm going to the library. I located some histories that go back to the earliest days of Taglios."

"Yeah?" One-Eye croaked, jerked himself out of a half-sleep. "Then find out for me why the hell the ruling gang are only princes. The territories they rule are bigger than most kingdoms around here."

"A question that never would have occurred to me," I said politely. "Or to any native of this end of the world, probably. I'll ask." If I remembered.

Nervous laughter came from the shadows in the back of the warehouse. Willow Swan. Goblin said, "He's playing tonk with some guys he knew in the old days."

Sahra said, "We should get him out of the city. Where can we keep him?"

"I need him here," I said. "I need to ask him about the plain. That's why we grabbed him first. And I'm not going off to some place in the country when I've finally started getting somewhere at the library."

"Soulcatcher might have him marked somehow."

"We've got two half-ass wizards of our own. Have them check him over. They add up to one competent—"

"You watch your mouth, Little Girl."

"I forget myself, One-Eye. You two together add up to half as much as either one alone."

"Sleepy has a point. If Soulcatcher marked him, you two ought to be able to find out."

One-Eye snapped, "Use your head! If she'd marked him, she'd already be here. She wouldn't be up there asking her lackeys if they'd found his bones yet." The little man climbed out of his chair, creaking and groaning. He headed for the shadows at the rear of the warehouse but not toward Swan's voice.

I said, "He's right." I headed to the back myself. I had not seen Swan up close for fifteen years. Behind me, Tobo started grilling his mother about Murgen. He was upset because his father had been indifferent.

Seemed to me there was a good chance Murgen did not understand who Tobo was. He had trouble with time. He had had that problem since the siege of Jaicur. He might think it was still fifteen years ago and he was stumbling away into a possible future.

Swan stared at me for a few seconds after I stepped into the light of the lamp illuminating the table where he was playing cards with the Gupta brothers and a corporal we called Slink. "Sleepy, right? You haven't changed. Goblin or One-Eye put some kind of hex on you?"

"God is good to the pure of heart. How are your ribs?"

Swan ran fingers through the remnants of his hair. "So that's the story." He touched his side. "I'll live."

"You're taking it well."

"I needed a vacation. Nothing's in my hands now. I can relax until she finds me again."

"Can she do that?"

"You the Captain now?"

"The Captain is the Captain. I design ambushes. Can she find you?"

"Well, son, this looks like the fabled collision between the unstoppable whatsis and the immovable thingee. I don't know where to lay my bets. Over here we got the Black Company with four hundred years of bad and tricky. Over there you got Soulcatcher with four centuries of mean and crazy. It's a toss-up, I guess."

"She doesn't have you marked somehow?"

"Only with scars."

The way he said that made me feel I knew exactly what he meant. "You want to come over to our side?"

"You're kidding. You pulled all that stuff this morning just to ask me to join the Black Company?"

"We pulled all that stuff this morning to show the world that we're still here and that we could do what we want, whenever we want, Protector or no Protector. And to take you so I can question you about the plain of glittering stone."

He looked at me for several seconds, then checked his cards. "There's a subject that hasn't come up in a while."

"You going to be stubborn about it?"

"You kidding? I'll talk your ear off. But I'll bet you don't learn a damned thing you didn't already know." He discarded a black knave.

Slink jumped on the card, laid down a nine-queen spread, discarded a red queen and grinned. He needed to see One-Eye about those teeth.

"Shit!" Swan grumbled. "I missed this game. How did you people learn? It's the simplest damn game in the world but I never met a Taglian who could figure it out."

I observed, "You learn fast when you play with One-Eye. Scoot over, Sin. Let me play while I pick this guy's brain." I pulled up a stool, studying Swan every second. The man knew how to get into a character. This was not the Willow Swan that Murgen wrote about or the Swan that Sahra saw when she visited the Palace. I picked up my five cards from the next deal. "This ain't a hand, it's a foot. How come you're so relaxed, Swan?"

"No stress. You can't have a worse hand than mine. I don't got no two cards of the same suit."

"No stress?"

"As of today I got nothing to do but lean back and take it easy. Just play tonk till my honey comes and takes me home."

"You're not afraid? Reports I've had said you're shakier than Smoke used to be."

His features hardened. That was not a comparison he liked. "The worst has happened, hasn't it? I'm in the hands of my enemies. But I'm still healthy."

"There's no guarantee you'll stay that way. Unless you cooperate. Darn! I'm going to have to rob a poor box if this keeps on." Play had not gotten all the way back to me before the hand ended. I did not win.

"I'll sing like a trained crow," Swan said. "Like a chorus. But I can't do you much good. I was never as close to the center as you may think."

"Possibly." I watched his hands closely as he dealt. It seemed like a moment when a skilled manipulator's ego might compel him to show himself how good he was at pulling fast moves. If he had any moves, he would not get them by me. I learned the game from One-Eye, too. "Prove it. Tell me how Soulcatcher kept you two alive long enough to get off the plain."

"That's an easy one." He completed a straight deal. "We ran away faster than the ghosts chasing us could run. We were riding those black horses the Company brought down from the north."

I had ridden those enchanted beasts a few times myself. That could be the answer. They could outdistance any normal horse and could run almost forever without tiring. "Maybe. Maybe. She didn't have any special talisman?"

"Not that she mentioned to me."

I looked down at another terrible hand. Grilling Swan could get expensive. I am not one of the better tonk players in the gang. "What happened to the horses?"

"Far as I know, they're all dead. Time or magic or wounds got them. And the queen bitch wasn't happy about that, either. She don't like walking and she ain't fond of flying."

"Flying?" Startled, I discarded a card I should have kept. That allowed one of the Guptas to go down and take me for another couple of coppers.

Swan said, "I think I'm going to like playing with you. Yeah. Flying. She's got a couple of them carpets that was made by the Howler. And she just ain't real good with them. I can tell you that from personal experience. Your deal. Ain't nothing like falling off of one of them suckers while it's hauling ass, even if you're only five feet high."

One-Eye materialized. He looked about as bright and alert as he ever did these days. "Room for one more?" His breath smelled of alcohol.

Swan grumbled, "I know that voice. No. I figured you out twenty-five years ago. I thought we got your ass at Khadighat. Or maybe it was Bhoroda or Nalanda."

"I'm quick on my feet."

Slink said, "You're in only if you show some money up front and you agree not to deal."

"And you keep your hands on top of the table all the time," I added.

"You smite me to the heart, Little Girl. People might get the idea you don't trust me not to cheat."

"Good. That'll save them a lot of time and pain."

"Little girl?" Swan asked. There was a whole different look in his eye suddenly.

"One-Eye's got diarrhea of the mouth. Sit down, old man. Swan was just telling us about Soulcatcher's magic carpets and how she doesn't like flying. And I'm wondering if we couldn't find some way to take advantage of that."

Swan looked from one of us to the other. I watched One-Eye's hands as he picked up his first bunch of cards. Just in case he might have done something to this deck sometime in the past. "Little girl?"

"Is there an echo in here?" Slink asked.

"Is that suddenly a problem?" I asked.

"No! No." Swan showed me the palm of his free hand. "I'm just getting a lot of surprises here. Soulcatcher thought she was pretty solid on the Company survivors. But I've already run into four people who are known to be dead, including the world's ugliest wizard and that Nyueng Bao woman who acts like she's in charge."

One-Eye growled, "Don't you go talking about Goblin that way. He's my pal. I'll have to stand up for him. Someday." He snickered.

Swan ignored him. "And you. That we had down as a man."

I shrugged. "Not many knew. And it's not important. The dope with the eye patch and smelly hat should've had sense enough not to mention it in front of an outsider." I glared.

One-Eye grinned, drew a card from the pile, discarded. "She's feisty, Swan. Smart, too. Designed the plan that pulled you in. You started on another one, Little Girl?"

"Several. I think Sahra will want the Inspector-General next, though."

"Gokhale? He can't tell us anything."

"Say it's personal. Swan. You know anything about Gokhale? He dabble in little girls like Perhule Khoji used to?"

One-Eye gave me an evil look. Swan stared. My mess-up this time. I had given something away.

Too late to fuss about it. "Well?"

"Actually, yes." Swan was pale. He focused on his cards, having trouble keeping his hands steady. "Those two and several others in that office. Common interests brought them together. The Radisha doesn't know. She doesn't want to know." He discarded out of turn. He had lost his zest for the game.

I realized what the problem was. He thought my speaking freely meant I expected to elevate him to a higher plane before long.

"You're all right, Swan. Long as you behave. Long as you answer questions when you're asked. Hell, I got to save you. There's a bunch of guys buried under the glittering plain that want to talk to you about that when they get back." Might be interesting to watch him talk it over with Murgen.

"They're still *alive?*" The idea seemed to stun him.

"Very alive. Just frozen in time. And getting angrier by the minute."

"I thought . . . Great God . . . shit."

"Do not speak so on the name of God!" Slink growled.

Slink was Jaicuri Vehdna, too. And much less lapsed than I. He managed prayers at least once a day and temple several times a month. The local Vehdna thought he was a Dejagoran refugee employed by Banh Do Trang because he had done the Nyueng Bao favors during the siege there. Most of our brothers endured genuine employment and worked hard to resemble pillars of the local community.

Swan swallowed, said, "You people ever eat? I ain't had nothing since yesterday."

"We eat," I said. "But not like you're used to. It's true what they say about Nyueng Bao. They don't eat anything but fish heads and rice. Eight days a week."

"Fish will do right now. I'll save the bitching till my belly's full."

"Slink," I said. "We need to send a kill team down to Semchi to watch the Bhodi Tree. The Protector's probably going to try to smash it. We could make some friends if we save it." I explained about the Bhodi disciple who burned himself and Soulcatcher's threat to turn the Bhodi Tree into kindling. "I'd like to go myself, just to see if the Bhodi nonviolent ethic is strong enough to make them stand around while somebody destroys their most holy shrine. But I have too much work to do here." I tossed my cards in. "In fact, I have work to do now."

I was tired but figured I could study Murgen's Annals for a few hours before I passed out.

As I walked away, Swan whispered, "How the hell does she know all that? And is she really a she?"

"Never checked personally," Slink said. "I have a wife. But she's definitely got some female habits on her."

What the devil did that mean? I am just one of the guys.

11

These were exciting times. I found myself eager to be up and outside, where things were happening. The impact of our boldness would have reached every cranny of the city by now. I gobbled cold rice and listened to Tobo complain, again, that his father had paid him no attention.

"Is there something I can do about that, Tobo?"

"Huh?"

"Unless you think I can go back there and tell him to shape up and talk to his kid, you're wasting your time and mine bitching about it. Where's your mother?"

"She left for work. A long time ago. She said they'd be suspicious if she didn't show up today."

"Probably would be. They'll be real edgy about everything for a while. How about instead of fussing about what's happened already, you spend some time thinking about what you'll do next time you see your father? And in the meantime, you can stay out of trouble by keeping notes for me whenever anybody questions the prisoner."

His glower told me he was no more excited about being offered work than any boy his age would be. "You're going out, too?"

"I have to go to work." It would be a good day to get to the library early. The scholars were supposed to be gone most of the day. There was supposed to be a big meeting of the bhadrhalok, which was a loosely associated group of educated men who did not like the Protector and who found the institution of the Protectorate objectionable. Jokingly, they referred to themselves as a band of intellectual terrorists. Bhadrhalok means, more or less, "the respectable people" and that was exactly what they thought they were. They were all educated, high-caste Gunni, which meant, right away, that a vast majority of the Taglian population regarded them with no sympathy at all. Their biggest problem with the Protector was that she held their self-confident, arrogant assumption of superiority in complete contempt. As revolutionaries and terrorists, they were less incandescent than any of the low-caste social clubs that existed on every residential block in the city. I doubt that Soulcatcher wasted two spies watching them. But they had great fun, fulminating and crying on one another's shoulders about the world going to hell in a goat cart driven by the demon in black. And every week or so it got most of the library crew out of my way.

I did what I could to encourage their seditious fervor.

I got off to a slow start. Not thirty yards from the warehouse exit I ran into two of our brothers doing donkey work for Do Trang while standing lookout. One made gestures indicating that they had something to report. Sighing, I strolled over. "What's the story, River?" The men called him Riverwalker. I did not know him by any other name.

"We got shadowtraps that's been sprung. We got ourselves some new pets."

"Oh, no. Darn." I shook my head.

"That's not good?"

"Not good. Run, report it to Goblin. I'll stick with Ran till you get back. Don't dawdle. I'm late for work." Not true, but Taglians have little sense of urgency, and the concept of punctuality is alien to most.

Shadows in the shadowtraps. Not a good eventuation, for sure. Near as we could determine, Soulcatcher had no more than two dozen manageable shadows left under control. As many more had gone feral in the remote south and were developing reputations as rakshasas, which were demons or devils but not quite like those my northern forebrethren knew. Northern demons seemed to be solitary beings of considerable power. Rakshasas are communal and pretty weak individually. But deadly. Very deadly.

In ancient myth, of course, they are much more powerful. They swat each other over the head with mountaintops, grow two heads for every one chopped off by a hero, and collect the beautiful wives of kings who are really gods incarnate but do not remember that fact. Things must have been much more exciting in olden times—even if they did not make a lot of sense from day to day.

Catcher would keep a close eye on her shadows. They were her most valuable resource. Which meant that if they had been sent out to spy, she should know exactly where each was supposed to have gone. At least that is the way I would have done it if I were committing irreplaceable resources. I did that for every single man we committed to Willow Swan's capture. I knew how they were going to get to their places and how they were going to get home and everything they were supposed to do in between. And just like I figured Soulcatcher might, I would have gone looking for them personally if they had failed to return home.

Goblin came hobbling into the early morning light, cursing all the way. He wore the all-covering brown wool of a veyedeen dervish. He hated the outfit, however necessary it was to disguise himself when he was outside. I did not blame him. The wool was hot. It was supposed to remind the holy men of the hell they were escaping by devoting themselves to chastity, asceticism and good works. "What the hell is this shit?" he growled. "It's hot enough to boil eggs out here already."

"The boys say we've caught something in our shadowtraps. I thought you might want to do something about that before Mama comes looking for her babies."

"Shit. More work—"

"Old man, you just had something in your mouth I wouldn't even want in my hand."

"Vehdna priss. Get the flock out of here before I give you a real language lesson. And bring home something decent to eat when you come back. Like maybe a cow."

More than once he and One-Eye had conspired to kidnap one of the sacred cattle that wander the city. To date, their efforts have come to naught because none of the men will go along. The majority have Gunni backgounds.

It took no time at all to learn that our shadow captives were not the only shadows that had run wild just before dawn. Rumor was rife. The stories of the murders the shadows committed banished news of the attack on the Palace and the self-immolation of the Bhodi disciple. The killings were closer to home and closer in time. And they were grotesque. The corpse of a man whose life has been devoured by a shadow is a twisted husk of the creature that was.

I insinuated myself into the crowd surrounding the doorway of a family where there had been multiple deaths. You can do that when you are little and limber and know how to use your elbows. I arrived just in time to watch them bring the bodies out. I was hoping they would be exposed to the public eye. Not that I wanted to see them myself. I saw plenty of those kinds of bodies during the Shadowmaster wars. I just thought the people ought to see what Soulcatcher could do. She needed all the enemies she could get.

The bodies were enshrouded already. But there was talk.

I traveled on, learning that most of the dead had been people who lived on the streets. And there had been a lot of those, taken in no obvious pattern whatsoever. It looked like Soulcatcher had sent the shadows out just to demonstrate that she had the power and the will to kill.

The deaths had evoked no great fear. People thought it was over. Most of them did not know any of the dead so were not angry, either. Curiosity and revulsion were the common emotions.

I considered turning back to tell Goblin to fix the captured shadows so they would go out killing again tonight and every night thereafter, till Soulcatcher tracked them down. She would not look for trappers if she thought her pets had gone rogue. And the shadows would create a lot more enemies for her before their terror ended.

At first it seemed the Greys had faded from the streets. They were less in evidence than usual. But as I skirted Chor Bagan, it became evident why. They had the place under siege, apparently on the assumption that any Black Company survivors, having been branded bandits by the Protector, would hide themselves amongst Taglios' homegrown thieves and villains. Amusing.

Sahra and I insist that we have as little to do with the criminal element as possible—over One-Eye's objections. And ignoring Banh Do Trang's occasional lapses. That element included folk of dubious morals and discipline who might serve us up for enough blood money to buy one more jar of illegal wine. I hoped they and the Greys had fun. I hoped somebody forgot the rules and their day turned bloody. That would make life easier for me and mine.

Any trip across town exposes you to the cruel truth about Taglios. Beggary exists there like nowhere else in the world. Were someone to sweep the city clean and organize the beggars into regiments, they would number more than the biggest army the Captain put together in the days of the Shadowmaster wars. If you look the least bit foreign or prosperous, they come at you in waves. Every attempt is made to exploit your pity. Not far from Do Trang's warehouse there is a boy with neither hands nor lower legs. Somehow, blocks of wood have been affixed in their place. He crawls around with a bowl in his mouth. Every cripple over the age of fifteen claims to be a wounded hero of the wars. The children are the worst. Often they have been maimed deliberately, their limbs deformed evilly.

They are sold to men who then feel they own them because they feed them a handful of toasted grain every few days.

A new mystery of the city is that men of that stripe seem to run the risk of cruel tortures and their own careers as deformed beggars. If they do not watch their back very, very carefully.

My route took me near one such. He had one arm he could use to drag himself around. The rest of his limbs were twisted ruins. His bones had been crushed to gravel but he had been kept alive by a dedicated effort. His face and exposed skin were covered with burn scars. I paused to place one small copper in his bowl.

He whimpered and tried to crawl away. He could still see out of one eye.

Everywhere you looked, life proceeded in the unique Taglian fashion. Every vehicle in motion had people hanging off it, sponging a ride. Unless it was the ricksha of a rich man, perhaps a banker from Kowlhri Street, who could afford outrunners armed with bamboo canes to keep people off. Shopkeepers often sat on top of their tiny counters because there was no other space. Workmen jogged hither and yon with backbreaking loads, violently cursing everyone in their way. The people argued, laughed, waved their arms wildly, simply stepped to the side of the street where no one was lying to defecate when the need came upon them. They bathed in the water in the gutters, indifferent to the fact that a neighbor was urinating in the same stream fifteen feet away.

Taglios is an all-out, relentless assault upon all the senses but engages none so much as it does the sense of smell. I hate the rainy season but without its protracted sluicings-out, Taglios would become untenable even for rats. Without the rains, the endemic cholera and smallpox would be far worse than they are—though the rainy times bring outbreaks of malaria and yellow fever. Disease of every sort is common and accepted stoically.

And then there are the lepers, whose plight gives new depth of meaning to horror and despair. Never do I find my faith in God so tested as when I consider the lepers. I am as terrified by them as anyone but I do know enough about some individuals to realize that very few are being visited by a scourge they deserve. Unless the Gunni are right and they are paying for evils done in previous lives.

Up above it all are the kites and crows, the buzzards and vultures.

For the eaters of carrion, life is good. Till the dead wagons come to collect the fallen.

The people come from everywhere, from five hundred miles, to find their fortunes. But Fortune is an ugly, two-faced goddess.

When you have lived with her handiwork for half a generation, you hardly notice anymore. You forget that this is not the way life has to be. You cease to marvel at just how much evil man can conjure simply by existing.

12

The library, created by and bequeathed to the city by an earlier mercantile prince who was much impressed by learning, strikes me as a symbol of knowledge rearing up to shed its light into the surrounding darkness of ignorance. Some of the city's worst slums wash right up against the wall enclosing its ground. The beggars are bad around its outer gates. Why is a puzzlement. I have never seen anyone toss them a coin.

There is a gateman but he is not a guard. He lacks even a bamboo cane. But a cane is unnecessary. The sanctity of the place of knowledge is observed by everyone. Everyone but me, you might say.

"Good morning, Adoo," I said as the gateman swung the wrought iron open for me. Though I was a glorified sweeper and fetch-it man, I had status. I appeared to enjoy the favor of some of the bhadrhalok.

Status and caste grew more important as Taglios became more crowded and resources grew less plentiful. Caste has become much more rigidly defined and observed in just the last ten years. People are desperate to cling to the little that they have already. Likewise, the trade guilds have grown increasingly powerful. Several have raised small, private armed forces that they use to make sure immigrants and other outsiders do not trample on their preserves, or that they sometimes hire out to temples or others in need of justice. Some of our brothers have done some work in that vein. It generates revenue and creates contacts and allows us glimpses inside otherwise closed societies.

Outside, the library resembles the more ornate Gunni temples. Its pillars and walls are covered with reliefs recalling stories both mythical and historical. It is not a huge place, being just thirty yards on its long side and sixty feet the other way. Its main floor is elevated ten feet above the surrounding gardens and monuments, which themselves cap a small knoll. The building proper is tall enough that inside there is a full-size hanging gallery all the way around at the level where a second floor should be, then an attic of sorts above that, plus a well-drained basement below the main floor. I find that interior much too open for comfort. Unless I am way down low or way up high, everyone can watch what I am doing.

The main floor is an expanse of marble, brought from somewhere far away. Upon it, in neat rows, stand the desks and tables where the scholars work, either studying or copying decaying manuscripts. The climate is not conducive to the longevity of books. There is a certain sadness to the library, a developing air of neglect. Scholars grow fewer each year. The Protector does not care about the library because it cannot brag that it contains old books full of deadly spells. There is not one grimoire in the place. Though there is a lot of very interesting stuff—if she bothered to look. But that sort of curiosity is not part of her character.

There are more glass windows in the library than anywhere else I have ever seen. The copyists need a lot of light. Most of them, these days, are old and their sight is failing. Master Santaraksita often goes on about the library having no future. No one wants to visit it anymore. He believes that has something to do with the hysterical fear of the past that began to build soon after the rise of the Shadowmasters, when he was still a young man. Back when fear of the Black Company gained circulation, before the Company ever appeared.

I stepped into the library and surveyed it. I loved the place. In another time I would gladly have become one of Master Santaraksita's acolytes. If I could have survived the close scrutiny endured by would-be students.

I was not Gunni. I was not high caste. The former I could fake well enough to get by. I had been surrounded by Gunni all my life. But I did not know caste from within. Only the priestly caste and some selected commercial-caste folks were permitted to be literate. Though familiar with the vulgate and the High Mode both, I could never pretend to have grown up in a priestly household fallen on hard times. I had not grown up in much of any kind of household.

I had the place entirely to myself. And there was no obvious cleaning that needed doing right away.

It ever amazed me that no one actually lived in the library. That it was more holy or more frightening than a temple. The kangali— the parentless and homeless and fearless boys of the street, who run in troops of six to eight—see temples as just another potential resource. But they would not trouble the library.

To the unlettered, the knowledge contained in books was almost as terrible as the knowledge bound up in the flesh of a creature as wicked as Soulcatcher.

I had one of the best jobs in Taglios. I was the main caretaker at the biggest depository and replicatory of books within the Taglian empire. It had taken three and a half years of scheming and several carefully targeted murders to put me into a position I enjoyed way too much. Always before me was the temptation to forget the Company. The temptation might have gotten me had I had the social qualifications to be anything but a janitor who sneaked peeks into books when nobody was looking.

In quick order I conjured the tools of my purported trade, then hurried to one of the more remote copying desks. It was out of the way, yet offered a good line of vision and good acoustics so I would not be surprised doing something both forbidden and impossible.

I had gotten caught twice already, luckily both times with *Tantric* books illuminated with illustrations. They thought I was sneaking peeks at dirty pictures. Master Santaraksita himself suggested I go study temple walls if that sort of thing appealed to me. But I could not help feeling that he began to harbor a deep suspicion after the second incident.

They never threatened me with dismissal or even punishment, but they made it clear I was out of line, that the gods punish those who exceed caste and station. They were, of course, unaware of my origins or associations, or of my disinclination to accept the Gunni religion with all its idolatry and tolerance for wickedness.

I dug out the book that purported to be a history of Taglios' earliest days. I would not have been aware of it had I not noticed it being copied from a manuscript so old that much of it had appeared to be in a style of calligraphy resembling that of the old Annals I was having so much trouble deciphering. Old Baladitya, the copyist, had had no difficulty rendering the text in modern Taglian. I have salvaged the moldy, crumbling original. I had it hidden. I had a notion that by comparing versions I could get a handle on the dialect of those old Annals.

If not, Girish could be offered a chance to translate for the Black Company, an opportunity he ought to pounce on considering the alternative available at that point.

I already knew that the books I wanted to translate were copies of even earlier versions, at least two of which had been transcribed originally in another language entirely—presumably that spoken by our first brothers when they came down off the plain of glittering stone.

I started at the beginning.

It was an interesting story.

Taglios began as a collection of mud huts beside the river. Some of the villagers fished and dodged crocodiles, while others raised a variety of crops. The city grew for no obvious reason beyond its being the last viable landing before the river lost itself in the pestilential delta swamps, in those days not yet inhabited by the Nyueng Bao. Trade from upriver continued overland to "all the great kingdoms of the south." Not a one of those was mentioned by name.

Taglios began as a tributary of Baladiltyla, a city great in oral histories and no longer in existence. It is sometimes associated with some really ancient ruins outside the village of Videha, which itself is associated with the intellectual achievements of a "Kuras empire" and is the center of ruins of another sort entirely. Baladiltyla was the birthplace of Rhaydreynak, the warrior king who nearly exterminated the Deceivers in antiquity and who harried the handful of survivors into burying their sacred texts, the Books of the Dead, in that same cavern where Murgen now lay entombed with all the old men in their cobwebs of ice.

Not all this was information from the book I was reading. As I went, I made connections with things I had read or heard elsewhere. This was very exciting stuff. For me.

Here was an answer for Goblin. The princes of Taglios could not be kings because they honored as their sovereigns the kings of Nhanda, who raised them up. Of course Nhanda was no more and Goblin would want to know why, in that case, the Taglian princes could not just crown themselves. There were plenty of precedents. From the looks of the history of the centuries before the coming of the Black Company, that had been the favorite pastime of anybody who could get three or four men to follow him around.

I overcame a powerful urge to rush ahead and look for the era when the Free Companies of Khatovar exploded upon the world. What had happened before that would help explain what had happened when they did.

13

A sudden, startled thrill ran through me. I was not alone anymore. A long time had passed. The sun had swung several hours across the sky. The quality of the light within the library had changed. It had become a much paler version of its morning self. Presumably the clouds had passed away.

I did not jump or, I hope, show any immediate outward reaction. But I did have to respond visibly to my awareness of the presence of whoever was standing behind me. Perhaps it was his breath that alerted me. The curry and garlic were strong. Certainly I never heard a sound.

I brought my heartbeat under control, smoothed my features, turned.

The Master of the Library, my boss, Surendranath Santaraksita met my gaze. "Dorabee. I believe you were reading." At the library they know me as Dorabee Dey Banerjae. An honorable name. A man of that named died beside me in a skirmish near the Daka Woods a long time ago. He did not need it anymore and I would do it no harm.

I did not speak. The truth would be hard to deny if the Master had been there long. I was halfway through the book, which was of the bound sort and contained no illustrations whatsoever, not even one *Tantric* passage.

"I have been watching you for some time, Dorabee. Your interest and skill are both evident. It's clear that you read better than most of my copyists. Yet it's equally obvious that you aren't of the priestly caste."

My face was still as old cheese. I was wondering if I should kill him and how I could dispose of the corpse if I did. Perhaps the Stranglers could be framed. . . . No. Master Santaraksita was old but still hale enough to throw me around if I tried to throttle him. Being small has definite disadvantages at times. He had eight inches on me but at the moment, that seemed like several feet. And someone else was moving around at the other end of the library. I heard voices.

I did not drop my eyes the way a menial should. Master Santaraksita already knew I was more than a curious sweeper, though a good one. I kept the place spotless. That was a Company rule. Our public characters had to be morally straight and excellent workers. Which did not make some of the men at all happy.

I waited. Master Santaraksita would decide his own fate. He would decide the fate of the library that he loved.

"So. Our Dorabee is a man of more talents than we suspected. What else do you do that we don't know about, Dorabee? Can you write, as well?" I did not answer, of course. "Where did you learn? It has long been the contention of many of the bhadrhalok that those not of the priestly caste do not have the mental facility to learn the High Mode."

Still I did not speak. Eventually he would commit to movement in some direction. I would respond accordingly. I hoped I could avoid destroying him and his brethren and stripping the library of whatever might be useful. That was the course One-Eye wanted to follow years ago. Never mind being subtle. Never mind not alerting Soulcatcher to what was happening right under her nose.

"You have nothing to say? No defense?"

"A pursuit of knowledge needs no defense. Sri Sondhel Ghosh the Janaka declared that in the Garden of Wisdom there is no caste." Albeit in an age when caste had much less meaning.

"Sondhel Ghosh spoke of the university at Vikramas, where all the students had to pass an exhaustive examination before they were allowed to enter the grounds."

"Do we suppose many students of any caste were admitted who were unable to read the *Panas* and *Pashids*? Sondhel Ghosh was not called the Janaka for nothing. Vikramas was the seat of Janai religious study."

"A janitor who knows about a religion long dead. We are indeed entering the Age of Khadi, where all is turned upon its head." Khadi is the favored Taglian name for Kina, in one of her less vicious aspects. The name Kina is seldom spoken, lest the Dark Mother hear and respond. Only the Deceivers want her to come around. "Where did you acquire this skill? Who taught you?"

"A friend started me out a long time ago. After we buried him, I continued to teach myself." My gaze never left his face. For a goofy old boffin, whose stuffiness was grist for the mockery of the younger copyists, he seemed remarkably flexible mentally. But then, he might be brighter than he seemed. He might realize that he could buy himself a float downriver to the swamps if the wrong words passed his lips.

No. Master Surendranath Santaraksita did not yet live in a world where one who read and cherished sacred texts also cut throats and trafficked with sorcerers, the dead and rakshasas. Master Surenranath Santaraksita did not think of himself that way, but he was a sort of holy hermit, self-consecrated to preserve all that was good in knowledge and culture. This much I had discovered already, through continuous observation. I had figured out, also, that we might not often agree on what was good.

"You just wish to learn, then."

"I lust after knowledge the way some men lust after pleasures of the flesh. I've always been that way. I can't help it. It's an obsession."

Santaraksita leaned a little closer, studying me with myopic eyes. "You are older than you seem."

I confessed. "People think I'm younger than I am because I'm small."

"Tell me about yourself, Dorabee Dey Banerjae. Who was your father? Of what family was your mother?"

"You will not have heard of them." I considered refusing to elaborate. But Dorabee Dey Banerjae did have a story. I had been rehearsing it for seven years. If I just stayed in character, it would all be true.

Stay in character. Be Dorabee caught reading. Let Sleepy worry about what to do when it was time for Sleepy to come back onstage.

"You denigrate yourself overmuch," Santaraksita said at one point. "I may have known your father . . . if he was the same Dollal Dey Banerjae who could not resist the Liberator's call for recruits when he raised the original legion that triumphed at Ghoja Ford."

I had named dead Dorabee's father already. I could not take that back now. How could he know Dollal, anyway? Banerjae was one of the oldest and most common of traditional Taglian surnames. Banerjaes were mentioned in the text I had been reading till moments ago. "That may have been him. I never knew him well. I do recall him boasting that he was one of the first to enroll. He marched off with the Liberator to defeat the Shadowmasters. He never came back from Ghoja Ford." I did not know much more about Dorabee's family. Not even his mother's name. In all Taglios how could it be possible I would encounter anyone who remembered the father? Fortune is indeed a goddess filled with caprice. "Did you know him well?" If that was so, the librarian might have to go—just that would make my exposure inevitable.

"No. Not well. Not well at all." Now Master Santaraksita seemed disinclined to say more. He seemed worrisomely thoughtful. After a moment he told me, "Come with me, Dorabee."

"Sri?"

"You brought up the university at Vikramas. I have a list of the questions the gate guards put to those who wanted to enroll. Curiosity impels me to subject you to the same examination."

"I know little about Janai, Master." If the truth were told, I was a bit shaky on the tenets of my own religion, always having been afraid to examine it too closely. Other religions do not stand up to the rigorous application of reason, for all we have things like Kina stalking the earth, and I really did not want to find myself stumbling over any boulders of absurdity protruding from the bedrock of my own faith.

"The examination was not religious in nature, Dorabee. It tested the prospective student's morals, ethics and ability to think. Janaka monks did not wish to educate potential leaders who would come to their calling with the stain of darkness upon their souls."

That being the case, I had to get into character very deeply indeed. Sleepy, the Vehdna soldier girl from Jaicur, had stains on her soul blacker than a shadow of all night falling.

14

"Then what did you do?" Tobo asked.

Around a mouthful of spicy Taglian-style rice, I told him, "Then I went out and made sure the library was clean." And Surendranath Santaraksita remained where he was, stunned into immo-

bility by the answers he had received from a lowly sweeper. I could
have told him that anyone who paid attention to the storytellers in
the street, the sermons of mendicant priests, and the readily available gratuitous advice of hermits and yogis, could have satisfied most
of the Vikramas questions. Darn it, a Vehdna woman from Jaicur
could do it.

"We got to kill him," One-Eye said. "How you want to do it?"

"That's always your solution these days, isn't it?" I asked.

"The more we get rid of now, the fewer there'll be around to ag-
gravate me in my old age."

I could not tell if he was joking. "When you start getting old,
we'll worry about it."

"Guy like that will be easy, Little Girl. He won't be looking for
it. Bam! He's gone. And nobody'll care. Strangle his ass. Leave a
rumel on him. Blame it on our old buddy Narayan. He's in town, we
need to put all kinds of shit off on him."

"Language, old man." One-Eye babbled on, putting a name to
animal waste in a hundred tongues. I turned my back. "Sahra? You've
been very quiet."

"I've been trying to digest what I picked up today. By the way, Jaul
Barundandi was distraught because you stayed home. Tried to take
your kickback out of my wages. He finally found Minh Subredil's
limit. I threatened to scream. He would've called my bluff if his wife
hadn't been around somewhere. Are you sure it's safe to let this librarian live? If it looked natural, no one would suspect—"

"It may not be safe but it could pay dividends. Master Santaraksita wants to make some kind of experiment out of me. To see if a
low-caste dog really can be taught to roll over and play dead. What
about Soulcatcher? What about the shadows? Did you learn anything?"

"She loosed everything she had. Just an impulse. No master plan
except to remind the city of her power. She expected the victims to
be immigrants who live in the streets. No one much cares about
them. Only a handful of shadows got back before dawn. Our captives
won't be missed until tomorrow."

"We could go catch a few more—"

"Bats," Goblin said, inviting himself to take a seat. One-Eye appeared to have dozed off. He still had hold of his cane, though. "Bats.
There's bats out there tonight."

Sahra offered a confirming nod.

Goblin said, "Back before we marched against the Shadowmasters, we killed all the bats. Had bounties on them big enough for bat hunters to make a living. Because the Shadowmasters used them to spy."

I recalled a time when crows were murdered relentlessly because they might be acting as Soulcatcher's far-flying eyes. "You're saying we should stay in tonight?"

"Mind like a stone ax, this old gal."

I asked Sahra, "What did Soulcatcher think about our attack?"

"It didn't come up where I could hear." She pushed some sheets from the old Annals across. "The Bhodi suicide bothered her more. She's afraid it might start a trend."

"A trend? There could be more than one monk goofy enough to set himself on fire?"

"She thinks so."

Tobo asked, "Mom, are we going to call up Dad tonight?"

"I don't know right now, dear."

"I want to talk to him some more."

"You will. I'm sure he's interested in talking to you, too." She sounded like she was trying to convince herself.

I asked Goblin, "Would it be possible for you to keep that mist thing going all the time so we could keep Murgen connected and any time we wanted, we could just send him where we needed to know about something?"

"We're working on it." He took off on a technical rant. I did not understand a word but I let him roll. He deserved to feel good about something.

One-Eye began to snore. The smart would stay out of reach of his cane anyway.

I said, "Tobo could keep notes all the time. . . ." I had had this sudden vision of the son of the Annalist taking over for the father, the way it goes in Taglian guilds, where trades and tools pass down generation after generation.

"In fact," One-Eye said, as though no time had passed since the last remark, and as though he had not been faking sleep a moment ago, "right now's the time you could play you a really great big ol' hairy-assed, old-time Company dirty trick, Little Girl. Send somebody down to the silk merchants' exchange. Have them get you some silk, different colors. Big enough to make up copies of them scarves the Strangers use. Them rumels. Then we start picking off the guys we don't like anyway. Once in a while we leave one of them scarves behind. Like with that librarian."

I said, "I like that. Except the part about Master Santaraksita. That's a closed subject, old man."

One-Eye cackled. "Man's got to stand by what he believes."

"It *would* get a lot of fingers pointing," Goblin said.

One-Eye cackled again. "It would point them in some other direction, too, Little Girl. And I'm thinking we don't want much more attention coming our way right now. I'm thinking maybe we're closer to figuring things out than any of us realizes."

"Water sleeps. We have to be taken seriously."

"That's what I'm saying. We use them scarves to take out informants and guys who know too much. Librarians, for instance."

"Would I be correct in my suspicion that you've been thinking about this for a while and by chance you just happen to have a little list all ready to go?" Very likely any such list would include all the people responsible for his several failed attempts to establish himself in the Taglian black markets.

He cackled. He took a swipe at Goblin with his cane. "And you said she's got a mind like a flint hatchet."

"Bring me the list. I'll discuss it with Murgen next time I see him."

"With a ghost? They got no sense of perspective, you know."

"You mean maybe he's seen everything and knows what you're really up to? Sounds like a perspective to me. Makes me wonder how far the Company might've gone if our forebrethren had had a ghost to keep an eye on you."

One-Eye grumbled something about how unfair and unreasonable the world was. He had been singing that song the whole time I had known him. He would keep it up after he became a ghost himself.

I mused, "You think we could get Murgen to winkle out the source of the stink that keeps coming from the back, there, where Do Trang hides his crocodile skins? I know it's not them. Croc hides have a flavor all their own."

One-Eye scowled. He was ready to change the subject now. The odor in question came from his beer- and liquor-manufacturing project, hidden in a cellar he and Do Trang thought nobody knew about. Banh Do Trang, once our benefactor for Sahra's sake, now was practically one of the gang because he had a powerful taste for One-Eye's product, a huge hunger for illegal and shadowy income, and he liked having tough guys on the payroll who would work hard for very little money. He thought his vice was a secret he shared only with One-Eye and Gota. The three of them got drunk together twice a week.

Alcohol is a definite Nyueng Bao weakness.

"I'm sure it's not worth the trouble, Little Girl. It's probably dead rats. Bad rat problem in this town. Do Trang puts rat poison out all the time. By the pound. No need to waste Murgen's time chasing rodents. You've both got better things to do."

I would be talking over a lot of things with Murgen if I could deal with him directly. If we could catch and keep his attention. I would like to know firsthand everything that ordinarily came to me through other people. I imply no malice, particularly from Sahra, but people do reshape information according to their own prejudices. Including even me, possibly, though until now, my objectivity has been peerless. All my predecessors, though . . . their reports must be read with a jaundiced eye.

Of course, most of them made the same observation in regard to their own predecessors. So we are all in agreement. Everyone is a liar but us. Only Lady was unabashedly self-congratulating. She missed few opportunities to remind those who came later how brilliant and determined and successful she was, turning the tide of the Shadowmaster wars when she had nothing to begin building upon but herself. Murgen was, putting it charitably, less than sane much of the time. Because I lived through many of the times and events he recollected, I have to say he did pretty good. Most of what he recorded *could* be true. I cannot contradict him. But a lot he set down does seem fanciful.

Fanciful? Last night I had a long chat with his ghost. Or spirit. Or ka. Whatever that was. If that was really Murgen and not some trick played on us by Kina or Soulcatcher.

We can never be one-hundred-percent certain that anything is exactly what it appears to be. Kina is the Mother of Deceit. And Soulcatcher, to quote a man far wiser and more foul of mouth than I, is a mudsucking lunatic.

15

"T his is excellent," I enthused again as Sahra summoned Murgen once more. She herself betrayed no enthusiasm for the task. Tobo's hovering did nothing to improve her temper. "Before he does anything else, I want to have him check on Surendranath Santaraksita."

"So you don't trust the librarian after all," One-Eye said. He chuckled.

"I think he's all right but why hand him a chance to break my heart if I can avoid it by keeping an eye on him?"

"How come it's got to be my eye?"

"There's not a sharper one available, is there? And you already turned down a chance to work on the Annals. I've got to do some heavy studying in those tonight. I might be on the track of something."

The little wizard grunted.

"I think I found something at the library today. If Santaraksita doesn't trip me up, I may have an outside view of the first coming of the Company by the end of the week." An independent historical source has been a goal almost as long as has been our desire for a look at uncontaminated editions of the earliest three volumes of the Annals.

Sahra had something else on her mind. "Barundandi wants me to bring Sawa to work, Sleepy."

"No. Sawa is on hiatus. She's sick. She has cholera, if that's what it takes. I'm finally starting to make some real headway. I'm not going to let that slide now."

"He's also been asking about Shiki." Back when Tobo had accompanied his mother to the Palace occasionally, she had called him Shikhandini, which was a joke Jaul Barundandi never got because he was not the sort to pay attention to historical mythology. One of the kings of legendary Hastinapur had had a senior wife who seemed to be barren. A good Gunni, he prayed and made sacrifice faithfully, and eventually one of the gods stepped down from heaven to tell him he could have what he wanted, which was a son, but he was going to get it the hard way, for the son would be born a daughter. And, as they say, it came to pass that the wife brought forth a daughter whom the king then named Shikhandin, a name that also existed in the female form Shikhandini. It is a long and not that interesting a story, but the girl grew up to become a mighty warrior.

The trouble started when it came time for the prince to take a bride.

Many of our public characters have obscure allusions or jokes built into them. That helped make things more interesting for the brothers playing the roles.

I asked, "Do we have any reason to snatch Barundandi? Other than his general sliminess?" I thought he was most useful right where he was. Any replacement was sure to be as venal and unlikely to be as kind to Minh Subredil. "And could we even get him out where we could touch him?"

Nobody suggested a strategic reason for grabbing the man. Sahra wanted to know, "Why do you ask?"

"Because I do think we could lure him. If we dress Tobo up pretty, then refuse to cooperate unless Barundandi meets him outside . . ."

Sahra was not offended. The ruse is a legitimate weapon of war. She looked thoughtful. "Maybe Gokhale instead?"

"Perhaps. Though he might want someone younger. We can ask Swan. I was thinking of catching Gokhale in that place where the Deceivers killed that other one." The enemy's leading personalities seldom left the Palace. Which was why we had chosen to go get Willow Swan.

Sahra began to sing. Murgen was reluctant again tonight. I said, "Murgen should look at that joy house, too. He'd be the best way for us to check it out." Though, no doubt, we could find several brothers willing to risk themselves in an extended recon.

Sahra nodded, did not break the rhythm of her lullaby.

"We might even . . ." No. We could not just burn the place once Gokhale had been inside long enough to become seriously engaged. Nobody would understand why I wanted to waste a perfectly good whorehouse—though a few might find a deadly fire highly amusing.

One-Eye looked like he was sleeping again but was not. Without opening his eyes, he asked, "You know where you're going, Little Girl? You got some kind of overall plan?"

"Yes." I was surprised to find that I really believed that. Intuitively, somewhere inside, though I had not known it consciously, I had engineered a master plan for the liberation of the Captured and the resurrection of the Company. And it was starting to come together. After all these years.

Murgen showed up muttering about a white crow. He was distracted. I asked the wizards, "You figured out how to anchor him here yet?"

"Always some damned thing," One-Eye grumbled. "Whatever you do, it's never enough."

"It can be done," Goblin admitted. "But I still don't see why we would want to."

"He hasn't been very cooperative. He doesn't want to be here. He's losing his connection to the real world. He'd rather sleep and wander those caverns." I took a stab in the dark. "And put on his white wings. Be Khadi's messenger."

"White wings?"

They did not read the Annals. "The albino crow that turns up sometimes. Sometimes Murgen is inside it. Because Kina puts him there. Or used to put him there and now he keeps stumbling back in, the way he kept stumbling around in time once Soulcatcher got him started."

"How do you know that?"

"I read sometimes. And once in a while I even read the Annals and try to figure out what Murgen didn't tell us. What he might not actually have known himself. Right now he may be enamored of being the white crow because that way he gets into actual flesh that ranges outside the caverns. Or he may just be falling under the influence of Kina as she wakes up again. But none of that ought to matter much right now. Right now we have a bunch of spying we need him to do. I want to be able to twist his arm if I have to."

The mission comes first. Murgen himself taught me that.

Sahra said, "Sleepy's right. Anchor him. Then I'll grab him by the nose and kick his behind until I've got his undivided attention." She seemed suddenly optimistic, as though taking a direct approach with her husband was some totally new concept fraught with unexpected hope.

She went straight to outright confrontation, drawing Tobo in to support her.

Maybe she *could* rebuild Murgen's ties with the outside world.

I turned to the others. "I found another Kina myth this morning.

In this one her father didn't trick her into going to sleep. She died. Then her husband got so upset that—"

"Husband?" Goblin squeaked. "What husband?"

"I don't know, Goblin. The book didn't name names. It was written for people who grew up in the Gunni religion. It assumes you know who they're talking about. When Kina died, her husband was so grief-stricken he grabbed up her corpse and started doing that stomping dance Murgen talks about her doing in his visions. He got so violent that the other gods were afraid he would destroy the world. So her father threw an enchanted knife that cut her up into about fifty pieces and every place one of the chunks fell became a holy place for Kina's worshippers. Just reading between the lines and guessing, I'd say Khatovar is where her head hit the ground."

"I got a notion One-Eye was on the right track back when he was going to desert and retire."

One-Eye gawked. Goblin saying something positive about anything he ever did? "The hell I was. I just had an attack of juvenile angst. I got over it and got responsible again."

"There's a new concept," I observed. "One-Eye responsible."

"For catastrophes and afflictions, maybe," Goblin said.

One-Eye said, "I don't get the Kina story. If she died back at the beginning of the world, how could she be giving us trouble for the last twenty or thirty years?"

"It's religion, dimwit," Goblin barked. "It don't got to make sense."

"Kina is a goddess," I said. "I guess gods can't ever be completely dead. I don't know, One-Eye. I didn't make it up, I just reported it. Look, the Gunni don't believe anybody dies really. Their soul goes on."

"Heh-heh-heh," Goblin chuckled. "If these Gunni got it right, you're in deep shit, runt boy. You got to keep going 'round on the Wheel of Life till you get it right. You got a lot of karma to work off."

"Stop. Now," I snapped. "We're supposed to be working."

Work. Not the favorite swear word of either man.

I told them, "You get Murgen nailed down. Or chained down. Whatever it takes to keep him under control. Then you help Sahra try to get through to him. I have a suspicion things are going to get exciting before long and we'll need him wide awake and cooperative."

One-Eye grumbled, "Sounds to me like you don't plan to be here looking over our shoulders."

I was up already. "Clever man. I have some reading and some translating to do. You can manage without me. If you concentrate."

One-Eye told Goblin, "We got to get that little bit into the sack with some guy'll pork her brains out." His cure for all ills, even at his age.

I paused to say, "When he's given everything else the once-over, have him search for Narayan and the Daughter of Night." I did not need to explain how badly we needed to keep those two from achieving their ends.

16

"I've got it!" I shouted, running back to the corner where Murgen's friends and family were trying to torment him into taking a broader interest in the world of the living. "I found it! I've got it!"

"I hope you ain't gonna give it to me," One-Eye grumbled.

My excitement was so loud and intense even Murgen, who was caught in the mist and being a real pain about his situation, paused to study me.

"I had a feeling, an intuition the other day, that the answer was in the Annals. In Murgen's Annals. And I'd just overlooked it. Maybe because it had been so long since I read them and I wouldn't have thought to look for it back then."

"And, behold!" One-Eye sneered. "There it was. In ink of gold on myrex-tinted paper, with little scarlet arrows saying, 'Here it is, Little Girl. The secret of the—'"

"Stuff it, dustbag," Goblin snapped. "I want to hear what Sleepy found." Though it would have been him doing the sarcasm if One-Eye had not beat him to it.

"It's the whole thing with the Nyueng Bao. Well, maybe not all of it," I said as Sahra scowled at me. "But the part with Uncle Doj and Mother Gota and why they came out of the swamp when they didn't have a debt of honor like your brother, Sahra." Sahra's brother Thai Dei was under the glittering plain with Murgen, serving as his bodyguard because of what Murgen and the Company had done to help the Nyueng Bao during the siege of Jaicur. "Sahra, you must know some of this."

"That may be true, Sleepy. But you'll have to tell us what you're talking about first."

"I'm talking about whatever it was that The Thousand Voices stole from the Temple of Ghanghesha sometime between the end of the siege and when Uncle Doj and your mother invited themselves to come stay with you here in Taglios. Murgen touches on it over and over, lightly, but I don't think he ever really caught on completely. Whatever it was that The Thousand Voices stole, Uncle Doj called it 'the Key.' From other internal evidence, I think it had to be another key to the Shadowgate, like the Lance of Passion." The Thousand Voices was what the Nyueng Bao called Soulcatcher. "I think if we had that key, we could open the way for the Captured."

If I was guessing right here, I had created a whole new line of inquiry: Why the Nyueng Bao?

Sahra began shaking her head slowly.

"Am I wrong? What is the Key, then?"

"I'm not saying you're wrong, Sleepy. I'm saying I don't want you to be right. There are things I wouldn't want to be true."

"What? Why?"

"Myths and legends, Sleepy. Ugly myths and legends. Some of them I'm not supposed to know. And I know I don't know them all. Probably none of the worst. Doj was their curator and keeper. As you are for the Black Company. But Doj never shared his secrets. Tobo, find your grandmother. Bring her here. Get Do Trang, too, if he's here."

Bewildered, the boy shuffled away.

A spectral whisper came out of the device where Murgen waited. "Sleepy may be right. I recall suspecting something like that and wondering if I could find a good history of the Nyueng Bao so I could figure it out. You'll need to question Willow Swan, too."

I said, "I'll do that later. Separately. Swan doesn't need to know what's happening. Are you paying attention now, Standardbearer? Do you have any idea where we're at and what we're doing?"

"I do." His tone was resigned, though. Like mine when I know I have to get up in the morning, want to or not.

"Tell me about the Temple of Ghanghesha, then. Both of you. Why would this Key have been kept there?"

Sahra did not want to talk about it. Her whole body said she was caught up in a ferocious internal struggle.

"Why is this so hard?" I asked.

"There is old evil in my people's past. I'm only vaguely familiar with it. Doj knows the whole truth. The rest of us just understand that our ancestors were guilty of a great sin and until we expiate it, our whole race is condemned to live in bitter destitution in the swamp. The temple was a holy place long before some Nyueng Bao began to adopt Gunni beliefs. It protected something. Possibly the Key you mentioned. The thing Uncle Doj has been looking for."

"Where did the Nyueng Bao come from, Sahra?" That question had intrigued me since childhood. Each few years hundreds of those strange people would pass through Jaicur on pilgrimage. They were quiet and orderly and stayed to themselves. And a year after they arrived from the north, they would pass through again, going back that way. Even at the height of the power of the Shadowmasters, that cycle had continued. Nobody knew where they went. Nobody ever cared.

"Out of the south somewhere, a long time ago."

"From beyond the Dandha Presh?" I could not imagine subjecting little children and old folks to the rigors of a journey of that magnitude. The pilgrimage had to be very important indeed.

"Yes."

"But there are no pilgrimages anymore." The one that had ended up with hundreds of Nyueng Bao dying in Jaicur was the last of which I was aware.

"The Shadowmaster and the Kiaulune wars made the next few times impossible. There's supposed to be a pilgrimage every four years. Each Nyueng Bao De Duang has to make the pilgrimage at least once as an adult. For a while the lack was no problem. But now the Protector will not permit the people to meet their obligations," Banh Do Trang rasped from his wheelchair, having arrived in time to catch the drift of my interrogation. "There are things we do not discuss with those who aren't Nyueng Bao."

I got the feeling he was saying the same thing twice at one time, one way for my benefit and another for Sahra's. This could be ticklish. We dared not offend Banh Do Trang, whose friendship we needed. If we lost him, we also risked losing Sahra, whose value to the Company could not be calculated.

Nothing is ever simple and straightforward.

I told the old man the way I had it figured. Ky Gota waddled in just as I started. My eyes widened as One-Eye gallantly offered her his seat. It is a world just chock-full of wonders. The little wizard went and got another seat, which he set next to Gota's. The two of them sat there leaning on their canes like a couple of temple gargoyles. A ghost of ancient beauty peeked out of the wide, permanent scowl that Gota used for a face.

I explained the situation. "But here's the mystery. Where is the Key today?"

Nobody volunteered that information.

"I'd think that if The Thousand Voices still had it, she'd be running down to Kiaulune every month to round up a new gaggle of killer shadows. It if *could* open the Shadowgate safely. And if Uncle Doj had it, he wouldn't be roaming around looking for it. He'd be back in the swamp blithely letting the rest of us go to *al-Sheil* in a handcart. Am I wrong? Mother Gota? You know the man. You must be able to offer something."

Able, perhaps. Willing, of course not. The big thing that stands out, to my ear, about the Company's sojourn in the south, is the stubborn silence of so many people. About everything. Like if we even discovered our own birthdays, that would be something we could use against them. The fact that the Company now consists almost entirely of native soldiers has not helped at all. Our life does not attract the knowledgeable, educated portion of the population. If a priest offered to sign on, we would send him downriver, knowing for certain that he was a spy.

"You got the damned gimmick?" One-Eye asked.

"Who?"

"You, Little Girl. The villainess, you. I didn't forget that you were Soulcatcher's guest for a while, when she caught you on the road coming back from running that message for Murgen. I haven't forgotten that when our sweet old Uncle Doj rescued you it was incidental. He was looking for his missing trinket, the Key. Not so?"

"That's all true. But I didn't bring anything away from that. Except a few new scars and the rags on my back."

"What we need to know then is has Soulcatcher been looking for the Key?"

"We don't know for sure. But she does fly down south occasionally and patrols the old ground like she's looking for something." We knew that, courtesy of Murgen. Though till now, her behavior had made no sense.

"So who else could've snatched this prize?" One-Eye did not press Gota for any information. The way to get around Gota was to ignore her. In time, she would insist that she be noticed.

I remembered a pale, ragged little girl who, though just four years old, had seemed ageless, silent and patient, confidently unfrightened by her captivity. The Daughter of Night. She never spoke to me once. She acknowledged my existence only when she had to, because if she irritated me too much, I might take all of what little food Soulcatcher allowed us. I should have strangled her then. But at that time I did not know who she was.

At that time I was having trouble remembering who I was. Soulcatcher had drugged me and gone down inside me and found half what made me me, then had tried *being* me in order to infiltrate the Company. I still wonder how well she really knows me. Certainly I do not want her to find out that I survived the Kiaulune wars. She might have the emotional weapons to crush me.

"Narayan came to get the Daughter of Night," I mused aloud. "But I caught only glimpses of him. An extremely skinny little man in a filthy loincloth who didn't look anything like the terrible monster he was supposed to be. It didn't occur to me it was him till I realized I wasn't going to be released, too. Since I couldn't see what they were doing, I don't know if they took anything with them. Murgen, you saw them then. I have it written down that you did. Did they take anything away that might have been this key?"

"I don't know. Believe it or not, you really do miss some things out here." He seemed piqued.

I realized I had not bothered to hear what he had to report. I asked.

"Not much useful," Sahra told me, cutting Murgen off before he could retell everything from the beginning.

"Can you find them now?" I foresaw trouble. There was an unwilling connection to Kina. If the dark goddess was stirring again, he would have to be careful not to attract divine attention. "We have these priorities regarding the Daughter of Night: Kill her. Failing that: Kill her sidekick. Failing that: Make sure she can't copy the Books of the Dead, which I'm sure she'll start doing again as soon as she develops a reliable connection with Kina. Finally: Recapture anything she and Singh might have carried off when Narayan rescued her."

One-Eye stopped nodding off long enough to clap his hands lazily. "Tear 'em up, Little Girl. Tear 'em up."

"Sarky old reprobate."

One-Eye snickered.

Goblin said, "You want another angle, find out from your library pals who makes bound blank books. Go to them and find out who's ordered some recently. Or bribe them to let you know when anybody does."

"Gosh," I said. "Somebody who actually uses his brain to think. The delight of the world is that its wonders never cease. Where the devil did Murgen go?"

Sahra said, "You just told him to find Narayan Singh and the Daughter of Night."

"I didn't mean right this second. I wanted to know if he found out anything about Chandra Gokhale we can use."

"Pressure getting to you, Little Girl?" One-Eye's tone was so sweet I wanted to pop him. "Relax. Now's the time when you don't want to force anything."

A couple of men from the duty crew, Runmust Singh and a Shadowlander dubbed Kendo Cutter by his squad mates, invited themselves into the staff meeting. Kendo reported, "There's all kinds of screaming going on out there tonight. I sent out word everybody should hole up someplace where there's plenty of light."

Sahra said, "The shadows are hunting."

I said, "We'll be all right here. But just to be safe, Goblin, why don't you make the rounds with Kendo and Runmust? We don't want any surprise. Sahra, will Soulcatcher let the shadows run completely wild?"

"To make her point? You're the Annalist. What do the books say about her?"

"They say she's capable of anything. She has no connection with the humanity of anyone else. It must be very lonely to be her."

"What?"

"We agree our next target should be Chandra Gokhale?"

Sahra eyed me oddly. That had been decided already. Unless some better opportunity fell into our laps, we would eliminate the Inspector-General, without whom the tax system and the bureau-

cratic side of government would stumble and stagger. He also seemed
the most vulnerable of our enemies. And his removal would leave
the Radisha more isolated than ever, cut off by the Protector on one
hand, the priests on the other, and unable to turn anywhere because
she was the Radisha, the Princess unapproachable, in some respects
a demi-goddess.

It had to be lonely to be her, too.

Subtlety and finesse.

I asked, "What did we do today to frighten the world?" Then I
realized that I knew the answer. It had been part of the plan for
capturing Swan. All the brotherhood would have avoided any risks.
Tonight there would be shows from buttons previously planted.
There would be more again tomorrow night. Smoke-and-light shows
proclaiming "Water sleeps," or "My brother unforgiven," or "All
their days are numbered." There would be more, somewhere, every
evening from now on.

Sahra mused, "Someone who wasn't one of us brought in another
prayer wheel and mounted it on a memorial post outside the north
entrance. It hadn't been noticed yet when I left."

"Same message?"

"I presume."

"That's scary. That could be a potent one. *Rajadharma*."

"It has the Radisha thinking already. That monk burning himself
definitely got her attention."

Story of my life. Here I spend months working out every tiny detail of a marvelous plan and I get upstaged by a lunatic with a fire
fetish.

"So those Bhodi nuts found a good message. You think we could
steal some of their thunder?"

One-Eye chuckled evilly.

"What?" I demanded.

"Sometimes I amaze myself."

Goblin, about to leave with Runmust and Kendo, observed, "You
been amazed at yourself for two hundred years. Mainly 'cause nobody
else bothers to get interested in insects."

"You better not go to sleep any time soon, Frogface—"

"Gentlemen?" Sahra said. Gently. Yet she grabbed the attention
of both wizards. "Can we stick to business? I need some sleep."

"Absolutely!" Goblin said. "Absolutely! If the old fart has an idea, let's get it out here before it dies of loneliness."

"You may continue your assignment."

Goblin stuck out his tongue but left.

"Amaze the rest of us, One-Eye," I suggested. I did not want him dozing off before he shared his wisdom.

"Next time one of those Bhodi loons lights himself up, we have the smoke and flames carry our message. 'Water Sleeps.' And a new one I thunk up, 'Nor Even Death Destroy.' You got to admit, that's got a nice religious ring to it."

"Indeed," I agreed. "What the heck does it mean?"

"Little Girl, don't you start in on me—"

The ghost of evils past whispered, "I found them."

Murgen was back.

I did not ask who. "Where?"

"The Thieves' Garden."

"Chor Bagan? The Greys have it under siege."

And they were still serious about getting the place cleaned out, Murgen said.

17

S ahra wakened me well before dawn, which is not my best time of day. When I opted for a military career, we were besieged in my hometown. I just knew that once we got out of there, we would sleep till noon, we would eat fresh food all the time and there would be plenty of it and never, ever, would we have to go out in the rain again. In the meantime, I took the best I could get, which was the Black Company during the siege, with the water fifty feet deep. The only thing resembling fresh food was the long pig Mogaba and his Nar friends were enjoying. Unless you counted the occasional lame rat or slow-witted crow.

"What?" I grumbled. Personally, I am convinced that even the priests of happy-go-lucky old Ghanghesha are not required to be pleasant before an hour much closer to noon than this was.

"I have to go to the Palace. You have to appear at the library. If we want to snatch Narayan and the girl right in front of the Greys, we need to start planning right now."

She was right. But that did not mean I had to accept it gracefully.

Every Company member inside Do Trang's complex, and Banh himself, gathered over a crude breakfast. Only Tobo and Mother Gota were absent. But they would have no part in any of this. I thought.

Nobody from outside could be included now, because shadows were on the prowl.

"We got a plan all worked out," One-Eye announced proudly.

"I'm sure it's one strike of genius after another," I replied as I made a groggy effort to collect a bowl of cold rice, a mango and a bowl of tea.

"First thing, Goblin goes up there in his dervish outfit. Then Tobo comes strutting along. . . ."

"Good morning, Adoo," I murmured distractedly as the gateman admitted me to the library grounds. I was worried about leaving Goblin and One-Eye to operate on their own. My mother instinct at work, they said, both showing nasty teeth as they reminded me that every hen has to trust her chicks on their own sometime. A point well made. Though few hens have to worry about their chicks getting drunk, forgetting what they are doing and wandering off in search of adventure in a city where there is not even one other skinny little black man or ugly little white character.

Adoo nodded his greeting. He never had anything to say.

Inside the library I went to work immediately, though only a couple of copyists had arrived before me. Sometimes Dorabee focused as intently as Sawa did. That helped turn off the worries.

"Dorabee? Dorabee Dey Banerjae!"

I started awake, amazed that I had fallen asleep. I had squatted down on my heels in a corner, in a fashion common amongst Gunni and Nyueng Bao but not common among Vehdna, Shadar or many of the ethnic minorities. We Vehdna favor sitting on the floor or on a cushion, cross-legged. Shadar like low chairs or stools. Not owning at least a crude stool is the truest mark of poverty amongst the Shadar.

I was in character even in my sleep.

"Master Santaraksita?"

"Are you ill?" He sounded concerned.

"Tired. I didn't sleep well. The *skildirsha* were hunting last night." I used the Shadowlander name for the shadows. That did not trouble Santaraksita. It had become part of the language under the Protectorate. "The screams kept waking me up."

"I understand. I did not enjoy a sound sleep myself, though not for that reason. I was unaware of the horror till I saw its marks this morning."

"The *skildirsha* show a proper respect for the priestly class, then."

The faintest twitch of his lip told me he had not missed the joke. "I am properly appalled, Dorabee. This is evil unlike any we have ever known. The blind misfortune of flood or plague or disaster we must endure stoically. And against the darkness even the gods themselves sometimes contend in vain. But to send out a pack of these shadows to do murder randomly and often, and for no reason even an insane man can comprehend, that is evil of the sort the northerners used to preach."

Dorabee managed a credible job of looking slack-jawed.

"I'm sorry. I'm exercised. You probably never saw any of the outsiders." He placed the same stress on "outsiders" that many Taglians used when they meant the Black Company specifically.

"I did. I saw the Liberator himself once when I was little. And I saw the one they called the Lieutenant after she came back from Dejagore. I was pretty far away but I remember it because that was the same day she killed all the priests. And the Protector. I saw her a couple of times." I was making it up as I went but that was the sort of thing most adult Taglians could claim. The Company had been in and out of the city for years before the final campaign against Longshadow and the fortress Overlook. I rose. "I'll get back to work now."

"You do your job well, Dorabee."

"Thank you, Master Santaraksita. I try."

"Indeed." He seemed to be having trouble getting something out. "I have decided that you will be allowed access to any books not in the restricted section." Restricted books were those not available in multiple copies. Only the most favored scholars were allowed near those. So far, I had been able to determine only a handful of the titles of the books so set aside. "When you have no other obligations."

Part of my day, every day, I spent just waiting to be told about something I needed to do.

"Thank you, Master Santaraksita!"

"I'll expect you to be able to discuss them."

"Yes, Master Santaraksita."

"We have set our feet upon an unknown road, Dorabee. An exciting and frightening journey lies ahead." His prejudices were such that he actually meant what he said. Me reading had twisted his universe all out of shape and now he was going to conspire in this perverted vermiculation.

I took my broom in hand. Exciting and frightening things would be happening elsewhere in my universe. And I hated every second that I was not there to control them.

18

The little dervish in brown wool seemed completely lost inside himself. He was busy talking to himself, paying no attention to the surrounding world. Most likely he was quoting to himself from the sacred texts of the Vehdna, as understood by his peculiar splinter sect. Though tired and irritable, the Greys did not challenge him immediately. They had been taught to honor all holy men, not just those already secure within the Shadar truths. Any devoted stalker after wisdom would find his path leading him to enlightenment eventually.

Tolerance of such seekers was common to all Taglians. The welfare of the soul and the spirit were of grave concern to most. The Gunni, indeed, considered the seeking of enlightenment to be one of the four key stages of an ideally lived life. Once a man successfully raised up and provided for his children, he should put all things material, all ambition and pleasure, aside. He should go into a forest to live as a hermit or become a mendicant seeker or in some other way should live out his final years looking for the truth and purifying his soul. Many of the greatest names in Taglian and southern history are those of kings and rich men who chose just such a path.

But human nature being human nature . . .

The Greys did not, however, let the dervish follow his quest into

Chor Bagan. A sergeant intercepted him. His associates surrounded the holy man. The sergeant said, "Father, you cannot go in that direction. This street has been closed to traffic by order of Minister Swan." Even dead, Swan had to take the blame for Soulcatcher's policies.

The dervish apparently failed to notice the Greys till he actually collided with the sergeant. "Huh?"

The younger Greys laughed. Men enjoy seeing their prejudices confirmed. The sergeant repeated his message. He added, "You must turn right or left. We're rooting out the evils infesting what lies straight ahead." He possessed a touch of wit.

The dervish looked first right, then left. He shivered, then announced, "All evil is the result of metaphysical error," in a raspy little voice and started along the street to the right. It was a very strange street. It was almost empty of humanity. In Taglios that was something seldom seen.

A moment later the Shadar sergeant squealed in surprise and pain. He began slapping his side.

"What's the matter?" another Grey asked.

"Something bit me . . ." He squealed again, which indicated that he was in a great deal of agony, for Shadar were proud of their ability to endure pain without outcry or even flinching.

Two of the sergeant's men tried to lift his shirt while a third clung to his arm in an effort to keep him immobile. He shrieked again.

Smoke began to boil out of his side.

The Greys were so startled they backed away. The sergeant went down. He went into convulsions. Smoke continued to boil up. It assumed a form none of the Greys wanted to see.

"Niassi!"

The demon Niassi began to whisper secrets no Shadar wanted to hear.

Grinning to himself, Goblin slipped into Chor Bagan. He disappeared long before anyone wondered if there might not be a connection between the sergeant's discomfort and the veyedeen dervish.

Greys arrived from all directions. Officers barked and cursed and drove them back to their stations before the denizens of Chor Bagan seized the opportunity to escape. Obviously this was a distraction meant to give their prey the chance to run.

A crowd had begun to gather, too. Among them was a Nyueng Bao boy who picked his moment, cut a purse and fled past the Greys, one of whom recalled him from the evening when one of their own got stoned. Discipline began to collapse.

The Grey officers tried. And managed rather well, considering. Only a few people escaped Chor Bagan. And a half-dozen slipped inside, among them a skinny little old man in the all-enveloping yellow of a leper.

One-Eye was not pleased. He was sure strategy had had nothing to do with it being him who had to assume the yellow. Goblin was up to something wicked.

The six raiders approached the target tenement from front and rear, in loose teams of three. One-Eye was around front. People cleared off fast when they saw the yellow. Lepers were held in absolute terror.

None of the men wanted to carry out a raid in broad daylight. It was not the Company way. But darkness was denied us till Soulcatcher pulled her shadows back off the streets. And the consensus of the Annalists and wizards was that it was less likely that the Daughter of Night could summon Kina's help during daylight. Daytime also offered a better chance of taking her by surprise.

Each team paused to make sure every man still wore his yarn bracelet before they stormed into the tenement. Each wizard set loose an array of previously prepared low-grade confusion spells that buzzed through the ramshackle structure like a swarm of drunken mosquitoes. The attackers passed inside, stepping over and around frightened, shivering families who, till now, had considered themselves wildly fortunate to have a roof over their heads, even if that meant renting floor space in a hallway. Both teams posted a man who would make sure no one went outside. Another two men met at the foot of the rickety stair. They would prevent movement up or down. Goblin and One-Eye met at the cellar entrance and shared a few complaints about being desperately undermanned, then a few exaggerated courtesies as each offered the other the opportunity to go down into the enemy's den first.

Goblin finally accepted on the basis of superior youth, quickness and alleged intelligence. He launched a couple of luminary floating stars into the pit, where the darkness was blacker than Kina's heart.

"Here!" Goblin said. "Ha! We've got—"

Something like a flaming tiger burst out of nowhere. It leaped at Goblin. A shadow drifted in from the side. It flicked something long and thin that looped around the little wizard's neck.

One-Eye's cane came down on Narayan's wrist hard enough to crack bone. The living saint of the Strangler lost his rumel, which flew across the cellar.

One-Eye's off hand tossed something over Goblin's head, toward the source of the tiger. A ghostly light floated up like a wisp of luminescent swamp gas. It moved suddenly, enveloping a young woman. She began to slap at herself, trying to wipe it off.

Goblin did something quick, while she was distracted. She collapsed. "Goddamn! Goddamn! It worked. I'm a genius. Admit it. I'm a fucking genius."

"Who's a genius? Who came up with the plan?"

"Plan? What plan? Success is in the details, runt. Who came up with the details? Any damned fool could've said let's go catch them two."

Both men tied limbs as they nattered.

One-Eye said, "Plan the details on this. We got to get out of here with these people. Through all the Greys in the world."

"Already covered. They've got so much trouble they won't have time to worry about any damned lepers." He started trying to get a yellow outfit over the head of the Daughter of Night. "Remind me to warn them back at the shop that this one can put together an illusion or two."

"I know that's the way its *supposed* to go." One-Eye began dragging Narayan Singh into another yellow outfit. In a moment Goblin would trade his brown for yellow, too. Upstairs, the four Company brothers, all of Shadar origin, were turning themselves into Greys. "I'm saying it ain't got a prayer of working."

"That because I planned it?"

"Absolutely. You're beginning to catch on. Welcome to reality."

"It goes to shit in our hands, you can blame it on Sleepy, not me. It was her idea."

"We got to do something about that girl. She thinks too damned much. Will you quit farting around? Them goddamn Greys out there are going to have time to go home for lunch."

"Don't hit him so hard. You want him to walk out of here under his own power."

"You talking to me? What the hell you doing with . . . get your hand out of there, you old pervert."

"I'm putting a control amulet over her heart, you dried-up old turd. So she won't embarrass us before we get her home."

"Oh, yeah. Sure you are. But why don't I look on the bright side? At least you're interested in girls again. She built as nice as her mother?"

"Better."

"Watch your mouth. The place might be haunted. And I got a suspicion maybe some of those ghosts can talk to each other, no matter what Murgen claims." One-Eye began to bully the groggy Narayan Singh up the steps.

"I do believe this is going to work," One-Eye crowed. The combination of Greys and lepers seemed the perfect device for exiting the Thieves' Garden—particularly now that the real Greys were running around distracted.

"I don't want to break your heart, old-timer," Goblin said. "But I think we done been fished." He was looking over his shoulder.

One-Eye looked back. "Shit!"

A small flying carpet dropped toward them, accompanied by crows making no sounds at all. Soulcatcher. And her very stance suggested mischievous glee.

She threw something.

"Spread out!" Goblin barked. "Don't let those two get away." He faced the descending carpet, heart in this throat. If it came to a direct face-off, he was going to get splattered like a stomped egg. He extended a gloved hand, caught the falling black globule, whipped his arm in a circle and launched the missile back into the sky.

Soulcatcher shrieked, outraged. The people of Talgios did not have that kind of nerve. She drove the carpet to one side, avoiding the black globe. And well she moved when she did.

Her luck had served her yet again. A screaming fireball ripped right through the space she had vacated, the same kind of fireball that had eaten all those holes in the Palace wall and had set the bodies of so many men burning like bad fat candles. She continued to dive. Two more fireballs barely missed her. She put a tenement between herself and the sharpshooters. She was extremely angry but did not let rage cloud her thinking.

Above her, her crows began bursting like soundless fireworks. Blood, flesh and feathers rained down.

In seconds she figured it out, conversing with herself in a committee of voices.

They had not been hiding inside Chor Bagan after all. She could not have caught anyone trying to slip away like this if they had not come in to retrieve something they did not want found. "They're here in the city. But we haven't found them. We haven't seen a trace or heard a rumor that they didn't want to reach our ears. Until now. That takes wizardry. That bold little one. That was the toad man. Goblin. Though the Great General of the Armies Mogaba assures us that he saw the body himself. Who else is alive? Could the Great General himself be less trustworthy than he would like us to believe?"

That was not possible. Mogaba had no other friends. He was committed in perpetuity.

Soulcatcher brought her carpet to earth, stepped off, folded its light bamboo frame, rolled the carpet around that, surveyed the street. They had come down this way. From up there. What could they have wanted desperately enough to have exposed themselves so thoroughly? Anything they thought that important would be something she was bound to find very interesting herself.

It took just one whispered word of power to illuminate the cellar. The squalor was appalling. Soulcatcher turned slowly. A man and his daughter, apparently. An old man and a young woman, anyway. One lamp. Discarded clothing. A few handfuls of rice. Some fish meal. Why the writing instruments and ink? What was this? A book. Somebody had just begun writing in it in an unfamiliar alphabet. She caught a spot of black movement in the corner of her eye. She whirled, crouching, fearing an attack by a rogue shadow. The *skildirsha* maintained an especially potent hatred for those who dared command them.

A rat fled, dropping the object of its curiosity. Soulcatcher knelt, picked up a long strip of black silk with an antique silver coin sewn into one corner. "Oh. I see." She began to laugh like a young girl catching on late to the meaning of an off-color joke. She collected the book, surveyed the scene once more before leaving. "Dedication sure doesn't pay."

Once in the street again, she reassembled her carpet, unconcerned about snipers. Those people would be long gone and far away. They knew their business. But crows should be tracking them.

She froze, staring upward but not really seeing the white crow on the peak of the tenement roof. "How did they find out where those two were?"

19

W hat happened?" Sahra demanded as soon as she came in, before she began shedding Minh Subredil's rags.

I was still Dorabee Dey Banerjae myself. "We lost Murgen somehow. Goblin thought they had him anchored, but he went away while we were all out and I don't know how to get him back."

"I meant what happened in the Thieves' Garden. Soulcatcher was out there. Whatever she tried to pull didn't work out but she came back a different person. I didn't get to hear everything she told the Radisha but I do know she found something or figured out something that changed her whole attitude. Like everything suddenly stopped being fun."

I said, "Oh. I don't know. Maybe Murgen can tell us. If we can get him back here."

Goblin joined us. He was pushing a sleeping One-Eye in Banh Do Trang's spare wheelchair. He announced, "They're resting peacefully. Drugged. Narayan was distraught. The girl took it pretty calmly. We need to worry about her."

"What's wrong with him?" I asked, indicating One-Eye.

"He's worn out. He's an old man. I want to see you have half the energy he does when you get to be half his age."

Sahra asked, "Why do we need to worry about the girl?"

"Because she's her mother's daughter. She doesn't have much skill with it yet because she hasn't had anybody to teach her, but she's got the natural ability to become a substantial sorceress. Maybe even as powerful as her mother but without Lady's rudimentary sense of ethics. It reeks off her—"

"'Tain't the only thing she reeks of, neither," One-Eye chirped. "First thing you do with that little honey, you throw her in a vat of hot water. Then throw in a couple, four lumps of lye soap and let her soak for a week."

Sahra and I exchanged glances. If she was bad enough to offend One-Eye, she had to be ripe indeed.

Goblin grinned from ear to ear but eschewed temptation.

I said, "I hear you ran into the Protector."

"She was on a roof or somewhere waiting for something to happen. She didn't get what she expected. A couple of fireballs and she ducked and stayed ducked."

"You made it home without being followed?" I knew the answer because I knew they knew the stakes. They would not have come anywhere near here had they had the slightest doubt that that was safe.

I had to ask, even knowing that if they had failed, the warehouse would be buried in Greys already.

"We were ready to deal with the crows."

"All but one," One-Eye grumbled.

"What?"

"I saw a white one up there. It didn't try to follow us, though."

Once again Sahra and I exchanged glances. Sahra said, "I'm going to change and relax and get something to eat. Let's meet in an hour. If you could find it in your heart, Goblin, you might try to get Murgen back here."

"You're the necromancer."

"You're the one who claimed he anchored him. One hour."

Goblin began grumbling to himself. One-Eye chuckled and made no offer to help. He asked me, "You ready to kill your librarian yet?"

I did not tell him so but I was slightly more open to the suggestion tonight. Surendranath Santaraksita seemed to suspect that Dorabee Dey Banerjae was something more than he pretended. Or maybe I was just paranoid enough to hear things Santaraksita never intended to say. "You don't worry about Master Santaraksita. He's being very good to me. Today he told me I can look at any book I want. Unless it's in the restricted stacks."

"Woo!" One-Eye breathed. "Somebody finally found the way to her heart. Who'd'a thunk a book would do it? Name the first one after me, Little Girl."

I waved a fist under his nose. "I'd knock out your last tooth and call you Mushy but I was brought up to respect my elders—even if

they're rambling, demented and senile." For all its One True God focus, my religion contains a strong taint of ancestor worship. Every
Vehdna believes his forefathers can hear his prayers and can inter-
cede with God and his saints. If he feels he has been properly treated.
"I'm going to follow Sahra's example."

"You holler if you want to get in practice for your new boyfriend."
His cackle ended abruptly as Gota limped around me. When I
glanced back, One-Eye appeared to be sound asleep again. Must
have been some other old fool running his mouth.

During the siege of Jaicur, I announced that never again would I be
picky about what I ate. That I would respond to anything offered me
with a smile of gratitude and a spoken "Thank you." But time has a
way of wearing away at such vows. I was nearly as sick of rice and
smoked fish as Goblin and One-Eye were. Breaking the tedium with
the occasional supper of rice and fish meal did not seem to help. I am
confident that it is their diet that makes the Nyueng Bao such a hu-
morless people.

I ran into Sahra, who had bathed and let her hair down and relaxed, looking a decade younger, so that it was easy to see how, a
decade earlier still, she could have been every young man's fantasy.
"I still have a little money I took off somebody who picked the wrong
side down south," I told her, waving a tiny piece of fish caught between two bamboo chopsticks. Nyueng Bao refuse to adopt innova-
tive utensils that have been in common use amongst everyone else
in this part of the world for centuries. Those who did the cooking in
Do Trang's complex were all Nyueng Bao.

"What?" Sahra was completely baffled.

"I'll give it up. If we can buy a pig with it." Vehdna are not supposed to eat pork. But I made the mistake of being born female, so I
probably do not have a seat reserved in Paradise anyway. "Or anything else that doesn't go through the water like this." I made a wig-
gly motion with one hand.

Sahra did not understand. Food was a matter of indifference to
her—so long as she got some. Fish and rice forever were perfectly
fine. And she was probably right. There are plenty of people out
there who have to eat chhatu because they cannot afford rice. And
others cannot afford any food at all. Though Soulcatcher seemed to
be thinning those out now.

Sahra started to tell me something about a rumor that another Bhodi disciple was going to present himself at the entrance to the Palace and demand an audience with the Radisha. But we were approaching the lighted area where we worked our wickednesses of evenings and she saw something there that made her stop.

I started to say, "Then we need to get somebody next to him—"

Sahra growled, "What the hell is *he* doing here?"

I saw it now. Uncle Doj was back, probably determined to invite himself into our lives again. His timing seemed interesting and suspect.

I also found it interesting that Sahra spoke Taglian when she was stressed. She had some definite points of contention with her own people, though around the warehouse nobody used Nyueng Bao except Mother Gota, who did so only to remain a pain.

Uncle Doj was a wide little man who, though on the brink of seventy, was mostly muscle and gristle, and in recent years, bad temper. He carried a long, slightly curved sword he called Ash Wand. Ash Wand was his soul. He had told me so. He was some sort of priest but would not bother to explain. His religion involved martial arts and holy swords, though. He was nobody's uncle in reality. Uncle was a title of respect among Nyueng Bao, and they all seemed to consider Doj a man worthy of the greatest respect.

Uncle Doj has meandered in and out of our lives since the siege of Jaicur, always more distraction than contribution. He could be underfoot for years at a stretch, then would disappear for weeks or months or years. This latest time he had been out of the way for more than a year. When he did turn up, he never bothered reporting what he had been doing or where he had been, but judging from Murgen's observations and my own, he was still searching for his Key diligently.

Curious, him materializing so suddenly after my epiphany. I asked Sahra, "Did your mother happen to leave the warehouse today?"

"That question occurred to me, too. It might be worth pursuit."

Very little warmth existed between mother and daughter. Murgen was not the cause but absolutely had become the symbol.

Uncle Doj was supposed to be a minor wizard. I never saw any evidence to support that, other than his uncanny skill with Ash Wand. He was old and his joints were getting stiff. His reflexes were fading. But I could not think of anyone who would remotely be his match.

Nor have I ever heard of anyone else dedicating his life to a piece of steel the way he has.

Maybe I did have evidence of his being a wizard, I reflected. He never had any trouble getting through the mazes Goblin and One-Eye had created to save us the embarrassment of unexpected walk-ins. Those two ought to tie him down till he explained how he did that.

I asked Sahra, "How do you want to handle this?"

Her voice was edged with flint. "Far as I'm concerned, we can lump him right in there with Singh and the Daughter of Night."

"The enemy of my enemy is my enemy, huh?"

"I never liked Doj much. By Nyueng Bao standards he's a great and honorable man, a hero due great respect. And he's the embodiment of everything I find distasteful about my people."

"Secretive, huh?"

She betrayed a hint of a smile. In that she was as guilty as any other Nyueng Bao. "That's in the blood."

Tobo noticed us watching and talking. He darted over. He was excited enough to forget he was a surly young man. "Mom. Uncle Doj is here."

"So I see. He say what he wants this time?"

I touched her arm gently, cautioning her. No need to start butting heads.

Doj, of course, was aware of our presence. I never saw a man so intensely aware of his environment. He might have heard every word we whispered, too. I put no store in the chance that time had weathered his sense of hearing. He gobbled rice and paid us no heed.

I told Sahra, "Go say hello. I need a second to put my face on."

"I ought to send for the Greys. Have them raid the place. I'm too tired for this." She did not bother to keep her voice down.

"Mom?"

20

I held Doj's eye. My face was cold. My voice held no emotion whatsoever as I asked, "What is the Key?" Bound, gagged, Narayan Singh and Daughter of Night watched and waited their turn.

The faintest flicker of surprise stirred in Doj's eyes. I was not the sort he expected to be a questioner.

I was in character again, a borrowed one based on a gang enforcer who had offended us a few years ago, Vajra the Naga. The gang was out of business and Vajra the Naga had gone on to a better world but his legacy occasionally proved useful.

Doj enjoyed the reasonable expectation that he would not be tortured. I had no intention of taking it that far. With him. The Company's fortunes and those of the Nyueng Bao had become so intermingled that I could not brutalize Doj without alienating our most useful allies.

Doj volunteered nothing. Nor did I expect him to be any more vocal than a stone. I told him, "We need to open the way onto the glittering plain. We know you don't have the Key. We do know where to start looking for it. We'll be pleased to return it to you once we release our brothers." I paused, giving him time to surprise me by replying. He did not.

"You are, perhaps, philosophically opposed to opening the way. We're going to disappoint you on that. The way will open. Somehow. You have only the option of participating or not participating."

Doj's eyes shifted, just for an instant. He wanted to read Sahra's stance.

Hers was plain. She had a husband trapped under the glittering plain. The wishes of the lone priest of some obscure, never-explained cult carried no weight with her.

Not even Banh Do Trang or Ky Gota offered demonstrative support, though both would favor him mainly out of decades of inertia.

"If you don't cooperate, then we won't return the Key when we're done with it. And *we* will determine what constitutes cooperation. The first step is to put an end to all of the normal Nyueng Bao equivocation and evasion and selective deafness."

Vajra the Naga was not a character I liked to adopt too often. A naga was a mythical serpent being that lived beneath the earth and had no sympathy whatever for anything human. The trouble with the character was that I could slip into it like it had been tailored for me. It would take only a small emotional distortion to turn me into Vajra the Naga.

"You have something we want. A book." I was betting a lot on my having reasoned out or intuited the course of various hidden events based upon what I had gotten from Murgen and his Annals. "It's about so-by-so and this thick, bound in tan vellum. The writing inside is in an untrained hand in a language no one has spoken for seven centuries. Specifically, it is a nearly complete copy of the first volume of the Books of the Dead, the lost sacred texts of the Children of Kina. Chances are you didn't know that."

Narayan and even the Daughter of Night reacted to that.

I continued, "The book was stolen from the fortress Overlook by the sorcerer called the Howler. He concealed it because he didn't want Soulcatcher to get it, nor did he want the child to have it. You either saw him hide it or stumbled onto it soon after he did. You concealed it somewhere you feel is safe. Ignoring the fact that nothing can remain hidden forever. Some eyes will discover anything eventually."

Once again I allowed Doj time for remarks. He chose to pass on the opportunity.

"You have a choice in all this. I remind you, though, that you're getting old, that your chosen successor is buried under the plain with my brothers, and that you have no allies more favorable than Gota, whose enthusiasm has to be suspect at this late date. You may choose to say nothing, ever, in which case truth will follow you into the darkness. But the Key will remain here. In other hands. Have you had enough to eat? Has Do Trang been a good host? Will somebody help our guest find something to drink? We shouldn't be scorned for our failures of hospitality."

"You didn't get a word out of him," One-Eye complained as soon as Doj was out of earshot.

"I didn't expect to. I just wanted him to have something to think about. Let's talk to these two. Scoot Singh over here, take the gag off and turn him so he can't get cues from the girl." She was spooky. Even bound and gagged, she radiated a disturbingly potent presence. Put her in the company of people already prepared to believe that she was touched by the dark divine and it was easy to understand why the Deceiver cult was making a comeback. Interesting, though, that that was a recent phenomenon. That for a decade she and Narayan had been fugitives painstakingly taking control of the few surviving Deceivers and evading the Protector's agents, and now, just as *we* feel we are up to tugging a few beards, *they* began making their survival known, too.

I had no trouble seeing where the Gunni imagination would find connections and portents and wild harbingers of the Year of the Skulls.

"Narayan Singh," I said in my Vajra the Naga voice. "You're a stubborn old man. You should have been dead long ago. Perhaps Kina does favor you. Which would suggest that here in my hands is where the goddess wants you to be." We Vehdna are good at blaming everything on God. Nothing can happen that is not the will of God. Therefore, He has already measured the depth of the brown stuff and has decided to toss you in. "And these are bloody hands, make no mistake."

Singh looked at me. He did not fear much. He did not recognize me. If our paths had crossed before, I had been too minor an annoyance for him to recall.

The Daughter of Night remembered me, though. She was thinking that I was a mistake she would not be making again. I was thinking maybe she was a mistake *we* ought not to make, however useful a tool she might become. She almost scared Vajra the Naga, who had been too dense to comprehend fear in personal terms.

"You're troubled by events but aren't afraid. You rely upon your goddess. Good. Let me provide assurances. We won't harm you. Assuming you cooperate. However much we owe you."

He did not believe a word of that and I did not blame him. That was the usual sort of "hold out a feather of hope" a torturer used to leverage cooperation from the doomed. "In this case, the pain will all be directed elsewhere."

He tried to turn to look at the girl.

"Not just there, Narayan Singh. Not only there. Though that's where we'll start. Narayan, you have something we want. We have several things we believe to be of value to you. I'm prepared to make an exchange, sworn in the names of all our gods."

Narayan had nothing to say. Yet. But I began to sense that his ears might be open to the right words.

The Daughter of Night sensed that, too. She squirmed. She tried to make some kind of noise. She was going to be as stubborn and crazy as her mother and aunt. Must be the blood.

"Narayan Singh. In another life you were a vegetable seller in the town called Gondowar. Every other summer you would go off to lead your company of *tooga*." Singh looked uncomfortable and puzzled.

This was nothing he expected. "You had a wife, Yashodara, whom you called Lily in private. You had a daughter, Khaditya, which was maybe just a little too clever a naming. You had three sons: Valmiki, Sugriva and Aridatha. Aridatha you've never seen because he wasn't born until after the Shadowmasters carried the able men of Gondowar off into captivity."

Narayan looked more uncomfortable and troubled than ever. His life before the coming of the Shadowmasters was a lost episode. Since his unexpected salvation, he had dedicated himself solely to his goddess and her Daughter.

"Those times were so unsettled that you have since proceeded on the reasonable assumption that nothing of your former life survived the coming of the Shadowmasters. But that assumption is a false one, Narayan Singh. Yashodara bore you that third son, Aridatha, and lived to see him become a grown man. Though she endured great poverty and despair, your Lily survived until just two years ago." In fact, until just after we located her. I still did not know for certain if some of my brothers had not grown overly zealous in their eagerness to locate Narayan. "Of your sons, Aridatha and Sugriva still live, as does your daughter Khaditya, though she has used the name Amba since she learned, to her horror, that her very father was the Narayan Singh of such widespread infamy."

By stealing Lady's baby, Narayan had ensured that his name would live on amongst those of the great villains. Everyone over a certain age knew the name and a score of evil stories burdening it— the majority of them fabrications or accretions of stories formerly attached to some other human demon whose ignominy had been nibbled up by time.

I had his attention despite his determination to remain indifferent. Family is critically important to all but a handful of us.

"Sugriva continues in the produce business, although his desire to escape your reputation led him first to move to Ayodahk, then to Jaicur when the Protector decided she wanted the city repopulated. He felt everyone would be strangers there and he could create a more favorable past for himself."

Both captives noted my unfortunate use of "Jaicur." Which did not give them anything they could use but which did tell them I was not Taglian. No Taglian would call that city anything but Dejagore.

I continued, "Aridatha grew into a fine young man, well-formed and beautiful. He's a soldier now, a senior noncommissioned officer in one of the City Battalions. His rise has been rapid. He has been noticed. There's a good chance he'll be chosen to become one of the career commissioned officers the Great General had been imposing on the army."

I fell silent. No one else spoke. Some were hearing this for the first time, though Sahra and I had started looking for those people a long time ago.

I got up and went out, got myself a large cup of tea. I cannot abide the Nyueng Bao tea-making ceremonies. I am, of course, a barbarian in their eyes. I do not like the tiny little cups they use, either. When I have some tea, I want to get serious about it. Make it strong and bitter and toss in a glob of honey.

I seated myself in front of Narayan again. No one had spoken in my absence. "So, living saint of the Stranglers, have you truly put aside all the chains of the earth? Would you like to see your Khaditya again? She was little when you left. Would you like to see your grandchildren? There are five of them. I can say the word and inside a week we can have one of them here." I sipped tea, looked Singh in the eye and let his imagination toy with the possibilities. "But *you* are going to be all right, Narayan. I'm going to see to that personally." I showed him my Vajra the Naga smile. "Will somebody show these two to their guest rooms?"

"That all you're going to do?" Goblin asked once they were gone.

"I'm going to let Singh think about the life he never lived. I'll let him think about losing what's left of that. *And* about losing his messiah. When he can avoid all those tragedies just by telling us where to find the souvenir he carried away from Soulcatcher's hideout down by Kiaulune."

"He won't take a deep breath without getting permission from the girl."

"We'll see how he handles having to make his own decisions. If he stalls too long and we get pressed, you can put a glamour on me that'll make him think I'm her."

"What about her?" One-Eye asked. "You going to personally work on her, too?"

"Yes. Starting right now. Put some of those choke spells on her. One on each wrist and ankle. And double them up around her neck." We had done some herding, amongst other things, over the years and One-Eye and Goblin, being incredibly lazy, had developed choke spells that constricted tighter and tighter as an animal moved farther away from a selected marker point. "She's a resourceful woman with a goddess on her side. I'd prefer to kill her and be done with it but we won't get any help from Singh if we do. If she does manage to escape, I want complete success to be fatal. I want near success to render her unconscious from lack of air. I don't want her having regular contact with any of our people. Remember what her aunt, Soulcatcher, did to Willow Swan. Tobo. Has Swan said anything that might interest us?"

"He just plays cards, Sleepy. He does talk all the time but he never says anything. Kind of like Uncle One-Eye."

Whisper. "You put him up to that, didn't you, Frogface?"

"Sounds like Swan to me," I said. I shut my eyes, began massaging my brow between thumb and forefinger, trying to make Vajra the Naga go away. His reptilian lack of connection was seductive. "I'm so tired—"

"Then why the hell don't we all just retire?" One-Eye croaked. "For a whole goddamned generation it was the Captain and his next year in Khatovar shit that beat us into the ground. Now it's you two women and your holy crusade to resurrect the Captured. Find yourself a guy, Little Girl. Spend a year screwing his brains out. We're not going to get those people out of there. Accept that. Start believing that they're dead."

He sounded exactly like the traitor in my soul that whispered in my mind every night before I fell asleep. The part about accepting that the Captured were never going to be coming back, anyway. I asked Sahra, "Can we call up our favorite dead man? One-Eye, ask him what he thinks of our plan."

"Bah! Frogface, you deal with this. I need a little medicinal pick-me-up."

Almost smiling despite her aching joints, Gota waddled out behind One-Eye. We would not see those two for a while. If we were lucky, One-Eye would get drunk fast and pass out. If we were not, he would come staggering out looking to feud with Goblin and we would have to restrain him. That could turn into an adventure.

"Well. Here's our prodigal." Sahra finally had Murgen back in the mist box.

I told him, "Tell me about the white crow."

Puzzled, "I go there sometimes. It's not voluntary."

"We took Narayan Singh and the Daughter of Night out of Chor Bagan today. There was a white crow there. You weren't here."

"I wasn't there." More puzzled. Even troubled. "I don't remember being there."

"I think Soulcatcher noticed it. And she knows her crows."

Murgen continued, "I wasn't there but I remember things that happened. This can't be happening to me again."

"Just calm down. Tell us what you know."

Murgen proceeded to report everything Soulcatcher said and did after she ducked our snipers. He would not tell us how he knew. I do not think he could.

Sahra said, "She does know that we have Singh and the girl."

"But did she guess why? The Company has an old grudge with those two."

"She'll need to see bodies to be convinced there was nothing more to it than that. She's still not completely satisfied that Swan is dead. A very suspicious woman, the Protector."

"A Narayan corpse would be easy—if we could make it credible. There're a million skinny, filthy little old men with green teeth out there. But we'd sure come up short on beautiful twenty-year-old women with blue eyes and skin paler than ivory."

"The Greys will definitely become more active now," Sahra said. "Whatever she suspects or doesn't, the Protector wants no one going about any tricky business in her city."

"A point the Radisha might argue. Which reminds me of something that's been knocking around the back of my head. Listen to this and tell me what you think."

21

As the Bhodi disciples made their way through the crowds, more than one onlooker reached out to slap their backs. The disciples took that with poor grace. It told them that many of the witnesses were there to be entertained.

The rite proceeded as before, but more quickly as it was evident that the Greys anticipated trouble and had instructions to head it off.

The kneeling priest in orange burst into flames just as the Greys began manhandling his assistants out of the way.

A gout of smoke leaped upward. A Black Company skull formed inside it, an evil eye seeming to stare deep into the souls of all the witnesses. A voice filled the morning. "All their days are numbered."

And the wooden curtain-wall shielding the reconstruction came to life. Glowing lime characters as tall as a man proclaimed "Water Sleeps," and "My Brother Unforgiven." They crawled slowly back and forth.

Soulcatcher herself materialized on the ramparts overhead. Her rage was palpable.

A second and larger cloud of smoke burst off the burning disciple. A face—the best representation of the Captain's that One-Eye and Goblin could manage—told the awed and silent thousands, "Rajadharma! The Duty of Kings. Know you: Kingship is a Trust. The King is the most exalted and conscientious servant of the people."

I began to slide away from there. This was sure to sting the Protector into some impulsive and self-defeating response.

Or maybe not. She did nothing obvious, though a sudden breeze came along. It blew the smoke away. But it fanned the flames consuming the Bhodi disciple. The smell of burning flesh spread out downwind.

22

When Master Santaraksita wanted to know why I was late, I told the truth. "Another Bhodi disciple set himself on fire in front of the Palace. I went to watch. I couldn't help myself. There was sorcery involved." I described what I had seen. As so many of the actual eyewitnesses also had, Santaraksita seemed both repelled and intrigued.

"Why do you suppose those disciples are doing that, Dorabee?"

I knew why they were doing it. It took no genius to fathom their motives. Only their determination remained a puzzle. "They're tying to tell the Radisha that she's not fulfilling her obligations to the Taglian people. They consider the situation so desperate that they've chosen to send their message by a means that can't be ignored."

"I, too, believe that to be the case. The question remains: What can the Radisha *do*? The Protector won't go away just because some people believe she's bad for Taglios."

"I have a great deal to do today, Sri, and I'm starting late."

"Go. Go. I must assemble the bhadrhalok. It's possible we can present the Radisha with some means of shaking the Protector's grip."

"Good luck, Sri." He would need it. Only the most outrageous good luck since the beginning of time was going to give him and his cronies the tools to undo Soulcatcher. Chances were good the bhadrhalok had no idea how dangerous an opponent they had chosen.

I dusted and mopped and checked the rodent traps and after a while noticed that most everyone had gone away. I asked old Baladitya the copyist where everyone was. He told me that the other copyists had ducked out as soon as the senior librarians had gone off to their bhadrhalok meeting. They knew that the bhadrhalok would do nothing but it would take them hours of grumbling and talking and arguing to get it done, so they made themselves a holiday.

It was not an opportunity to be refused. I began examining books, even going so far as to penetrate the restricted stacks. Baladitya knew nothing. He could not see three feet in front of his face.

23

Jaul Barundandi partnered Minh Subredil with a young woman named Rahini and sent them to work in the Radisha's own quarters, under the direction of a woman named Narita, a fat, ugly creature possessed by an inflated conception of her own importance. Narita complained to Barundandi, "I need six more women. I'm supposed to clean the council chamber again after I complete the royal suite."

"Then I suggest you pick up a broom yourself. I'll be back in a few hours. I expect to see progress. I've given you the best workers available." Barundandi went elsewhere to be unpleasant to someone else.

The fat woman took it out on Subredil and Rahini. Subredil did not know who Narita was. The woman had not worked in the royal chambers before. As Subredil steered a mop around, she whispered, "Who is this woman who is so bitter?" She stroked her Ghanghesha.

Rahini glanced right and left but did not raise her eyes. "You must understand her. She is Barundandi's wife."

"You two! You aren't being paid to gossip."

"Pardon, ma'am," Sahra said. "I didn't understand what to do and didn't want to trouble you."

The fat woman scowled for a moment but then turned her displeasure in another direction. Rahini smiled softly, whispered, "She's in a good mood today."

As the hours passed and her knees and hands and muscles began to ache, Sahra realized that she and Rahini had been delivered to Barundandi's wife more for who they were than for the work they could do. They were not bright and they were not among the more attractive workers. Barundandi wanted Narita to believe that these were the kind of women he always employed. Elsewhere, no doubt, he and his chief assistants would take full advantage of their bit of power over the unfortunate and the desperate.

It was not a good day for exploring. There was more work than three women could possibly complete. Sahra got no chance to collect additional pages from the hidden Annals. Then, not many hours after the day started, conditions within the Palace became much less relaxed. The high and the mighty began to show themselves, moving rapidly here and there. Rumor came, apparently passing right through stone walls. Another Bhodi disciple had burned himself to death outside and the Radisha was completely distraught. Narita herself confided, "She's very frightened. Many things are happening over which she has no control. She has gone to the Anger Chamber. She does so almost every day now."

"The Anger Chamber?" Sahra murmured. She had not heard of this before, but till recently she never worked this close to the heart of the Palace. "What is that, ma'am?"

"A room set aside where she can tear her hair and clothing and rage and weep without having her emotions poison surroundings used for other purposes. She won't come out until she can face the world in complete calm."

Subredil understood: It was a Gunni thing. Only Gunni would come up with an idea like that. Gunni religion personified everything. It had a god or goddess or demon, a deva or rakshasa or yaksha or whatever for everything, usually with several aspects and avatars and differing names, none of whom were seen much nowadays but who had been very busy way back when.

Only an extremely wealthy Gunni would come up with a conceit like an Anger Chamber—a Gunni cursed with a thousand rooms she did not know how to use.

Later in the day Subredil contrived to be allowed to service the freshly evacuated Anger Chamber. It was small and contained nothing but a mat on a polished wooden floor and a small shrine to ancestors. The smoke was thick and the smell of incense was overpowering.

24

A good thing I didn't have any pages on me, too," Sahra told me. "The Greys started searching us going out. That woman Vancha tried to steal a little silver oil lamp. She'll spend all morning tomorrow being 'punished' by Jaul Barundandi."

"Does Barundandi's boss know what he does?"

"I don't think so. Why?"

"We could trick him into betraying himself. Get him tossed out."

"No. Barundandi is the devil we know. An honest man would be harder to manipulate."

"I loathe the man."

"That's because he's loathsome. Not unlike other men in similar positions of petty power. But we're not here to reform Taglios, Sleepy. We're here to find out how to release the Captured. And to torment our enemies when doing that doesn't jeopardize our primary mission. And we did a great job of that today. The Radisha was crushed by our messages."

Sahra told me what she had discovered. Then I told her about my own small triumph. "I got into the restricted stacks today. And I found what I think might be the original of one of the Annals we've got hidden in the Palace. It's in terrible shape but it's all there and it's still readable. And there may be more volumes. I only got through part of the restricted stack before I had to go help Baladitya find his slippers so his grandson could lead him home."

I had the book right there on the table. I patted it proudly. Sahra asked, "Won't it be missed?"

"I hope not. I replaced it with one of the moldy discards I've been saving."

Sahra squeezed my hand. "Good. Good. Things have gone well lately. Tobo, would you find Goblin? I have an idea to run past him."

I said, "I'll see how our guests are doing. Somebody might be ready to whisper confidences in my ear."

But only Swan wanted my ear and he did not have confidences in mind. In his way he was as incorrigible as One-Eye, yet he had a style that did not offend me. I do not think Swan had an evil bone in him. Like so many people, he was a victim of circumstance, struggling to keep his head up in the turbulence of the river of events.

Uncle Doj was displeased with his circumstances even though he was not a prisoner. "We can certainly get along without that book," I told him. "I doubt that I could read it, anyway. Mostly I want to make sure it doesn't get back to the Deceivers. What we really need is your knowledge."

Doj was a stubborn old man. He was not yet ready to make deals or to look for allies.

Before I left I asked, "Will it all die with you? Will you be the last Nyueng Bao to follow the Path? Thai Dei can't if he's buried under the glittering plain." I winked. I understood Doj better than he thought. His problem was not a conflict with his morality, it was a matter of control. He wanted to do everything his way, no strings.

He would come around if I kept reminding him of his mortality and his lack of a son or an apprentice. Nyueng Bao are famous for their stubbornness but even they will not sacrifice all their hopes and dreams rather than adjust.

I visited Narayan just long enough to offer a reminder that our interest did not lie in harming him. But the only reason we had for keeping the Daughter of Night healthy was our hope of his cooperation. "You can be stubborn for a while yet. We have several tasks to wrap up before you become our main interest and we concentrate on murdering your dreams."

That was my whole focus with each of our prisoners. Make them put their hopes and dreams on the line. Maybe I could weasel my way into history, as famous or infamous as Soulcatcher and Widowmaker, as Stormshadow and Longshadow, remembered forever as the Dreamkiller.

I had a vision of myself drifting through the night like Murgen, disembodied but dragging along a bottomless bag of black night into which I stuffed all the dreams I stole from restless sleepers. I was a real old-time rakshasa, there.

The Daughter of Night did not look up when I went to view her. She was in a cage Banh Do Trang used for keeping large animals of the deadliest sort. Sometimes leopards, but mostly tigers. A fully grown male tiger was worth a fortune in the apothecary market. She was shackled as well. The cats never were. In addition, I believe, a little opium and nightshade were used to season her food. Nobody wanted to underestimate her potential. Her family had a dire history. And she had a goddess on her shoulder.

Reason told me to kill her right now, before Kina wakened as much as she could. That would buy me the rest of my lifetime free of the end of the world. It would take the dark goddess generations to create another Daughter of Night.

Reason also told me that if the girl died, the Captured would spend the rest of time in those caverns under the glittering plain.

Reason told me, after a moment watching her, that she was not just ignoring me. She did not know I was there. Her mind was elsewhere. Which was not a comfortable feeling at all. If Kina could turn her loose, the way Murgen was loose. . . .

25

Master Santaraksita paused to tell me, "It was good of you to care for Baladitya yesterday, Dorabee. I had forgotten him in my eagerness to assemble the bhadrhalok. But you should be careful or his grandson will begin expecting you to walk the old man home for him. He tried it with me."

I did not look into his eyes, though I did want to see what was there. There was a tightness in his voice that told me he had something on his mind. But I had taken too many liberties with Dorabee already. He would not stare into the eyes of the priestly caste. "I but did the right thing, Master. Are we not taught to respect and aid our elders? If we do not when we are young, who will respect and aid us when we ourselves become frail?"

"Indeed. Nevertheless, you continue to amaze and intrigue me, Dorabee."

Uncomfortable, I tried to change the subject by inquiring, "Was the meeting of the bhadrhalok productive, Master?"

Santaraksita frowned, then smiled. "You're very subtle, Dorabee. No. Of course not. We're the bhadrhalok. We talk. We don't act." For a moment he mocked his own kind. "We'll still be debating what form our resistance should take when the Protector perishes of old age."

"Is it true what they say, Master? That she's four hundred years old, yet fresh as a bride?" I did not need to know, I just needed conversation to nurture Santaraksita's surprising interest in me.

"That seems to be the common belief, handed down from the northern mercenaries and those travelers the Radisha adopted."

"She must be a great sorceress indeed, then."

"Do I detect a note of jealousy?"

"Would we all not like to live forever?"

He looked at me oddly. "But we shall, Dorabee. This life is only a stage."

Wrong thing to say, Dorabee Dey. "I meant in this world. I find myself largely content to remain Dorabee Dey Banerjae."

Santaraksita frowned slightly but let it go. "How are your studies coming?"

"Wonderfully, Master. I'm especially fond of the historical texts. I'm discovering so many interesting facts."

"Excellent. Excellent. If there's anything I can do to help . . ."

I asked, "Is there a written Nyueng Bao language? Or was there ever?"

That took him from the blind side. "Nyueng Bao? I don't know. Why in the world would you—"

"Something I've seen a few times near where I live. Nobody knows what it means. The Nyueng Bao down there won't talk. But I never heard of them being literate."

He rested a hand on my shoulder for a moment. "I'll find out for you." His fingers seemed to be trembling. He murmured something unintelligible and hurried away.

26

Word was in that the Bhodi disciples were not happy with us for stealing their thunder at the Palace gate. I wondered what they would think when the news arrived about our behavior at Semchi. That seemed to be coming together perfectly for us. Unless Soulcatcher was thinking farther ahead than we could detect.

Murgen had Slink's party well on the way to the village. And moving faster than the group the Protector had sent to destroy the Bhodi Tree. That group outnumbered our brothers but did not expect any resistance. In a few days it would turn really nasty down there.

As the weather had here. Storm season had arrived. I had been delayed coming home by a ferocious thunderstorm that flooded some streets and sent down hail an inch in diameter. The kangali and other children went out and tried to gather up the ice, barking in pain every time a hailstone found unprotected skin. For a short while the air was almost tolerably cool. But then the storm moved on and the heat returned worse than it had been before. The stench of the city welled up. One storm was not enough to sluice it clean, only to turn everything over. In a few days the insects would be more miserable than ever before.

I hugged my burden and told myself I would not have to stay in this cesspool much longer.

"One more to locate and I'll have everything I need from the library." My new acquisition lay open for public viewing. Of course no one could read it. Not even me. But I was confident that I now possessed another original of the three missing Annals. Perhaps the very first, since it was so alien. The other seemed to be inscribed in the same alphabet, much modified and somewhat like that used in the discarded volume I had rescued. If the language was the same, I would be able to figure it out eventually.

One-Eye cackled. "Yeah. Everything but somebody to translate that stuff for you. Everything but your new boyfriend." He insisted that Master Santaraksita was out to seduce me. And that Santaraksita would be brokenhearted if he succeeded and discovered that I was female.

"That's enough of that, you filthy old thing."

"Sacrifice for the cause, Little Girl." He started to offer some graphic advice. He had been drinking again. Or was drinking still.

Sahra arrived. She tossed a large bundle of pages my way. "Can it, One-Eye. Find Goblin. There's work to do." Of me she demanded, "Why do you put up with that?"

"He's harmless. And he's for sure too darned old to change. And if he's nagging me, he's not getting into something that's going to get us all killed."

"So you're sacrificing for the cause."

"Something like that. That was quick." Goblin had arrived. "What happened to One-Eye?"

"Taking a leak. What do I have to do now?"

Sahra said, "I can get into the Anger Chamber. The rest is up to you."

"You do this and you'll never be able to get back into the Palace. You know that, don't you?"

"What're we talking about?" I asked.

Sahra said, "I think we can kidnap the Radisha. With a little luck and a lot of help from Goblin and One-Eye."

"Goblin's right. You do that, we'd all better be a hundred miles away by the time the word gets out. I have a better idea. If we have to give away the fact that we can get inside the Palace, do it by sabotaging Soulcatcher. Get to one of her carpets, rig it to come apart under her when she's two hundred feet up and moving fast."

"I like the way you think, Sleepy. Put that on the list, Sahra. I want to be there. It'd be like the time the Howler flew into the side of the Tower at Charm. Man, he must've been going at least three times as fast as a horse could run when he hit that wall. Blauw! Hair, teeth and eyeballs all over the—"

"He walked away from that, you idiot." One-Eye was back. "He's out there under the plain with our guys right now." A unique odor suggested that One-Eye had taken a moment out to award himself some medicinal refreshment.

"Stop it. Now." Sahra was cranky tonight. "Our next step will be to neutralize Chandra Gokhale. We've already decided that. These other things we can worry about down the road."

I observed, "We'll need to freshen up our evacuation drill in case we need to get out of Taglios in a hurry. The more active we get, the more likely it becomes that something will go wrong. If it does, we'll have Soulcatcher breathing down our necks."

Goblin observed, "She isn't stupid, she's just lazy."

I asked Sahra, "Did she call in her shadows yet?"

"I don't know. I didn't hear anything."

Goblin grumbled. "What we really need is a formula for doing without sleep. For about a year. Let me see Minh Subredil's Ghanghesha."

Sahra sent Tobo to fetch the statue. The boy could be much less unpleasant when he was in a group.

Silence struck as Banh Do Trang rolled in, pushed by one of his own people. He smiled at a private joke. He enjoyed startling us. "One of my men tells me that we have a couple of outsiders caught in the confusion net. They appear to be harmless. An old man and a mute. Somebody will have to get them out and send them on their way without making them suspicious."

That news gave me a little chill but I did not suspect the truth till poor overworked Tobo and Goblin—the latter going along but staying out of sight while the boy led the intruders to safety—returned and Goblin reported, "I think your boyfriend followed you home, Sleepy."

"What?"

"There was this terrified old man who tried to impress Tobo with the fact that he was a librarian." A lot of Taglians would have been impressed. The ability to read was almost a sorcery in itself. "He called his sidekick Adoo. You told us—"

One-Eye began to howl. "The Little Girl's a regular heartbreaker! Damn, I'd give anything to be there when that old fool slides his hand into her pants and don't find what he's looking for."

I was embarrassed. I do not think I have been embarrassed about anything since the first time my uncle Rafi slipped his hand under my sari and did find what he was after. That darned fool Santaraksita! Why did he have to go complicating things like this?

"That's enough of that!" Sahra snapped. "There's supposed to be a meeting of the Privy Council tomorrow. I think we can use it to get to Gokhale. But I'll need to take Sawa and Shikhandini."

"Why?" I asked. I had no desire to go back inside the Palace ever again.

"That's great," One-Eye enthused. "You don't show at the library tomorrow, that old goat is gonna pine and whine and wonder what happened, if it's all his fault even though he knows there's no way you could know he tried to follow you home. You'll have your hook set, Little Girl. All you have to do is pull him in."

Sahra snapped, "I said—"

"Wait a minute. He may have a point. Suppose I do play Santaraksita's game? To the point where I get him to do my translations for me? We could even add him to our collection. I don't think he has much family. Why don't we take a closer look, see how long it might be before people wondered why he was missing."

"Oh, you're wicked, Little Girl," One-Eye said. "You're really wicked."

"You could find out someday, you keep riding me."

"About Gokhale?" Sahra asked.

"All right. Why are we taking me and Tobo both?"

"Tobo to put an idea into his head so he gets an itch he's going to have to go scratch. You to cover us. Just in case. I'll have Tobo carry his flute." Tobo's flute was a small version of the fire-projecting bamboo. "He can turn it over to you once we're inside." Tobo had carried that flute every time he had accompanied his mother into the Palace. We try to think ahead. "Also, I want to keep you fresh in Jaul Barundandi's mind. I'll definitely have to have you along when I snatch the Radisha. Goblin, what can you do with my Ghanghesha?"

No one else on earth would have dared hand the little wizard a straight line like that. But Sahra was Sahra. She did not have to pay the price.

I started to leave. I had other things to do. Tobo asked, "Is it all right if I show your Annals to Murgen? He wants to read them."

"You two starting to get along now?"

"I think so."

"Good. You can let him see them. Tell him not to be too critical. If he is, I won't come out there and dig him up."

27

Narayan seemed thoroughly puzzled by my continued interest. I do not believe he remembered me at all. But he now knew that I was female and had been the young man Sleepy that he had encountered, only rarely, ages ago.

"You've had time to reflect. Have you decided to help us yet?"

He looked at me with pure venom, yet without obvious personal hatred. I was just a particularly unpleasant obstacle delaying the inevitable triumph of his goddess. He had gotten his mind back into a rut.

"All right. I'll see you again tomorrow night. Your son Aridatha has a leave day coming up. We'll bring him around to visit you."

There was a guard watching the Daughter of Night. "What're you doing here, Kendo?"

"Keeping an eye on—"

"Go away. And don't come back. And spread the word. *Nobody* guards the Daughter of Night. She's too dangerous. Nobody even goes near her unless Sahra or I tell them to. And then they don't do it alone."

"She don't look—"

"She wouldn't, would she? Start hiking." I went to the cage. "How long would it take for your goddess to create all the right conditions for the birth of another like you? If I decide to kill you?"

The girl's gaze rose slowly. I wanted to cringe away from the power in her eyes but I held on. Maybe she should be getting even more opium than she was already.

"Reflect upon your value. And upon my power to destroy it." I felt puffed up. That was the kind of thing the devas, or lesser gods, blathered at one another on the fringes of the epics spun by the professional storytellers.

She glared. There was so much power in her eyes that I decided Kendo ought to spend a little time in private with Goblin and One-Eye, making sure he had not been taken in already.

"I think that without you there never will be a Year of the Skulls. And I *know* that you're still alive only because I want something from Narayan, who loves you like a father." Singh *was* her father, for all practical purposes. Croaker had been denied the chance by cruel Fortune. Or, more accurately, by the will of Kina.

"Keep well, dear." I left. I had a lot of reading to get done. And some writing if I got the chance. My days were always full and all too often they got confused. I decided to do things, then forgot. I told others to do things, then forgot that, too. I was beginning to look for-ward to the time when our successes—or sufficiently spectacular failures—forced us out of town. I could sneak off somewhere where nobody knew me and just loaf for a few months.

Or for the rest of my life if I wanted.

I had no trouble understanding why every year a few more of our brothers gave up and faded away. I only hoped a little notoriety would bring them back.

I studied the pages Sahra had brought out for me but the transla-tion was difficult, the subject matter was uninspiring, and I was tired. I kept losing my concentration. I thought about Master Santaraksita. I thought about going back up to the Palace, armed. I thought about what Soulcatcher would do now that she knew she did not have us trapped inside the Thieves' Garden. I thought about getting old and being alone and had a suspicion that that fear might have something to do with why some brothers remained with the Company no mat-ter what. They had no other family.

I have no other family.

I will not look back. I am not weak. I will not relax my self-con-trol. I will persevere. I will triumph over myself and will conquer all adversity.

I fell asleep rereading my own recollections of what Murgen had reported about the Company's adventure on the glittering plain. I dreamed about the creatures he had encountered there. Were they the rakshasas and Nagas of myth? Did they have anything to do with the shadows, or with the men who evidently created the shadows from hapless prisoners of war?

28

I have a bad feeling about this," I told Sahra as she and Tobo and I started the long walk. "You're sure the shadows are all off the streets?"

"Quit fussing, Sleepy. You're turning into an old woman. The streets are safe. The only monsters out here are human. We can han-dle those. You'll be safe in the Palace if you just stick to your charac-ter. Tobo will be safe as long as he remembers that he's not really

Shikhandini and desperate for his mother to keep her job. It's in the nature of men like Jaul Barundandi that they do their bullying inside your head, not physically. They'll take 'no' for an answer. And I won't lose my job over it. My work is being noticed by others. Especially by Barundandi's wife. Now, get yourself into character. Tobo, you too. You particularly. I know Sleepy can do this when she concentrates on it."

Tobo was clad as a budding young woman, Minh Subredil's daughter, and I hoped we could get him back inside the warehouse unnoticed by Goblin and One-Eye, because they would ride him mercilessly. With the investment of a little artifice on his mother's part, Tobo made a very attractive young woman.

Jaul Barundandi thought so, too. Minh Subredil was the first worker called forward and Barundandi never bothered with his customary grumble about taking Sawa as part of the package.

Sawa had trouble keeping a straight face later when we found Barundandi's wife Narita waiting to pick women to work for her. One glance at Shiki was enough. Minh Subredil's family definitely belonged under her direct supervision.

Minh Subredil had done a good job of ingratiating herself with Narita. For the very good reason that Narita was in charge of cleaning those parts of the Palace of most immediate interest to us.

Sawa had not worked for Narita in the past. Subredil explained Sawa to Narita, who seemed more patient than she had the few times I had seen her before. Narita said, "I understand. There're plenty of simple things that need doing. The Radisha was particularly restless last night. These days when she has trouble sleeping, she breaks things and makes messes."

The woman actually sounded sympathetic. But the Taglian people loved their ruling family and seemed to feel that they deserved more room than the man on the street. Perhaps because of the burdens they bore, always in the past with maximum respect for *Rajadharma*.

Subredil maneuvered me into a spot whence I could observe well without being noticed. She and Narita brought me several brass treasures that needed cleaning. The ruling family had to be very fond of brass. Sawa cleaned tons of it. But Sawa could be trusted not to damage anything.

Shiki came to me and asked, "Will you take care of my flute for me, Aunt Sawa?" I took the instrument, studied it briefly, pasted on an idiot grin and tooted on the thing a few times. Just so everybody would know it was a real flute and not imagine that it might be a small fireball thrower, capable of making life both brief and painful for the first half-dozen people who got too close to a flautist in a bad temper.

Barundandi's wife asked Shiki, "You play the flute?"

"Yes, ma'am. But not very well."

"I was quite a skilled player when I was a girl . . ." She noticed her husband peeking in for the second time this morning and began to suspect he was interested in more than just the progress of the day's work. "Subredil, I don't think it's wise for you to bring your daughter here." And a moment later, she growled, "I'll be back in a minute. I have to talk to that man. I have to straighten him out."

The moment she stepped out, Minh Subredil moved with startling rapidity. She vanished into the Radisha's Anger Chamber. I had to admire her. Her mind never seemed clearer than when she was in a dangerous position. I suspected she actually enjoyed her role as a Palace menial. And the more dangerous the times, the more effective she seemed.

Despite a massive workload and Narita's frequent trips away to sabotage her husband's efforts to weasel in close to Shikhandini, or to draft Shiki into a different working group, in mid-afternoon we left the Radisha's personal suite for the gloomy chambers where the Privy Council assembled. There was a rumor that the Bhodi disciples were about to send another suicidal goof to the gateway. The Radisha wanted to forestall that somehow.

We were supposed to get the place ready for a Council session.

The Bhodi rumor had had its birth in the mind of Ky Sahra. It was supposed to be the device by which we could bring Shikhandini face-to-face with Chandra Gokhale.

We had almost two hours before the staffers appeared, the quiet little men who wrote everything down. Then the Purohita arrived, accompanied by the ecclesiastical members of the Privy Council. The Purohita did not deign to note our existence even though Shiki mistook him for Gokhale and batted her eyes till Subredil signed her off. I could hear the excuse that would come later: All old men looked alike.

Neither Arjuna Drupada nor Chandra Gokhale considered themselves old.

We continued our work, ignored. The folk of the Palace, particularly the inner circle, were lucky we had other things we wanted to do with our lives. Had we not cared about our own survival, we could have slaughtered scores of them. But getting rid of the Purohita would not mean much in the grand scheme. The senior priests would replace him with another old man just as nasty and narrow of mind before Drupada's bones got cold.

Chandra Gokhale came in and he did not overlook the help. Sahra must have gleaned a few suggestions from Willow Swan about what the old pervert liked, because he stopped dead, staring at Shikhandini like somebody had clubbed him between the eyes. Shiki had the role down perfectly. She was a shy virgin and a flirt at the same time, as though her maidenly heart had been smitten instantly. God apparently fashioned men so that they would swallow that sort of bait ninety-nine times out of ten.

Barundandi's timing was good. He came to move us out of the meeting chamber just as the Protector swooped in like some dark, angry eagle. Gokhale watched our departure with moon eyes. Before we completed our evacuation, he was whispering to one of his scribes.

Jaul Barundandi, unfortunately, had a sharp eye for some things. "Minh Subredil, I believe your daughter has charmed the Inspector-General of the Records."

Subredil appeared surprised. "Sir? No. That can't be. I won't let my child stumble into the trap that destroyed my mother and condemned me to this cruel life."

Sawa caught Subredil's arm. Apparently she had become frightened by that intense outburst, but in reality she squeezed, warning Subredil not to say anything that Barundandi might remember if Chandra Gokhale disappeared.

We might want to consider a change of plan. We did not want anyone to have any reason to connect anything outside with any of us.

Subredil's outburst faded. She became embarrassed and anxious to be elsewhere. "Shiki. Come on."

I was ready to kick Shikhandini's bottom myself. She was being a positive slut. But she did respond to her mother's command.

Sawa sort of settled down out of the way with the last of her dirty brass, in hopes of being overlooked while the Privy Council covened, but Jaul Barundandi was alert. "Minh Subredil. Bring your sister-in-law." He tried to flirt with Shikhandini. He got a look of disgust for his trouble.

Minh Subredil got me going, then went after her daughter. "What did you think you were doing in there?"

"I was just having fun. The man is a disgusting old pervert."

Softly, as though not meant for Barundandi's ears while the words really were, Subredil said, "Don't ever have fun like that again. Men like that will do whatever they like with you and there isn't anything anybody can do about it."

That warning was not all acting. The last thing we needed was one of the mighty dragging Shikhandini into a dark corner to do a little groping.

That was not supposed to happen. It was unthinkable, supposedly. And for ordinary people that was mostly true. But not so at a level where men began to believe that they existed outside the usual rules.

"Narita!" Barundandi called. "Where have you gotten to? That damned woman. She's slipped off to the kitchen again. Or she's gone somewhere to sneak a nap."

I heard the Radisha behind us, in the meeting chamber, but could not make out individual words. An angry voice responded. That had to be Soulcatcher. I wanted to be somewhere a little farther away. I started moving.

Sawa, of course, did things others did not always understand. Subredil grabbed hold and started to fuss. Barundandi told her, "Take this bunch to the kitchen, get something to eat. If Narita is there, tell her I want her."

The moment he was out of sight, I announced, "Sawa is going to wander off." Sawa was not completely happy with the pages Subredil kept bringing Sleepy. Subredil could not read them, worked in a rush and seemed incapable of collecting anything interesting.

I hoped I remembered the way. Even when you wear the yarn bracelet, the Palace is a confusing place and I had not roamed it since the days when the Captain was the Liberator and a great hero of the Taglian people. And even then, I had been only an occasional visitor.

As soon as I began to feel unsure, I got out a small piece of chalk and began to leave tiny marks in the Sangel alphabet. I had managed to learn a little of that language during our years in the far south but it had been a struggle. I hoped anyone who discovered the marks would not recognize what they were.

I did find the room where the old books were hidden. It was obvious that someone came there often. The dust was disturbed badly, which in itself would raise questions if discovered. I tried to drag out the book that looked the oldest. Darn, that thing was heavy. Once I got it open, I found that the pages were real stubborn about tearing. They were not paper at all, which never has been very common. I could tear them only one at a time. Which maybe explained why Subredil just grabbed whatever came easiest. She would not have time to pick and choose.

I worried that I had been away too long myself, convinced that Barundandi or his wife must have noticed that I was missing. I hoped it did not occur to them to wonder why Subredil was not making a scene because she had lost track of me.

Even so, I continued to tear pages until I had all I thought the three of us could carry away.

I hid everything in an unused room not far from the service postern, uncertain how we would recover it heading out, then took myself way down inside Sawa, almost to the point of incapacitating confusion.

They found me dirty and tearstained and still trying to find the way back to the meeting chamber, "they" being some of the other day workers. In moments I was reunited with Subredil and Shikhandini. I clung to my sister-in-law like a wood chip desperate to shed the embrace of a rushing flood.

Jaul Barundandi was not happy. "Minh Subredil, I accepted this woman here for your sake, out of kindness and charity. But lapses of this sort are not acceptable. No work got done while we were searching . . ." His voice trailed off. The Radisha and the Protector were headed our way, following a most unusual route. This was backstairs country. Which meant nothing whatsoever to Soulcatcher, of course. That woman had no sense of class or caste. There was the Protector and beneath the Protector there was everyone else.

Sawa just sort of folded up and squatted with her face in her lap. Subredil and Shikhandini and Jaul Barundandi partially tried to get out of the way, partially gawked. Shiki had not seen either woman before.

Sawa crossed her fingers out of sight in her lap. Subredil whispered prayers to Ghanghesha. Jaul Barundandi shivered in terror. Shikhandini stared with a teen's inability to feel appropriate fear.

The Radisha paid us no heed. She stamped past talking about ripping the guts out of Bhodi disciples. Her voice contained almost no emotional conviction. The Protector, though, slowed down and considered us all intently. For an instant I found myself almost overcome by the dread that she really could read minds. Then she went on and Jaul Barundandi ran along behind, forgetting us and Narita both because the Radisha barked some command back his way.

Sawa rose and whimpered, "I want to go home."

Subredil agreed that it was enough of a day.

Neither the Greys nor the Royal Guards were searching anyone. A good thing, too. I carried so much paper in my small clothes I could fake a normal walk for only a few dozen yards.

29

I got through my part of the evening meeting quickly and ran off to my own little corner so I could compare my newly acquired pages with those of the book I had stolen from the library that I thought was an exact copy—if not the genuine original—of the true first volume of the Annals of the Black Company. I was so cheerful I am sure One-Eye must have had great fun talking about me behind my back.

It did not occur to me to stick around to see how our temptation of Chandra Gokhale played out.

The story I got later was, Gokhale had a man try to follow Shiki home. When that man did not report back within a reasonable time—on account of he ran into Runmust and Iqbal Singh someplace he should not have been and ended up taking the long swim downriver—Gokhale headed for the joy house that specialized in serving him, his associates and those who shared their select but hardly rare tastes in pleasure. Riverwalker and several other brothers picked him up when he left the Palace. He was accompanied by two companions who would regret their wishes to ingratiate themselves

with the Inspector-General by joining him in an evening of indul-
gence.

Murgen followed events closely, too. Knowing that he would do
so, I felt at ease snuggling up with my new acquisitions.

It took me over an hour to conclude that what I had brought out
today was indeed a later version of the first ever Annal and most of
another hour to realize that I would not be able to winkle out the
book's secrets without skilled help. Or a lot more time than I had.

Chandra Gokhale apparently died in that joy house. Likewise,
his two companions. There were witnesses. People saw them strangled. Then a red rumel got left behind in the killers' haste to get
away.

The Greys arrived almost immediately. They loaded the corpses
into a cart, saying the Protector wanted Gokhale's back in the Palace
instantly. But the Greys stopped being Greys moments after they left
the pleasure house. Their course led them toward the river rather
than toward the Palace. The extra bodies vanished into the flood.

A white crow dozing on a rooftop wakened when they started
downhill. It stretched and followed them.

30

Murgen was there when Soulcatcher received the news. The report reached the Palace in a remarkably short time and was
unusually complete. The Greys worked hard to please their mistress.

The party bringing Gokhale to the warehouse had not yet arrived.

Murgen had been asked to look around the Protector's quarters
while he was there. We knew nothing about them. Nobody ever
went into her suite. Not since Willow Swan had gone to his reward.

Murgen would have to be questioned about how she lived in private.

Soulcatcher did not retreat there, however. She went out looking for the Radisha right away.

The Radisha knew something had happened to Gokhale but she
had not had detailed reports. The women settled in the receiving
chamber of the Radisha's austere suite. Soulcatcher told what she

knew. She used a very businesslike voice. It was said sometimes that the Protector was her most dangerous and least stable when she stopped being capricious and seemed calmest and most serious.

"It seems the Inspector-General shared some habits with Perhule Khoji. In fact, I'm now assured that his particular weakness was common amongst the senior men of his ministry."

"There were rumors."

"And you did nothing?"

"Chandra Gokhale's private amusements, loathsome as I found them personally, did not prevent his performing perfectly as Inspector-General of the Records. He was particularly adept at generating revenue."

"Indeed." Soulcatcher's businesslike manner wavered momentarily. Murgen would report his amusement at the thought she might actually have a moral opinion. "He was attacked in the same manner as Khoji was."

"Suggesting somebody might have a grudge against the ministry as a whole? Or that the Deceivers pick men of his particular weakness as ceremonial targets?"

"Deceivers didn't kill Gokhale. Of that I'm sure. This was done by the people who lured Swan out and killed him. If they killed him."

"If?" The Radisha was startled by the implication.

"We saw no corpse. Note that we have no body this time, either. Men disguised as our men were right there to haul the body away. That's two members of the Privy Council lost in less than a week. Organizationally, they were the most important. They made the machinery work. If the Great General was anywhere nearby, I'd predict that he would be their next target. That gaggle of priests means nothing. They do nothing. They control nothing. My sister proved that if they're killed, they can be replaced by other do-nothings within minutes. Nobody can replace Swan or Gokhale. The Greys are beginning to unravel already."

Murgen made a mental note to mention that Willow Swan might have been less a puppet than he led the world to believe.

"Why couldn't it be the Stranglers?" the Radisha asked.

"Because those people cut the head off that particular serpent the other day." She described events in the Thieves' Garden. Obviously, she had not bothered to share the news before. It was clear that the Protector considered the Princess a necessary but junior partner in her enterprise. "In a matter of days these people, whom we thought ruined forever, have cut the head off one enemy and have crippled the other seriously. There is a dangerous mind behind this."

Not dangerous at all. Not even that lucky. But a sufficiently paranoid mind will discern patterns and threats where only fortune has conspired. Soulcatcher was ever alert for evils as great as her own.

"We knew they couldn't remain in the darkness forever," the Radisha said. She corrected herself hastily. "*I* knew. The Captain reminded me often enough." She did not need to bring up the past and her belief in mistakes she had made. That devil was buried deep, hundreds of miles away. A much more immediate danger was right there in the room with her.

The Protector was a mistake she had abandoned hope of living long enough to correct. Blind to the consequences at the time, she had chosen to mount the tiger. Now her sole choice was to hang on for the rest of the ride.

Soulcatcher said, "We have to recall the Great General. If we can get his troops into the city before our enemies make their next move, we'll have the manpower to hunt them down. You should send the orders immediately. And once the courier is safely off, we should announce that the Great General is returning. Their special dislike for Mogaba should cause them to delay their other plans till they can gather him in as well."

"You think you know what they'll do?"

"I know what I'd do if I came down with the kind of sudden, burning ambition that seems to have taken them over. I wonder if there hasn't been some kind of coup or something?"

Exasperated, the Radisha demanded, "What will they do next?"

"I'll keep that to myself for now. Not that I don't trust you." Soulcatcher probably had abiding suspicions about herself. "I just want to make sure I've identified enough of a pattern to begin tapping into the workings of this new mind. I'm quite talented at that, you know."

The Radisha knew, to her own despair. She said nothing. Soulcatcher sat silently herself, as though waiting for the Princess to speak. But the Radisha had nothing to say.

The Protector mused, "I wonder who it could be? I knew the wizards of old. Neither one has the ambition or imagination or drive, even though both do have the hardness."

The Radisha made a squeak of sound. "The wizards?"

"The two little men. The day-and-night pair. They aren't much of anything but lucky."

"*They* survived?"

"I said they're lucky. Do you recall anyone who didn't go onto the plain who looked like a potential leader? I don't."

"I thought all those people were dead."

"As did I, in most cases. Our Great General claims to have seen most of their bodies personally. But the Great General identified them assuming that the two wizards had been killed first. Hmm. Here I had begun to be suspicious of him. Perhaps his only crime is that he's a fool. Can you think of anyone?"

"Not inside the Company I knew. But there was a Nyueng Bao who had something to do with the Standardbearer's wife. A priest of some sort. He seemed to be totally obsessed with weapons and the martial arts. I ran into him only a few times. And he's never been accounted for in any reports."

"A Master of the Path of the Sword? That would explain a lot. But I killed them all when I— Have you noticed how people keep turning up alive when there's every reason to believe that they're dead?"

An actual smile tried to gnaw its way out of the Radisha's mouth. The woman talking could be considered the mother of all those whose deaths had been celebrated prematurely. "There's sorcery afoot. Nothing should be any great surprise."

"You're right. You're absolutely right. And that's a blade that can have more than one edge." Soulcatcher rose to leave. Her voice changed, became cruel. "More than one edge. A Master of the Path of the Sword. It's been a long time since I visited those people. They may be able to tell me something useful." She stalked out of the room.

The Radisha remained motionless for several minutes, clearly troubled. Then she got up and went to her Anger Chamber. She settled herself there. The unseen spy went after the Protector. She, he discovered, had gone directly to the ramparts. She assembled her small, single-rider carpet, all the while arguing with herself in a dozen querulous voices.

He barely listened. He was too surprised and shocked. There was a white crow up there. It was watching the Protector, who remained unaware of Murgen's presence although, historically, she had been more sensitive to him than to any of the living except her sister. But the bird had no trouble seeing Murgen. It examined him with first one eye, then with the other. Then it winked deliberately. And then it launched itself into the night when the Protector's rookery took flight to accompany her on her travels.

But I am the white crow!

The disorientation was brief but as frightening as it had been years ago, when first Murgen had started stumbling around outside his flesh.

31

I said, "Better get Uncle Doj before we go any farther with this, Tobo." I spotted Kendo Cutter and Runmust. "You guys finally back? How did it go?"

"Perfect. Just like you planned it."

Sahra asked, "You have my present?"

"They're lugging him in now. He's still out cold."

"Drop him right here where I can chat with him when he comes around." Sahra had a wicked gleam in her eye.

I chuckled. "Soulcatcher thinks we're following some grand, carefully orchestrated master plan exquisitely fashioned by a great strategic mastermind. If she knew we were just stumbling around in the dark hoping we stay lucky until we can open the way for the Captured—"

One-Eye barked, "You telling me you masterminds don't got a next step ready to go, Little Girl?"

"We have several." I did. "And I'm sure the next one hasn't ever occurred to Soulcatcher as being within the realm of possibility. I'm going to bring Master Santaraksita home for supper and give him a chance to sign up for the adventure of a lifetime."

"Heh-heh! I knew it."

Uncle Doj joined us. He was seriously peeved about the way he had been treated lately.

I told him, "One of our friends just reported a conversation between The Thousand Voices and the Radisha. The process of reasoning is beyond my imagination but The Thousand Voices has decided that all her troubles recently are the fault of a Master of the Path of the Sword who should've been killed a long time ago. When last seen, she was off to visit the folks at the Vinh Gao Ghang temple to ask about the man. You may be familiar with that temple."

Doj lost color. His sword hand trembled for an instant. His right eyelid twitched. He turned toward Sahra.

Sahra told him, "It's true. What can she learn there?"

"Speak the tongue of The People."

"No."

The Master of the Path of the Sword accepted what he could not control. You would have to say he was somewhat less than gracious about it, though, if you wanted to report the whole truth.

I said, "You still have a book we want. And you could tell us a great deal that we could use, I think."

He was a stubborn old man. He was determined not to let me stampede him into anything.

I said, "The Thousand Voices has sent for Mogaba. She means to have the army come dig us out. If I could, I'd like to get out of Taglios before she starts. But we have a lot to do and a lot to find out before we can go. Your help would be invaluable. As I keep reminding you, you have people under that plain, too. . . . Huh?"

"What? Sleepy?" Sahra said. "Goblin! See what's the matter with her!"

"I'm all right. I'm fine. I just had what you call an epiphany, I think. Listen. All the evidence indicates that Soulcatcher thinks the Captured are dead. Which would mean that she believes Longshadow is dead. We know he's not, which is why we're not worried right now. But if she doesn't know, why isn't she amazed that the world hasn't been overrun by shadows?"

I got a lot of blank looks for my trouble, even from the wizards.

I said, "Look, what it means is, it doesn't matter if Longshadow is dead or alive after all. As long as he stays inside the Shadowgate. There isn't a doomsday sword hanging over the world, certain to fall when the madman croaks. Somebody besides the cleverest wizards will survive."

The less clever wizards caught on then. They brightened up dramatically. Not that either had ever cared much what became of the world after they staggered out of it.

What to do about the Shadowmaster had never been a significant issue to us because there were always more immediate obstacles to overcome before he could become a major concern.

Sahra said as much. "If we can't open the way, there's no point in worrying about how we can keep it closed to those not in our favor."

"I wonder how the Shadowmasters did it? Brute force? The Black Company was still in the far north and the Lance of Passion was up there with them." I stared at Uncle Doj. Others began to do so, too. I wondered aloud, "Could it be that the great shame of the Nyueng Bao isn't nearly as ancient as I thought? Could it be that it just goes back a couple of generations? To about the time that the Shadowmasters appeared, practically manifesting themselves overnight?"

Uncle Doj closed his eyes. They stayed that way for a while. When the old priest opened them again, he glared at me. "Come walking with me, Stone Soldier."

Chandra Gokhale, Inspector-General of the Records and favorer of very young girls, chose that moment to groan. I told Doj, "Indulge me for a few minutes, Uncle. I have a guest to entertain. I promise not to take too long."

Goblin knelt beside the minister, patted his face gently, helped Gokhale to a sitting position. The Inspector-General began to puff up for a bluster storm. As his mouth opened, I leaned down to whisper, "Water sleeps."

Gokhale's head jerked around. In a moment he recalled where he had seen me before. Goblin told him, "All their days are numbered, buddy. And it looks like some of you got a few less days than some others do." Gokhale recognized him, too, though he was supposed to be dead. And when he remembered where he had seen Sahra before, he began to tremble.

Sahra asked, "Would you recall abusing Minh Subredil on several occasions? Subredil certainly remembers. What I think we'll do to requite that is to return it fivefold. The brothers will install you in a tiger cage in a moment. You'll be well treated otherwise. And in a few days maybe we'll bring in the Purohita to keep you company." She chuckled so wickedly I felt a chill. "For all the rest of their days, calling the Heaven and the Earth and the Day and the Night, like brothers, Chandra Gokhale and Arjuna Drupada."

Part of that was some Nyueng Bao formula I didn't understand. But I got the point. And so did Gokhale. He would be caged all the rest of his days with the man he most loathed.

Sahra chuckled again.

She made me nervous when she got like that.

32

I watched the old priest closely as we eased through the spell net surrounding the warehouse. He did not have a yarn amulet. His head twitched and jerked. His feet kept wanting to change direction but his will hacked a way through the illusions. Possibly that was a result of his training on the Path of the Sword. I recalled, though, that Lady had insisted he was a minor wizard.

"Where are we going, Uncle? And why are we going there?"

"We go where no Nyueng Bao ear will hear what I tell you. Old Nyueng Bao would label me a traitor. Young Nyueng Bao would call me a lying fool. Or worse."

And I? I was generally a proponent of the latter view whenever I heard him preaching about his path to inner peace through obsessively continuous preparation for combat. His philosophy had appealed only to a very few of Banh Do Trang's employees, all Nyueng Bao, all too young to have witnessed actual warfare. I understood that the Path of the Sword was not militaristic, but others had trouble grasping that fact.

"You want to maintain your image as an old stiff-neck who wouldn't be caught dead helping a subhuman *jengali* fall and break her skull."

It was too dark to tell but I thought he smiled. "That's an extreme way of stating it but it approximates the facts." His Taglian, never poor, improved now that he had no other audience.

"Are you overlooking the fact that every bit of darkness out here might harbor a bat or crow or rat, or even one of the Protector's shadows?"

"I have nothing to fear from those things. The Thousand Voices already knows everything I'm going to tell you."

But she might not want me to know, too.

We walked in silence for a long time.

Taglios seldom fails to amaze me. Doj cut across a wealthy section, where whole families fort up in estates surrounded by guarded walls. Their youths were out on Salara Road, which grew up ages ago to provide them with their diversions. Reason insisted that beggars ought to be plentiful where the wealth was concentrated, but that was not the case. The extremely poor were not allowed to offend the sight of the mighty with their presence.

There, as everywhere, odors assailed the nostrils but these scents were sandalwood, cloves and perfumes.

After that, Doj led me into the dark, crowded streets of a temple district. We stepped aside to let a band of Gunni acolytes pass. The boys were bullying the people living in the streets. I thought we might have trouble with them, too, which would have ended with them suffering a lot of pain, but a brake on their misbehavior saved them from its consequences. That arrived in the form of three Greys.

The Shadar do not disdain the caste system entirely but they do hold to the notion that the highest caste must include not just the priests and men qualified by birth to become priests, but also, certainly, any men of the Shadar faith. And that faith, which is an extremely heretical and Gunni-infected bastard offshoot of my own One True Faith, contains a strong strain of charity toward the weak and the unfortunate.

The Greys methodically applied their bamboo canes and invited the youths to take up any complaints with the Protector. The acolytes were smarter than they pretended. They got the hell out of there before the Greys used their whistles to invite all their friends to the caning.

All part of night in the city. Doj and I drifted onward.

Eventually he led me to a place called the Deer Park, which is an expanse of wilderness near the center of the city. It had been created by some despot of centuries past.

I told Doj, "I really don't need all this exercise." I wondered if he had some goofball plan to murder me and leave the body under the trees. But what would be the point?

Doj was Doj. With him, you never knew.

"I feel more comfortable here," he said. "But I never stay long. There is a company of rangers charged with keeping squatters out. They consider anyone not Taglian and high caste a squatter. This is good. This log has shaped itself to my posterior."

The log in question tripped me. I got back onto my feet and said, "I'm listening."

"Sit. This will take a while."

"Leave out the begats." Which was a Jaicuri Vehdna colloquialism having to do with difficulties memorizing scripture, which you have to do as a child. I meant, "Don't bother telling me whose fault it was and why they're such bloody villains for it. Just tell me what happened."

"Asking a storyteller not to embellish is like asking a fish to give up water."

"I do have to go to work tomorrow."

"As you will. You are aware, are you not, that the Free Companies of Khatovar and the roving bands of Stranglers who murder for the glory of Kina share a common ancestry?"

"There's enough suggestion in our recent Annals to allow for that interpretation," I admitted. Caution seemed indicated.

"My place amongst the Nyueng Bao would correspond roughly with yours as Annalist of the Black Company. It includes, as well, the role of the priest in the Strangler band—whose secondary obligation is to maintain a sound oral history of the band. Over the centuries the *toog* have lost their respect for education."

My own studies suggested that a great deal of evolution had taken place in my Company during those same centuries. Probably a lot more than had been the case with the Deceiver bands. They had stayed inside one culture that had not changed a lot. Meanwhile, the Black Company kept moving into stranger and stranger lands, old soldiers being replaced by young foreigners who had no connection with the past and no idea that Khatovar even existed.

Doj seemed to echo my thoughts. "The Strangler bands are pale imitations of the original Free Companies. The Black Company retains the name and some of the memories, but you're philosophically much farther from the original than the Deceivers are. Your band is ignorant of its true antecedents and has been kept that way willfully, mainly through the manipulations of the goddess Kina, but also, to a lesser extent, by others who didn't want your Company to become what it had been in another time."

I waited. He did not volunteer to explain. Doj was difficult that way.

He did, I suppose, do something that was even harder for him. He told the truth about his own people. "Nyueng Bao are the almost pure-blooded descendants of the people of one of the Free Companies. One that chose not to go back."

"But the Black Company is supposed to be the only one that didn't go back. The Annals say—"

"They tell you only what those who recorded them knew. My ancestors arrived here after the Black Company finished laying the land to waste and moved on north, already having lost sight of its divine mission. Deserting in its own way, through ignorance of what it was supposed to be. By then it was already three generations old and had made no effort to maintain the purity of its blood. It had just fought the war which is the first that your Annalists remember and was almost completely destroyed. That seems to be the fate of the Black Company. To be reduced to a handful, then to reconstitute itself. Again and again. Losing something of its previous self each time."

"And the fate of your Company?" I noted that he did not mention a name. No matter, really. No name would mean anything to me.

"To sink ever deeper into ignorance itself. I know the truth. I know the secrets and the old ways. But I'm the last. Unlike other Companies, we brought our families with us. We were a late experiment. We had too much to lose. We deserted. We went and hid in the swamps. But we've kept our lineage pure. Almost."

"And the pilgrimages? The old people who died in Jaicur? Hong Tray? And the great, dark, terrible secret of the Nyueng Bao that Sahra worries about so much?"

"The Nyueng Bao have many dark secrets. All the Free Companies had dark secrets. We were instruments of the darkness. The Soldiers of Darkness. The Bone Warriors charged with opening the way for Kina. Stone Soldiers warring for the honor of being remembered for all eternity by having our names written in golden letters in glittering stone. We failed because our ancestors were imperfect in their devotion. In every company there were those who were too weak to bring on the Year of the Skulls."

"The old people?"

"Ky Dam and Hong Tray. Ky Dam was the last elected Nyueng Bao captain. There was no one to take his place. Hong Tray was a witch with the curse of foresight. She was the last true priest. Priestess."

"Curse of foresight?"

"She never foresaw anything good."

I sensed that he did not want to get into that subject. I recalled that Hong Tray's final prophecy involved Murgen and Sahra, which certainly was an offense to all right-thinking Nyueng Bao—and was not yet a prophecy completely fulfilled, probably.

"The great sin of the Nyueng Bao?"

"You had that idea from Sahra, of course. And she, like all those born after the coming of the Shadowmasters, believes that 'sin' is what caused the Nyueng Bao to flee into the swamps. She believes wrongly. That flight involved no sin, but survival. The true black sin occurred within my own lifetime." His voice tightened up. He had strong feelings about this.

I waited.

"I was a small boy just taking my first small steps on the Path of the Sword when the stranger came. He was a personable man of middle years. His name was Ashutosh Yaksha. In the oldest form of the language Ashutosh meant something like Despair of the Wicked. Yaksha meant much the same as it does in Taglian today." Which was "good spirit." "People were prepared to believe he was a supernatural being because he had a white skin. A very pale, white skin, lighter than Goblin or Willow Swan, who sometimes get some sunlight. He wasn't an albino, though. He had normal eyes. His hair wasn't quite as blond as Swan's is. In sum, he was a magical creature to most Nyueng Bao. He spoke the language oddly but he did speak it. He said he wanted to study at the Vinh Gao Ghang temple, the fame of which had reached him far away.

"When pressed about his origins, he insisted that he hailed from 'The Land of Unknown Shadows, beneath the stars of the Noose.'"

"He claimed to have come off the glittering stone?"

"Not quite. That was never clear. There or beyond. No one pressed him hard. Not even Ky Dam or Hong Tray, though he troubled them. Very early we learned that Ashutosh was a powerful sorcerer. And in those days many of the older people still knew about the origins of the Nyueng Bao. It was feared that he might have been sent to summon us home. That proved to be untrue. For a long time Ashutosh seemed to be nothing but what he claimed, a student who wanted to absorb whatever wisdom had accumulated at the temple of Ghanghesha. Which had been a holy place since the Nyueng Bao first entered the swamp."

"But there's a but. Right? The man was a villain after all?"

"He was indeed. In fact, Ashutosh was the man you knew later as Shadowspinner. He was there to find our Key, sent by his teacher and mentor, whom you came to know as Longshadow. At a young age this man had stumbled across rumors that not all the Free Companies had returned to Khatovar. What he understood from that, that nobody else realized, was that each Company still outside must possess a talisman capable of opening and closing the Shadowgate. An ambitious man could use that talisman to recruit rakshasas he could send out to do evil for him. The power to kill becomes the ultimate power in the hands of a man who has no reservations about employing it."

"So this Ashutosh Yaksha found the Key?"

"He only assured himself that it existed. He wormed his way into the confidence of the senior priests. One day someone let something drop. Soon afterward, Ashutosh announced that he had received word that his teacher, mentor and spiritual father, Maricha Manthara Dhumraksha, impressed by his reports on the temple, had chosen to come visit. Dhumraksha turned out to be a tall, incredibly skinny man who always wore a mask, apparently because his face was deformed."

"You heard a name like Maricha Manthara Dhumraksha and you didn't suspect something?"

I could not see Doj in the darkness but I could feel his unhappy frown. He said, "I was a small child."

"And the Nyueng Bao aren't interested in anything not their own. Yes. I'm Vehdna, Uncle, but I recognize the names Manthara and Dhumraksha as those of legendary Gunni demons. Even though you walk amongst lesser beings, you might keep your ears open. That way, when a nasty *jengali* sorcerer pulls your leg, you'll at least have a clue."

Doj grunted. "He had a golden tongue, Dhumraksha did. When he discovered that each decade, as the custom was then, a band of the leading men understood a pilgrimage south—"

"He invited himself along and tricked somebody into letting him examine the Key."

"Close. But not quite. Yes. You did guess correctly. The pilgrimage went to the very Shadowgate. The pilgrims would spend ten days there waiting for a sign. I don't believe anyone knew what that might be anymore. But the traditions had to be observed. The pilgrims, however, never took the actual Key with them. They carried a replica charged with a few simple spells meant to fool an inattentive thief. The real Key stayed home. The old men didn't really want a sign from the other side."

"Longshadow got in a hurry."

"He did. When the pilgrims arrived at the Shadowgate, they found Ashutosh Yaksha and a half-dozen other sorcerers waiting. Several were fugitives from that northern realm of darkness where the Black Company was then in service. When Dhumraksha used the false key, his band found themselves under attack from the other side of the Shadowgate. Before the gateway could be stopped up, using the power of Longshadow's true name, three of the would-be Shadowmasters had perished. The one called the Howler, cruelly injured, had fled. The survivors quickly became the feuding, conquering monsters your brothers found in place when they arrived. And the same disaster caused the Mother of Night to reawaken and begin scheming toward a Year of the Skulls once more."

"And that's the great sin of the Nyueng Bao? Letting themselves be hoodwinked by sorcerers?"

"In those days there was little contact with the world outside the swamp. Banh Do Trang's family managed all outside trade. Once a decade a handful of the older men traveled to the Shadowgate. About as frequently, Gunni ascetics would enter the swamp hoping to purify their souls. These Gunni hermits were obviously crazy or they wouldn't have come into the swamps in the first place. They were always tolerated. And Ghanghesha found a home."

"Where does The Thousand Voices fit?"

"She learned the story from the Howler around the time we were trapped in Dejagore. Or soon afterward. She came to the temple soon after we returned, the best of us exhausted, our old men all dead, including our Captain and Speaker, and witch Hong Tray with them. There was no one but me left who knew everything—though Gota and Thai Dei knew some, and Sahra a little, they being of the family of Ky Dam and Hong Tray. The Thousand Voices went to the temple while I was away. She used her power to intimidate and torture the priests until they surrendered the mysterious object that had been given them for safekeeping ages ago. They didn't even know what it was anymore. They really can't be blamed but I can't help blaming them. And there you have it. All the secrets of the Nyueng Bao."

I doubted that. "I doubt that seriously. But it's a basis from which to work. Are you going to cooperate? If we get Narayan Singh to divulge what he did with the Key?"

"If you'll undertake a promise never to tell anyone what I told you here tonight."

"I swear it on the Annals." This was too easy. "I won't say a word to a soul." But I did not say anything about not writing it down.

I did not extract an oath from him.

Sometime, eventually, he would face the moral dilemma that had swallowed the Radisha once it seemed that the Company would fulfill its obligation to her and it was coming time for her to deliver on her own commitments. Once Uncle Doj had his own people out from under the glittering stone, his reliability as an ally would turn to smoke.

Easily dealt with when the time came, I thought. I told Doj, "I still have to work tomorrow. And it's a whole lot later now than it was an hour ago."

He rose, evidently relieved that I had not asked many questions. I did have a few in mind, such as why the Nyueng Bao had risked more frequent pilgrimages to the Shadowgate once the Shadowmasters were in power, adding women and children and old people to the entourage. So I asked anyway, while we were walking.

He told me, "The Shadowmasters permitted it. It added to their feelings of superiority. And it let us keep them thinking that we didn't have the real Key, that we were searching for it. Our own people believed that was what we were doing. Only Ky Dam and Hong Tray knew the whole truth. The Shadowmasters were hoping we'd find it for them."

"The Thousand Voices figured it out."

"Yes. Her crows went everywhere and heard everything."

"And in those days she had a very sneaky demon at her beck and call." I continued to pester him all the way back to the warehouse, cleverly trying to find his remaining secrets by coloring in more map around the blank places.

I did not fool him a bit.

Before I dragged off to bed, I visited Sahra, Murgen and Goblin one more time. "You people get all of that?"

"Most of it," Murgen said. "This weary old slave has been doing some other chores, too."

"Think he told the truth?"

"Mostly," Sahra admitted. "He told no lies that I noticed, but I don't think he told the whole truth."

"Well, of course not. He's Nyueng Bao right down to his twisted toe bones. And a wizard besides."

Before Sahra got indignant, Goblin told me, "There was a white crow out there with you."

"I saw it," I said. "I figured it was Murgen."

Murgen said, "It wasn't Murgen. I was there disembodied. Same as now."

"What was it, then? *Who* was it?"

"I don't know," Murgen replied.

I did not entirely believe him. Maybe it was a false intuition but I was sure he had a strong suspicion.

33

Master Santaraksita hardly waited till there were no eavesdroppers before he approached me. "Dorabee, your record is beginning to look bad. Two days ago you were late. Yesterday you didn't show up at all. This morning you don't look alert and ready for work."

I was not. I would have been testy with anyone else. In this case I barely noticed that his words were not spoken in a tone in keeping with their content. I sensed relief in him at my return and a lingering whiff of a fear that I would not. I lied. "I had a fever. I couldn't stay on my feet for more than few minutes at a time. I tried to come in but I was so weak I got lost for a while and eventually ended up just going home."

"Should you even be here today, then?" Changing course, sounding overly worried.

"I have a little more strength today. I have a lot of work to do. I really want to keep this job, Sri. None other would put me so close to so much wisdom."

"Where is home, Dorabee?" I had collected my broom. He was following me. Eyes were following us, some with a knowing look that told me Santaraksita may have pursued other young men in the past.

I was ready for this one because I knew he had tried to follow me. "I share a small room near the waterfront in the Sirada neighborhood with several friends from the army." A common situation throughout Taglios, where men outnumber women almost two to one because so many men have come in from the Territories, hoping to make their fortunes.

"Why didn't you go home when you came back, Dorabee?"

Oh-oh. "Sri?"

"Your mother, your brother, your sisters, and their wives and husbands and children all still dwell in the same place where you lived as a child. They believed you were dead."

Oh, darn! He had gone to see them? The busybody. "I don't get along with those people, Sri." Which was an outright lie on behalf of Dorabee Dey Banerjae. The man I had known had been very close to his family. "When I came back from the Kiaulune wars, I was so horribly changed that they wouldn't have recognized me. Had I gone home, it wouldn't have been long before they found out things about me that would've caused them to disown me. I preferred to let them think Dorabee was dead. The boy they remembered no longer exists anyway."

I hoped he would interpret that according to his own wishful thinking.

He bit. "I understand."

"I'm grateful for your concern, Sri. If you will excuse me?" I went to work.

I worked briskly, deep in thought. What I needed to do required me to let myself be seduced. I had no experience along those lines, from either of the possible viewpoints. But the old men tell me I am clever, and after a while I thought I saw a way by which events could proceed as desired without Surendranath Santaraksita putting himself in a position of emotional or moral risk greater than he had when he tried to follow me home and I had to send Tobo out to rescue him. Which, of course, he did not know.

I had a weak spell toward mid-morning, at a point where old Baladitya could repay his small debt by being solicitous. By the time Master Santaraksita manufactured a reasonable excuse to put himself into my proximity, I had collected myself and was back at work.

A few hours later I contrived to throw up my lunch, then made a show of cleaning up. I suffered dizzy spells later still. The last occurred after most of the librarians and copyists had gone home, despite the threat of further showers. The afternoon storm had not been as terrible as most. Taglians generally viewed that as a bad omen.

Santaraksita played his part perfectly. He was beside me before my spell was over. Nervously, he suggested, "You'd better quit now, Dorabee. You've put in more than your day's work. The rest will be here tomorrow. I'll walk along with you to make sure you're all right."

A relapse threatened as I began to protest that that was not necessary. So I said, "Thank you, Sri. Your generosity knows no bounds. What about Baladitya?" The old copyist's grandson had failed to show again.

"He's practically on our way. We'll just leave him off first." I tried to think of some small act or something I could say that would encourage Santaraksita's fantasy, but could not. That proved unnecessary, anyway. The man was determined to hook himself. All because I knew how to read.

Weird.

Riverwalker just happened to be hanging around outside when Master Santaraksita, Baladitya and I left the library grounds. I made a little gesture to let him know we were going to do it. More signs and gestures along the way let him know that the old man should be rounded up as soon as Santaraksita and I left him. He was a witness who could say that the Master Librarian had been seen last in my company. And he might be useful.

Not far from the warehouse, I suffered another mild spell. Santaraksita put an arm around me to help. I drifted back into my safe place some and went on with the game. By now we were surrounded, at a distance, by Company brothers. "Just straight ahead," I told Santaraksita, who was becoming confused by the outer web of spells. "Just hold my hand."

Moments later a gentle tap at the base of the Master Librarian's skull let me step away from my uncomfortable role.

"Here I'm known as Sleepy. I'm the Annalist of the Black Company. I brought you here to assist in the translation of material recorded by some of my earliest predecessors."

Santaraksita began to fuss. Kendo Cutter placed a hand over his mouth and nose so he could not breathe. After several such episodes, even a member of the priestly class recognized the connection between silence and unimpeded breathing.

I told him, "We have a pretty cruel reputation, Sri. And it's rightly deserved. No, I'm not Dorabee Dey Banerjae. Dorabee did die during the Kiaulune wars. Fighting on our side."

"What do you want?" In a shaky voice.

"Like I said, we need to translate some old books. Tobo, get the books from my worktable."

The boy went away grumbling about why was it always he who had to run and fetch.

Master Santaraksita was very put out when he discovered that some of what I wanted translated had been pilfered from his own restricted stacks. In fact, when I told him, "I want to start with this one," and showed him what I believed to be the earliest of the Annals, he lost some color.

"I'm doomed, Dorabee . . . I'm sorry, young man. Sleepy, was it?"

"Haw!" One-Eye bellowed, having appeared only moments before. "Did you ever go sniffing up the wrong tree. My little darling Sleepy, here, is all girl."

I smirked. "Darn! Here we go again, Sri. Now you have to get your mind around the fact that a *woman* can read. Ah. Here's Baladitya. You'll be working with him. Thank you, River. Did you run into any trouble?"

Santaraksita began to balk again. "I won't—"

Kendo silenced him again.

"You'll translate and you'll work hard at it, Sri. Or we won't feed you. We aren't the bhadrhalok. We quit talking about it a long time ago. We're doing it. It's just your misfortune to get caught up in it."

Sahra arrived. She was soaked. "It's raining again. I see you landed your fish." She collapsed into a chair, considered Surendranath Santaraksita. "I'm exhausted. My nerves were on edge all day. The Protector returned from the swamp at noon. She was in a totally foul mood. She had a huge argument with the Radisha, right in front of us."

"The Radisha stood up to her?"

"She did. She's reached her limit. Another Bhodi disciple came this morning but the Greys stopped him from burning himself. Then the Protector announced that she was going to take the night away from us by letting the shadows run loose from now on. That's when the Radisha started screaming."

Santaraksita looked so completely appalled by the implications of Sahra's revelations that I had to laugh. "No," he insisted. "It's not funny." Then we discovered that he was not really concerned about the shadows. "The Protector is going to clip my ears. At the very least. These books weren't supposed to be in the library at all. I was supposed to have destroyed them ages ago, but I couldn't do that to any book. Then I forgot about them. I should've locked them up somewhere."

"Why?" Sahra snapped. She did not get an answer.

I asked her, "Did you make any headway?"

"I didn't get a chance to pick up any pages. I did get into the Radisha's suite. I did eavesdrop on her and Soulcatcher. And I did pick up a little other information."

"For example?"

"For example, the Purohita and all the sacerdotal members of the Privy Council will be leaving the Palace tomorrow to attend a convocation of senior priests in preparation for this year's Druga Pavi."

The Druga Pavi is the biggest Gunni holiday of the Taglian year. Taglios, with all its numerous cults and countless minorities, boasted some holiday almost every day, but the Druga Pavi beggared all the rest.

"But that doesn't come up until after the end of the rainy season." I had a funny feeling about this.

"I got a premonition from it myself," Sahra admitted.

"River, take the Master and copyist and make sure they're as comfortable as we can make them here. Have Goblin provide them with chokers and make sure they understand how they work." I asked Sahra, "Did you happen to hear about this before or after Soulcatcher got back from terrorizing the swamp?"

"After, of course."

"Of course. She suspects something. Kendo. As soon as it's light out tomorrow, I want you to head for the Kernmi What. See what you can find out about this meeting without giving away how interested you are. If you see a lot of Greys or other Shadar around, don't bother. Just get back here with that word."

"Suppose this's a genuine opportunity?" Sahra asked.

"It'll stay genuine as long as they're outside the Palace. Won't it?"

"Maybe it would be best to just kill them. Put some flash buttons on the corpses. That would make Soulcatcher really mad."

"Wait. I'm having a thought. It might just be straight from *al-Shiel*." I waved a finger in the air as though counting musical beats. "Yes. That's it. We need to hope the Protector *is* trying to bait a trap with the Purohita." I explained my thinking.

"That's good," Sahra said. "But if we're going to make it work, you and Tobo will have to go inside with me."

"And I can't. There's no way I can miss work the day after Master Santaraksita disappears. Get Murgen. See if he was around the Palace today. Find out if there's a trap and where it's at. If Soulcatcher is going to be away, maybe you and Tobo can do it on your own."

"I don't want to belittle your genius, Sleepy, but this is something I've thought about a lot. Off and on for years. The possibility is partly why I keep trying to worm my way closer to the center of things. The truth is, it can't be managed by fewer than three people. I need Shiki and I need Sawa."

"Let me think." Sahra got Murgen's attention while I thought. Murgen seemed to be more alert and more interested in the outside world now, particularly where his wife and son were concerned. He must have begun to understand. "I've got it, Sahra! We can have Goblin be Sawa."

"Ain't no fucking way," Goblin said. He repeated himself four or five times in as many languages, just in case somebody missed his point. "What the fuck is the matter with you, woman?"

"You're as small as I am. We rub a little betel-nut juice on your face and hands, dress you up in my Sawa outfit, have Sahra sew your mouth shut so you can't shoot it off every time the urge hits you, nobody will know the difference. As long as you keep looking down, which is what Sawa mostly does."

"That may be a solution," Sahra said, ignoring Goblin's continued protests. "In fact, the more I think about it the better I like it. No disrespect meant but in a major pinch, Goblin would be a lot more useful than you would."

"I know. There you go. And I could go ahead and be Dorabee Dey besides. Isn't it wonderful?"

"Women," Goblin grumbled. "Can't live with them but they won't go away."

Sahra said, "You'd better start learning Sawa's quirks from Sleepy." To me she said, "There'll be plenty of work for Sawa. I made sure. And Narita is eager to get her back. Tobo, you need to get some sleep. Nobody's connected you with Gokhale but you'll still need to be alert."

"I really don't like going up there, Mom."

"You think I do? We all have—"

"Yes. I think you do. I think you keep going up there because you want the danger. I think it might be hard for you when you do have to stop taking risks. I think when that happens, we're all going to have to watch you close so you don't do something that might get us all killed along with you."

That was a kid who had been doing a lot of thinking. Maybe with a little help from one or more uncles. Sounded to me like he might be riding knee to knee with the truth, too.

34

I settled into a chair outside the cage where Narayan Singh was being kept. He was awake but he ignored me. I said, "The Daughter of Night still lives."

"I know that."

"You do? How?"

"I'd know if you'd harmed her."

"Then you need to know this. She isn't going to stay unharmed a whole lot longer. The only reason she's healthy now is that we want your cooperation. If we can't get it, then there's not much reason to keep on feeding her. Or you, either. Though I do intend to keep my word about taking care of you. Because I'd want you to see everything you value destroyed before you're allowed to die yourself. Which reminds me. Aridatha couldn't be with us tonight. His captain was concerned that there might be some unrest. Another Bhodi disciple planned to burn himself. So we'll have to wait until tomorrow night."

Narayan made a sound like a whispered moan. He did not want to have to acknowledge my existence, for existence, and mine in particular, was making him very unhappy. Which made me happy, though I had no personal grudge. My enmity was all very sanitary, very institutional, very much on behalf of my brothers who had been injured. And on behalf of my brothers who were imprisoned beneath the earth.

I suggested, "Maybe you should go to Kina for guidance."

Such a look he gave me. Narayan Singh had no sense of humor and did not recognize sarcasm when it struck from the grass and sank its fangs in his ankle.

I told him, "Just to recap: I don't have much patience left. I don't have much time left. We've leaped onto the tiger's back. The big catfight is coming."

Catfight. Universal male slang for a squabble amongst women.

Oh, really?

It had just occurred to me. We were all women in this fight. Sahra and I. The Radisha and Soulcatcher. Kina and the Daughter of Night. Uncle Doj was as close to a principal as any man was right now. And Narayan, though he was mainly the Daughter of Night's shadow.

Strange. Strange.

"Narayan, when the fur starts flying, I won't be much interested in looking out for your friend. But I'm definitely going to take care of you."

I started to leave.

"I can't do this thing." Singh's voice was almost inaudible.

"Work on it, Narayan. If you love the girl. If you don't want your goddess to have to start all over from scratch." I thought I had that much power. By killing the right people, I could lay Kina down to sleep for another age. And I would if I could not get my own brothers out of the ground.

I found Banh Do Trang awaiting me in the little corner where I worked and slept. He did not look well, which was not surprising. He was not too many years younger than Goblin and did not have Goblin's wondrous resources. "Can I be of any service, Uncle?"

"I understand Doj told you the story of our people." The best he could manage was a hoarse whisper.

"He told me *a* story. There're always doubts left behind when any Nyueng Bao shares a secret with me."

"Heh. Heh-heh. You're a bright young woman, Sleepy. Few illusions and no obvious obsessions. I think Doj was as honest with you as he could compel himself to be. Assuming he was honest with me when he consulted me afterward. He finally heard me when I told him that this's a new age. That that was what Hong Tray wanted to show us when she chose the *jengal* to become Sahra's husband. We're all lost children. We must join hands. That, too, is what Hong Tray wanted us to understand."

"She could've said so."

"She was Hong Tray. A seeress. A Nyueng Bao seeress. Would you have her issue blunt rescripts like the Radisha and Protector?"

"Absolutely."

Do Trang chuckled. Then he seemed to fall asleep.

Was that that? I wondered. "Uncle?"

"Uh? Oh? I'm sorry, young woman. Listen. I don't think anyone else has mentioned it. Maybe no one else but Gota and I have seen it. But there's a ghost in this place. We've seen it several times the past two nights."

"A ghost?" Was Murgen getting so strong people were starting to see him?

"It's a cold and evil thing, Sleepy. Like something that's happiest skulking around the mouths of graves or slithering through a mountain of bones. Like that vampire child in the tiger cage. You should be very wary of her. And I think I should find my way to bed. Before I fall asleep here and your friends begin to talk."

"If they're going to gossip about me, I can't think of anyone I'd rather have them connect me with."

"Someday when I'm young again. Next time around the Wheel."

"Good night, Uncle."

I thought I might read for a while but I fell asleep almost instantly. Sometime during the night I discovered that Do Trang's ghost did exist. I awakened, instantly alert, and saw a vaguely human shimmer standing nearby, evidently watching me. The old man had done a good job describing it, too. I wondered if it might not be Death Himself.

It went away as soon as it sensed my scrutiny.

I lay there trying to put it together. Murgen? Soulcatcher spying? An unknown? Or what it felt like, the girl in the tiger cage out for an ectoplasmic stroll?

I tried reason but was still too tired to stick with it long.

35

There was something wrong with the city. In addition to its extraordinarily clean smell. The rain had continued throughout most of the night. And in addition to the stunned looks on the faces of street-dwellers, who had survived their worst night yet. No. It was a sort of bated-breath feeling that got stronger as I approached the library. Maybe it was some sort of psychic phenomenon.

I stopped. The Captain used to say you had to trust your instincts. If it felt like something was wrong, then I should take time to figure out why I felt that way. I turned slowly.

No street poor here. But that was understandable. There were dead people around here. The survivors would be clinging to whatever shelter they could find, afraid the Greys would replace the shadows by day. But the Greys were absent, too. And traffic was lighter than it should be. And most of the tiny one-man stalls that sprawled out into the thoroughfare were not in evidence.

There was fear in the air. People expected something to happen. They had seen something that troubled them deeply. What that might be was not obvious, though. When I asked one of the merchants who was bold enough to be out, he ignored my question completely and tried to convince me that there was no way I could manage another day without a hammered-brass censor.

In a moment I decided he might be right. I paused to speak to another brass merchant whose space lay within eyeshot of the library. "Where is everyone this morning?" I asked, examining a long-spouted teapot sort of thing with no real utility.

A furtive shift of the merchant's eyes toward the library suggested there was substance to my premonitions. And whatever had spooked him had taken place quite recently. No Taglian neighborhood remains quiet and empty for long.

I seldom carry money but did have a few coins on me this morning. I bought the useless teapot. "A gift for my wife. For finally producing a son."

"You're not from around here, are you?" the brass smith asked.

"No. I'm from . . . Dejagore."

The man nodded to himself, as if that explained everything.

When I started to move on, he murmured, "You don't want to go that way, Dejagoran."

"Ah?"

"Be in no hurry. Find a long way around that place."

I squinted at the library. I saw nothing unusual. The grounds appeared completely normal, though some men were working on the garden. "Ah." I continued forward only till I could slide into the mouth of an alley.

Why were there gardeners there? Only the Master Librarian ever brought them in.

I caught glimpses of something wheeling above the library. It drifted down to settle on the ironwork of the gate, above Adoo's head. I took it for a lone pigeon at first but when it folded its wings, I saw that it was a white crow. And a crow with a sharper eye than Adoo had. But Adoo was accustomed to posting himself in the gateway.

That constituted another warning sign.

The white crow looked right at me. And winked. Or maybe just blinked, but I preferred the implication of intelligence and conspiratorial camaraderie.

The crow dropped onto Adoo's shoulder. The startled gateman nearly jumped out of his sandals. The bird evidently said something. Adoo jumped again and tried to catch it. After he failed, he ran into the library. Moments later Shadar disguised as librarians and copyists rushed out and began trying to bring the crow down with stones. The bird got the heck out of there.

I followed its example, heading in another direction. I was more alert than I had been in years. What was going on? Why were they there? Obviously they were lying in wait. For me? Who else? But why? What had I done to give myself away?

Maybe nothing. Though failing to show up to be questioned would count as damning evidence. But I was not lunatic enough to try to bluff my way through whatever it was the Greys were trying to do.

The milk was spilt. No going back. But I did want to mourn the one volume of ancient Annals I had not yet been able to locate and pilfer.

All the way home I tried to reason out what had brought out the Greys. Surendranath Santaraksita had not been missing long enough to cause any official interest. In fact, some mornings the Master Librarian did not arrive until much later than this. I gave it up before I threw my brain out of joint. Murgen could go poking around down there. He could find the answer by eavesdropping.

36

Murgen was busy eavesdropping even though it was daytime. He was worried about Sahra and Tobo. And maybe even a little about Goblin. I found One-Eye, hung over but attentive, at the table where the mist engine resided. Mother Gota and Uncle Doj were there as well, tense and attentive themselves. Which told me that Sahra was determined to go ahead with our most daring stroke yet. To my amazement, One-Eye hustled over—in reality, a slow shuffle—and patted me on my back. "We heard you were coming in, Little Girl. We were scared shitless they were going to get you."

"What?"

"Murgen warned us there was a trap. He heard some of the Grey bosses talking about it when he was scouting to see what Sahra was headed into. The old bitch Soulcatcher herself was out there waiting for you. Well, not exactly you personally, just somebody who goes around stealing books that aren't supposed to be there in the first place."

"You've lost me good, old man. Start someplace where I can see a couple of landmarks."

"Somebody followed you and your boyfriend yesterday. Somebody more suspicious of him than of you. Evidently a part-time spy for the Protector."

We knew there were informants out there getting paid piecework rates. We tried not to be vulnerable to them.

"Also evidently with a boner for your boyfriend."

"One-Eye!"

"All right. For your boss. More or less literally. He went and told the Greys that this dirty old man was about to force perversions on one of the youths who worked for him. A few Greys went to the library and started poking around and asking questions and quickly discovered that some funds had gone missing, and Santaraksita as well, when they started dragging people out of bed and pulling them in. Then they discovered several books missing also, including some great rarities and even a couple that were supposed to have been removed from the library years ago but had not been. *That* got back to Catcher. She got her sweet little behind down there in about ten seconds and started threatening to eat people alive and hurting anybody whose looks she didn't like."

"And I almost walked into the middle of it." I mused, "How did they know the books were gone? I replaced them with discards." But maybe Master Santaraksita, if he was a crook, had been doing that, too.

If he had been corrupt, he had had me fooled.

We would have to talk.

"Near as Murgen could find out, Dorabee Dey Banerjae isn't suspected of anything worse than naïveté. Surendranath Santaraksita, though, is in deep shit. Soulcatcher is going to kill him one limb at a time and let him watch the crows eat as they go. And after that she's going to get nasty." One-Eye grinned a grin in which just the one lonely tooth loomed. Not exactly a recommendation of his talents as the Company dental specialist.

"Say what you like about Soulcatcher, she doesn't put up with any corruption."

Which was just another black mark in her ledger as far as One-Eye was concerned.

"I'm safe," I said. "Here's food for thought. A white crow was waiting at the gate, possibly to warn me. It made a definite attempt to communicate. So what's the story with Sahra?"

"She's going ahead. That Jaul Barundandi is a real dimwit. He bought Goblin's feeble imitation of your Sawa character. Then he tried to get Tobo away from Sahra. Sahra threatened to tell his wife."

Minh Subredil was going to have trouble staying employed if she kept up the bad attitude.

"The cover team in place?"

"Little Girl, who's been doing this shit since before your great-grandmother was born?"

"You always check again. And keep on checking. Because sooner or later, you're going to save someone who overlooked something. Is the evacuation team operational?" Chances were good we were going to have to leave Taglios long before I wanted. Soulcatcher soon would be hunting us hard.

One-Eye said, "Ask Do Trang. He said he'd take care of it. You might find it interesting to note that Catcher dropped the watch on Arjana Drupada when the library jumped to the head of her list and she needed trustworthy people there."

"She doesn't have enough to go around?"

"Not that she trusts. Most of those she's had watching the Bhodi disciples so she can head them off before they pull any more suicide stunts."

"Then we have to hit Drupada—"

"Go teach your granny to suck eggs, Little Girl. Like I said, who was playing these games when Granny's mommy was still shitting her nappies?"

"Who's covering the warehouse, then?" Having so many things in the air meant that every brother had to be occupied somewhere. Soulcatcher was not alone in facing manpower limitations.

"You and me, Little Girl. Pooch and Spiff are around somewhere, being a mixture of sentries and couriers."

"You're sure Drupada is clean?"

"Murgen checks every half hour. Much as he'd rather be haunting his honey. Friend Arjana is clean. For now. But how long will it last? And Murgen's also been keeping an eye on Slink at Semchi. Checking him every couple of hours. Looks like that's going to happen today, too. Soulcatcher is going to shit. She's just going to shit rocks. We're going to do everything but stroll up and bite her on the tit today."

"Language, old man. Language."

Uncle Doj murmured something.

One-Eye hastened to the mist projector.

37

Despite her enthusiasm the night before, Sahra had been worried about having Goblin along, playing Sawa's role. The little man was not reliable. He was bound to do something. . . .

She did not give him enough credit. He had not survived so long by doing stupid things in tight places. He was determined to be more completely Sawa than ever I had played the role. He did nothing on his own. Minh Subredil guided him completely. But over his conservative role-playing he laid a glamour of disinterest. Jaul Barundandi and everyone else merely gave the idiot woman a glance and concentrated on Shiki, who appeared particularly attractive this morning. Who carried her flute hung on a thong around her neck. Anyone who tried to use force would suffer a cruel surprise.

The flute was not new but the Ghanghesha that Shiki carried was. Today even Sawa carried a statue of the god. Jaul Barundandi mocked Subredil. "When will you start carrying a Ghanghesha in each hand?" This was after he had been threatened because of Shiki and he was not feeling kindly.

Subredil bent and whispered to her Ghanghesha, something about pardoning Barundandi because at heart he was a good man who needed help finding his anchor within the light. Barundandi heard some of that. It disarmed him for a while.

He turned the madwoman and her companions over to his wife, who had developed an almost proprietary interest lately. Subredil, in particular, made her look good because she got so much work done.

Narita, too, noted the Ghanghesha. "If religious devotion will win you a better life next time around the Wheel, Subredil, you're headed for the priestly class for sure." Then the fat woman frowned. "But didn't you leave your Ghanghesha here yesterday?"

"Ah? Ah! Ah! I did? I thought I lost that one forever. I didn't know what had become of it. Where is it? Where is it?" She had prepared for this, though the Ghanghesha had been left behind intentionally.

"Easy. Easy." Subredil's love affair with her Ghanghesha amused everyone. "We took good care of it."

There was a lot of work scheduled for the day, which was good. It helped pass the time. Nothing else could be done till much later, and even then, luck would have to play a big part. Another dozen Ghangheshas would not have been out of place where the need for luck went.

During the noon break, over kitchen scraps, Subredil's party heard rumors of the Protector's rage over someone having stolen some books from the royal library. She was out there now, investigating personally.

Subredil shot warning looks at her companions. No questions. No worrying about the people they could not possibly help.

Later in the day there were more rumors. The Purohita and several members of the Privy Council, along with bodyguards and hangers-on, had been treated to a wholesale slaughter on the very steps of the Kernmi What, in what sounded like a full-scale military assault supported by heavy sorcery. Reports were vague and confused because everyone but the attackers had been trying to find somewhere safe to hide.

Subredil tried to take that into account but could not control her anger entirely. Kendo Cutter was too violent a man to have been in charge. And too devout a Vehdna. The Gunni were not going to be pleased about bloodshed happening on the very steps of a major temple.

There was much talk about the signs and portents thrown up as cover and diversion while the attackers faded away. There would be no doubt who had been responsible, nor even who was next on the list of the doomed. Any smoke cloud that did not declare "Water Sleeps" thundered "My Brother Unforgiven."

It had been rumored only for a day that the Great General had been summoned to Taglios to deal with the dead who refused to lie down. To the people in the street, it looked like the Company would be waiting.

Sahra was worried. Soulcatcher was sure to abandon the library when she heard about the attack. If she returned to the Palace extremely agitated, Sahra's operation might have to be abandoned because the sorceress would be too alert.

The Radisha stormed through not long after the news began to make the rounds. She was distraught. She headed directly for her Anger Chamber. Sawa looked up from the brasswork she was cleaning, just for an instant, apparently badly troubled. Subredil set her mop aside and went to see what was wrong. No one else paid them any attention.

Not much later, when Jaul Barundandi dropped in to see how the work was going and somehow got into an argument with Narita, Sawa wandered away when no one was looking. No one noticed right away because Sawa almost never did anything to be noticed and today she wore charms reinforcing that.

Shiki drifted closer to her mother. She looked pale and troubled and kept touching her flute. She whispered, "Shouldn't be we going?"

"It isn't time. Place your Ghanghesha." Shiki was supposed to have done that hours ago.

Rumor rushed through, pursued by uglier rumor still. The Protector had returned and she was in a frothing rage. She was visiting her shadows now. It was going to be another night of terror in the streets of Taglios.

The women started talking about the possible wisdom of finishing work before the Protector decided she had to see the Radisha. The Protector would not respect the privacy of the Princess. She made no secret of her contempt for Taglian custom. Even Narita seemed to hold the opinion that it would be best not to be where you could be seen when the Protector was in a mood.

At that point Shiki discovered that her aunt was missing.

"Damn it, Subredil!" Narita fumed. "You promised you'd watch her closer the last time this happened."

"I'm sorry, mistress. I became so frightened. She probably decided to go to the kitchen. That was what she was trying to do when she got lost last time."

Shiki was going already. Not more than a minute later, she called, "I found her, Mother."

When the rest of the women arrived, they found Sawa seated against a wall, brass lamp in her lap, unconscious, with vomit all over her. "Oh, no!" Subredil cried. "Not again." And in a whirlwind of nonsense and apparently vain efforts to get Sawa's attention, she got across the hint of a fear that Sawa might be pregnant after having been abused by one of the Palace staff.

Narita was away in seconds, fuming. Subredil and Shiki were right behind her, supporting Sawa between them, heading for the servants' postern. Nobody noticed that none of the women were carrying their Ghangheshas, not even the one that Subredil had forgotten the day before.

Because of the state Sawa was in, and the state Narita was in, and the imminent explosion of displeasure expected from the Protector, the women managed to draw their pay, then to escape without having to deal with Barundandi's kickback lieutenant. Again.

They were able to lay Sawa inside a covered ox cart not long after they got into the twisty streets downhill from the Palace. Subredil
had to caution Shiki repeatedly against celebration.

38

E verything we did must have been seen by somebody," I told the
gathered troops. "When word gets out that the Radisha has vanished, all those people are going to remember and try to help. Soulcatcher is supposed to have a knack for separating wheat from chaff."

"Also a knack for calling up the kind of supernatural assistance
that can pick your particular trail out of a thousand," Willow Swan
volunteered. He was present because he had agreed to take care of the
Radisha. She was going to be in a state when she awakened and discovered that her demons had caught up with her at last.

Banh Do Trang wanted to know, "Are you going to flee or not?"
The old man was at the edge of collapse. He had been working since
before dawn.

"Can we?" I asked.

"You could go this instant if the situation became totally desperate. It will be a few hours yet before the barges are completely provi-
sioned, however."

Nobody wanted to go, though. Not just yet. A lot of the men had
developed ties. Everyone had unfinished business. That was life. The
same situation had come up time and again over the course of the
Company's history.

Sahra said, "You still haven't gotten Narayan to give you the Key."

"I'll talk to him. Is River back yet? No? What about Kendo? How
about Pooch and Spiff?" We had people running all over on special
assignments. Good old One-Eye had sent our last two men, the
barely competent Pooch and Spiff, to assassinate Adoo the gateman
because Murgen had been able to determine that it had been he who
had caused all the excitement at the library. More, Adoo knew the
general neighborhood where I lived.

One-Eye informed me, "Kendo Cutter is coming through the
web right now. Arjana Drupada appears to be reasonably healthy for
a man with a dozen knife wounds. Hang on."

Murgen was whispering something. It was thundering and hailing outside. I could not hear a word.

"It's started at Semchi, Murgen says. Slink hit them just as they were starting to pitch camp. Cut them off from their weapons."

"Darn!" I swore. "Darn-darn-darn!"

"What's the matter with you, Little Girl?"

"He should've waited until they tried to do something to the Bhodi Tree. This way, nobody will know why we jumped them."

"There's why you don't have you a man."

"What?"

"You ask too much. You sent Slink out there to kill some people. Unless you told him it's got to be a show, all our guys allowed to fight only left-handed or something, he's going to do it fast and dirty and with as little risk to our own guys as he can."

"I thought he understood—"

"Did you *assume*, Little Girl? At this late stage in your career? You, who's got to run a checklist on lacing your own boots?"

He had me. And he had me good. I tried to change the subject. "If we decide to evacuate, we're going to have to run somebody out there to warn Slink and tell him where to rendezvous."

"Don't try to change the subject."

I turned away. "Kendo. Does he need medical attention?"

"Drupada? He's not bleeding that much anymore."

"Then let's take him back to meet his new roommate." One-Eye catching me out had me feeling particularly evil. This seemed like a good time to take it out on the enemy. "The rest of you, take real good care of the Radisha. We don't want her coming up with a hangnail anybody can blame on us."

Cutter bobbed his head and muttered something under his breath.

"Hey, pervert!" I called to the Inspector-General of the Records. "I don't want you ever to say that the Black Company don't cater to its guests, so here's your very own human play toy. Maybe a little longer in the tooth than you prefer but it's only until the Protector gets around to rescuing you."

Kendo planted a boot in Drupada's behind and shoved. Into the cage the Purohita went. He and Gokhale backed off into opposite corners and glared at one another. Human nature being what it is, each man probably thought the other was responsible for his dismay.

I told Kendo, "Relax now. Get something to eat. Take a nap. But stay away from the girl."

"Hey, I got it the first time, Sleepy. And more so now she's started sleepwalking. So ease up."

"Give me a reason."

"Why don't we just skrag her?"

"Because we need Singh to help open the way through the Shadowgate. And he won't unless he feels confident that we'll be good to the Daughter of Night."

"I don't know any of the Captured that well. Don't feel like you've got to save them on my account."

"I feel like we have to save them on the Company's account, Kendo. Just the same as we'd be doing if it was you out there."

"Sure. Right." Kendo Cutter was one of those people who tended to look on the dark side no matter what.

"Get some rest." I went to talk with Narayan while I waited for Murgen to generate some report on what was happening inside the Palace.

I did not want to run away but knew it was very close to time for the Company to go. We had to see what Soulcatcher's reaction to the kidnapping would be. And we had to get Goblin out of the Palace.

If Soulcatcher did not come after us like a screaming monsoon storm, I was going to get really worried about what she was up to.

"I've had a real good day, thank you, Mr. Singh. A whole lot of planning and a little inspired improvisation fell into place all at once. Just one thing more could make the day perfect." I sniffed the air. It smelled like One-Eye and friends were cooking up a new batch. Probably so they could take a little something along when we had to run.

I kicked a bundle of hides of some kind over beside the bars of Singh's cage, settled myself. I caught him up on the latest gossip. Including, "None of your people seem to be worried about you two. Maybe you were just a little *too* secretive. Be kind of pathetic if the whole cult faded away because everyone just sat around waiting to find out what was going on."

"I've been told that I'm free to deal with you." There was no cringe to the man tonight. He had gotten a little backbone somewhere. "I'm prepared to discuss the object you seek if I receive absolute assurances that the Black Company will never do the Daughter of Night any harm."

"Never is an awful long time. You're out of luck." I got up. "Goblin's been wanting to work on her just forever. I'm going to let him pull a few fingers off now to show you we have no conscience or remorse where certain old enemies are concerned."

"I offered you what you asked."

"You offered me a delayed death warrant. If I agree to that kind of nonsense, ten years from now the blackhearted witch will start poisoning us and we'll be stuck with the disastrous choice of keeping our word and accepting destruction or breaking our word and seeing our reputation destroyed. I'm certain you don't know much northern mythology. There's an old religion up there that tells how a leading god allowed himself to be slain so his family would no longer be bound by a promise he made foolishly to an enemy, who wore it like a turtle's shell."

Narayan stared at me, cold as a cobra, waiting for me to crack. And I did, a little, because I bothered to explain. One-Eye has told me a hundred times that I should not explain. "I just don't want that artifact badly enough to commit my people to the level of vulnerability that you're asking. In particular, I won't undertake commitments for those of us who are buried. On the other hand, maybe you'd like to undertake commitments whereby, assuming you get out of this alive, you guarantee never to be a pain in the Company neck ever again. Whereby you agree to go to the Captain and the Lieutenant and beg their forgiveness for stealing their child."

The very suggestion appalled the living saint of the Deceivers. "She's the Child of Kina. The Daughter of Night. Those two are irrelevant."

"Evidently we don't have anything to talk about yet. I'll send you a few fingers for breakfast."

I went to see if Surendranath Santaraksita was being a good fellow and pursuing the tasks I had suggested he could use to help overcome the tedium of his captivity. To my surprise I found him hard at work, with old Baladitya assisting, translating what I had presumed to be the first volume of the lost Annals. They had a whole stack of sheets already done.

"Dorabee!" Master Santaraksita said. "Excellent. Your friend the foreigner keeps telling us we can't have any more real vellum when we're done with these last few sheets. He wants us to use those ridiculous bark books they still employ out in the swamps."

Before there were modern paper and vellum and parchment, there was bark. I do not know what kind of tree it came from, just that the inner bark was removed carefully, treated and pressed and used to write on. To make a book, you stacked the bark sheets, drilled a hole down through the upper-left-hand corner of the stack, then bound everything together with a cord or ribbon or length of very light chain. Banh Do Trang would favor bark because it was both cheap, traditional and hardier than animal products.

"I'll talk to him."

"There's nothing earthshaking in there, Dorabee."

"My name is Sleepy."

"Sleepy isn't a name. It's a disease, or a misfortune. I prefer Dorabee. I'll use Dorabee."

"Use whatever you like. I'll know who you're talking to." I read a couple of sheets. He was right. "This is tedious stuff. This looks like an account book."

"That's what it is, mainly. The things you want to know are just the things the writer assumes any reader of his own time would know already. He wasn't writing for the ages, or even for another generation. He was keeping track of horseshoe nails, lance shafts and saddles. All he has to say about their battle is that the lower-ranking officers and noncommissioned officers failed to demonstrate an adequate enthusiasm for appropriating weapons lost or abandoned by the defeated enemy, preferring to wait till the next dawn to begin gleaning. As a consequence, stragglers and the local peasantry managed to scavenge all the best."

"I notice he doesn't bother to name a single name, person or place." I had begun reading while the Master talked. I could listen and read at the same time even though I was a woman.

"He does give mileage and dates. The context suggests the appropriate systems of measure. It can be figured out. But what I've already started to wonder, Dorabee, is why we've all been deathly afraid of these people all our lives. This book gives us no reason to be afraid. This book is about a troop of crabby little men who marched off somewhere they didn't want to go for reasons they didn't understand, fully believing that their unstated mission would last only several weeks or, at most, a few months. Then they would be able to go home. But the months piled into years and the years into generations. And still they didn't really know."

The material also suggested we needed to revise our old belief that the Free Companies exploded into the world at the same time, in a vast orgy of fire and bloodshed. The only other company mentioned was noted to have returned years before the Black Company marched, and in fact, several senior Company noncoms had served as private soldiers in that earlier, unnamed band.

"I can see it," I grumbled. "We're going to translate these things, find out all sorts of things, and not be an inch closer to understanding anything."

Santaraksita said, "This's much more exciting than a meeting of the bhadrhalok, Dorabee."

Then Baladitya spoke for the first time. "Do we have to starve to death here, Dorabee?"

"Nobody's brought you anything to eat?"

"No."

"I'll just see about that. Don't be startled if you hear me shouting. I hope you enjoy fish and rice."

I took care of that, then hid in my corner for a while. I was feeling a little depressed after having seen Master Santaraksita's work. I suppose that sometimes I invest too much in my goals, then suffer a correspondingly huge disappointment when things do not work out.

39

Tobo woke me. "How can you sleep, Sleepy?"

"I guess I must be tired. What do you want?"

"The Protector has finally started to grumble about the Radisha. Dad wants you to come keep track yourself. So you don't have to record anything third-hand."

At the moment, my name felt entirely appropriate. I just wanted to lie down on my pallet and dream about finding another kind of life.

Trouble was, I had been doing this since I was fourteen. I did not know anything else. Unless Master Santaraksita was willing to let bygones by bygones and take me back at the library. Right after we buried Soulcatcher in a fifty-foot-deep hole we filled in with boiling lead.

I dragged a stool in between Sahra and One-Eye, leaned forward with my elbows on the table and stared into the mist where Murgen appeared to report when it suited him. One-Eye was fussing at Murgen even though Murgen was away. I said, "Anybody would think you were worried about Goblin, the way you're carrying on."

"Of course I'm worried about Goblin, Little Girl. The runt borrowed my transeidetic locuter before he went up there this morning. Not to mention he still owes me several thousands pais for . . . well, he owes me a bunch of money."

My recollection had it the other way around. One-Eye always owed everyone, even when he was doing well. And several thousand pais is not exactly a fortune, a pai being a tiny seed of such uniform weight that it is used as a measure for gems and precious metals. It takes almost two thousand of them to equal a northern ounce. Since One-Eye had not specified gold or silver, the standard assumption would be that he had meant coin-grade copper. In other words, not very much.

In other words still, he was worried about his best friend but he could not say so because he had a century-long history of reviling the man in public.

If there was any such magical instrument as a transeidetic locuter, One-Eye invented it an hour before he loaned it to Goblin.

He muttered, "That ugly little turd gets himself killed, I'm gonna strangle him. He can't leave me holding the bag on—" He realized he was thinking out loud.

Sahra and I both made mental notes to investigate the bag metaphor. It sounded like there were business plans afoot. Secret plans. Surprise, surprise.

Murgen materialized practically nose to nose with me. He murmured, "Soulcatcher is out of patience. A flock of crows just brought the news from Semchi. She's in a complete black mood. She says she's going into the Radisha's Anger Chamber after her if she doesn't come out in the next two minutes."

"How's Goblin?" One-Eye barked.

"Hiding," Murgen replied. "Waiting for sunrise." He was not go-

ing to try leaving during the night, the way we had planned originally. Soulcatcher had loosed her shadows, just to punish Taglios for
irritating her. We had a few traps out, randomly distributed through
likely neighborhoods, but I did not expect to catch anything. I figured our luck along those lines was about used up.

Goblin was armed with a shadow-repellent amulet left over from
the Shadowmaster wars but did not know if it was any good anymore.
Being bright and full of forethought, it had not occurred to any of us
to test it on real shadows while we had some in stock.

You cannot think of everything.

But you should make the effort.

One of the Royal Guards actually tried to stop the Protector when
her patience failed and she went to dig the Radisha out of her hide-
away. He went down without a sound, stricken by a casual touch. He
would recover eventually. The Protector was not feeling particularly
vindictive. For the moment.

She crashed through the door of the Anger Chamber. And
howled in frustration before the pieces finished falling. "Where is
she?" The power of her rage wilted the onlookers.

A subassistant chamberlain, bowing almost double, continuing
to bob and get lower, whined, "She was in there, O Great One!"

Someone else insisted, "We never saw her leave. She has to be in
there."

From somewhere, echoing, almost as if coming from some distance
in time as well as place, there was the sound of brief laughter.

Soulcatcher turned slowly, her stare a cruel spear. "Come closer.
Tell me again." Her voice was compelling, chilling, terrible. She
stared into one pair of eyes after another, making full use of the fear
so many had that she could read the deepest secrets in their minds.

None of the Radisha's people changed their stories.

"Out of here. Out of this whole apartment. Something happened
here. I want no distractions. I want nothing disturbed." She turned
again, slowly, extending a sorceress's senses to feel the shape of the
past. It was more difficult than she anticipated. She had been loafing
for too long, falling out of practice and getting out of shape.

The remote laughter sounded again for an instant, seeming just
a touch closer.

"You!" Soulcatcher snapped at a fat woman, one of the house-keepers. "What are you doing?"

"Ma'am?" Narita was barely able to croak her response. In a moment, she would lose control of her bladder.

"You just pushed something into your left sleeve. Something off the altar." A single white candle, almost consumed, still burned in the tiny shrine to ancestors. "Come here." Soulcatcher extended her gloved right hand.

Narita could not resist. She stepped toward the dark woman, so trim and evilly feminine in her leather. Idly, Narita hated her for maintaining that sleek body.

"Give it to me."

Reluctantly, Narita removed the Ghanghesha from her sleeve. She began to babble about not wanting her friend to get into trouble, making no sense at all, failing to realize that if she had not tried to conceal the Ghanghesha, the Protector would have overlooked it entirely.

Soulcatcher stared at the little clay figurine. "The cleaning woman. It belongs to the cleaning woman. Where is she?"

Far, mocking laughter.

"She's a day employee, ma'am. She comes in from outside."

"Where does she live?"

"I don't know, ma'am. I don't think anybody does. Nobody ever asked. It never mattered."

One of the other staffers offered, "She was a good worker."

Soulcatcher continued to examine the Ghanghesha. "Something's odd here. . . . Now it does matter. To me. Find out."

"How?"

"I don't care! Be creative! But do it." Soulcatcher hurled the clay figurine to the floor. Shards flew in every direction.

A wisp of a ghost of darkness curled up and stood like a rampant cobra a foot high for an instant. Then it struck. At the Protector.

The staffers squealed and began trampling one another, trying to get away. They had not seen a shadow before but they knew what a shadow could do.

The laughter was closer now, louder and lasting longer.

Soulcatcher offered a convincing squeal of surprise and fright, like a young woman who has just stepped on a snake. Her apparel and the handful of generalized protective spells that always surrounded her saved her from becoming a victim of her own cruelest weapon.

Even so, for a minute she was like a child swatting mosquitoes as the shadow enthusiastically strove to terminate their relationship. Failing to reclaim control of the shadow, Soulcatcher destroyed it. The necessity told her that a pretty clever mind had prepared it, probably hoping that she would be too angry to pay close attention for just that instant needed. . . .

"Woman! Come back here!" The Protector extended a hand in the direction Narita had fled. Somehow, a single strand of the woman's hair had become entwined through Soulcatcher's fingers. Those fingers shimmered momentarily. The air became charged. The other staffers whimpered and wished they had even had the nerve to try to run.

Narita reappeared slowly, taking short zombie steps. "Here!" Soulcatcher said. She pointed at a spot on the Anger Chamber floor. "The rest of you. Go away. Quickly." She did not have to add any encouragement. "Fat woman. Tell me everything about the creature who always carried the Ghanghesha."

"I've told you everything I know," Narita whined.

"No. You have not. Start talking. She may have kidnapped the Radisha."

Soulcatcher regretted mentioning that the instant the words left her helmet.

The laughter sounded like it was coming from just out in the hallway, a diabolic snickering. The Protector's head twitched toward that direction. She sensed no threat. It could wait a minute.

"Her name is Minh Subredil." It took Narita only another thirty seconds to relate everything she knew about Minh Subredil, her daughter Shikhandini and her sister-in-law Sawa.

"Thank you," Soulcatcher snarled. "You've been most unhelpful. And for that, I shall provide an appropriate reward." She gripped the fat woman's throat in her right hand, squeezed.

As Narita went limp, that laughter sounded once more. There might have been a word there, too. Ardath? Or perhaps Silath? Or might it have been . . . ? No matter. Soulcatcher would not listen to that, just to the mockery. She hurled herself toward the sound but when she burst into the hallway, there was nothing to see.

She started to call for Guards, for Greys, but recalled that she had just slain the one person other than herself who knew for sure that the Radisha had disappeared.

The Radisha had shut herself away from the world. *That* was all anybody really needed to know. The Princess could live forever right there in her Anger Chamber. She did not need to venture forth ever again. She had her good friend the Protector to handle the boring chores of managing her empire for her.

More laughter, apparently from nowhere and everywhere. Soul-catcher stamped away. This was not over yet.

A white crow dropped out of the murk near the ceiling of the hall-way, flapped heavily, landed beside the fat woman. It held its beak poised beneath her nostrils momentarily, as though checking for breath. Then it flapped away suddenly, sharp ears having caught the sound of a stealthy footfall.

A shivering Jaul Barundandi eased into the chamber. He knelt beside the woman. He took her hand. He remained there, tears streaking his cheeks, until he heard the Protector returning, arguing with herself in a variety of voices.

40

W hat do you know about that?" I said to Sahra. "Narita tried to cover for you. And then Barundandi got all broken up about what happened to her."

Sahra waggled a finger. She was thinking. "Murgen. What do you know about that white crow?"

Murgen hesitated before responding. "Nothing." Which meant he was telling an approximate truth but he had some definite ideas. Sahra and I both knew him that well.

Sahra said, "Suppose you tell me what you think is going on, then."

Murgen faded away.

"What the heck is that?" I snapped at One-Eye. "You were sup-posed to rig this thing so he has to do what he's told."

"He does. Most of the time. He could be carrying out a previous instruction."

But the old fool sounded to me like he had no idea what Murgen was doing.

Soulcatcher worked quickly, then summoned the staff members who had been present when she had broken into the Anger Chamber. "The continuing excitement was too much for this poor woman. I've tried to resurrect her but her soul refuses to respond. She must be happy where she is now." There were no witnesses to contradict her, though remote laughter mocked her. "I did find the Radisha. She'd fallen asleep. She has retreated into the Anger Chamber and does not wish to be disturbed again. Not for a long time. I should have honored her wishes before. We would have avoided this disaster." She indicated the fat woman.

Even the staffers who had looked into the Anger Chamber earlier and had seen nothing had to admit that someone was inside now, moving around angrily, muttering the way the Radisha did and looking very much like the Radisha in glimpses caught through cracks in the poorly restored door.

The Protector suggested, "Let's all turn in for the night. Tomorrow we'll begin repairing the mess I made." She watched her audience intently, feeling for anyone who could cause trouble.

The staff departed. They were relieved just to be away from Soulcatcher.

Soulcatcher sat down and thought. There was no way to tell what was going through her mind till she began muttering in a committee of voices. Then it was clear that she was trying to work out the mechanics of the abduction. She seemed willing to give considerable weight to the possibility that the Radisha had stage-managed the whole thing herself.

A very suspicious woman, the Protector.

One by one she found and questioned each of the people who had dealt with Minh Subredil, Sawa and Shikhandini, beginning with Jaul Barundandi and finishing with Del Mukharjee, the man Barundandi usually trusted to collect the kickbacks from the outside workers. "You will cease that," the Protector informed Mukharjee. "You and anyone else involved. If it happens again, I will put you into a glass ball and hang you above the service postern with your whole body turned inside out. I'll add a couple of imps to feed on your entrails for the six months it will take you to die. Do you understand?"

Del Mukharjee understood the threat just fine. But he had no idea whatsoever why the Protector would want to interfere with his livelihood.

The Protector had a passion about corruption.

In time the Protector reasoned that three women had come into the Palace and three women had gone away again. It seemed very likely that the three who had departed were not the three who had entered. And no one the Radisha's size had gone out since.

Which meant that someone with some answers might still be inside.

Chuckling wickedly, Soulcatcher began to look for evidence that someone had slipped off into the untenanted wilds of the Palace.

Goblin was asleep on a dusty old bed. Occasionally his snores would turn to sneezes and snorts when too much dust got into his nostrils.

A squawk had him bouncing up so suddenly he almost collapsed from light-headedness. He spun around. He saw nothing. He heard soft laughter, then a bizarre, squawking voice that sounded almost familiar. "Wake up. Wake up. She is coming."

"Who's coming? Who's talking?"

There was no response. He did not feel any strong sorcerous presence. It was a puzzle.

Goblin had a good idea who might be coming, though. Not many women were likely to be hunting him here in the middle of the night.

He was ready. His little pack was carrying the two books Sleepy most wanted to save. Taking all three was physically impossible. His traps were set. All he had to do was move on into the now-empty part of the Palace that had been occupied by the Black Company back when its staff and leadership had been quartered there. There were ways to get out unnoticed. He and One-Eye had found them in olden times. The trouble was, he had no desire to be on the streets after dark, amulet or no.

Soulcatcher gave up most of her sense of touch when she chose to wrap every inch of her body in leather and helmet. She never noted the touch of or resistance of the strand of spider silk stretched across the corridor. But she did have a marvelously well-developed sense for personal danger. Before the Ghanghesha hit the floor, she was moving to defend herself. It was such reflexes that made it possible for creatures like her, her sister Lady, and the Howler, to have survived for so long. This time she had the proper controlling spells ready, hung about her, sparkling like spanking-new tools.

The shadow trapped inside the figurine barely got its bearings before it was attacked itself, seized and constrained, then twisted and crushed down into a whining, seething ball completely enclosed inside one of the Protector's gloved hands. A merry young voice called, "You'll have to do better than that."

Soulcatcher continued to move forward, amused by the idea of tossing the shadow back into someone's face. The trail began to grow indistinct, then disorienting. Experimentation showed her the cause was external. The corridor had been strewn with cobwebs of spells so subtle that even she might not have noticed had she just been hurrying along. "Oh, you clever devils. How long has this been here? Ah. A very long time indeed, I see. You were still in favor when you started this. Have you been hiding here all along? I certainly couldn't find you in the city if you never were out there."

In another voice entirely, she asked, "What have we here? It smells like somebody very frightened is hiding behind this door. And he didn't even bother to lock it. How stupid does he think I am?"

She shoved the door with her toe.

A clay Ghanghesha plummeted from its place atop the door. Soulcatcher giggled. She was even quicker to recapture this shadow, which she squeezed down inside her other hand. Then she pushed into the room.

There was no one there anymore. That was easy to sense. But there was a curious feel to the place. It demanded an investigation.

She generated a small light, stood in place, turned slowly while she read the history of the room for subtle clues. A great deal had happened there. Much of the recent history of the Black Company had been shaped in that room. It retained a strong smell of old fear she identified eventually with the long-dead Taglian court wizard, Smoke.

All this she debated with herself in a committee of argumentative voices. In the end, she seemed entertained. Most of the time life was a great entertainment for Soulcatcher.

"And what do we have here?" Something with inked characters on it peeped from beneath a dusty old bed where someone had been lying until minutes ago. Thoughtlessly, she reached for the object, opening her hand to grasp it. "Damn! That was stupid!" She wasted several minutes regaining control of the shadow. It was very agile this time. She stuffed it into the hand restraining the other. The two were extremely unhappy in there. One thing shadows seemed to hate more than the living was other shadows.

What Soulcatcher had found was a book with half the pages torn out. It was alone. "So this is what became of those. I was never quite sure who took them. I wonder if they got any use out of them?"

As she was about to depart, the Protector glanced at the damaged book once more. "Been taking these pages a few at a time. That would take a long time. Which means they've been coming in and out of the Palace for a long time. Which therefore suggests that the Radisha didn't engineer her own disappearance. Oh, well. She's gone. It amounts to the same thing. Let's catch our little rat and let him play with our little friends."

Unlike Soulcatcher, Goblin could not see in the dark. But he had the advantage of knowing where he was going. He did manage to stay ahead and did slide out of one of the old hidden exits. There was a little light outside from a fragment of moon peeking through scurrying young clouds trying to catch up with Mother Storm. Goblin laid the last Ghanghesha on the cobblestones in plain sight, then ran. The books on his back beat against him, pounding the breath out of him. He muttered something about the good news being that it was all downhill from here. The bad news was that it was dark out, there were shadows on the prowl, and he was not so sure about the quality of his fifteen-year-old amulet. He had to hope that in a city this vast, none of the handful of nightstalkers would cross his path while he was huffing and puffing and concentrating on staying ahead of Soulcatcher.

It did not occur to him that she might have recovered the shadows he had left in ambush, that they might be after him, too.

Soulcatcher stepped into the night close enough behind to glimpse a flicker of her quarry vanishing into the shadows between structures across the open area outside the Palace. She spied the abandoned Ghanghesha and several other small items that looked like they had been dropped in the rush to get away. She tossed her two shadows into the air and stomped her heel down on the clay figurine at the same time. This would set a pack of small deaths on the little man's heels.

By now, she was reasonably certain that she was chasing the wizard called Goblin.

She screamed. The pain in her heel was beyond anything she had ever experienced. As she collapsed, trying to will her throat to seal itself, she watched three ferociously bright balls of light streak into the night in pursuit of the shadows she had sent to claim Goblin. Still fighting the incredible pain, she produced a dagger and used its tip to dip another fireball out of her heel. Already it had eaten all the way to the bone and in, and had done some damage as high as her ankle—despite her normal protection.

"I'll be crippled," she snarled. "He lulled me. He set me up so I'd think this would be another easy shadow trap." None of her voices were amused now. "Clever little bastard will pay for this."

The fallen fireball burned its way into the cobblestones. Still ignoring her pain, Soulcatcher tried to stand. She discovered that she was not going to be able to walk. She was, however, not losing any blood. The fireball had cauterized her wound. "My beloved sister, if you weren't already dead, I'd kill you for inventing those damned things."

Laughter echoed down off the ramparts of the Palace.

A flicker of white glided after Goblin.

"I think I'll kill *somebody* anyway." Soulcatcher made her way toward the Palace entrance on hands and knees, muttering continuously. She had isolated her pain in a remote corner of her mind and was now concentrating on being angry about what this odyssey was doing to her beautiful leather pants and gloves.

41

C an you believe that?" I asked. "She was as mad about ruining her outfit as she was about losing Goblin and getting hurt."

One-Eye chuckled, immensely relieved because Goblin had gotten away. "I believe it."

"What? You, too?"

"It's a northern thing. Everything she wears is leather. You people are all goofy about stuff like that. She probably has to fly five thousand miles every time she wants a new pair of pants. Means she's really got to watch her waist and behind. Unlike some—hey! No punching! We're all on the same side here."

"Do you believe this little pervert?" I asked Sahra.

"You go ask Swan." One-Eye showed me his tooth. The one he was about to lose. "He'll tell you the woman's got her good points."

Sahra remained all business. "What are we going to do if she just pretends the Radisha is all right? How many people normally see the Princess? Not many, I know. And there's no Privy Council anymore. We've seen to them. Except for Mogaba."

"We've got to see about him, too," One-Eye grumbled.

"Let's not overreach. The Great General will be harder to take than the others were."

I mused, "She wouldn't actually have to keep the Radisha in hiding very long. Maybe two weeks, while she builds a new Council, handpicked to woof 'Yes, ma'am!' and 'How high?' when she tells them to jump."

One-Eye blew out a bushel of air. "She's right. Maybe we should've considered that."

I said, "I did consider it. Having the Radisha under our control looked like the best deal. We can trot her out any time Soulcatcher gets too bizarre. And Soulcatcher will realize that. She won't let temptation carry her too far. Not until she sorts us out."

"She will do everything she can to find and recover the Radisha," Sahra said. "I'm sure of that. Which means we need to hurry up and get out of the city."

I said, "I have one little thing to do before I go. Don't anybody wait on me. Murgen. Be a pal and put a little real effort into finding out about this other white crow."

I did not await his response. Now that Goblin seemed safe, I was eager to interview our newest prisoner.

Someone had taken some effort to make the Radisha comfortable. Nor had she been forced into a cage. Presumably, One-Eye had provided a sampler of choker spells.

I studied her while she remained unaware of my presence. She had had a formidable reputation when first the Company had come to Taglios. She had put up a good struggle, too, but the years had worn her down. She looked old and tired and defeated now.

I stepped forward. "Have they treated you well so far, Radisha?"

She showed me a weak smile. There was a twinkle both of anger and sarcasm in her eye.

"I know. It's not the Palace. But I've enjoyed worse. Including chains and no roof at all."

"And animal hides?"

"I've lived here for the last six years. You get used to it." It had been longer than that but I was not taking time to be precise.

"Why?"

"Water sleeps, Radisha. Water sleeps. You were expecting us. We had to come."

At that point it became completely real to her. Her eyes grew big. "I've seen you before."

"Many times. Lately, around the Palace. Once upon a time, long ago, around the Palace also, with the Standardbearer."

"You're the idiot."

"Am I? Perhaps one of us—"

She began to grow angry then.

I told her, "That won't help. But if you need to rage to feel better, consider this. The Protector is covering up your disappearance already. The one person who knew for sure—not counting us villains, of course—is dead already. There'll be more deaths. And you'll begin making the most outrageous pronouncements from the anonymity of your Anger Chamber. And in six months the Protector will be so solidly in control, behind her Greys and those who think they can profit from an alliance with her, that you won't matter anymore." As long as Soulcatcher could come to an accommodation with Mogaba.

I did not mention that.

The Radisha began to speak quite rudely of her ally.

I let her run for a while, then offered another slogan: "All their days are numbered."

"What the hell does that mean?"

"Sooner or later we're going to get everyone who injured us. You're right. It's not really sane. But it's the way we are. You've seen it happening lately. Only the Protector and the Great General are still running free. All their days are numbered."

The reality sank in a little deeper. She was a captive. She did not know where. She did not know what was going to happen. She did know that her captors were willing to pursue their grudges to insane lengths, just as they had promised they would before she made the mistake of letting herself be seduced by Soulcatcher's deadly promises.

"You have no designated heir, do you?"

The change of direction startled her. "What?"

"There isn't any clear-cut line of succession."

Again, "What?"

"At the moment I don't just hold you hostage, I have the entire future of Taglios and the Taglian Territories firmly under my thumb. You don't have a child. You brother has no child."

"I'm too old for that now."

"Your brother isn't. And he is still alive."

I left her then, to think, her mouth hanging open.

I considered seeing Narayan Singh again, decided I would seem too eager. I was too tired, anyway. You do not treat with a Deceiver without full command of your faculties. Sleep was the lover whose arms I needed to wrap me up.

42

I was playing tonk with Spiff and JoJo and Kendo Cutter, an interesting mix. At least three of us took our religion somewhat seriously. JoJo's real name was Cho Dai Cho. He was Nyueng Bao and, in theory, One-Eye's bodyguard. One-Eye did not want a bodyguard. JoJo did not want to be a bodyguard. So they did not see much of one another, and the rest of us saw as little of JoJo as we did of Uncle Doj. JoJo complained, "You're just ganging up on the dumb swamp boy. I know."

I said, "Me get in cahoots with a heretic and an unbeliever?"

"You'll ambush them after you finish picking my bones."

I had been having an unusual run of luck.

Everybody resents it when their favorite mark gets lucky.

I said, "I can't get used to this not having to go to work." JoJo discarded a six I needed to fill to the inside of a five-card straight. "Maybe this is my day."

"Be a good time to get out and find you a man, then."

"Goblin. You're still alive. As mad as Soulcatcher was last night, I figured she would have you for a midnight snack before you got halfway home."

Goblin gave me his big frog grin. "She's gonna walk funny for a while. I couldn't believe she actually stomped on it." His grin faded. "I've been thinking. Maybe nailing her that way was a mistake. I could've led her somewhere where we could've got her in a cross-fire—"

"She would've been looking for that. In fact, her suspecting something like that was probably one reason she didn't keep chasing you. You want to sit in?"

All three of my companions glowered. Goblin was not One-Eye but they did not trust him a bit. They knew with the confidence of ignorance that Goblin was just more clever when he cheated. The fact that his history was one of losing more than he won was just a part of the cover-up.

You might have noticed that the human animal is fond of forming and clinging to prejudices, remaining their steadfast curator in the face of all reason and contradiction.

"Not this time." Goblin could take a hint. He would also take them some other way sometime and laugh himself silly behind his hand. And it would serve them right. "Got work to do. I'm already getting complaints from everybody about a ghost that was all over the warehouse last night. Got to scope it out."

I had a losing hand. Or foot. I tossed it in. "He's making me feel guilty for loafing." I collected my winnings.

"You can't quit now," Kendo grumbled.

"You proved your point. Women can't play cards. I stay here much longer, I won't have a copper left to my name. Then you wouldn't get a birthday present this year."

"Didn't get one last year, either."

"I must've played tonk with you then, too. So many of you do it, I have a hard time keeping track of which ones of you guys keep beating up on me."

They all grumbled now.

Goblin said, "Maybe I can sit in, just for a hand or two."

"That's all right. You better help Sleepy. Or Sleepy can help you." The grumbling stopped till we were out of earshot.

Goblin chuckled. So did I. He said, "We ought to get married."

"I'm too old for you. See if Chandra Gokhale can fix you up."

"Aren't those two like a couple of starving rats?" Gokhale and Drupada were at one another constantly. Their squabbles had not yet devolved into anything physical only because they had been warned in the strongest of terms that the winner of any fight would be punished terribly.

"Maybe one of them will kill and eat the other one," I said. "If we're lucky."

"You're a dreamer, for sure."

"What's your opinion on this ghost?"

He shrugged.

"You know it's the girl, don't you?"

"I'm pretty sure."

"You think she's going through the same thing Murgen did when he started? Falling through time and everything?"

"I don't know. There's a difference. Nobody ever saw anything with Murgen."

"Can you stop her from doing it?"

"Spooking you out?"

"In the sense that I'm scared she'll go out and get help, sure."

"Ooh. I didn't think about that."

"Do think about it, Goblin. What about the white crow? Could she be the white crow?"

"I thought Murgen was the white crow."

He knew better. "Murgen's here, being Sahra's recon slave."

"It wouldn't be the first time Murgen was in the same place, looking at things from two different times."

"He tells me he can't remember being the crow."

"Maybe that's because he hasn't done it yet. Maybe it's a Murgen from next year or something."

I did not know what to say to that. That possibility had not occurred to me. And Murgen had done that sort of thing before.

"On the other hand, personally I don't think it's Murgen or the brat." He grinned his big toad grin. He knew I would stub my toe on that.

I did. "What? You little rat. Who is it, then?"

He shrugged. "I got a couple ideas but I'm not ready to talk about them yet. You got the Annals. All you need to follow my reasoning is right in there." He began giggling, pleased with himself for stumping the Annalist at her own game. So to speak. "Ha-ha." He spun around, dancing. "Let's go beat up on Narayan Singh. Whoa. Look who's here. Swan, you're too damned old to wear your hair that long. Unless you're going to comb it all up on top there to kind of cover the thin spot."

I held a finger above Goblin's dome, pointing down. He had not had a crop come in during my lifetime.

Swan said, "Kind of looks like your widow's peak is sagging back a little, too. Probably comes of banging your head on the bottoms of so many tables." Swan looked at me, an eyebrow raised. "He been in the ganja or something?"

"No. He just hasn't gotten over the fact that he went toe to toe with your girlfriend and came out ahead on points." Swan had suggested a good point indirectly, though. With hemp such a common weed, it was a wonder that Goblin and One-Eye had not gotten in on the entertainment side of that crop.

Goblin understood what I was thinking without me saying a word. He told me, "We don't have anything to do with it because it screws up your head."

"And that water-buffalo urine you brew back there doesn't?"

"That's pure medicine, Sleepy. You ought to try it. It's chock-full of stuff that's good for you."

"My diet is just fine, Goblin. Except for the fish and the rice."

"That's what I'm saying. We take up a collection, buy us a pig . . . never mind what Sahra says. There ain't nothing sweeter than some fatback and beans—"

Swan had invited himself to accompany us in our seventy-foot trek to Narayan's cage. He said, "I'll kick in on that myself. I haven't tasted bacon in over twenty years."

"Shit," Goblin said. "You're going to kick in? Man, you don't even have a name anymore. You're dead."

"I could run up to the Palace, dig around under my mattress. Times haven't been all bad for me."

"You won't marry me, Sleepy," Goblin said, "then you oughta marry Swan. He's got a hoard put back and he's too damned old to bother you with any of that man stuff. Narayan Singh. Get your skinny, shit-smelling ass up from there and talk to me."

Swan whispered, "Survival must be a real powerful drug."

"I expect it is when you're Goblin's age," I agreed.

"I guess it is at any age."

"Meaning?" I asked.

"Meaning, I guess, I should've headed back north a long time ago. I got nothing going for me here. I should've started moseying when Blade and Cordy went down. But I couldn't. And it wasn't just Soulcatcher twisting my arm."

"Umm?"

"I'm a loser. We were all losers. All three of us. We couldn't even make it as soldiers in the old empire. We deserted. Blade got his ass thrown to the crocodiles for smarting off to the priests back in his home country. We never had no real start-up, any of us. Me and Cordy only headed on down here because once we got to running, it took a long time to stop. Now I don't have my friends anymore, I don't have anybody to goose me into doing things."

I did not enlighten him about the health of Blade and Mather, who were among the Captured, but I did point out, "You can't be entirely inadequate. You've had some kind of commission or other from the Taglian throne practically since you got here."

"I'm an outsider. I make a great fall guy. Everybody knows who I am and everybody can recognize me. So the Protector or the Radisha puts me out front where I can take the heat for all their unpopular decisions."

"Now they'll need to find somebody else."

"Don't give me that look. I wouldn't join the Black Company if you promised to marry me and make me Captain, too. You guys got doom written all over you."

"What do you want?"

"Me? Since I don't got the stones or the young body to go home anymore—and home wouldn't be there when I showed up anyway—what I'd like to do is what we tried to do when we first came down here. Set me up a little brewery, spend my last few years making people's lives a little easier."

"I'm sure Goblin and One-Eye would be happy to take on a partner."

"Them two? No way. They'd drink up half the product. They'd

get drunk and get in a fight and start throwing the barrels at each other—"

He had a point. "You have a point. Though they've shown considerable self-control lately."

"It helps you pay attention if your fuckup will get you killed. I'm always surprised by this guy." He meant Narayan Singh. "He looks like such a trivial little wart. There're ten thousand that look just like him out there on the streets right now and not one will ever do anything more important than starve to death."

"If I thought it would do any good, I'd starve this one to death, too. Narayan. I'm back. Are you going to talk to me today?"

Singh raised his eyes. He seemed serene, at peace. That could be said for Stranglers. They never had trouble with their consciences. "Good morning, young woman. Yes. We can talk. I took your advice. I went to the goddess. And she approved your petition. Frankly, I was surprised. She set down no special conditions for making a bargain. Other than that the lives and well-being of her chief agents remain unimpaired."

Swan was more taken aback than I was. "You got the right guy here, Sleepy?"

"I don't know. I figured they'd still try to weasel a little even after they couldn't stall anymore." This required a little thought. Or a lot of thought. And maybe some worry. "I'm definitely pleased, Narayan. Definitely. Where's the Key?"

Narayan smiled a smile almost as ugly as One-Eye's. "I'll take you to it."

"Aha," I murmured. "I see. The first shoe drops. Fine. When will you be ready to travel?"

"As soon as the girl recovers. You may have noticed she's been sick."

"Yes, I did. I thought it must be her time of the month." A horrible, *horrible* thought occurred to me. "She's not pregnant, is she?"

The look on Singh's face told me that notion was completely unthinkable to him.

"That's good. But it doesn't matter, Narayan. As long as we're conspiring together, Deceivers and Black Company, you two aren't going to be a team. It's a sad truth, Narayan Singh, but I just don't trust you. And her I wouldn't trust if she was in her grave."

He smiled like he knew a secret. "But you expect us to trust you."

"Based on the well-known fact that once it has sworn a thing, the Company always keeps its word. Yes." A slight exaggeration, of course.

Narayan glanced at Swan for just a second. He smiled again. "I guess that's just going to have to be good enough for me."

I pasted on my most scintillating false smile. "Wonderful. We're in business together. I'll get some people ready for an expedition. Do we have far to go?"

Smile. "Not far. Just a few days south of the city."

"Ha. The Grove of Doom. I should have guessed."

I led Swan away. I rejoined the fellows at the card table. "I want Singh's son brought in as soon as we can get him." It could not hurt to have a little extra ammunition.

43

I don't know what to do with myself, not having to work," Sahra told me. She and Tobo were huddled in front of the mist box, sharing what they could with Murgen. I was pleased to see mother and son getting along.

I suggested, "There's always work for those who want to put out the buttons that'll remind everyone about us after we're gone. There's always something that needs lugging down to the river."

"To paraphrase Goblin, I don't miss work so much I'm actually going to volunteer to do some. Was there something?"

"The guys just brought in Singh's son. Good-looking fellow. They also brought in a couple of rescripts they found posted on the official announcement pillars. Put up since the Radisha went into seclusion."

"What do they say?"

"Mainly that she's willing to pay some pretty big rewards for information leading to the apprehension of any member of the gang of vandals masquerading as members of the long defunct Black Company and causing public disorders."

"Will anybody believe that?"

"If she says it often enough. I don't care about her telling tall tales. I care about the reward offers. There're people out there who'd sell their mothers. She puts a couple of no-goods on the street throwing money around and bragging about how they cashed in, somebody who really knows something might decide to bet the long odds."

"Then why don't we just go? There isn't that much more we can do here anyway, is there?"

"We can get Mogaba."

"Let the world think that. Start a rumor. Start a bunch of rumors about the Great General *and* about the Radisha. While we evacuate. When are you leaving to get the Key?"

"I'm not sure. Soon. I'm stalling for time. So a message can get through to Slink."

Sahra nodded. She smiled. "Good thinking. Singh will have something up his sleeve."

Willow Swan suddenly invited himself to join us. "The girl is having some kind of a problem."

I scowled at him. Sahra did the same but was polite enough to ask, "The Daughter of Night? What kind of problem?"

"I think she's having a fit. A seizure, like."

"Perfect timing," I grumbled. At the same time, Sahra yelled for Tobo to get Goblin. I growled, "What were you doing anywhere near her, Swan?"

He showed some color and said, "Uh . . ."

"Aw, you dumb mudsucker! Lady did you in. You panted after her for years. Then you put the screws to a dozen million people by letting Lady's baby sister threaten to blow in your ear. Now you're going to let Lady's brat put a ring in your nose and make an even bigger idiot out of you? You really are stupid and pathetic, Swan!"

"I was just—"

"Thinking with something that isn't your brain. As though you're some dopey fifteen-year-old. This woman isn't some cute little virgin, Swan! She's worse than your worst nightmare. Come here."

He came. I moved suddenly, violently, the way I had wanted to do so many times with my uncles. The tip of my dagger penetrated the skin underneath his chin. "You really want to die a really stupid, humiliating, pointless death? Let me know. I'll arrange it. Without the rest of us having to pay the price again."

One-Eye's cackle filled the air. "Ain't she a wonder, Swan? You ought to think about her instead of your usual black widows." He was in Do Trang's spare wheelchair again but getting around under his own power.

"I could arrange something pointless and humiliating for you, too, old man."

He just laughed at me. "You invited this soldier Aridatha down here to meet his long-lost daddy, Sleepy. You ought to be dealing with him instead of here flirting with Swan."

He could be maddening at times. And he loved it. If he could find any kind of lever at all. . . . I told Swan, "You explain to One-Eye what you mean about the girl. One-Eye, deal with it. Solve it. Short of killing her. Singh won't give me the Key if we kill the skinny little . . . witch."

44

Darn. Aridatha Singh was almost enough to make me change my mind about swearing off men. He was gorgeous. Tall, well-proportioned, a beautiful smile that showed magnificent teeth even when he was under stress. His manners were perfect. He was a gentleman in every sense but condition of birth.

I told him, "Your mother must have been a marvel."

"Excuse me?"

"Nothing. Nothing. Around here, I'm called Sleepy. You're Aridatha. That's enough of an introduction."

"Who are you people? Why am I here?" He did not bluster or threaten. Amazing. Few Taglians ever recognized that as a waste of time.

"It isn't necessary for you to know who we are. You're here to meet a man who is also our prisoner. Don't mention the fact that you'll be released after your interview. He won't be. Come with me."

Moments later Aridatha Singh remarked, "You're a woman, aren't you?"

"I was the last time I checked. We're here. This is Narayan. Narayan! Get up! You have a visitor. Narayan, this is Aridatha. As promised."

Aridatha looked at me, trying to understand. Narayan stared at the son he had never seen and saw something there that made him melt, just for an instant. And I knew that I could reach him if I could keep it from looking like I was asking him to betray Kina.

I stepped back and waited for something to happen. Nothing did. Aridatha kept glancing back at me. Narayan just stared. Out of patience at last, I asked Narayan, "Shall I send people to collect Khaditya and Sugriva as well? And their children, too?"

This threatened Narayan and told Aridatha that he had been abducted because he belonged to a particular family. I recognized the instant the truth occurred to him. There was an entirely different look in his eyes when he glanced back at me again.

I said, "Not much good can be said about this man, from my point of view, but you can't call him a bad father. Fate never gave him the chance to be good or bad." Except to the girl, for whom he had done everything possible, to her complete indifference. "He's very loyal."

Aridatha realized that this was not about him at all. That he was a lever meant to get some kind of movement out of Narayan Singh. *The* Narayan Singh, the infamous chief of the Strangler cult.

Aridatha won my heart all over again when he squared up his shoulders, stepped forward and offered his father a formal greeting. There was no warmth in it but it was absolutely proper.

I watched them try to find some common ground, some point at which to start. And they found it quickly enough. We had not found any evidence, ever, to disdain Narayan Singh's affections for his Lily. Aridatha thought quite highly of his mother.

"The man's a piece of work, isn't he?"

I was startled. I had not heard a sound. But Riverwalker was behind me. River did not have much talent for light-footing it. Which left me with the perfectly scary notion that Aridatha Singh really was having an effect on me. "Yes. He is. And I don't quite know why."

"Well, I'll tell you. He reminds me of Willow Swan. A bedrock-decent guy. Only smart. And still young enough to be unspoiled by life."

"River! You should hear yourself talk. You're halfway intelligent."

"Don't mention it front of the guys. One-Eye will figure out why he can't cheat me at tonk more'n half the time." He considered Aridatha again. "Pretty, too. Better keep him away from your librarian. They'll elope on you."

Another broken heart. "You think? What kind of clues . . ."

"I don't know. I could be wrong."

"When does he have to be back? Can we keep him all night?"

"You figuring on testing him out?"

River did not usually rag me much, so I knew I had to be asking for it somehow. "No. Not that way. The villain in me came up with an idea. We introduce him to the Radisha before we turn him loose."

"Now you're matchmaking?"

"No. Now I'm showing a four-square guy that his ruler isn't in the Palace. He can make the rumors credible. Because he can tell the truth."

"Couldn't hurt."

"You keep an eye on those two here. I'll go talk to the Woman."

Riverwalker raised an eyebrow. Nobody but Swan used that term to describe the Radisha anymore. "You're picking up bad habits."

"Probably."

45

I found the Radisha lost inside herself. Not asleep, not meditating, just wandering around inside, probably feeling immensely guilty about having been relieved by her recent lack of stress. I felt a moment of compassion. She and her brother might be our foes but they were sound people at heart. *Rajadharma* had been bred into them.

"Ma'am?" She was due respect but I could not use princely titles. "I need to speak to you."

She raised her eyes slowly. They seemed to be knowing, caring eyes even in despair. "Were all of my household staff my enemies?"

"We didn't choose to become your enemies. And even today we honor and respect the royal office."

"You would, of course. To remind me of my folly. Like the Bhodi and their self-immolations."

"Our quarrel with you won't ever be as great as our quarrel with the Protector. We could never find a path to peace with her. You'd never unleash the *skildirsha* on the city. She would. And the depth of her evil is such that she doesn't see the wickedness in what she's doing."

"You're right. Do you have a name? If she was safely a few hundred years in the past, we might consider her a goddess. A power capable of smashing kingdoms out of whimsy, the way a child might kick over an anthill just to see the bugs scramble."

"I'm called Sleepy. I'm the Annalist of the Black Company. I'm also the villain who plans most of your misfortunes. This situation wasn't an intentional part of the master plan but the opportunity presented itself. Now it looks like we might've outmaneuvered ourselves."

The Radisha had become focused. "Go on."

"The Protector has chosen to cover up your disappearance. Officially you're in your Anger Chamber purifying yourself and asking the gods and your ancestors to calm your heart and give you wisdom in the coming troubled times. You have taken breaks to issue some fairly bewildering rescripts, though. My brothers brought back these two. My brothers are illiterate, so they couldn't select for content. But these are probably representative. I'll have more brought in if you like."

The Radisha read the announcement of rewards first. It was straightforward and sensible. "This must make you uncomfortable."

"It does."

"She doesn't have the money. What is this? A ten-percent reduction in the rice allowance? We don't have a rice ration. We don't need to ration rice."

"No, you don't. Though everybody who wants rice can't afford it. And some of us who would be happy to see the last of the stuff don't get to eat anything else."

"You know what this is?" The Radisha pounded her right forefinger against the rescript like she was trying to peck a hole through. "I'll bet. All those strange personalities. They don't just come out as voices. Or she was in an especially strange humor when she dictated these. She has those spells. When the voices seem to take over completely. They never last long."

Ah, I said to myself. This is an interesting tidbit, worth pursuing later. "Would you care to counter with something more sound? I don't have the manpower to cover the entire city but I can see that new rescripts are posted in the more important places."

"How do you prove they're genuine? Anyone can take a piece of treated *naada* and write something on it."

"I'm working on that. We have a guest, a highly respected soldier from one of the City Battalions. We brought him in to visit another prisoner. I thought he might pass the word that you're our prisoner, too."

"Interesting. You know what she'll do, don't you? Call your bluff. Produce an imitation or illusory version of me and challenge you to produce your Radisha. Which you won't do because you're not really interested in getting killed. Correct?"

"We can deal with that. The Protector has a serious handicap. Nobody believes anything she says. They've started thinking that way about you, too, because you're beginning to come across as her stooge. Why did you always have such a hateful and treacherous attitude toward the Company?"

"I'm not her stooge. You have no idea how many of her mad schemes I've managed to stifle."

I did not tell her that we did. I had her angry enough to talk, but prodded just a little more. "Why did you hate my brothers before they ever came down the river?"

"I didn't *hate*—"

"Maybe I chose the wrong word. There was something. The Annalists before me all sensed it and knew you'd turn on the Company as soon as you felt safe from the Shadowmasters. You weren't as obsessed as Smoke was but you shared his disease."

"I don't know. I've wondered about that a lot the last decade. It went away after I gave the order to turn on you. But Smoke and I weren't the only ones. The whole principality felt the same. There was a memory of a time before, when the Company—"

"There was no such time. Not that anybody bothered to record in the histories and documents of those days. The little I've been able to decipher of our own Annals from back then is dully routine. The only terrible battle I found came when the Company was three generations old. It took place not far from here and the Company lost. It was almost wiped out. Its three volumes of Annals fell into enemy hands. They've been in Taglian libraries ever since. From the

moment the Company returned to Taglios, access to those has been
denied us. All kinds of crazy things were done to keep us from getting to those books. People died because of those books. And from
all I can see, the real secret that's hidden there, that had to be kept
at all cost, was that nothing extraordinary happened during those
early years. It was *not* an age of rapine and endless bloodshed."

"How could all the people of a dozen states remember something
that never happened and become terrified that it was going to happen again?"

I shrugged. "I don't know. We'll ask Kina how she did it. Right
before we kill her."

The Radisha's expression told me she was thinking she was not
alone in her ability to believe the impossible.

I said, "You want to shake loose from your lunatic friend? You
want to get off the hook with us? You want to get your brother back?"
Presumably the possibility that the Prahbrindrah Drah still lived had
grown significant in her recent thoughts.

The Radisha opened and closed her mouth several times. Never
an attractive woman, age and present circumstances conspired to
make her almost repulsive.

I should condemn? Time was doing no favors for me, either.

I said, "It can be managed. All of it."

"My brother is dead."

"No, he's not. No one outside the Company knows. Not even
Soulcatcher. But the people she trapped out there under the plain
are frozen in time. Sort of. I don't understand the mystic science involved. The point is, they're there, they're healthy, and they can be
brought back out. I've just made a deal that will give us the Key we
need to open the way."

"You can bring my brother back?"

"Cordy Mather, too."

The light was not good but I detected the rush of color to her
neck. "There are no secrets from you people, are there?"

"Not many."

"What do you want from me?"

I never expected to be at this point with the Woman. Despite her
down-to-earth, sensible, businesslike reputation. So I didn't have a
ready answer. But I did manage to come up with a wish list quickly.
"You could step out in public someplace where a whole lot of people

would see you and recognize you and repudiate the Protector. You could exculpate the Black Company. You could fire the Great General. You could announce that you've been under Soulcatcher's evil spell for fifteen years but now you've finally made your escape. You could make us the good guys again."

"I don't know if I can do that. I've been afraid of the Black Company for too long. I'm still afraid."

"Water sleeps," I said. "What's the Protector done for you?"

The Radisha had no answer for that.

"We can bring back your brother. Think of the pressure that would take off you. *Rajadharma.*"

In a tightly controlled voice, the Radisha snapped, "Don't say that! That tears my entrails out and strangles me with them."

Exactly what I had wished on her a time or two when I was in a less forgiving mood.

Aridatha Singh looked at me oddly. "He wasn't anything like I thought Narayan Singh would be." Seeing his sovereign had not impressed him nearly so much as seeing his father had.

"Not many people are once you get to know them. River, you want to take this man back where you found him?" It was night, yes, but we still had those two protective amulets left over from the Shadowmaster wars. They definitely looked like they were still good. I wished we had another hundred but Goblin and One-Eye could not make them anymore. I am not sure why. They shared no trade secrets with me. I suppose they were just too old.

I worry a lot when I consider a future without them in it. And a future without One-Eye cannot be far away.

O Lord of Hosts, preserve him until the Captured are delivered and all our quarrels are resolved.

46

Men were charging everywhere around the warehouse. Some were continuing frenetic preparations for the Company's evacuation. Some were getting ready to accompany Narayan and me to the Grove of Doom to collect the Nyueng Bao Key. The Nyueng

Bao, Do Trang's confederates and the handful still attached to the Company somehow, seemed to be doing a lot of nervous moving around just to be moving. They were scared and worried.

Banh Do Trang had suffered a stroke during the night. One-Eye's prognosis was not encouraging.

I told Goblin, "I'm not saying she had anything to do with it but Do Trang was the first one to realize that the girl was roaming around outside her flesh."

"He's just old, Sleepy. Nobody did it to him. You ask me, he's really way overdue. He hung on here because he cares about Sahra. She's all right now. It looks like her husband might actually be freed. And he's too old to run away. Soulcatcher is going to find this place eventually, once Mogaba arrives and starts searching. I wouldn't be surprised if Do Trang just decided that dying was the best thing he could do for everyone right now."

I did not want Do Trang to go, for all the reasons none of us like to see those close to us die, but also because he was, in his quiet way, the best friend the Company had had in generations.

Like everyone else, I tried to lose myself in work. I told Goblin, "Even if she's totally innocent, I want the girl fixed so she can't wander. Whatever you have to do short of permanently crippling or killing her."

Goblin sighed. Lately that was all he did when someone gave him more work. I guess he was too tired to squawk anymore.

"Where is One-Eye?"

"Uh—" Furtive look around. A whisper. "Don't say I said anything. I think he's trying to figure out how to take his equipment with us."

I shook my head and walked away.

Santaraksita and Baladitya called out to me. They had accepted their situation and were applying themselves with a will. The Master Librarian seemed particularly excited about facing a real academic challenge for the first time in years. He said, "Dorabee, in all the excitement I forgot to mention that I did get an answer to your question about a written Nyueng Bao language. There was one. And not only was there one, this oldest book is written in an antique dialect of that language. The others were recorded in an early Taglian dialect, although the original of the third volume does so employing the foreign alphabet instead of native characters."

"Which argues that the invader alphabet had well-defined pho-
netic values that at the time must have been more precise than those
of the native script. Right?"

Santaraksita gawked. After a moment he said, "Dorabee, you
never cease to amaze me. Absolutely correct."

"So have you discovered anything interesting?"

"The Black Company came off the plain, which was called Glittering Stone even then, and mostly minced around from one small
principality to the next, squabbling internally over whether or not
they were going to sacrifice themselves to bring on the Year of the
Skulls. There was plenty of enthusiasm among the priests attached
to the Company but not much among the soldiers. Many of those apparently volunteered as a way to escape something called The Land
of Unknown Shadows, not because they wanted to bring on the end
of the world."

"The Land of Unknown Shadows, eh? Anything else?"

"I've developed some very good information on the price of
horseshoe nails four centuries ago and on the scarcity of several medicinal plants that are now found in every herb garden."

"Earthshaking stuff. Stay with it, Sri."

I meant to tell him he had to evacuate with the rest of us but decided not to upset him right away. He was having a good time. No
point making him face a choice between abduction and being put to
death just yet.

Uncle Doj materialized. "Do Trang wants to see you."

I followed him to the tiny room the old man had built for himself in a remote corner of the warehouse. On the way, Doj warned me
that Do Trang was unable to speak. "He's already seen Sahra and
Tobo. I think he was fond of you, too."

"We're going to get married in the next life. If the Gunni are
right."

"I am ready to travel."

I stopped. "What?"

"I'm going with you to the Grove of Doom."

"You'd better not have some crazy idea about snatching the Key."

"I agreed to help. I'll help. I want to be there to make sure the
Deceiver keeps his word. The Deceiver, Miss Sleepy. Deceiver. Also,
I agreed to turn over that volume of the Books of the Dead. Its hid-
ing place is on the way."

"Very well. The presence of Ash Wand will be a comfort to me and a vexation to my enemies."

Doj chuckled. "It will indeed."

"We won't be coming back here."

"I know. When we leave, I'll be carrying everything I wish to retain. You won't need to pretend with Do Trang. He knows his path. Do him the honor of an honest farewell."

I did more. I became all teary for the first time in my adult life. I rested my head on the old man's chest for a minute and whispered my thanks for his friendship and renewed my promise to see him in the next life. A small heresy but I do not think God has been monitoring me too closely.

Banh lifted a hand weakly and stroked my hair. And after that I got up and went away somewhere to be alone with my grief for a man who, it seemed, had never been that close, yet who was going to have a major impact on the rest of my life. I understood that after the tears stopped, I would never be quite the same Sleepy again. And that that was one legacy Do Trang wanted to leave behind.

47

The biggest problem I expected with the evacuation was one that came up every time the Company picked up and moved out after having been settled in one place for a long time. Roots had to be torn up. Ties had to be severed. Men had to abandon the lives they had created for themselves.

Some just would not go.

Some who did go would tell someone where they were headed.

The nominal strength of the Company was somewhat over two hundred people, a third of whom did not live in Taglios at all but maintained identities at scattered locations where they could aid brothers who were traveling. Overall, it was very much like what the Deceivers used to do. Partly that was intentional, because those people had spent centuries finding the safest ways.

Early on, couriers went out carrying code words to all our distant brothers to warn them that a time of trouble was coming. Nobody would be told what was happening, only warned that something was and that it was going to be big. Once that code word arrived, it would already be too late to drop out of anything.

Behind the couriers, eventually, would come the majority of the men, in driblets small enough not to attract attention, disguised a dozen ways, departing Taglios in what I considered their order of plausible risk. The last to leave town would be those with the heaviest entanglements. All the men would pass through a series of checkpoints and assembly points, each time being informed only of an immediate destination. The key hope, though, was that Soulcatcher would not begin to catch on until those who were going to go were well away.

Those who refused to go would be excused—if they remained loyal to the Company interests in the city. It would be useful to have a few agents on hand after the Company appeared to have gone.

That, too, was something the Deceivers had done for generations.

There would be flashy smoke shows. The demon Niassi would be much more prevalent, putting a damper on Grey efficiency. The men who stayed—I would not know who they were because I would be among the first to leave—would be expected to undertake what was supposed to look like a series of random assaults, break-ins and acts of vandalism that later would begin to appear to be part of a terror campaign meant to peak during the Druga Pavi. If Soulcatcher took the bait, she would spend her time preparing to ambush us there.

If not, every hour bought was an hour farther down the road my brothers would be before the Protector realized that we had done the unexpected again. And even then, I expected her to look in the wrong places for a long time.

48

My party was the first to leave Taglios. We went the morning Banh Do Trang died. With me went Narayan Singh, Willow Swan, the Radisha Drah, Mother Gota and Uncle Doj, Riverwalker, Iqbal Singh with his wife Suruvhija and two children and baby, and his brother Runmust. In addition, we had several goats with small packs and chickens tied to their backs, two donkeys, one or the other of which Gota rode much of the time, and an ox cart drawn by a beast we strove hard to keep looking sadder and scruffier than it really was. Most everyone adopted some form of disguise. The Shadar trimmed their hair and beards and the whole family adopted Vehdna dress. I stayed Vehdna but became a woman. The Radisha became a man. Uncle Doj and Willow Swan shaved their heads and became Bhodi disciples. Swan darkened himself with stain but there was no way to change his blue eyes. Gota had to do without Nyueng Bao fashions.

Narayan Singh remained exactly the same, virtually indistinguishable from thousands of others just like him.

We looked bizarre, but even stranger bands collected to share the rigors of the road. And we would collect together only when we camped. On the road we stretched out over half a mile, one Singh brother out front, the other in back, while River stayed fairly close to me. The brothers carried a pair of devices given them by Goblin and One-Eye. If Narayan, the Radisha or Swan strayed far from a line running between them, choke spells would begin constricting around their throats.

None of the three had been informed of that. We were all supposed to be friends and allies now. But I believe in trusting some of my friends more than others.

On the Rock Road that the Captain had had built between Taglios and Jaicur, we did not catch the eye at all. But a crowd like that, with a baby and an ox cart and regular Vehdna prayers and whatnot, is not swift. Nor did the season help. I became thoroughly sick of the rain.

The last time I traveled down the Rock Road I rode a giant black stallion that covered the distance between Taglios and Ghoja on the River Main in a day and a night without hurrying.

Four days after leaving the city we were still at least that long from the bridge at Ghoja, which would be our first dangerous bottleneck. In the afternoon Uncle Doj chose to announce that we had come as close as the road would carry us to the place where he had hidden the copy of the Book of the Dead.

"Aw, darn," I said. "I was hoping it would be way farther down the road. How are we going to explain having a book if we get stopped?"

Doj showed me his palms and a big smile. "I'm a priest. A missionary. Blame it on me." Despite the hardships, he was happy. "Come help me dig it up."

"What is this place?" I asked two hours later. We had come into something that might have come from one of Murgen's old nightmares about Kina. Twenty yards of woods formed a palisade all around it.

"It's a graveyard. During the chaos of the first Shadowlander invasion, before the Black Company came, possibly even before you were born, one of the Shadowlander armies used this as a camp, then as a burial ground. They planted the trees to conceal the tombs and monuments from enemy eyes." Noting my appalled expression, he added, "Down there they have different customs for dealing with the dead."

I knew that. I had been there. I had seen it. But never had I seen it so concentrated, nor exuding such an air of depression. "This is grim."

"A spell makes it seem that way. They thought they would come back and turn the place into a memorial after they won the war. They wanted to keep people away."

"I'm willing to go along with their wishes. This is too creepy for me."

"It's not that bad. Come on. This shouldn't take more than a few minutes."

It did, but not a lot longer. It was a matter of pulling the door away from one of the fancier tombs and digging out a bundle wrapped in several layers of oilskins.

"This is a place worth remembering," Doj said as we went away. "People around here won't come near it. People from farther away don't know about it. It's a good hideout."

"I can't wait."

"You'll love the Grove of Doom, too."

"I've been there. I didn't like it, either, but at the time I was too worried about Stranglers to be scared of ghosts or ancient goddesses."

"It's another good place to hide."

I am not suspicious by nature the way Soulcatcher is but I am suspicious occasionally. I am particularly suspicious of reticent old Nyueng Bao who suddenly turn chatty and helpful. "The Captain hid out there once," I said. "He didn't find the place congenial, either. What're you up to?"

"Up to? I don't understand."

"You understand perfectly, old man. Yesterday I was just another *jengali*, albeit one you had to tolerate. Today, suddenly, I'm getting unsolicited advice. I'm being offered the benefit of your accumulated wisdom, like I'm some kind of apprentice. You want me to take a turn carrying that?" He was, after all, an old man.

"As the pace and pressures have increased and events have taken unexpected—but usually favorable—twists, I've begun reflecting more intently on the wisdom of Hong Tray, on the foresight she showed, even upon her devilish sense of humor, and I believe I'm finally beginning to grasp the full significance of her prophecies."

"Or of mass quantities of bullfeathers. Tell it to Sahra and Murgen next time you see them. And put a little honest sentiment into your apologies."

My attempt to be unpleasant did not subdue him. That took the arrival of the afternoon rains, a little early, a lot heavy, supported by a truly ferocious fall of hail. Along the road, dashing out from under the trees where we had left our own party, a score of travelers tried to collect the ice before it melted. Taglians never see snow, and rainy-season storms provide the only time they ever see ice—unless they travel far down into what used to be the Shadowlands, to the higher elevations of the Dandha Presh.

Scavenging hailstones was a young people's game. The old folks pushed under the trees as far as they could get, wearing their rain gear. The baby would not stop crying. She did not like the thunder. Runmust and Iqbal tried to keep an eye on the children as well as to watch unknown travelers closely. They were convinced that anyone met on the road might be an enemy spy. Which seemed a perfectly sensible attitude to me.

Riverwalker prowled, cursing the rain. That also seemed a perfectly sensible attitude.

Uncle Doj did a fine job of not drawing attention to his burden. He settled beside Gota. She began to gripe but without her usual enthusiasm.

I sat down near the Radisha. We were calling her Tadjik these days. I said, "Have you begun to understand why your brother found life on the road so appealing?"

"I trust you're being sarcastic?"

"Not entirely. What was the worst crisis you faced today? Your feet get wet?"

She grunted. She got the point.

"I believe it was the politics he resented. The fact that no matter what he considered doing, there were always a hundred selfish men who wanted to subvert his vision for their own profit."

"You knew him?" the Radisha asked.

"Not well. Not to philosophize with. But he wasn't a man who kept his views secret."

"My brother? Being away must've changed him a lot more than I thought it could, then. He never revealed his inner self while he lived in the Palace. That would have been too risky."

"His power was more secure out there. He didn't have to please anyone but the Liberator. His men came to love him. They would've followed him anywhere. Which got most of them killed when you turned on the Company."

"He's *really* alive? You aren't just manipulating me for your own ends?"

"Of course I am. Manipulating you, that is. But it *is* true that he's alive. All the Captured are. That's why we left Taglios even though we had your side on the run. We want our brothers out before we do anything more."

I heard a whisper. "Sister. Sister."

"What?"

The Radisha had not spoken. She eyed me inquisitively. "I didn't say it."

I glanced around apprehensively, saw nothing. "Must just be the rain in the leaves."

"Uhm." The Radisha was not convinced, either.

Hard to believe. I really missed Goblin and One-Eye.

I found Uncle Doj again. "Lady insisted that you're a minor wizard. If you have any talent at all, please use it to see if we're being watched or followed." Once Soulcatcher started looking for us outside Taglios, it should not take long for her crows and shadows to find us.

Uncle Doj grunted noncommittally.

49

Real fear found us the morning after next, just when it seemed we had every reason to be positive. We had made good time the day before, there were no crows around yet, and it looked like we would reach the Grove of Doom before the afternoon rains, which meant we could complete our business there and get clear before night fell. I was happy.

A band of horsemen appeared on the road south of us, headed our way. As they drew nearer, it became evident that they were uniformly clad. "What should we do?" River asked.

"Just hope they aren't looking for us. Keep moving." They showed no interest in travelers ahead of us, though they forced everyone off the road. They were not galloping but were not dawdling, either.

Uncle Doj drifted nearer the donkey not carrying Gota. Ash Wand lay hidden amidst the clutter of tent and tent poles that formed that animal's burden. Several precious fireball projectors were among the bamboo tent poles, too.

We had very few of those left now. We would have no more until we fetched Lady out of the ground. Goblin and One-Eye could not create them themselves—though Goblin admitted privately that the opposite would have been the case even just ten years ago.

They were too old for almost anything that required flexible thought and, especially, physical dexterity. The mist projector was, in all probability, the last great contribution they would make. And most of the nonmagical construction on that had been accomplished using Tobo's young hands.

I caught a glint of polished steel from the horsemen. "Left side of the road," I told River. "I want everybody over there when we have to get out of their way."

But I spoke too late. Point-man Iqbal had already jumped off to the right. "I hope he has sense enough to get back across after they pass by."

"He isn't stupid, Sleepy."

"He's out here with us, isn't he"

"That's a fact."

The band of horsemen turned out to be what I expected: the forerunners of a much larger troop which, in turn, proved to be the vanguard of the Third Territorial Division of the Taglian Army.

The Third Territorial Division was the Great General's personal formation. Which meant that God had chosen to bring us face-to-face with Mogaba.

I tried not to worry about what sort of practical joke God was contemplating. Only He knows His own heart. I just made sure my whole crowd was on the left side of the road. I got us loosened up even more. Then I worried about which of us might be recognizable by Mogaba or any veterans who had been around long enough to recall the Kiaulune and Shadowmaster wars.

None of us were memorable. Few of us went back far enough to have crossed paths with the Great General. That is, except Uncle Doj, Mother Gota, Willow Swan . . . right! And Narayan Singh! Narayan had been a close ally of the Great General in the days before the last Shadowmaster war. Those two had had their wicked heads together innumerable times.

"I will need to alter my appearance."

"What?" The skinny little Deceiver had materialized beside me, startling me. If he could sneak up like that . . .

"This will be the Great General, Mogaba. Not so? And he might recognize me even though it has been years since last we stood face-to-face."

"You astonish me," I admitted.

"I do what the goddess desires."

"Of course." There is no God but God. Yet every day I had to deal with a goddess whose impact on my life was more tangible. There were times when I had to struggle hard not to think. In Forgiveness He is Like the Earth. "Suppose you just borrow some clothing and get rid of your turban?" Though doing nothing struck me as the perfect solution with him. As noted before, Narayan Singh resembled the majority of the poor male Gunni population. I thought Mogaba would have trouble recognizing him even if they had been lovers. Unless Narayan gave himself away. And how could he do that? He was the Master Deceiver, the living saint of the cult.

"That might work."

Singh drifted away. I watched him, suddenly suspicious. He could not be unaware of his own natural anonymity. Therefore he must be trying to create a predisposed pattern of thought inside my mind.

I wished I could just cut his throat. I did not like what he did to my thinking. I could easily become obsessed with concerns about what he was really doing. But we needed him. We could not collect the Key without him. Even Uncle Doj did not know exactly what we were seeking. He had never actually seen, or even known about, the Key before it was stolen. I hoped he would recognize it if he saw it.

I might spend a little time thinking how we could get around my having given him such solid guarantees that he was willing to travel with us and trust us not to murder the Daughter of Night while they were separated.

The cavalry finished clattering past. They had paid us no heed, since we had not insisted on getting in their way. Behind them a few hundred yards came the first battalion of infantry, as neat, clean and impressive as Mogaba could keep them while on the march. I received several offers of temporary marriage but otherwise the soldiers were indifferent to our presence. The Third Territorial was a well-disciplined, professional division, an extension of Mogaba's will and character, nothing like the gangs of ragged outcasts that constituted the Company.

We were a military nil anyway. We could not get together and fight our weight in lepers today, let alone deal with formations like the Third Territorial. Croaker's heart would be broken when we dragged him out of the ground.

My optimism began to fade. With the soldiers hogging the road, we traveled much slower. The landmarks showing the way to the Grove of Doom were in sight but still hours away. The cart and the animals could not be pushed on muddy ground.

I began to watch for a place to sit out the rain, though I did not recall any good site from previous visits to the area. Uncle Doj was no help when I asked. He told me, "There is no significant cover closer than the grove."

"Someone should go scout that."

"You have reason for concern?"

"We're dealing with Deceivers." I did not mention that Slink and the band from Semchi were supposed to meet us there. Doj did not need to know. And Slink might have gotten slowed down if he had to duck around Mogaba's army and patrols.

"I'll go. When I can leave without arousing curiosity."

"Take Swan. He's the most likely to give us away." The Radisha was a risk, too, though thus far she had shown no inclination to yell for help. But Riverwalker was close enough to grab her by the throat if she even took a deep breath.

She was not stupid. If she intended to betray us, she meant to wait till she could manage it with some chance of surviving the attempt.

Uncle Doj and Willow Swan managed to drift away without attracting attention, though Uncle had to go without Ash Wand. I joined River and the Radisha. I noted, "This country is a lot more developed than it used to be." When I was young, most of the land between Taglios and Ghoja was deserted. Villages were small and poor and supported themselves on minimal tracts of land. There were no independent farms in those days. Now the latter seemed to be everywhere, founded by confident and independence-minded veterans or by refugees from the tortured lands that once lay prostrate under the heels of the Shadowmasters. Many of the new farms crowded right up to the road right-of-way. They made getting off the road difficult at times.

The force moving north numbered about ten thousand, men enough to occupy miles and miles of roadway even without the train and camp followers coming on behind. Soon it was obvious we would not reach the Grove of Doom before the rains came and might not get there before nightfall.

Given any choice at all, I did not want to be anywhere near the place after dark. I had gone in there by night once before, ages ago, as part of a Company raid meant to capture Narayan and the Daughter of Night. We murdered a lot of their friends but those two had gotten away. I remembered only the fear and the cold and the way the grove seemed to have a soul of its own that was more alien than the soul of a spider. Murgen once said that being in that place at night was as bad was walking through one of Kina's dreams. Though of this world, it had a powerful otherworldly taint.

I tried to ask Narayan about it. Why had his predecessors chosen that particular grove as their most holy place? How had it been different from other groves of those times, when humanity's impact on the face of the earth had been so much less?

"Why do you wish to know, Annalist?" Singh was suspicious of my interest.

"Because I'm naturally curious. Aren't you ever curious about how things came to be and why people do the things they do?"

"I serve the goddess."

I waited. Evidently he deemed that an adequate explanation. Being somewhat religious myself, I could encompass it even though I did not find it satisfying.

I offered a snort of disgust. Narayan responded with a smirk. "*She* is real," he said.

"She is the darkness."

"You see her handiwork around you every day."

Not true. "Untrue, little man. But if she ever gets loose, I think we will." This discussion had become terribly uncomfortable suddenly. It put me in the position of admitting the existence of a god other than my god, which my religion insisted was impossible. "There is no God but God."

Narayan smirked.

Mogaba did the one good thing he had ever done for me. By turning up in person he saved me the rigorous and embarrassing mental gymnastics necessary to reconfigure Kina as a fallen angel thrown down into the pit. I knew it could be done. Elements of Kina myth could be hammered into conformity with the tenets of the only true religion, given a quick coat of blackwash, and I would have completed a course of religious acrobatics elegant enough to spark the pride of my childhood teachers.

Mogaba and his staff traveled three quarters of the way toward the rear of the column. The Great General was mounted, which was a surprise. He was never a rider before. The greater surprise, though, was the nature of his steed.

It was one of the sorcerously bred black stallions the Company had brought down from the north. I had thought they were all dead. I had not seen one since the Kiaulune wars. This one not only was not dead, it was in outstanding health. Despite its age. It also appeared bored by the business of travel.

"Don't gape," Riverwalker told me. "People get curious about why other people are curious."

"I think we can afford to stare some. Mogaba will feel like he deserves it." Mogaba looked every bit the Great General and mighty warrior. He was tall and perfectly proportioned, well-muscled, well-clad, well-groomed. But for the dust of silver in his hair, he looked little older than he had been when first I saw him, right after the Company captured Jaicur from Stormshadow. He had had no hair then, having preferred to shave his head. He seemed in a good humor, not a condition I had associated with him in the past, when all his schemes had come to frustration as the Captain just seemed to bumble around and do the one thing that would undo all his efforts.

As the Great General came abreast, his mount suddenly snorted and tossed its head, then shied slightly, as though it had stirred up a snake. Mogaba cursed, although he was never in any danger of losing his seat.

Laughter dropped out of the sky. And a white crow fell right behind it, alighting precariously atop the pole carried by the Great General's personal standardbearer.

Cursing still, Mogaba failed to note that his steed turned its head to watch me as I passed.

The darned thing winked.

I had been recognized. The beast must be the very one I had ridden so long ago, for so many hundreds of miles.

I began to get nervous.

Someone amongst Mogaba's personal guard launched an arrow at the crow. It missed. It fell not far from Runmust, who shouted angrily before he thought. Now the Great General vented his spleen upon the archer.

The horse continued to watch me. I fought an urge to run. Maybe I could get through this yet. . . .

The white crow squawked something that might have been words but were just racket to me. Mogaba's mount jumped enough to freshen the well of vituperation. It faced forward and began to trot. The ultimate effect was to divert attention from us southbound scrubs.

Everybody but Iqbal's Suruvhija stared at the ground and walked a little faster. Soon we were past the worst danger. I drifted over beside Swan, who was still so nervous he stuttered when he tried to crack a joke about pigeons coming to roost on the Great General while he was still alive.

Laughter passed overhead. The crow, up high, was almost indistinguishable against the gathering clouds. I wished I had someone along who could advise me about that thing.

For a generation, crows have not been good omens for the Company. But this one seemed to have done us a favor.

Could it be Murgen from another time?

Murgen would be watching, I was sure, but that crow had no way to communicate. So maybe so. . . .

If so, this encounter would have been an adventure for him, too, what with him knowing that if we got caught, his chances for resurrection plummeted to zero.

50

The passages of the Great General held us up long enough that we could not leave the road unremarked until after the rains began falling hard enough to conceal our movements from everyone except someone extremely close by. We left the road unnoticed then. Our travel formation collapsed into a miserable pack. Only Narayan Singh showed real eagerness to get to the grove. And he did not hurry. Not often long on empathy, I found myself pitying Iqbal's children.

Swan pointed out, "It'd be to Singh's advantage to get us there just after night falls."

"Darkness always comes."

"Uhn?"

"A Deceiver aphorism. Darkness is their time. And darkness always comes."

"You don't seem particularly bothered." He was hard to hear. The rainfall was that heavy.

"I'm bothered, buddy. I've been here before. It isn't what you'd call a good place." I could not state that fact with sufficient emphasis. The Grove of Doom was the heart of darkness, a spawning ground for all hopelessness and despair. It gnawed at your soul. Unless you were a believer, apparently. It never seemed to trouble those for whom it was a holy place.

"Places are natural, Sleepy. People are good and evil."

"You'll change your mind after you get there."

"I got a sneaking suspicion I'm gonna drown first. Do we got to be out in this?"

"You find a roof, I'll be glad to get under it." Big thunder had begun fencing with swords of lightning. There would be hail before long. I wished I had a better hat. Maybe one of those huge woven-bamboo things Nyueng Bao farmers wear in the rice paddies.

I could just make out Riverwalker and the Radisha. I followed them hoping they were following someone they could see. I hoped we did not have anyone get disoriented and lost. Not tonight. I hoped the guys from Semchi were where they were supposed to be.

Iqbal appeared in the gloom as the hail began to fall. He bent over to try to ease the sting of the missiles. I did the same. It did not help much.

Iqbal shouted, "Left, down the hill. There's a stand of little evergreens. Better than nothing at all."

Swan and I dashed that way. The hailstones kept getting bigger and more numerous as the thunder got louder and the lightning closer. But the air was cooling down.

There is a bright side to everything.

I slipped, fell, rolled, found the trees the hard way, by sliding in amongst them. Uncle Doj and Gota, River and the Radisha were in there already. Iqbal was an optimist. I would not have called those darned things trees. They were bushes suffering from overweening ambition. Not a one was ten feet tall and you had to get down on your belly in the damp and needles to enjoy their shelter. But their branches did break the fall of the hailstones, which rattled and roared through the foliage. I started to ask about the animals but then heard the goats bleating.

I felt a little guilty. I do not like animals much. I had been shirking my share of their caretaking.

Hailstones dribbled down through the branches and rolled in from outside. Swan picked up a huge example, brushed it off, showed it to me, grinned and popped it into his mouth.

"This is the life," I said. "When you're with the Black Company, every day is a paradise on earth."

Swan said, "This would be a superb recruiting tool."

As those things always do, the storm went away. We crawled out and counted heads and discovered that not even Narayan Singh had gone missing. The living saint of the Stranglers did *not* want to leave us behind. That book really was important to him.

The rain dwindled to a drizzle. We clambered out of the muck, many communing bluntly with their preferred gods while we formed up. We did not spread out much now, except for Uncle Doj, who managed to disappear into a landscape with almost no cover.

Over the next hour we ran into several landmarks I recognized from Croaker's and Murgen's Annals. I kept an eye out for Slink and his companions. I did not see them. I hoped that was a good omen rather than a bad.

The later it got, the more peachy it seemed to Narayan Singh. I was afraid he would curse us all by betraying a genuine smile. I considered mentioning his children's names just to let him know he was weighing on my mind.

My divination skills were flawless. It was dusk when we reached the grove. We were all miserable. The baby would not stop crying. I was developing a blister from walking in wet boots. With the possible exception of Narayan, not a soul amongst us remained mission-oriented. Everybody just wanted to drop somewhere while somebody else got a fire going so we could dry out and get something to eat.

Narayan insisted that we press on to the Deceiver temple in the heart of the grove. "It'll be dry there," he promised.

His proposal aroused no enthusiasm. Though we were barely inside its boundary, the smell of the Grove surrounded us. It was not a pleasant odor. I wondered how much worse it was back in the heyday of the Deceivers, when they murdered people there often and in some numbers.

The place possessed strong physic character, an eerieness, a creepiness. Gunni would blame that on Kina because this was one of the places where a fragment of her dismembered body had fallen, or something such. Despite the fact that Kina was also supposed to be bound in enchanted sleep somewhere on or under or beyond the plain of glittering stone. Gunni do not have ghosts. We Vehdna do. Nyueng Bao do. For me, the grove was haunted by the souls of all the victims who died there for Kina's pleasure or glory or whatever reason Stranglers kill.

Had I mentioned it, Narayan or one of the more devout Gunni would have brought up the matter of rakshasas, those malignant demons, those evil night-rangers jealous of men and gods alike. Rakshasas might pretend to be the spirit of someone who had passed on, merely as a tool for tormenting the living.

Uncle Doj said, "Like it or not, Narayan is right. We should move into the best shelter available. We would be no less safe there than here. And we would be free of this pestilential drizzle." The rain just would not go away.

I considered him. He was old and worn out and had less reason to want to move on than any of us younger folks. He must have a reason to want to go on. He must know something.

Doj always did. Getting him to share it was the big trick.

I was in charge. Time for an unpopular decision. "We'll go ahead."

Grumble grumble grumble.

The temple projected a presence more powerful than that of the Grove. I had no trouble locating it without being able to see it. Walking close behind, Swan asked me, "How come you never tore this place down when you were on top?"

I did not understand his question. Narayan, just ahead of me, overheard it and did understand. "They tried. More than once. We rebuilt it when no one was watching." He launched a rambling rant about how his goddess had watched over the builders. It sounded like a recruiting speech. He kept it up until Runmust swatted him with a bamboo pole.

It was one of *those* poles, too, though Narayan did not know. The grove was a very dark place, perfect for an ambush by shadows. Runmust was not going to go quietly.

I could not help wondering what evils Soulcatcher was up to now that she had complete freedom to work her will upon Taglios.

I hoped the people who stayed behind completed their missions, particularly those tasked to penetrate the Palace again. Jaul Barundandi had to be recruited and brought in too deep to run before his rage subsided sufficiently for reason to reassert itself.

51

The baby continued to cry, burrowing into her mother's breast without looking for nourishment. The noise worried everyone. Anyone who wished to visit misfortune upon us would have no trouble tracking us. We would be unlikely to hear them sneaking up, because of the crying and the sound of drizzle falling from branch to branch in the waterlogged trees. River and the Company Singhs kept their hands on their weapons. Uncle Doj had recovered Ash Wand and was keeping it handy despite the risk of rust.

The animals were as thrilled as the infant was. The goats bleated and dragged their feet. The donkeys kept getting stubborn, but

Mother Gota knew a trick or three for getting balky beasts of burden moving. A considerable ration of pain was involved.

The rain never ended.

Narayan Singh took the lead. He knew the way. He was home.

I felt the dread temple loom before us although I could not see it. Narayan's sandals whispered as they scattered soggy leaves. I listened intently but heard nothing new until Willow Swan started muttering, nagging himself for having followed up on the one original idea he had ever had. If he had ignored it, he could be rocking beside a fireplace in his own home, listening to his own grandkids cry, instead of tramping through the blue miseries on yet one more mystery quest where the best he could look forward to was to stay alive longer than the people dragging him around. Then he asked me, "Sleepy, you ever consider throwing in with that little turd?"

Somewhere, an owl screamed.

"Which one? And why?"

"Narayan. Bring on the Year of the Skulls. Then we could all finally sit back and relax and not have to slog around in the rain and shit anymore."

"No. I haven't."

The owl screamed again. It sounded frustrated.

What sounded like crow laughter answered it, taunting.

"But that's what the Company set out to do in the first place, isn't it? To bring on the end of the world?"

"A handful of the senior people did, apparently. But not the guys who actually had to do the work. There's a chance they didn't have any idea what it was all about. That they marched because staying home might be a less pleasant option."

"Some things never change. I know that story by heart. Careful. These steps are slicker than greased owl shit."

He had heard the birds conversing, too. That was a northern saying that lost something in translation.

Rain or no, the goats and donkeys flat refused to move any nearer the Deceiver shrine, at least until a light took life inside the temple doorway. That came from a single feeble oil lamp, but in the darkness it seemed almost bright.

Swan observed, "Narayan knows right where to look, don't he?"

"I'm watching him. Every minute." For what good keeping a close eye on a Deceiver would do.

To tell the truth, I was counting on Uncle Doj. Doj would be much harder to trick. He was an old trickster himself. As a trickmaster, I needed to stick to what I knew, which was designing wicked plots and writing about them after they ran their course.

Something flapped overhead as I entered the temple. Owl or crow, I did not turn quickly enough to discover the truth. I did tell Runmust and Iqbal, "Keep a close watch while I check this out. Doj. Swan. Come with me. You know more about this place than anyone else."

Below, River and Gota swore vilely as they strove to keep the goats under control. Iqbal's sons had fallen asleep where they stood, indifferent to the ongoing rain.

Narayan blocked my advance just steps inside the temple. "Not until I complete the rituals of sanctification. Otherwise you'll defile the holy place."

It was not my holy place. I did not care if I defiled it. In fact, that sounded like an amusement to be indulged—just before I had the place torn down yet again and this time plowed under. But I did have to get along. For the moment. "Doj. Keep an eye on him. Runmust. You, too." He could pick the living saint off with his bamboo if the Deceiver tried to be clever.

"We have an understanding," Narayan reminded me. He seemed troubled. And not by me. He kept poking around like he was looking for something that was supposed to be there but just was not.

"You make sure you hold up your end, little man." I stepped back outside, into a drizzle that had become more of a heavy, falling mist.

"Sleepy," Iqbal whispered from the base of the steps. "Check what I found."

I barely heard him. The baby continued to crank. Long-suffering Suruvhija rocked her and hummed a lullaby. She was not much more than a girl herself and, I suspected, not very bright. I could not imagine any woman being happy with her life, but Suruvhija seemed content to go where Iqbal led. A breeze stirred the branches of the grove. "What?" Of course I could not see. I descended the temple steps into the damp, chilly darkness.

"Here." He shoved something into my hands.

Pieces of cloth. Fine cloth, like silk, six or seven pieces, each with a weight in one corner.

I smiled into the face of the night. I snickered. My faith in God was restored. The demon had betrayed her children again. Slink had gotten to the grove in time. Slink had been sneakier than any Deceiver. Slink had done his job. He was out there somewhere right now, covering us, ready to offer Narayan another horrible surprise. I felt much more confident when I went back inside and yelled at Narayan, "Get your skinny ass moving, Singh. We've got women and children freezing out here."

Narayan was not a happy living saint. Whatever he was looking for, under cover of fortifying the temple against the defiling presence of unbelievers, just was not there to be found.

I was tempted to toss him the captured rumels. I forbore. That would only make him angry and tempt him to go back on his agreement. I did tell him, "You've had time enough to sanctify the whole darned woods against the presence of nonbelievers, don't you think? You forget how miserable it is out here?"

"You should cultivate patience, Annalist. It's an extremely useful trait in both our chosen careers." I forbore mentioning that we had been patient enough to get him tucked into our trick bag. Then his exasperation surfaced for a moment. He hurled something to the floor. He was not out of control by much but it was the first time I ever saw him less than perfectly composed when he was supposed to be the master of the situation. He whispered something as he beckoned me. I do believe he took his goddess's name in vain.

This new version of the temple was scarcely a shadow of what Croaker and Lady had survived. The present idol was wooden, not more than five feet tall and unfinished. The offerings before it were all old and feeble. The temple as a whole did not possess the sinister, grim air of a place where many lives had been sacrificed. These were lean times for Deceivers.

Narayan persisted in his search. I could not bring myself to break his heart by telling him the friends he expected to meet must have fallen foul of the friends I'd hoped to meet. You need to keep a certain amount of mystery in any relationship.

I said, "Tell me where it's all right to spread out and where you'd rather we didn't and I'll see that we do our best to honor your wishes."

Narayan looked at me like I'd just sprouted an extra head. I told him, "I've been thinking a lot lately. We're probably going to be working together for a while. It'd make things easier for everybody if we all made the effort to respect one another's customs and philosophies."

Narayan scooted off. He began the process of laying a fire and of telling people where they could homestead. The temple was not that big inside. There would not be much room to spread out there.

Singh would not turn his back on me.

"You spooked him good," Riverwalker told me. "He'll spend the whole night with his back to the wall, trying to stay awake."

"I hope my snoring helps. Iqbal, don't do that." The fool had actually started helping Mother Gota set up to do some cooking. That old woman was a menace around a cook fire. She was already under a ban throughout the Company. She could boil water and give it a taste to gag you.

Iqbal grinned a grin that told the world he needed to consult One-Eye about his teeth. "We're setting this up for me."

"All right." Much better. Much much better.

After she finished helping Iqbal, the old woman helped milk the goats. Now I understood how Narayan felt. Maybe I should keep my back to a wall and watch my dozing, too.

Gota was not even complaining.

And Uncle Doj had stayed outside, presumably to enjoy the refreshing weather and cheerful woods.

52

It was dry in that wicked temple but it never got warm. I do not believe a brushfire could have routed the chill that inhabited that place, that gnawed into your bones and soul like an ancient and ugly spiritual rheumatism. Even Narayan Singh felt it. He hunched over the fire, twitching, as though he expected a blow from behind at any minute. He muttered something about his faith having been tested enough.

I do not belong to an empathetic and compassionate brotherhood. Those who offend us must look forward to moments of extreme discomfort, should God in His magnanimity see fit to present us with the opportunity to provide it. And our antipathy toward Narayan Singh was so old it had become ritual. So it was not with any commiseration that I told him, "We're prepared to make the exchange. Our First Book of the Dead for your Key."

His head came up. He stared at me directly, the true Narayan behind the masked Narayan considering me coldly. Wariness took life in the corners of his eyes. "How could—"

"Never mind. We have it. A swap was the deal. And we're ready to swap now."

Calculation began to replace caution. I would have bet a handsome sum he was assessing his chances of murdering us in our sleep so he would not have to keep his side of the bargain.

"It would be, perhaps, a less elegant solution than mass murder, Narayan, but why not just do the deal the way we agreed?" I shivered. The temple seemed to be getting colder, if that was possible. "In fact, I'll give you a bonus. Once you hand over the Key, you can go. Away. Free. As long as you vow not to screw with the Black Company anymore." A vow he would make in an instant, I was sure, such vows being worth the bark they are written on when they spring from the mouths of Deceivers. Kina would not expect him to keep faith with an unbeliever.

"A truly generous offer, Annalist," Singh replied. Suspiciously. "Let me sleep on it."

"By all means." I snapped my fingers. Iqbal and Runmust broke out the shackles. "Put the goatbells on him tonight, too." We had several of those, to go with several goats. Once attached to Narayan's shackles, they made a racket whenever he moved. He was a stealthmaster, but not master enough to keep the bells from betraying him. "But don't be surprised if I don't feel as generous when light and warmth return to the world. Darkness always comes, but the sun also rises."

I had my blanket around me already. I pulled it tighter and lay down, squirmed a little in a vain attempt to get comfortable, then fell into the sort of evil-haunted dreams apparently experienced by anyone who passes the night in the Grove of Doom.

I was aware that I was dreaming. And I was familiar with the dreamscapes, though I had never visited them myself. Both Lady and Murgen had written about them. The visual elements did not trouble me terribly. But nothing had prepared me for the stench, which was the stink of thousand-week-old battlefields, worse than any stench I remembered from the siege of Jaicur. Countless crows had come to banquet there.

After a while I began to feel another presence, far off but approaching, and I was afraid, not wanting to come face-to-face with Narayan's dreadful goddess. I wanted to run but did not know how. Murgen had drawn upon years of experience when he eluded Kina.

Then I realized I was not being stalked. This presence was not inimical. In fact, it was more aware of me than I of it. It was amused by my discomfort.

Murgen?

'Tis I, my apprentice. I thought you'd dream here tonight. I was right. I like being right. It's one of the joys of bachelorhood I had forgotten until I became a haunt.

I don't think Sahra would appreciate—

Of course not. Forget that. I don't have time. There're things you should know and I won't be able to reach you again directly until you enter the dark roads on the glittering plain. Listen.

I "listened."

Life in Taglios was proceeding normally. The scandal at the royal library and disappearance of the chief librarian had been played into a major distraction by the Protector. Soulcatcher was more interested in consolidating her position than in rooting out remnants of the Black Company. After all these years she still did not take us as seriously as we wanted. Or she was completely confident that she could root us out and exterminate us any time she felt like bothering.

That being a possibility, Murgen's advice was sound. We should keep moving fast while that option was available.

The best news was that Jaul Barundandi had shown an eager willingness to attach himself to the cause in hopes of avenging his wife. His initial assignment, to be carried out only if he was confident he could manage without getting caught or leaving evidence, was to penetrate the Protector's quarters and steal, destroy, or somehow incapacitate the magical carpets she had stolen from the Howler. If those could be denied her, our position would improve dramatically. He was also to recruit allies—without telling them that he was helping the Black Company. The ancient hysterical prejudice remained potent.

It sounded wonderful but I counted on nothing. Men driven solely by a need for revenge are flawed tools at best. If he let the obsession consume him, he would be lost to us before he could do any of the quiet, long-term things that make an inside man such a treasure.

The bad news was bad indeed.

The main party, traveling by water, had passed through the delta and was now ascending the Naghir River, meaning it was way ahead of us in terms of time still needed to reach the Shadowgate.

One-Eye had suffered a stroke two nights earlier, during a drunken knock-down-drag-out with his best friend Goblin.

Death did not claim him. Goblin's swift intercession had prevented that. But now he suffered from a mild paralysis and the sort of perplexing speech problems that sometimes come after a stroke. The latter made it difficult for One-Eye to communicate to Goblin what Goblin needed to know to cope with the problem. The words One-Eye wanted to say or write were not the words that came out.

A problem that is maddening enough for the ordinary Annalist, coping only with time constraints and native stupidity.

You cannot prepare yourself enough. The inevitable is always a shock when it lowers its evil wing.

As if responding to a great joke, the circling crows rattled with dark, mocking laughter. The skulls in the bonefield grinned, enjoying the grand joke, too.

There were more minor bits of news. Once Murgen exhausted his store, I asked, *Can you reach Slink if he's here? Can you put a thought into his empty head?*

Possibly.

Try. With this.

My idea amused Murgen. He hurried off to haunt Slink's certain-to-be-strange dreams. The crows scattered, as though there was nothing interesting keeping them around anymore.

I continued to people the place of nightmare, hoping I would not become a regular, as had befallen Lady and Murgen. I wondered if Lady still went there, making her interment that much more a session in hell.

A crow landed high up in a barren tree, against the face of what passed for a sun in that place. I could not distinguish it but it seemed different from the other crows.

Sister, sister. I am with you always.

Terror reached down inside me and squeezed my heart with a fist of iron. I shot bolt upright. Panic and confusion swamped me as I grabbed for my weapons.

Doj stared at me from beyond the fire. "Nightmares?"

I shivered in the cold. "Yes."

"They're the bad side of staying here. But you can learn to shut them out."

"I know what to do about them. Get away from this godforsaken place as soon as I can. Tomorrow. Early. Right after the Deceiver turns over the Key and you authenticate it."

I thought I heard faint crow laughter in the night outside.

53

I took my turn on watch. I discovered that I was not the only one with problem dreams. Everyone slept poorly, including Narayan. Iqbal's baby never stopped whimpering. The goats and donkeys, though not allowed inside, also bleated and snorted and whimpered all night long.

The Grove of Doom is just plain a Bad Place. No way around that. Some things *are* black and white.

Morning was not much more pleasant than night had been. And even before breakfast, Narayan tried to sneak away. River-walker showed remarkable restraint in bringing him back still able to walk.

"You were going to run out on me now?" I demanded. I had a good idea what he really had in mind but did not want him to suspect I knew what had become of the friends he had expected to rescue him. "I thought you wanted that book back."

He shrugged.

"I had a dream last night. And it wasn't a good dream. It took me places I didn't want to go, with beings I didn't want to see. But it was a true dream. I came away with the certainty that neither of us has any chance of getting what we want if we don't fulfill our ends of our bargain. So I'm here to tell you I'm playing it straight up, the Book of the Dead for the Key."

Narayan betrayed a flicker of annoyance at my mention of a dream. No doubt he had hoped for divine guidance and had failed to receive it last night. "I just wanted to look for something I left here last time I visited."

"The Key?"

"No. A personal trinket." He squatted beside the cook fire, where Mother Gota and Suruvhija were preparing rice. The Radisha, to the amazement of all, was trying to help. Or, better put, was trying to learn what was being done so she could help at another time. Neither woman offered the Princess's status any special respect. Gota snarled and complained at the Radisha exactly as she would have done with the rest of us.

I watched Narayan eat. He used chopsticks. I had not noticed that before. Paranoid me, I searched my memory, trying to remember if Singh had used the customary wooden spoon in the past. Uncle Doj, like all Nyueng Bao, used chopsticks. And he claimed they constituted some of his deadliest weapons.

I was going to go crazy if I did not get Narayan out of my life for a while.

He smiled as though he was reading my mind. I think maybe he put too much faith in my word on behalf of the Company. "Show me the book, Annalist."

I looked around. "Doj?"

The man appeared in the temple doorway. What was he up to in there? "Yes?"

"The Master Deceiver wishes to see the Book of the Dead."

"As you wish." He descended the leaf-strewn outer steps, rummaged through one of the donkey packs, came up with the oilskin package we had retrieved from the Shadowlander tomb. He presented it to the Deceiver with a bow and a flourish, stepped back and crossed his arms. I noted that in some mystic manner. Ash Wand had found its way onto his back. I recalled that Doj's adopted family bore Narayan Singh and the Strangler cult an abiding grudge. Deceivers had murdered To Tan, the son of Sahra's brother Thai Dei. Thai Dei lay buried beneath glittering stone with the Captured.

Uncle Doj had offered no promises to Narayan Singh.

I wondered if Singh knew all that. Most of it, probably, though the subject never arose in his presence.

I noted, also, that without plan or signal, my other companions had placed themselves so that we were surrounded by armed men. Only Swan seemed unsure of his role. "Settle and have some rice," I told him.

"I *hate* rice, Sleepy."

"We're going places where there'll be a little more variety. I hope. I've eaten rice till it's coming out my ears, too."

Narayan opened the oilskins reverently, set them aside one by one, ready to be reused. The book he revealed was big and ugly but not much distinguished it from volumes I saw every day when I was Dorabee Dey Banerjae. Nothing branded it the most holy, most sacred text of the darkest cult in the world.

Narayan opened it. The writing inside was completely inelegant, erratic, disorganized and sloppy. The Daughter of Night had begun inscribing it when she was four. As Narayan turned the pages I saw that the girl was a fast learner. Her hand improved rapidly. I saw, too, that she had written in the same script used to record the first volume of the Annals. Were both in the same language?

Where was Master Santaraksita when I needed him?

Out on the Naghir with Sahra and One-Eye. No doubt complaining about the accommodations and the lack of fine dining. Too bad, old man. I have the same problems here.

"Satisfied that it's genuine?" I asked.

Narayan could not deny it.

"So I've lived up to my half of the bargain. I have, in fact, made every effort to facilitate it. The game is back to you now."

"You have nothing to lose, Annalist. I still wonder how I would get away from here alive."

"I won't do anything to keep you from leaving. If revenge is absolutely necessary, it'll be that much sweeter down the road." Narayan tried to read my true intentions. He was incapable of accepting anything at face value. "On the other hand, there's no way you'll go anywhere if you don't produce the Key. And we'll know if you try to pass off a substitute." I looked at Doj.

Narayan did the same. Then he settled into an attitude of prayer and sealed his eyes.

Kina may have responded. The grove did turn icy cold. A sudden breeze brought a ghost of the odor from the place of the bones.

Singh shuddered, opened his eyes. "I have to go into the temple. Alone."

"Wouldn't be a back way out of there, would there?"

Singh smiled softly. "Would it do me any good if there were?"

"Not this time. Your only way out of here is not to be a Deceiver."

"So be it. There'll be no Year of the Skulls if I don't take a chance."

"Let him go," I told Doj, who stood between Narayan and the temple. River and Runmust, I noted, now had bamboo in hand, in case the little man made a break.

"He's been in there a long time," River complained.

"But he's still there," Doj assured us. "The Key must be well hidden."

Or not there anymore, I did not say. "What're we looking at here?" I asked Doj. "I'm not clear on what this Key is. Is it another lance head?" The Lance of Passion had opened the plain to Croaker, then had ushered the Captured to their doom.

"I've only heard it described. It's a strangely shaped hammer. He's about to come out."

Narayan appeared. He seemed changed, invigorated, frightened. Riverwalker gestured with his bamboo. Runmust raised his slowly. Singh knew what those poles could do. He had no chance if he tried to run now.

He carried what looked like a cast-iron war hammer, old, rusty, and ugly, with the head all chipped and cracked. Narayan made it seem heavier than it looked.

"Doj?" I asked. "What do you think?"

"Fits the description, Annalist. Except for the head being all cracked."

Singh said, "I dropped it. It cracked when it hit the temple floor."

"Feel it, Doj. If there's any power there, you ought to be able to tell."

Doj did as I said once Singh surrendered the hammer. The Nyueng Bao seemed startled by its weight. "This must be it, Annalist."

"Take your book and start running, Deceiver. Before temptation makes me forget my promises."

Narayan clutched the book but did not move. He stared at Suruvhija and the baby.

Suruvhija was using a red silk scarf to dab spit-up off the infant's chin.

Fools! Idiots!

54

While we were getting ready to travel, one of Iqbal's kids—the older boy—noticed a particularly deep flaw in the head of the hammer. The rest of us had been too busy congratulating ourselves and deciding what the Company would do once we brought the Captured forth from the plain. The boy got his father's attention. Iqbal summoned Runmust and me.

Being old folks, it took us a while to see what the boy meant. Us having bad eyes and all.

"Looks like gold in there."

"That would explain the weight. Doj. Come here. You ever hear anything about this hammer being gold inside?"

Iqbal began prying with a knife. A fragment of iron fell away.

"No," Doj said. "Don't damage it any more."

"Everybody calm down. It's still the Key. Doj, study it. Carefully. I don't want all the years and all the crap we went through to go to waste now. What?" Weapons had begun to appear.

"Look who's here," Swan said. "Where did those guys come from?"

Slink and his band had arrived. I exchanged looks with Slink. He shrugged. "Gave us the slip."

"I'm not surprised. We screwed up here. He knew somebody was out there." Suruvhija still had the red scarf draped over her shoulder. "Folks, we need to get traveling. We want to get across the bridge at Ghoja before the Protector starts looking for us." From the beginning I had pretended that getting across that bridge would give us a running chance.

I told Slink, "You guys did a great job at Semchi."

"Could've been better. If I'd thought about it, I'd've waited till they damaged the Bhodi Tree. Then we'd have been heroes instead of just bandits."

I shrugged. "Next time. Swan, tell that goat we're going to eat it if it don't start cooperating."

"You promise?"

"I promise we'll get some real food when we get to Jaicur."

55

Our crossing at Ghoja was another grand anticlimax. We all worked ourselves into a state of nerves before we reached the bottleneck. I sent Slink forward to scout and did not believe a word, emotionally, when he reported the only attention being paid anyone went to those few travelers who argued about paying a two-copper pais toll for use of the bridge. These tightwads were commended to the old ford downstream from the bridge. A ford that was impassable because this was the rainy season. Traffic was heavy. The soldiers assigned to watch the bridge were too busy loafing and playing cards to harass wayfarers.

Some part of me was determined to expect the worst.

Ghoja had grown into a small town serving those who traveled the Rock Road, which was one of the Black Company's lasting legacies. The Captain had had the highway paved from Taglios to Jaicur during his preparations for invading the Shadowlands. Prisoners of war had provided the labor. More recently, Mogaba had used convicts to extend the road southwestward, adding tributaries, to connect the cities and territories newly taken under Taglian protection.

Once we were safely over the Main, I began to ponder our next steps. I gathered everyone. "Is there any way we could forge a rescript ordering the garrison here to arrest Narayan if he crosses the bridge?"

Doj told me, "You're too optimistic. If he's going south, he's already ahead of us."

Swan added, "Not to mention that if he fell into the Protector's hands, she'd find out everything he knows about you."

"The voice of an expert heard."

"I didn't take the job voluntarily."

"All right. She could, yes. He knows where we're headed. And why. And that we have the Key. But what does he know about the other bunch? If he doesn't get caught, won't he try to intercept them so he can do something about getting the Daughter of Night away from them?"

No one found any cause to disagree.

"I suggest we remind one another of that occasionally, so it gets said sometime when Murgen is around to hear it." Sahra never promised to spare Narayan's ragged old hide. Maybe she could ambush him and take back that unfinished first Book of the Dead.

Swan pointed out, "That crow is still following us."

A small but lofty fortification overlooked the bridge and ford from the south bank. The bird was up top watching us. It had not moved since our crossing. Maybe it wanted to rest its bones, too.

River whispered, "We still have one bamboo pole with crow-killing balls in it."

"Leave it alone. It doesn't seem to mean any harm. For now, anyway." I was sure it had tried to communicate several times. "We can take it out if anything changes."

At Ghoja we heard nothing but the traditional grumbling about those in charge. Rumors concerning events in Taglios seemed so exaggerated that no one believed a tenth of anything they heard. Later, after we reached Jaicur and were taking it easy for a while, the temper of rumor began to change. It now carried a subtle vibration suggesting the great spider at the heart of the web had begun to stir. It would be a long time before any concrete news caught up but the general consensus was that we should get going right now and not dawdle along the way.

Runmust discovered that a man answering Narayan's description had been seen lurking in the vicinity of the shop operated by his now-pseudonymous offspring, Sugriva. "The man does have a weakness. Should we kill Sugriva while we're here?"

"He's never done anything to us."

"His father did. It would be a reminder to him."

"He doesn't need reminding. If Narayan is so dim that he thinks we're done with him now, let him. Just let me be there to see the look on his face when we catch him again."

Narayan had stood out in Jaicur because the city was still very nearly a military encampment. People would remember us as well, if asked during the next few weeks.

I roamed around looking for my childhood a few times but nothing that I remembered, people or places, good or evil, remained. That past survived nowhere but within my mind. Which was the one place I wished that it could die.

56

The practical rules of Company field operations resemble those obeyed by stage magicians. We would prefer our audience saw nothing at all but we do realize that invisibility is impractical. So we try to show the watcher something other than what he is looking for. Thus the goats and donkeys. And, south of Jaicur, all new looks and identities for everybody, with the enlarged party breaking up into two independently traveling "families," plus a group of failed southern fortune-hunters dragging home in despair and defeat after having had their spirits crushed by the Taglian experience. There were quite a few men of the latter sort around. They had to be watched. Many were not above taking advantage of weaker parties if they thought they could manage it. The roads were not patrolled anymore. The Protector did not care if they were safe.

Doj and Swan, Gota and I formed the advance party. We looked weak but that old man was worth four or five ordinary mortals. We had only one scrape. It was over in seconds. Several blood trails led off into the brush. Doj had chosen to leave no one dead.

The land became less hospitable and rose steadily. In clear air it was possible to look ahead and catch the faintest glimpse of the peaks of the Dandha Presh, still many days' journey south of us. The paved road ended alongside an abandoned work camp. "They must've run out of prisoners," Swan observed. The camp had been stripped of everything portable.

"What they ran out of is enemies Soulcatcher thought were worth an investment in a road. She could always find people she doesn't like and use them up in an engineering project." And she had done so on the western route, which was being followed by the rest of the Company. They would have paved footing all the way to Charandaprash. Their road, and the waterways serving it, had remained under construction until just a few years ago, when the Protector evidently decided the Kiaulune wars really were over, that it was not necessary to make life easy for the Great General and his men, and bullied the Radisha into no longer spending the money.

I wondered what the Radisha's perspective would be. I suspected she had believed she was in charge right up to the moment we disappeared her. Then she had begun getting an education, here amongst her faithful subjects.

We reached Lake Tanji, which I love. The lake is a vast sprawl of icy indigo beauty. When I was a lot younger, we fought our deadliest encounter with the things that had given the Shadowmasters their names there. More than a decade later you could still see places where rock had melted. If you went exploring some of the narrow gulches scarring the hillsides, you could find clutches of human bones that had come back to the surface with time.

"This is a place of dark memory," Doj remarked. He had been here for that battle, too. And so had Gota, who had stopped complaining long enough to deal with her memories also.

She really did have a lot of pain these days.

The white crow streaked overhead. It dropped down the slope ahead, vanished into the ragged foliage of a tall mountain pine. We saw that bird almost every day now. There was no doubt it was following us. Swan swore that it had tried to strike up a conversation with him once when he was out in the brush relieving himself.

When I asked what it wanted, he said, "Hey, I got the hell out of there, Sleepy. I've got problems enough. I don't need to get known as a guy who gossips with birds, too."

"It might've had something interesting to say."

"Without a doubt. And if it *really* wants to tell somebody something badly enough, it'll come talk to you."

Right now Swan looked down the slope and said, "It's hiding from something."

"But not from us." I looked back up the slope. The ground appeared untouched up there. There was no sign of other travelers. Below me, downhill, the meandering track appeared occasionally upon the slope and along the shore, both of which were deserted. This was no longer a popular route. "I could retire beside that lake," I told Swan.

"Must not be the best place or somebody would've beaten you to it."

He had a point. This country was far emptier now than it had been twenty years ago. Then there had been villages around the lake.

"There you go," Swan said, looking back.

"What?" I looked. It took a moment. "Oh. The bird?"

"Not just a bird. A crow. The regular kind of crow."

"Your eyes are better than mine. Ignore it. If we don't pay it any special attention, it shouldn't have any reason to concentrate on us." My heartbeat was rising, though.

Maybe it was just a feral crow and had nothing to do with Soulcatcher. Crows are not fastidious about their dining.

Or maybe the Protector had, at last, begun looking for us outside of Taglios.

White crow in hiding, black crow in the air, searching. What did it mean?

Not much we could do about it, whatever. Though Uncle Doj had a calculating eye whenever he looked up at the black crow.

It lost interest after a while. It went away. I told the others, "That shouldn't be a problem. Crows are smart, for birds, but one by itself can't remember a lot of instructions or carry much information back. If it is one of hers." We had to assume that it was. Crows were much less common than they used to be. Those remaining always seemed to be under Soulcatcher's control. Her control was probably why they were dying out.

If this one *was* a scout for the Protector, it would be days yet before it could report.

Doj observed, "If it was suspicious, we can expect to have shadows around in a few days."

That would be Soulcatcher's best means of scouting us. Shadows traveled faster than crows, could be given much more complex instructions and could bring back far more information. But could Soulcatcher control them so far away? The original Shadowmasters had had major difficulties managing their pets over long distances.

We passed along the shores of Lake Tanji. Each of us seized an opportunity to bathe in the icy water. The old road then led us on to the Plain of Charandaprash, where the Black Company had won one of its greatest triumphs and the Great General had suffered his most humiliating defeat—through no fault of his own. Though a capricious history would not recall the blame due his cowardly master, Longshadow. Wreckage from that battle still lay scattered across the slopes. A small garrison watched over the approaches to the pass through the Dandha Presh. It showed no interest in clearing any mess or, even, in monitoring traffic. Nobody looked my group over. Nobody asked questions. We were assessed an unofficial toll and warned that the donkey might find the footing treacherous in the high pass because there was still ice on the rocks up there. We did learn that there had been heavier traffic than usual lately. That told me that Sahra's group had encountered no insuperable difficulties and was ahead of us, as it should be, even with all the old men and reluctant companions.

The mountains were far colder and more barren than the highlands we had crossed. I wondered how the Radisha was handling it, about her thoughts concerning the empire she had acquired, mostly thanks to the Company. Doubtless her eyes had been opened some.

They needed a lot of opening. She had spent most of her life cooped up inside the Palace.

The white crow turned up every few days but its darker kinfolk did not. Maybe the Protector was preoccupied elsewhere.

I wished I had Murgen's talent for leaving his body. I had not had so much as a good dream since leaving the Grove of Doom. I knew exactly as little as everyone else. And that was extremely frustrating after having had easy access to secrets from afar for so long.

Nights in the mountains get really cold. I told Swan I was tempted to take up his suggestion that we go off somewhere and set up housekeeping in our own tavern and brewery. When it got really cold, a few lesser sins did not seem to matter.

57

The timing of events in Taglios is uncertain because the principal reporter, Murgen, had maintained such a casual relationship with the concept for the last decade and a half. But his sketchy descriptions of events in the city following our departure are of more than passing interest.

At first the Protector suspected nothing. The stay-behinds

planted smoke buttons and started rumors but with a declining enthusiasm the Taglian peoples began to sense. At the same time, though, the populace developed an abiding suspicion that the Protector had done away with the reigning Princess. The people became less tractable by the hour.

The arrival of the Great General and his forces guaranteed the peace. Moreover, it freed the Protector to go hunting enemies instead of spending her time making sure her friends remained intimidated enough to continue supporting her. In just days she found the Nyueng Bao warehouse on the waterfront, empty now except for a few cages occupied by missing members of the Privy Council, none of whom were in shape to resume their duties. An armamentarium of booby traps came with the prodigal ministers, of course, but none of those were clever enough to inconvenience Soulcatcher herself. Quite a few Greys were not so fortunate. The Protector took rather a heartless view of those who did fall victim to the Company legacy. "Better to get the dimwits winnowed out now, when the broader risk is minimal," she told Mogaba. The Great General's attitude complemented hers precisely.

Questions asked in the neighborhood produced no information of substance, however vigorously they were put. The Nyueng Bao merchants had been careful to maintain a veil around themselves and their businesses. They had even employed the magical in their quest for greater anonymity. Wisps of confusion spells persisted yet.

"I smell those two wizards," Soulcatcher muttered. "But you promised me that they were dead, didn't you, Great General?"

"I saw them die myself."

"You'd better hope you don't irritate *me* so much you don't survive to see them die again, for real." Her voice was that of a spoiled child.

The Great General did not respond. If Soulcatcher frightened him, he showed no sign. Neither did he betray any anger. He waited, reasonably confident that he was too valuable to become the victim of an evil caprice. Perhaps, in his heart of hearts, he thought the Protector was not equally valuable.

"There's no trace of them," Soulcatcher mumbled later, in a voice academically cool. "They're gone. Yet the impression of their presence persists, as bold as a bucket of blood thrown against a wall."

"Illusion," Mogaba said. "I'm sure you'd find a hundred instances in the Black Company Annals of where they drew an enemy's eye in one direction while they moved in another. Or made someone believe their numbers were far greater than they actually were."

"You'd find as many instances in my diaries. If I bothered to keep any. I don't, because books are nothing but repositories for those lies the author wants his reader to believe." The voice she used now was the antithesis of academic. It was that of a man who knew, from painful experience, that education just taught people sneakier ways to rob you. "They aren't here anymore but they may have left spies."

"Of course they did. It's doctrine. But you'll have a hell of a time finding them. They won't be people anyone else would suspect."

Jaul Barundandi and two of his assistants laid out a dinner while the Protector and her champion talked. Their presence attracted no notice. Paranoid though she was, Soulcatcher paid little heed to the furniture. Every staffer had been interrogated in the hours following the Radisha's disappearance and no inside accomplices had been found.

The Protector was not unaware that she was not as beloved of the staff as the Radisha had been. But she was not troubled. No mundane attacker had any genuine hope of penetrating her personal defenses. And these days she had no peer in this world. Sheer perversity and protracted elusiveness had put her in a position to elect herself queen of the world. If she wanted to bother.

Someday, when she got her head organized, she was going to have to think about that.

Halfway through a rare meal Soulcatcher paused in mid-chew. She told Mogaba, "Find me a Nyueng Bao. Any Nyueng Bao. Right now. Right away."

The lean black man showed no emotion as he rose. "May I ask why?"

"Their headquarters was inside a Nyueng Bao warehouse. Nyueng Bao have been associated with the Company since the fighting at Dejagore. The last Annalist married one of them. He had a child by her. The association may be more than historical happenstance." She knew a great deal more about Nyueng Bao than she was willing to share, of course.

Mogaba inclined his upper body in a ghost of a bow. Mostly he was comfortable working with Soulcatcher. Mostly he approved of her thinking. He went in search of someone who could catch him a couple of swamp monkeys.

The servants hovered around the Protector, perfectly attentive. Idly, she noted that these three were among the same half dozen who struggled to make her life easier wherever she happened to be in the Palace. In fact, one or more always followed her on her exploratory safaris into the maze of abandoned corridors that made up the majority of the Palace, just in case she needed something. Lately they had brought life into her personal quarters, which for so long had been as chill and barren and dusty as the empty sectors.

It was their nature. It was bred into them. They must serve. Without the Radisha to fulfill their need for a master, they had had to turn to her.

Mogaba was away hours longer than she liked. When the man did deign to return, her voice of choice was spoiled-brat querulous. "Where have you been? What took you so long?"

"I've been demonstrating how hard it is to catch the wind. There are no Nyueng Bao anywhere in the city. The last time anyone can remember seeing any of them was the day before yesterday, in the morning. They were going aboard a barge that later headed downriver, toward the swamps. Evidently the swamp people have been leaving Taglios since *before* the Radisha disappeared and you hurt your heel."

Soulcatcher growled. She did not want to be reminded that she had been tricked. The heel itself was reminder enough.

"The Nyueng Bao are a stubborn people."

"Famous for it," Mogaba agreed.

"I've visited them twice before. Each time they failed to appreciate my full message. I suppose I'll have to go preach to them again. And round up any fugitives they've taken in." It was an obvious conclusion, that the Company survivors had retreated into the swamps. The Nyueng Bao had taken in fugitives before. And supportive evidence was available if the Protector cared to dig. The barges carrying the majority of the Company had gone downriver. You had to go down into the delta to get to the Naghir River, which was the principal navigable waterway leading into the south.

Soulcatcher popped up. She rushed out with the bounce and enthusiasm of a teenager. Mogaba settled down to contemplate the remains of his meal, which had not yet been cleared away. One of the servants murmured, "We thought you might wish to continue, sir. Should you prefer otherwise, we will clear away instantly."

Mogaba looked up into a bland face that projected eagerness to serve. Nevertheless, he had a momentary impression that the man was measuring his back for a dagger.

"Take it away. I'm not hungry."

"As you wish, sir. Girish, take the leftovers to the charity postern. Make certain the beggars there know that the Protector is thinking of them."

Mogaba watched the servants depart. He wondered what had given him the impression that that man was insincere. The truth supposedly lay in a man's deeds, and that one never behaved as anything less than a totally devoted servant.

Soulcatcher stamped into her personal suite. The more she thought about the Nyueng Bao, the more enraged she became. What would it take to teach those people? That seemed like something they could work out between them before the sun came up. A night of shadow-terror ought, at the very least, to put them into a mood to pay attention.

Soulcatcher understood herself better than outsiders believed she did. She wondered why she was in so foul a temper, which seemed to go beyond her usual caprice and irritability. She belched, hammered her chest with a fist to loosen another burp. Maybe it was the spicy food. She sensed bad heartburn coming. She felt a little light-headed, too.

She climbed to the parapet where she kept the only two flying carpets left in the world. That could be reached only by the route she followed. She would go down there and make those swamp monkeys pay for the heartburn, too. Dinner had been a Nyueng Bao ethnic specialty consisting of big, ugly mushrooms, uglier eels, and unidentifiable vegetables in a blisteringly spicy sauce, served upon a bed of rice. It had been a favorite of the Radisha's, served often. The kitchens had not changed their routines, because the Protector did not care about the menu.

The Protector belched again. The growing heartburn seared her insides.

She jumped on the larger carpet. It creaked under her weight. She ordered it to head downriver. Fast.

A few miles out, four hundred feet above the rooftops, streaking faster than a racing pigeon, sabotaged frame members under the carpet began to snap. Once the first went, the stress became too much for the others. The carpet disintegrated in seconds.

A burst of light flared, bright enough to be seen by half the city. The last thing Soulcatcher saw, as she arced toward the surface of the river, was a huge circle of characters declaring "Water Sleeps."

Just before the flash leaped through his window, a bemused Mogaba discovered a folded, sealed letter on his spartan cot. Belching, glad he had eaten no more of that spicy food, he broke the wax and read "My brother unforgiven." Then the unexpected lightning grabbed his attention. He read the slogan in the sky, too. All the labor he had invested in learning to read over the past few years was to be rewarded thus?

What now? If the Protector was gone? Pretend she was in hiding, too, and make the deceit a double veil?

He belched again, settled down on his cot. He did not feel well at all. That was a baffling new feeling for him. He never got sick.

58

A chatty youngster of native stock and a more than customarily ambitious disposition interviewed us at the military control point we encountered at the southern end of the pass. He was not yet old enough to be pompously officious but he would get there. Personally, he seemed more interested in foreign news than in contraband or wanted men. "What's going on up north?" he wanted to know. "We've seen a lot of refugees lately." He examined our meager possessions without ever looking inside anything.

Gota and Doj rattled at one another in Nyueng Bao and pretended not to understand the young man's accented Taglian. I shrugged and responded in Jaicuri at first, which is close enough to Taglian for the two peoples to understand one another most of the time, but here it only frustrated the young official. I had no desire to stand around gossiping with a functionary. "I do not know about others. We have had nothing but decades of misfortune and suffering.

We heard there were opportunities down here so we abandoned the Land of Our Sorrows and came."

The official assumed I meant a particular country, as I had hoped, rather than recognizing that the Land of Our Sorrows was the Vehdna way of describing where a convert lived before he became acquainted with God.

"You say there are many others doing the same as us?" I tried to sound troubled.

"Recently, yes. Which is why I feared something might be afoot."

He feared for the stability of the empire to which he had attached himself. I could not resist a prank. "There were rumors that the Black Company had surfaced in Taglios and was warring with the Protector. But there are always crazy stories about the Black Company. They never mean anything. And they had nothing to do with our decision."

The young man became more unhappy. He passed us through without further interest. I did not bother commending him but he was the only official we had encountered since leaving Taglios who was making a serious effort to perform his duties. And he was doing it only in hopes of getting ahead.

I never had to bring out the richly complex legend I have invented for our foursome, in which Swan was my second husband, Gota the mother of my deceased first spouse and Doj her cousin, all of us survivors of the wars. The story would have played in any region where there had been any extended fighting. Splatchcobbled family survival teams were not at all uncommon.

I complained, "I worked on weaving us a history all the way down here and I never got to use it. Not once. Nobody's doing their job."

Doj smiled and winked and vanished into the broken ground beside the road, off to reclaim the weapons we had hidden before approaching the checkpoint.

"Somebody should do something about that," Swan declared. "Next vice-regal subofficer I see, I'll march right up and give him a piece of my mind. We all pay taxes. We have a right to expect more effort from our officials."

Gota woke up long enough to call Swan an idiot in Taglian and Nyueng Bao. She told him he ought to shut up before even the God of Fools renounced him. Then she closed her eyes and resumed snoring. Gota had begun to concern me. She had shown less life every day for the past few months. Doj seemed to think she believed she no longer had anything to live for.

Maybe Sahra could get her going again. We should be joining up with the others before long. Maybe Sahra could get her excited about rescuing Thai Dei and the Captured.

I was troubled about consequences. All these years I had striven toward the undertaking we would launch before long, and now, for the first time, I had begun to wonder what success might really mean. Those people buried out there never were paragons of sanity and righteousness. They had had almost two decades to ferment in their own juices. They were unlikely to entertain much brotherly love toward the rest of the world.

And then there was the guardian demon Shivetya and, somewhere, the enchanted and enchained thing worshipped by Narayan Singh and the Daughter of Night. Not to mention the mysteries and dangers of the plain itself. And all the perils we did not yet know.

Only Swan had any experience of that. He had nothing positive to report. Nor had Murgen at any time over the years, though his experiences had been dramatically different from Swan's. Murgen had experienced the glittering plain in two worlds at once. Swan seemed to have experienced the version in our world in sharper focus. Even after so many years he could describe particular landmarks in exquisite detail.

"How come you never talked about this before?"

"I never hid it, Sleepy. But there just don't seem to be much percentage in volunteering anything in this world. If I admit anything I know about that place, next thing I'll know is, good old Willow Swan is elected to go back up there as the guide for a gang of invaders guaranteed to irritate the shit out of whatever spirits haunt the place. Am I right? Or am I right?"

"You aren't as stupid as you let on. I thought you didn't see any spirits."

"Not the way Murgen claimed he saw them but that don't mean I didn't feel them creeping around. You'll find out. You try to sleep at night when you feel hungry shadows calling you from a few feet away. It's like being inside a zoo with all the predators in the world slavering just the other side of the bars. Bars that you can't see and can't even feel and so have no way of knowing if they're trustworthy.

And all this jabber ain't doing my nerves any good at all, neither, Sleepy."

"We may never have to go up there, Swan—if the Key we've got is a fake or isn't any good anymore. Then there won't be anything we can do but maybe set up your brewery and pretend we never heard of the Protector or the Radisha or the Black Company."

"Be still, my heart. You know goddamn well that thing's going to be the true Key. Your god, my gods, somebody's gods have got a boner for Willow Swan and they're gonna keep making sure that whatever happens, it's gonna be the worst possible thing and it's gonna happen to me. I oughta run out on you now. I oughta turn you in to the nearest royal official. Only that would let Soulcatcher know that I'm still alive. Then she'd get real nasty, asking me why I didn't turn you in three, four months ago."

"Not to mention you'd probably get yourself dead long before you could unearth an official who cared enough to listen to you."

"There's that, too."

Doj came back with the weapons. We passed them around, resumed traveling. Swan continued eloquently describing himself as the firstborn son of Misfortune.

He went through these spells of high drama.

A half mile down the road we encountered a small peasants' market. A few old folks and youngsters who could not contribute much on the farm waited to take advantage of travelers still shaking from the miseries of the mountains. Fresh foods in season were their hot sellers but they retailed gossip at no charge as long as you contributed a few snippets of your own. They found doings beyond the Dandha Presh particularly intriguing.

I asked a young girl, who looked like she could be the little sister of the customs official back up the road, "Do you remember many of the people who came through here? My father was supposed to have come down ahead of us, to find us a place to settle." I proceeded to describe Narayan Singh in detail.

The child was a lighthearted thing, without a care or concern. Chances were she did not recall what she had eaten for breakfast. She did not remember Narayan but went off to find someone who might.

"Where was she when I was young enough to get married?" Swan grumbled. "She'll be pretty when she's older and she doesn't have a brain in her head to complicate things."

"Buy her. Bring her along. Raise her up right."

"I'm not as pretty as I used to be."

I tried to think of someone who was. Not even Sahra qualified.

I waited. Swan muttered. Doj and Gota wandered around, Uncle swapping tales and Mother examining the wares for sale. Except for the produce, those were feeble. She did acquire a scrawny chicken. The one positive of our travel team was that there were no Gunni or Shadar to complicate mealtime. Only Gota, who kept trying to do the cooking. Maybe I could murder the chicken in her sleep and get it roasted before she woke up.

The girl brought a very old man. He was no help, either. He seemed interested only in telling me what he thought I wanted to hear. But it did seem possible that Narayan had come through the pass some time before we had.

I hoped Murgen was on the job and had alerted the others to the possibilities.

Doj and Gota headed on down the road before I finished with the locals, surprised that my command of the language was adequate to the task. Evidently Gota was tired of riding. The donkey certainly could use the break.

"Is that a pet?" the small girl asked.

"It's a donkey," I said, really astonished that I had been having so little trouble communicating. They had donkeys down here, did they not?

"I know that. I meant the bird."

"Huh! Well." The white crow was perched on the donkey's pack. It winked. It laughed. It said, "Sister, sister," and flapped into the air, then glided on down the mountain.

Swan said, "I was just thinking I found an up side to this trip. It's not raining down here."

"Maybe I'll see if they'll let *me* have the child. In exchange for your strong back."

"We're getting a little too domestic here, Goodwife . . . Sleepy? Didn't you ever have a real name?"

"Anyanyadir, the Lost Princess of Jaicur. But even now my wicked stepmother has discovered that I still live and has summoned the princes of the rakshasas to bargain with them for my murder. Hey! I'm kidding. I'm Sleepy. And you've known me practically since I started being Sleepy, off and on. So just let it be."

59

Once we cleared the mountains, it was no long journey to the site of Kiaulune. Incredible destruction had been wrought there during the Shadowmaster wars, then during the Kiaulune wars between the Radisha and those who chose to keep faith with the Black Company. A pity most of the wreckage had been cleared away even before Soulcatcher decided she could declare victory and go north to claim her new place as Protector of All the Taglias. The Radisha should have seen it at its worst, to understand what she had wrought by betraying her contract with the Company. But the worst now existed only in the memories of survivors. The once-clamorous valley now boasted a sizable town and a checkerboard of new farms peopled by a mixture of natives, former prisoners of war and deserters from every conceivable faction. Peace had broken out and was being enthusiastically exploited on the presumption that it could not possibly last.

The transition from the old Kiaulune, once called Shadowcatch, and the new, simply called the New Town, saw one thing remain unchanged. Over there on the far slope of the valley, miles and miles away, beyond the crumbled, brush-strewn ruins of once-mighty Overlook, where the land quickly changed from rich green to almost barren brown, was the dreaded thing called the Shadowgate. It did not stand out but I felt its call. I told my companions, "We have to be careful not to get in a hurry now. Haste could be deadly."

The Shadowgate was not just the only way we could get up onto the plain to go free the Captured, it was also the only portal through which the shadows imprisoned up there could escape and begin treating the whole world the way their cousins had the destitute of Taglios. And that gate was in tender shape. The Shadowmasters had injured and weakened it badly when gaining access to the shadows they enslaved.

"We're in complete agreement on that," Uncle Doj replied. "All the lore emphasizes the need for caution."

There had been some disagreement between us lately. He had resumed his romance with the idea of the Company Annalist becoming his understudy in the peculiar role he played among the Nyueng Bao. The Company Annalist who had no great interest in the job but Doj was one of those people who just have grave difficulties getting their minds around the concept "No!"

"That's new," I said, indicating a small structure a quarter mile below the Shadowgate, beside the road. "And I don't like its looks." It was hard to tell from so far but the structure looked like a small fortification built of stone salvaged from the rubble of Overlook.

Doj grunted. "A potential complication."

Swan observed, "We keep standing around looking like spies, somebody's going to get unpleasant with us."

A point not without substance, although those in charge seemed awfully lax. It was obvious that trouble had not visited in a while. Quite probably not since the Black Company left. "Somebody— probably named me, because I'm the only one here who looks like what she says she is—will have to go scout around." The original plan had been for everybody to camp in the barrens not far downhill from where that new structure now stood.

I was troubled. Someone should have been watching for us to come out of the mountains. I hoped that was just Sahra's oversight. She had been married to the Company for an age but never did learn to think like a soldier. If nobody offered good advice, or she chose to ignore the advice she was given because, like many civilians, she could not grasp why all the little horsepuckey things have to be done, she might not have thought it important to watch for us.

I prayed it was as simple as that.

Nobody demanded that I give them the role of scout. Poor me. More sore feet while the rest of them loafed around in the shade of young pines.

The white crow materialized minutes after I turned the knee of a hill and the others were out of sight. It swooped at me and squawked. It swooped at me again. I tried to swat it like it was some huge, really annoying bug. It laughed and came back, now squawking what sounded like words.

I got it. Finally. The bird wanted me to follow it. "Lead on, fell

harbinger, never forgetting that I'm not Gunni and therefore hobbled by no holy ban against eating meat." I had enjoyed, if that is the
proper word, crow stew several times during the lowest lows of my
military career.

The crow had only my interests at heart. It led me straight to a
large tent village on a hillside overlooking the near outskirts of the
New Town. Our people had to be only some of the refugees housed
there but Sahra's hand was obvious everywhere. The layout was neat
and orderly and clean. Exactly as the Captain's rules insisted, though
those are honored mainly in the breech when he is not around.

I suffered an immediate conflict. Charge ahead to see everyone I
had missed for months? Or run back and collect my traveling companions? Once I started grabbing, it might be hours before—

My choice got made for me. Tobo spotted me.

My first warning was a shout. "Sleepy!" A mass of churning arms
and legs charged in from the left and collected me in a totally unexpected hug.

I wriggled loose. "You've grown." A lot. He was taller than me
now. And his voice had deepened. "You won't be able to be Shiki
anymore. The great men of Taglios will be brokenhearted."

"Goblin says it's time I start breaking the girls' hearts, anyway."
There was not much doubt that he would have the power to do that.
He was going to be a handsome man who had no lack of confidence.

Uncharacteristically, I slipped an arm around his waist and
walked down toward where other familiar faces had begun to appear.
"How was your journey?"

"Mostly kind of fun, except when they made me study, which was
about all the time. Sri Surendranath is worse than Goblin but he says
I could be a scholar. So Mother always backs them up whenever anybody wants to make me study. But we got to see a lot of neat things.
There was this temple in Praiphurbed that was completely covered
with carvings of people doing it all different ways—oh, I'm sorry." He
reddened.

Tobo had a mental image of me as a sort of chaste nun. And most
of my adult life would not contradict that view. But I am not against
interpersonal adventures, I am just not interested myself. Probably
because, Swan insists, I have not yet run into the man whose animal
presence completely overwhelms my intellectual reluctance. Swan
being a leading authority in his own mind.

He keeps volunteering. Who knows? Maybe someday I will be-come curious enough to experiment, just to find out if I can be touched without running to my away place to hide.

Now the others were wishing me welcome with a sincerity that set another place inside me, a small, warm place, all aglow. My com-rades. My brothers. All kinds of rattle and chatter inundated me. Now we were going to do something. Now we were going to get somewhere. Now we were going to kick some ass if we had to. Sleepy was here to figure it all out and tell everybody where and when to stick the knife.

"God knows all the secrets and all the jokes," I said, "and I wish He'd share the secret of the joke that explains why He created such a scruffy bunch of hired killers." I used a little finger to get rid of a tear before anybody realized that it was not raining. "You guys look pretty fat for having been on the road so long."

Somebody said, "Shit, we been here waiting for you for a whole fuckin' month. Some of us. The slowest ones got here last week."

"How's One-Eye doing?" I asked as Sahra wriggled through the throng.

"He's fucked up," a voice volunteered. "How'd you know . . . ?"

I exchanged hugs with Sahra. She said, "We were starting to worry." A question clung to the edge of her statement.

"Tobo. Your grandmother and Uncle Doj are waiting in the woods back up the road. Run up and tell them to come on down."

"Where're the rest?" somebody demanded.

"Swan is with them. The rest are behind us somewhere. We broke up into three groups after we reached the highlands. There were crows around. We didn't want to give them anything obvious to watch."

"We did the same thing after we left the barges," Sahra told me. "Did you see many crows? We saw only a few. They might not have been the Protector's."

"The white one keeps turning up."

"We saw it, too. Are you hungry?"

"You kidding? I've been eating your mother's cooking since we left Jaicur." I looked around. People were watching who were not Black Company. They might only be refugees, too, but the enthusi-asm of my reception was sure to cause talk.

Sahra laughed. It sounded more like the laughter of relief than that of good humor. "How is Mother?"

"I think there's something wrong, Sahra. She's stopped being nasty, bitter old Ky Gota. Most of the time she's lost inside herself. And those times when she is completely aware, she almost has manners."

"In here." Sahra lifted a tent flap. It was the largest tent in the encampment. "And Uncle Doj?"

"A step slower but still Uncle Doj. He wants me to turn Nyueng Bao and be his apprentice. Like I have a lot of free time being Murgen's apprentice. He says it's just because he doesn't have anybody else to pass his responsibilities on to. Whatever they are. He seems to think I should sign on before he tells me what for."

"Did you get the Key?"

"We did. Uncle Doj has it in his pack. But Singh got away. Not unexpectedly. Did he turn up here? We picked up rumors along the way that gave me the idea that he was ahead of us and gaining ground. You do still have the girl?"

Sahra nodded. "But she's a handful. I think bringing her south again put her in closer touch with Kina. Common sense tells me we should break our promise and kill her." She settled on a cushion. "I'm glad you're here. I'm completely worn out. Keeping these people under control when there's so little for them to do . . . it's a miracle that we haven't had any major incidents. . . . I bought a farm."

"You what?"

"I bought a farm. Not far from the Shadowgate. They tell me the soil is lousy, but it's a place where most of the men can stay out of sight and keep out of trouble and even stay busy building housing or working the ground so we'll eventually be self-supporting. Half the gang is over there now. Most of these guys here would be, too, except that Murgen said you were going to arrive today. You made good time. We didn't expect you for several more hours."

"Does that mean you're all caught up on what's going on in the world outside?"

"I have a particularly talented husband who doesn't always share everything with me. And I don't always share him with the others. And we both probably shouldn't be that way. There're a thousand things we need to talk about, Sleepy. I don't know where to start. So why not just with, how are you?"

60

The brotherhood had to begin moving.

Goblin burst into the tent uninvited and gasped out the news that Murgen said my feted arrival had caught the eyes of official informants and had aroused the suspicions of the local authorities. Those folks had been disinclined to investigate the refugee camp before only due to a complete lack of ambition. I sent Kendo and a dozen men to secure the southern end of the pass through the Dandha Presh, both to guarantee a favorable welcome for those coming down behind me and to help keep anyone from strolling off northward with news about where we were. I sent several small teams off to capture senior officers and officials before they could become organized. There was no real, fixed, solid governmental structure here because the Protector favored the rule of limited anarchy.

It was obvious that these former Shadowlands, despite their proximity to the glittering plain, were no more than an afterthought to the powers in Taglios. The troubles in the region had been settled with a vengeance. The Great General had won the reputation he had desired. There were few troops and no officials of any renown here now. It looked like a safe, remote province suitable for rusticating human embarrassments deemed not worth exterminating.

Even so, regionwide, there were many more of them than there were of us and we were out of battle practice ourselves. Brains, speed and ferocity would have to sustain us till we gathered the whole clan and completed preparations to follow the road up the south side of the valley.

"So, now you've had your power fix and you've got time to talk, how the hell are you, Sleepy?" Goblin asked. He looked exhausted.

"Worn to the bone from traveling but still full of vinegar. It's nice to talk to somebody where I don't have to lean over backwards to look them in the eye."

"Walk in the goddamn door talking that shit. I knew there was a reason I didn't miss you."

"You say the sweetest things. How's One-Eye?"

"Getting better. Having Gota here will hurry it up. But he's never going to be completely right. He's going to be slow and shaky and have spells where he'll have trouble remembering what he's doing. And he'll always have trouble communicating, especially when he's excited."

I nodded, took a deep breath, said, "And it's going to happen again, isn't it?"

"It could. It often does. It doesn't have to, though." He rubbed his forehead. "Headache. I need some sleep. You can drive yourself crazy trying to deal with something like this."

"If you need sleep, you'd better get it now. Things are starting to happen. We'll need you fresh when it gets exciting."

"I knew there was another reason I didn't miss you. You haven't been here long enough to blow your nose and already people and things are flying all over, getting ready to beat each other in the head."

"It's my perky personality. Think I should visit One-Eye?"

"Up to you. But he'll be heartbroken if you don't. He's probably already all bent out of shape because you came and saw me first."

I asked how to find One-Eye and left Goblin. I noted that refugees not associated with the Company were sneaking out of the camp. There were signs of excitement over in the New Town, too.

Gota, Doj and Swan were nearing the camp from the uphill side. Tobo larked around them like an excited pup. I wondered where Swan would stand once the real excitement started. He would stay neutral as long as he could, probably.

"You look better than I expected," I told One-Eye, who was actually doing something when I ducked into his tent. "That spear? I thought you lost it ages ago." The weapon in question was an elaborately carved and decorated artifact of extreme magical potency that he had begun crafting back during the siege of Jaicur. Its designated target then had been the Shadowmaster Shadowspinner. Later, he had continued improving it so he could use it against Longshadow. That spear was so darkly beautiful that it seemed a sin to use it just to kill someone.

One-Eye took his time collecting himself. He looked up at me. There was less of him than there was when last I had seen him, and even then he had been just a shell of the One-Eye I remembered from when I was young.

"No."

Just that one word. None of the usual creative invective or accusations and insults. He did not want to embarrass himself. The results of the stroke were more crippling emotionally than physically. He had been master of his surroundings for two hundred years, far beyond the dreams of men, but now he could not count on being able to speak a complete, coherent sentence.

"I'm here. I've got the Key. And things have begun to happen already."

One-Eye nodded slowly. I hope he understood. There had been a woman in Jaicur, she was a hundred nineteen when she died, they said. In all my years I never saw her do anything but sit in a chair and drool. She understood nothing anyone said to her. She had to be changed like a baby. She had to be fed like a baby. I did not want that to happen to One-Eye. He was old and cantankerous and a major pain more often than not, but he was a fixture of my universe. He was my brother.

"That other woman. That married one. She does not have the fire." His words were a ghost of speech. When he talked, his hands shook too badly to hold his tools.

"She's afraid to succeed."

"And afraid not to. You are busy, Little Girl." He beamed because he had gotten that out without much trouble. "You do what you must. But I have to talk to you again. Soon. Before this happens to me again." He spoke slowly and with great care. "You are the one." He was tiring, so great was his mental effort. He beckoned me closer, murmured, "Soldiers live. And wonder why."

Someone threw the tent flap back. Brilliant light burst inside. I knew it was Gota without being able to see. Her odor preceded her. "Try not to make him talk too much. He's worn out."

"I have seen this problem before." Cold, yet civil. More animated than she had been for some time but still not the caustic, frequently irrational Gota of last year. "I will be of more value here." Her accent was much less heavy than usual. "Go kill someone, Stone Soldier."

"Been a while since anybody called me that."

Gota bowed mockingly as she waddled past. "Bone Warrior. Soldier of Darkness, go forth and conjure the Children of the Dead from the Land of Unknown Shadows. All Evil Dies There an Endless Death."

I stepped outside, baffled. What was that all about?

Behind me, "Calling the Heaven and the Earth and the Day and the Night."

I thought I had heard that formula before but could not recall the place or the context. Surely it was sometime when a person of the Nyueng Bao conviction was being particularly cryptic.

The excitement had increased. Someone had stolen some horses already . . . had *acquired* them. Let us not leap too far with our conclusions. Several riders were charging around, unguided by any rational plan. Something should have been in place for a situation like this. I grumbled, "This's what happens when nobody wants to take charge. You three men! Get over here! What in the name of God are you doing?"

After listening to their hemming and hawing, I gave some orders. They galloped off with messages. I murmured, "There is no God but God. God is the Almighty, Boundless in Mercy. Show Mercy unto me, O Lord of the Seasons. Let mine enemies be even more confused than my friends." I felt like I was inside the eye of a storm of screwups.

My fault? All I did was show up. If I was likely to have that effect, someone should have met me away from witnesses and led me to Sahra's farm. That might have given us time to get into shape, with nobody the wiser.

We really had very little formal organization, no declared chain of command, and no established table of responsibility. We had no real policies other than fixed enmities and an emotional commitment to release the Captured. We had deteriorated into little more than a glorified bandit gang and I was embarrassed. It was partly my fault.

I rubbed my behind. I had a distinct feeling the Captain was going to catch up on years' worth of chew-outs. I could make all the excuses I wanted about only being a stand-in for Murgen while he was buried, but I had been chosen as his understudy. And the Annalist is often the Standardbearer, too, and the Standardbearer is generally designated because those in command think he is capable of becoming Lieutenant and possibly, eventually, Captain. Which meant that Murgen had seen something in me a long time ago and the Old Man had not found cause to disagree with him. And I had done nothing with that but have a good time designing torments for our enemies while a woman who was not a pledged member of the Company assumed most of its leadership by default. Sahra's courage and intelligence and determination were beyond reproach but her skills as a soldier and commander were less so. She meant well but she did not understand strategies not designed around her own needs and desires. She wanted to resurrect the Captured, of course, but not for the benefit of the Black Company. She wanted her husband back. To Sahra, the Company was just a means of achieving her ends.

We were about to pay the price of my reluctance to step forward and serve the interests of the Company.

We were hardly more than the gang of thugs the Protector claimed us to be. I was willing to bet that any determined resistance we encountered hereabouts was likely to shatter what little family spirit the Company had left. We would have to pay for forgetting who and what we were. And my anger, mainly at myself, made me seem twice life-size. I stomped around screaming and foaming at the mouth and before long had bullied everyone into doing something useful.

And then a sorry bunch of ragamuffins trudged out of the New Town and headed for the refugee camp like a reluctant flock of geese, honking and straggling all over. They numbered about fifty and carried weapons. The steel was more impressive than the soldiers carrying it. The local armorer did his job well. Whoever trained recruits did not. They were more pathetic than my gang. And my guys had the advantage of having knocked people over the head before and so had little reluctance to hurt someone again. Particularly if that someone threatened them.

"Tobo. Go get Goblin."

The boy eyed the approaching disorder. "I can handle that clusterfuck, Sleepy. One-Eye and Goblin have been teaching me their tricks."

Scary idea, a frenetic teenager with their skills and their lunatic lack of responsibility. "That might well be. You might be a god. But I didn't tell you to handle it. I told you to go get Goblin. So move it."

Red anger flooded his face but he went. If I had been his mother, he would have argued until the wave of southerners rolled over us.

I walked toward the soldiers, painfully conscious that I still wore the rags I had had on since the day we sneaked out of Taglios. Nor was I equipped with anything remarkable in the way of weapons. I carried a stubby little sword that never had been much use for anything but chopping wood. I was always at my best as the kind of soldier who stands off at a distance and plinks the enemy when he is not looking.

I found a suitable spot and waited, arms crossed.

61

No grand effort had been made to train these troops or clothe them well. Which reflected the Protector's disdain for petty detail. What threat could the fledgling Taglian empire possibly face out here at the edge of beyond, anyway? There were no threats from beyond the borders.

The officer leading the pack was overweight, which also told me something about the local military. Peace had persisted for a decade but times were not yet so favorable that this country could support many fat men.

Huffing and puffing, the officer could not speak first. I told him, "Thank you for coming. It shows initiative and a mind capable of recognizing the inevitable swiftly. Have your men stack their weapons over there. Assuming everything goes the way it should, we'll be able to let them go home in two or three days."

The officer gulped some more air while he strove to understand what he was hearing. Evidently this little person had some mad notion that she had the upper hand. Though he had no way of telling if I was he, she or it.

I allowed the rags at my throat to fall open long enough for him to see the Black Company medallion I wore as a pendant on a silver chain. "Water sleeps," I told him, sure rumor had had plenty of time to carry that slogan to the ends of the empire.

Though I failed to intimidate him into ordering his men to disarm instantly, I did buy a few moments for the rest of the gang to gather. And a grim-looking band of cutthroats they were. Goblin and Tobo came down to stand beside me. Sahra shouted at her son from somewhere behind us but he ignored her. He had decided he was one of the big boys now and that stinking Goblin kept encouraging his fantasies.

I said, "I suggest you disarm. What's your name? What's your rank? If you don't get rid of the weapons, a lot of people will get hurt and most of them are going to be you. It doesn't have to be that way. If you cooperate."

The fat young man gulped air. I do not know what he had expected. This was not it. I was not it. I expect he was used to bullying refugees too battered by fate to even consider resisting another humiliation.

Goblin cackled. "Here's your chance, kid. Show us what you got."

"Here's one I've been practicing when nobody was around." Tobo kept on talking but in a whisper so soft I could not make out the words. In a few seconds I did not care about the words, anyway. Tobo began turning into something that was no gangly teenage boy. Tobo began turning into something I did not want to be around.

The kid was a shapeshifter? Impossible. That stuff took ages to master.

At first I thought he was going to become some mythical being, a troll, an ogre, or some misshapen and befanged creature still essentially human in shape, but he went on to become something insectoid, mantislike but big and really ugly and really smelly and getting bigger and uglier and smellier by the second.

I realized I did not smell so good myself. Which is usually a clue that you smell pretty awful to those around you, since you are not normally aware of your own odor.

Like most of what you saw from his teachers, Tobo was presenting an illusion, not undergoing a true transformation. But the southerners did not know that.

I was part of an illusion of my own. Goblin's huge grin told me who was behind the little practical joke, too. He was not too far over the top with it, either, so I might not have noticed had I not been alerted by what was happening with Tobo.

I seemed to be becoming some more-traditional nightmare. Something like what you might expect to see if for generations they had been saying that the Black Company was made up of guys who ate their own young when they could not roast yours.

"Have your men stack their weapons. Before this gets out of hand."

Tobo made a clacking noise with his mouth parts. He sidled forward, rotating his bug head oddly as he considered where to start munching. The officer seemed to understand instinctively that predators take the fat ones first. He discarded his weapons where he stood, having no inclination to get any closer to Tobo.

I said, "Men, you might help these fellows dispose of their tools." My own people were as stunned as the native soldiers were. I was stunned myself but remained plenty scared enough to take advantage while we retained the upper hand psychologically. I went around to the other side of the soldiers, putting them between horrors. Horrors they were not yet sure were entirely illusions. Sorcerers conjured some pretty nasty creatures sometimes. Or so I have heard.

That must be true. My brothers had told me about the ones they had seen. The Annals told me about more.

The southerners began to give up their weapons. Spiff or Wart or somebody remembered to make them lie down on their bellies. Once a handful got it started, the rest found themselves short on the will to resist, too.

Sahra could not hold back anymore. She tied into Goblin. "What are you doing to my son, you crazy old man! I told you I don't want him playing with—"

A *Ssss!* and a *Clack!* erupted from Tobo. A claw on the tip of a very long limb snipped at Sahra's nose.

The kid was going to be sorry about that stunt later.

Uncle Doj hustled up. "Not now, Sahra. Not here." He pulled her away. His grip evidently caused her considerable distress. Her anger did not subside but her voice did. The last thing I heard her say was something unflattering about her grandmother, Hong Tray.

I said, "Goblin, enough with the show. I can't talk to this man if I look like a rakshasa's mother."

"It ain't me, Sleepy. I'm just here to watch. Take it up with Tobo." He sounded as innocent as a baby.

Tobo was preoccupied, having altogether too much fun playing the scary monster. I told Goblin, "You're going to be teaching him that stuff, you'd better put some time into getting across the concept of self-discipline, too. Not to mention, you need to teach him not to bullshit people. I know who's doing what to whom here, Goblin. Stop it."

I was not disappointed to discover that Tobo had some talent. It was almost inevitable, actually. It was in his blood. What troubled me was the time of life when Goblin and, presumably, One-Eye had chosen to lure his talent into the open. In my opinion, Tobo was at exactly the wrong age to become all-powerful. If no one controlled him while he learned to rule himself, he could become another perpetual adolescent chaotic like Soulcatcher.

"All part of the program, Sleepy. But you need to understand that he's already more mature and more responsible than you or his mother want to admit. He's not a baby. You have to remember that most of what you see in him is him showing you what he thinks you expect to see. He's a good kid, Sleepy. He'll be all right if you and Sahra don't mother him to death. And right now he's at an age when you have to back off and let him stub his toes or regret it later."

"Child-rearing advice from a bachelor?"

"Even a bachelor can be smart enough to know when the child-rearing part is over. Sleepy, this boy has a big, hybrid talent. Be good to him. He's the future of the Black Company. And that's what that old Nyueng Bao granny woman foresaw when she first saw Murgen and Sahra together, back during the siege."

"Marvelous reasoning, old man. And your choice of time to bring that to my attention is typically, impeccably inconvenient. I've got fifty prisoners to deal with. I've got a pudgy little new boyfriend here and I need to convince him that he ought to help me talk his fellow captains into cooperating with us. What I don't have is time to deal with the difficult side of Tobo's adolescence. Pay attention. In case you haven't noticed, we're no longer a secret. The Kiaulune wars have started up again. I wouldn't be surprised if Soulcatcher herself didn't turn up someday. Now get me out of this imaginary ugly suit so I can do whatever I have to do."

"Oh, you're so forceful!" Goblin made the illusion go away. He made the one surrounding the boy fade, too. Tobo seemed surprised that he could be overruled so easily, but the little wizard softened the blow to his ego by immediately engaging him in a technical critique of what he had accomplished.

I was impressed by what I had seen. But Tobo as the future of the Company? That made me real uncomfortable, despite its questionable reassurance that the Company did have a future.

62

I stirred the fat officer with a toe. "Come on. Hop up here. We need to talk. Spiff, let the rest of these people sit up as soon as their weapons are cleared away. I'll probably let them go home in a little while. Goblin, you want to go face the music with Sahra? Get that out of the way so it isn't just waiting for a bad time to blow up on us?"

The fat officer got his feet under him. He looked very, very unhappy, which I could understand. This was not his best day. I took hold of his arm. "Let's you and me take a walk."

"You're a woman."

"Don't let it go to your head. Do you have a name? How about a rank or title?"

He offered a regional name about a paragraph long, filled with the unmanageable clicks that mess up a language otherwise already unfit for the normal human tongue. As proof of my assertion, I offer my inability to manage it at much more than a pidgin level despite having spent years in the area.

I picked out what sounded like it identified his personal place in the genealogy of a nation. "I can call you Suvrin, then?" He winced. I got it after a moment. Suvrin was a diminutive. No doubt he had not been called that by anyone but his mother for twenty years.

Oh, well. I had a sword. He did not.

"Suvrin, you've probably heard rumors to the effect that we're not nice people. I want to put your mind at ease. Everything you've ever heard is true. But this time we're not here to loot and pillage and rape the livestock the way we did last time. We're really just passing through, we hope with minimal dislocation for everybody, both us and you. What I need from you, assuming you'd rather cooperate than lie in a grave being walked on by some replacement who will, is a bit of official assistance aimed at hurrying us on our way. Have I been going too fast for you?"

"No. I speak your language well."

"That's not what I—never mind. Here's what's happening. We're going to go up on the glittering plain—"

"Why?" Pure fear filled his voice. He and his ancestors had lived in terror of the plain since the coming of the Shadowmasters.

I offered a bit of nonsense. "For the same reason the chicken crossed the road. To get to the other side."

Suvrin found that concept so novel he could think of no response.

I continued, "It'll take us a while to get ready. We have to assemble provisions and equipment. We have to scout some things.

And not all of our people have arrived yet. I'd just as soon not fight a war at the same time. So I want you to tell me how to avoid that."

Suvrin offered an inarticulate grumble.

"What's that?"

"I never wanted to be in the army. My father's doing. He wanted me away from the family, someplace where I couldn't embarrass him, but he also wanted me doing something he felt to be in keeping with the family dignity. He thought if I was a soldier, there'd be nothing I could mess up. We had no enemies who could embarrass me."

"Stuff happens. Your father should know that. He's lived long enough to have a grown-up son."

"You don't know my father."

"You might be surprised. I've met plenty just like him. Probably some that were way worse. There's nothing new in this world, Suvrin. And that includes all kinds of people. How many more soldiers are there around here? How many all told on this side of the mountains? Do any of them have any special loyalty to Taglios? Will they abandon Taglios if the pass is closed?" The Territories south of the Dandha Presh were vast but weak. Longshadow had exploited them mercilessly for more than a generation, then the Shadowmaster and Kiaulune wars had devastated them.

"Uh . . ." He wriggled but not hard. Just enough to satisfy his self-image.

We spent the remainder of the day together. Suvrin made the transitions from grudging prisoner to nervous accomplice to helpful ally. He was easily led, overresponding to modest praise and expressions of gratitude. My guess was that he had not had many nice things said to him during his young life. And he was scared to death that I would demolish him the instant he did fail to cooperate.

We sent the rest of the soldiers home as soon as our men stripped the New Town armory. Most of the weapons stored there looked like they had been picked up off old battlefields and treated with contempt ever since by the armorer whose work I had so much admired earlier.

I found the man and drafted him. He was a prima donna, a master with an artist's attitude. I figured One-Eye could tame him.

Suvrin accompanied me when I went across to the farm Sahra had acquired. Poor leader though he was, Suvrin really was in charge of all the armed forces in the Kiaulune region. Which said very little for the quality of his men or for the wisdom and commitment of his superiors. But I decided to keep him handy. He was useful as a symbol, if nothing else.

When I went across I insisted that everyone else make the move, too. I wanted everyone not out on picket duty or patrol in one place so we could respond quickly, in strength, to any threat.

I told Suvrin, "I've neutralized the whole province except for that little fort below the Shadowgate. Right?" That stronghold had sealed its gate. The men inside would not respond to the messenger I sent.

Suvrin nodded. He was having second thoughts, too late.

"Will they leave if you tell them to go?"

"No. They're foreigners. Left by the Great General to keep the road to the Shadowgate closed."

"How many?"

"Fourteen."

"Good soldiers?"

Embarrassed, "Much better than mine." Which might only mean that they could march in step.

"Tell me about their fort. How are they set for water and provisions?"

The fat man hemmed and hawed.

"Suvrin, Suvrin. You have to think about this."

"Uh . . ."

"You can't get in any deeper than you already are. You can only do your best to get back out. Too many people have seen you cooperating already. I'm sorry, buddy. You're stuck." I fought sliding into the character of Vajra the Naga, seductive as it was. It was so blessedly useful.

Suvrin made a sound suspiciously like a whimper.

"Courage, Cousin Suvrin. We live with it every day. All you can do is put on a death's-head grin and tug on their beards and yank out their tail feathers. Here we go. This looks like the place." A poorly built structure had loomed out of the darkness. Light leaked out through the roof and walls both. I wondered why they bothered. Maybe it was still under construction. I could make out the vague shapes of tents beyond it.

Something stirred on the rooftree as I pulled the door hanging aside so Suvrin could enter. The white crow. A soft chuckle came from the bird. "Sister, sister. Taglios begins to waken." The thing took wing. I watched it fade in the light of a rising fragment of moon. That had been pretty clear.

I shrugged and went inside. I could worry about the white crow next week, once I finally got a chance to go to bed. "Are any of you guys aware that we're at war? That under similar circumstances every army since the dawn of time has put out sentries to watch for people sneaking up?"

Several dozen faces watched me blandly. Goblin asked, "You didn't see anybody?"

"There's nothing out there to see, old man."

"Ah. And you got here alive, too." Which remark left me to understand that there were dire traps out there, held in abeyance only by the alert decision-making of sentries I not only overlooked but whose presence I never suspected.

"All I can say to that is, somebody must have taken a bath sometime since the turn of the century." The same could not be said for most of the crowd inside that shelter. Which might be the reason the roof and walls were so porous. "This is my new friend Suvrin. He was the captain of the local garrison. I blew in his ear and he decided he wanted to help us so we would go away before the Protector shows up and makes life tough for everybody."

Somebody in back said, "You could blow in mine and—ow! What the fuck you hit me for, Willow?"

Vajra the Naga said, "Knock it off. Swan, keep your hands to yourself. Vigan, I don't want to hear your mouth again. You should know better. What've you guys done to get ready to knock over that tower over by the Shadowgate?"

Nobody said a word.

"You guys obviously did something while you were waiting around." I gestured at our surroundings. "You managed to build a house. Badly. Or a barracks. But you didn't do anything else? There're no scouts out? No planning got done? No preparations got made? Was there something going on that I haven't heard about yet?"

Goblin sidled up. In an uncharacteristic tone he murmured, "Don't press these issues. Now isn't the time. Just tell people what to do and send them out to do it."

I trust the little wizard's wisdom occasionally. "Sit down. Here's what we'll do. Dig out whatever fireball launchers we have left. Vigan, pick ten men. Carry the heaviest launcher yourself. The others can carry lighter ones. If there aren't enough to go around, bring bows. We'll go take care of this right now. Vigan, choose your team."

The man who had made the mistake of irritating me rose. In a surly tone he named his helpers. Chances were all of them had irritated him sometime recently. It rolls downhill.

In the few minutes it took Vigan to get ready, I had the others tell me things they thought I ought to know.

63

I had the men encircle the little fort. We carried torches and made no effort to sneak. Per instructions, Vigan carried the heaviest piece of bamboo. It had an interior diameter of three inches. He told me, "There's supposed to be only a couple, three balls left in this one."

"That ought to be enough. Right here should be fine." A good archer with a strong bow might cause us trouble but those were exceeding rare in modern Taglian armies. Mogaba was a warrior. He believed real men got in close, where they could get splattered with each other's blood when they fought. It was a blind spot we had exploited more than once during the Kiaulune wars and would exploit again until he figured it out.

Goblin shuffled into position behind us. Tobo did, too. They said nothing, which must have been a trial for the boy. He talked in his sleep.

"What do I do?" Vigan asked.

"Let them have one. Through the stonework right above the gate." Louder, I said, "Stand fast. Nobody do anything until I tell you."

The first two times Vigan turned his hand release crank, nothing happened.

"Is it empty?" I asked.

"It's not supposed to be."

Goblin advised, "Try again, then. It's been over ten years since it was used. Maybe it just needs to be loosened up."

I mused, "I'll bet nobody's bothered to keep the mechanism clean. And you folks wondered why I wanted to hire an armorer. Go ahead. Crank it again. Carefully, so you don't lose your aim."

Whack! Crackle-crackle-crackle-sizzle! into the distance. The fireball ripped right through the little fortification's two outside walls and whatever lay between them. Stone steamed and ran. The scarlet ball wobbled through the air for several miles more, gave up the last of its momentum, gradually darkened as it drifted to earth beyond the ruins of Overlook.

"Move to the left a few yards, drop your aiming point five feet, then do it again."

Vigan was having fun now. There was a bounce to his step as he moved to his new position. This time it took only one extra turn of the crank to get the fireball launched.

A blistering, lime-colored ball ripped through the fortification. It hit something significant inside. It had almost no energy left when it appeared on the far side.

A gout of steam blew out the top of the tower. "Must've gotten a water barrel," I said. Water and the fireballs made a wicked combination resulting in storms of superheated steam. "Suvrin, where are you?" Two fireballs should have gotten their attention inside, should have gotten the survivors to thinking. Now I could begin placing my shots. "Suvrin! Have you ever been inside that rockpile?"

The fat man came forward reluctantly. When he was close by me, his face was in the light. The garrison inside would remember him. He wanted to lie to me, too, I could see. But he did not have the courage. "Yes."

"What's the layout? It doesn't look like it could be that complicated."

"It isn't. Animals and storage on the ground floor. They can pile up stuff behind the gate so you can't knock it in. They live on the second floor. It's just one big room. There's a stove for cooking and pallets for sleeping and racks of weapons and that's about it."

"And the roof is basically just a fighting platform, right? Wait a minute, Vigan. Don't spend any more fireballs than we have to. Let them think for a while now. Maybe they'll give up. They know I didn't hurt Suvrin's men. Tobo, circle around and tell all the men that if they have to launch a fireball, we need it to go through the second level. Preferably low. They'll probably get down on the floor when death starts coming through."

"Can I shoot one of those things, Sleepy?"

"Get the message out first." I watched him scoot off. He did not expose himself unnecessarily. Faces could be seen occasionally behind the archers' embrasures over yonder. A couple of arrows had come out and fallen harmlessly. I told Goblin, "If anybody had been paying attention, we'd have the place mapped down to the last cot and table and we'd know exactly where to aim every fireball to get the best effect."

"You're absolutely right again. Just as you always are. Be quiet for a second. There's something going on here. Those men aren't as scared as they should be."

As he spoke, I glimpsed a face peeking over the parapet. A moment later the white crow plummeted out of the night. It knocked the leather helmet off the soldier.

I yelled, "Everybody wake up! They're about to pull something!"

Goblin had started muttering already. He was doing something odd with his fingers.

Men jumped up atop the little fort. Each had something in hand, ready to throw. A half-dozen fireballs squirted their way without my approval. One grenadier went down but not before he launched his missile.

Glass, I saw. Same type One-Eye had used to make firebombs, years ago. We still had a few of those, too. But throwing firebombs at us out here would be pointless. We were too far away to be reached.

"Aim low!" I yelled. "Shadows coming!" That was not a shout that had been heard for an age but it was one the veterans remembered and could respond to without ever thinking.

Goblin was already wobbling across the slope in as near a sprint as his old bones could manage, still muttering and wiggling his fingers. Pink sparks leaped between his fingers and slithered around amongst his few remaining hairs. He grabbed a skinny little bamboo pole from one of the men. It had been painted with black stripes, meaning that its dedicated purpose was use against shadows.

Fireballs flew. Some peppered the fortress. Some dove after the shadows that spilled out of the breaking glass containers. Suvrin began whimpering behind me. I told him, "Don't run. They'll get you for sure. They love a fleeing victim."

There was a lot of screaming inside the fortress. Fireballs streaking through had found human targets. In their way, the fireballs were almost as bad as the killing shadows.

One of my men began shrieking when a shadow found him. But he was the only one. Goblin's spell helped some. The quick use of fireballs helped more.

Goblin began loosing fireballs from the pole he had snagged but sent them racing northward instead of toward the stubborn little fort. He quit after only a few tries. He came back to me. "They've done their job, those brave boys in there. They got their warning away." He was as sour as a lemon slice under the tongue.

"So I take it Soulcatcher didn't die when she hit the water." I had heard the news from Taglios only up to the part where the Protector's carpet had fallen apart in midair, with her streaking along four hundred feet above the river. The break coming at that point had not been because anyone was trying to make things particularly dramatic, it was just because there was too much going on to have a lot of time left for catching up. Especially where Murgen was concerned. Murgen seemed to be employed full time easing Sahra's frights and concerns.

"She was one of the Ten Who Were Taken, Sleepy. Those people don't hurt easy. Hell, she survived having her head cut off. She carried it around in a box for about fifteen years."

I grunted. Sometimes it was hard to remember that Soulcatcher was much more than just an unpleasant, distant senior official. "They likely to have any more surprises in there?" I meant the question for Suvrin but Goblin answered.

"If they did, they would've used them. You thinking about going in after them?"

"Oh, heck no! Somebody might get hurt. Somebody besides them. Suvrin, go over there and tell them if they surrender in the next half hour, I'll let them go. If they don't, I'll kill them all before the hour is up."

The fat man started to protest. Vigan poked his behind with the tip of a dagger. I told Suvrin, "If they do anything to you, I'll avenge you."

"That's a big weight off my heart."

Goblin asked, "How are you going to avenge anybody? Considering you're not going to go in there after them."

"That's what we have wizards for. This looks like a wonderful opportunity for you to give Tobo some on-the-job training."

"Am I surprised? Not hardly. For a hundred years it's been, 'What do we do now?' 'I don't know. Let's let Goblin handle it.' I oughta just take a hike and let you figure it out for yourself."

"I'm tired. I'm going to sit down here and rest my eyes until Suvrin gets back."

I heard Goblin tell Vigan to put another heavyweight fireball into the corner of the fortification, along the length of the wall so all its energy would be spent devouring the pale limestone. There was a solid *thump!* swiftly followed by the smell of superheated limestone. As I drifted away, Goblin muttered something about burning them out.

64

T he surface of the river was not friendly when Soulcatcher hit it but neither was the impact like hitting stone from the same altitude. Her fall had been long enough to allow her time to prepare for the landing.

Even so, the collision was brutal enough to extract her consciousness temporarily. But she had prepared for that, too, between curses. When consciousness returned she was drifting downriver with the flood, head above the surface. It being the rainy season, the river was high and the current brisk. It took a great effort to complete the swim to the south bank. By the time she crawled out of the flood and collapsed, she was a half-dozen miles downstream from where she had gone in, which was outside the city proper, in a domain best known for its jackals, of both the two- and four-legged varieties. It was said that leopards still hunted there at night, the occasional crocodile could be found along the shore, and it was not that many years since a tiger had come visiting from down the river.

The Protector experienced no difficulties with any mad or hungry thing. A hundred crows perched around her, standing guard. Others flapped about in the darkness until squadrons of bats had gathered. Birds and bats together discouraged the scavengers and predators till Soulcatcher awakened and in a fit of pique, sent an entire band of jackals racing away with their pelts aflame.

She stumbled toward home, regaining strength slowly, muttering about growing old and less resilient. A tremor entered the voice she chose to inveigh against the predations of time.

Eventually she reached the home of a moneylender, where she commandeered transportation back to the Palace. She arrived there somewhat after the breakfast hour in a temper so foul that the entire staff made a point of becoming invisible. Only the Great General came to inquire after her well-being. And he went away when she started snarling and snapping.

Though she reveled in her paranoia, Soulcatcher did not suspect that her accident had been anything else until she examined her remaining carpet preparatory to another effort to fly off to entertain the Nyueng Bao. Then she discovered that the light wooden-frame members on which the carpet was stretched had been weakened by strategic saw cuts.

The who and probable why became clear within seconds. She sent out a summons to Jaul Barundandi and his associates.

Surprise. Barundandi was nowhere to be found. He had been called out of the Palace for a family emergency, he had said, just moments after her return. So the Greys reported when told to investigate.

"What an amazing coincidence. Find him. Find the men he worked with regularly. We have a great deal to discuss."

Greys scattered. One bold captain, however, remained behind to report, "Rumor in the city says the Bhodi intend to resume their self-immolations. They want the Radisha to come out and address their concerns personally."

The news did not improve Soulcatcher's temper. "Ask them if they would like me to donate the naphtha they need. I'm feeling particularly charitable today. Also ask them if they can hold off starting long enough for the carpenters to put up grandstands so more of the Radisha's good subjects can enjoy the entertainment. I don't care what those lunatics do. Get out of here! Find that Barundandi slug!" The voice she used was informed with a potent lunacy.

Jaul Barundandi's luck was mixed. He managed to avoid the attentions of the bats and crows and shadows the Protector released when the Greys had no immediate success in locating him, but an informer eventually betrayed him when the reward for his capture grew large enough. The lie was that he had attacked and severely wounded the Radisha, that only the Protector's swift intercession with her most powerful sorcery had saved the Princess's life. The Radisha's situation remained grave.

The Taglian people loved their Radisha. Jaul Barundandi discovered that he had no friends but his accomplices and it was one of those who betrayed him in exchange for a partial reward (the Grey officers pocketing the bulk) and a running start.

Jaul Barundandi suffered terrible torments and tried hard to cooperate so the pain would stop but he could tell the Protector nothing that she wanted to know. So she had him put into a cage and hung fifteen feet above the place where the Bhodi disciples generally chose to give up their lives and issued a rescript encouraging passersby to throw stones. It was her intent that he hang there indefinitely, his suffering neverending, but sometime during the first night, somehow, someone managed to toss him a piece of poisoned fruit while leaving his betrayer and a murdered Grey below, each with a piece of paper in his mouth bearing the characters for "Water Sleeps." Crows savaged both corpses before they were discovered.

It was the last time Black Company tokens would be seen but their appearance was sufficient to provoke the Protector almost beyond reason. For days the still-loyal remnants of the Greys remained extremely busy making arrests, most of them of people unable to guess what they had done to irk Soulcatcher.

She never did get to the Nyueng Bao swamp despite having made necessary repairs to her remaining carpet. Taglios became more fractious by the hour. She had to devote her entire attention to keeping the city tamed.

Then came the faithful and tattered little shadow that had made its way through mountains and forests, over lakes and rivers and plains, in order to bring her news of what was happening in the nethermost south.

Soulcatcher screamed a scream of rage so potent that the entire city became informed of it instantly. Immigrants began to rehearse the wisdom of a return to the provinces.

The Great General and two of his staff officers broke through the door to the Protector's apartment, certain she needed rescuing. Instead, they found her pacing furiously and debating herself in half a dozen voices. "They have the Key. They must have the Key. They

must have murdered the Deceiver. Maybe they made an alliance
with Kina. Why would they go down there? Why would they go onto
the plain after what happened to the last group? What keeps pulling
them out there? I've read their Annals. There's nothing in those.
What do they know? The Land of Unknown Shadows? They cannot
have developed an entirely new and independent oral tradition
since they served me in the north. If it's important one of them will
record it. Why? Why? What do they know that I don't?"

Soulcatcher became aware of Mogaba and his men. The latter
looked around nervously, trying to figure out where the voices were
coming from. When Soulcatcher became excited, those seemed to
come from everywhere at once.

"You. Have you caught me any terrorists yet?"

"No. Nor shall I unless an angry family member comes forward
because he thinks it would be a good way to get even. There won't
be more than a handful left here and those probably don't know each
other. I gather, from what I overheard, that they've gone back to
Shadowcatch." He had worked for the Shadowmaster Longshadow.
He could not get out of the habit of calling Kiaulune by the name
given it by his previous employer.

"Exactly. We're back where we were fifteen years ago. Only now
they have the Radisha and the Key." Her tone left no doubt she
placed the blame entirely on him.

Mogaba was not bothered. Not immediately. He was accustomed
to being blamed for the shortcomings of others and he did not believe the remnants of the Black Company could offer any real threat
any time soon. They had been beaten down too thoroughly and had
been away from it too long. They were more military than the Deceivers only inside their own fantasies. Even the comic-opera functionaries down there ought to be able to wear them down and bury
them eventually. They would find no aid or sympathy in the Shadowlands. The people down there really did remember the Black
Company's last visit. "The Key? What is that?"

"A means of passing through the Shadowgate unharmed. A talisman that makes it possible to travel on the plain." Her voice had
become pedantic. Now it became angry. "I possessed that talisman at
one time. Long ago I used it to go up there and explore. Longshadow
would have been unmanned had he known. More unmanned than
the eunuch he already was. But it disappeared in the early excite-

ment around Kiaulune. I suspect that Kina clouded my mind while the Deceiver Singh stole both it and my sister's darling daughter. I can't imagine why that rabble would want to go onto the plain after the previous disaster but if it's something they want to do, it's something I want to prevent. Prepare for a journey."

"We can't leave Taglios unsupervised for as long as it would take us to travel all the way to Shadowcatch. We don't have the stallion anymore, even if it could carry double."

Soulcatcher was baffled. "What?"

"The black stallion from the north. The one I've been using all these years. It's vanished. It broke down its stall and ran off. I told you that last month." She did not recall that, obviously.

"We'll fly."

"But—" Mogaba hated flying. In the days when he had been Longshadow's general he had had to fly with the Howler almost daily. He still loathed those times. "I thought the larger carpet was the one that was destroyed."

"The small one will carry both of us. It'll be hard work. I'll have to rest a lot. But we'll still be able to get down there and back before these people know we're gone and try to take advantage. A week for the round trip. Ten days at the outside."

The Great General had a few dozen reservations but kept them behind his teeth. The Protector was worse than Longshadow had been about suffering opinions she did not want to hear.

Soulcatcher said, "We'll adopt disguises once we get there and go among them. I want you to keep an eye out for a hammer, so by so, made of cast iron but far heavier than it ought to be."

Mogaba bowed slightly. He said nothing about how difficult it would be for either of them to blend in with the crowd they would be chasing.

Soulcatcher told him, "Prepare your men. They'll have to keep Taglios under control for a couple of weeks."

Mogaba withdrew, saying nothing about the proposed time changing already. In his position it was necessary to do a lot of saying nothing.

The Protector watched him go, amused. He did not conceal his thinking nearly as well as he believed. But she was ancient in her wickedness and had studied the dark side of humanity so thoroughly that she could almost read minds.

65

The little fortress settled in upon itself slowly, as though made of wax only slightly overheated. As soon as I fell asleep and could not interfere, Goblin handed the magical siege work over to Tobo, who did a creditable job of rooting the enemy survivors out of their shelter. The wicked little thing had been taking lessons a lot longer than he and his teachers would admit.

The garrison was bringing out its dead and wounded when a shout awakened me. I sat up. Morning had begun to arrive. And the world had changed.

"What's Spiff's problem?" I asked.

One of my veterans had recognized one of theirs.

The devil himself arrived to explain. "The guy in charge. That's Khusavir Pete, Sleepy. You remember, we thought he was killed when the Bahrata Battalion got wiped out in the ambush at Kushkhoshi."

"I remember." And I recalled something that Spiff did not know, a fact I shared only with Murgen, who had been the ghost in the rushes while the slaughter was taking place. Khusavir Pete, at that time a sworn brother of the Company, had led our largest surviving force of allies into a trap that efficiently took us out of the Kiaulune wars. Khusavir Pete had cut a deal. Khusavir Pete had betrayed his own brothers. Khusavir Pete was high on my list of people I wanted to meet again, though until just now I had been the only one who knew that he had survived and that his treachery had been rewarded with a high post, money and a new name. But just seeing him had some of the men figuring it out fast.

"You should've asked her to change your face, too," I told him when they flung him down bleeding in front of me. "Though you've had a better run than you probably expected when she turned you." I held his eyes with mine. What he saw convinced him it would not be worth his trouble to deny anything. Vajra the Naga had come out to play.

More and more of the men gathered around, most of them not getting it until I explained how Khusavir Pete had been seduced by Soulcatcher into betraying and helping destroy more than five hundred of our brothers and allies. Would-be greetings quickly became imaginative suggestions of ways whereby we might reduce the traitor's life expectancy. I let the man listen until some of the troops tried to lay hands on. Then I told Goblin, "Hide him somewhere. We may have a use for him yet."

The excitement was over. I had indulged in a decent meal. My attitude much improved, I took the opportunity to renew my acquaintance with Master Surendranath Santaraksita. "This life seems to agree with you," I told him as I arrived. "You look better now than you did when we left the city." And that was true.

"Dorabee? Lad, I thought you were dead. Despite their endless assurances." He leaned closer and confided, "They aren't all honest men, your comrades."

"By some chance did Goblin and One-Eye offer to teach you to play tonk?"

The librarian managed to look a little sheepish.

"Not to play with them is a lesson everyone has to learn."

Sheepishness transformed into impishness. "I think I taught them a little something, too. Card tricks were one of my hobbies when I was younger."

I had to laugh at the idea of those two villains getting taken themselves. "Have you discovered anything that would be useful to me?"

"I've read every word in every book we brought along, including all of your company's modern chronicles written in languages known to me. I found nothing remarkable. I have been amusing myself by trying to work backward into the chronicles I can't read by comparing materials repeated in more than one language."

Murgen had done a lot of that. He had had a thing about copying stuff over, in cleaner drafts, and one of his great projects had been to revise Lady's and the Captain's Annals for accuracy, based on evidence provided by other witnesses, while rendering them into modern Taglian. We have all done that to our predecessors, some, so that every recent volume of the Annals is really an unwilling collaboration.

I said, "We drag a lot of books around, don't we?"

"Like snails, carrying your history on your back."

"It's who we are. Cute image, though. Doesn't all that study get dull after a while?"

"The boy keeps me sharp."

"Boy?"

"Tobo. He's a brilliant student. Even more amazing than you were."

"Tobo?"

"I know. Who would expect it of a Nyueng Bao? You're destroying all my preconceptions, Dorabee."

"Mine are taking a beating, too." Tobo? Either Santaraksita had an unsuspected talent for inspiring students or Tobo had suffered an epiphany and had become miraculously motivated. "You sure it's Tobo and not a changeling?"

The demon himself popped in. "Sleepy. Runmust and River-walker and them are on their way over. Good morning, Master Santaraksita." Tobo actually seemed excited to be there. "I don't have any other duties right now. Oh, Sleepy, Dad wants to talk to you."

"Where?" Things had been happening too fast. There had been no chance to catch up with Murgen.

"Goblin's tent. Everybody but Mom thought that would be the safest place to keep him."

I had no trouble picturing Sahra being irritated about not being able to share the occasional private moment with her husband.

When I ducked out, the young man and the old were already settling with a book. I glared a warning at Santaraksita which, it developed, was both wasted and unnecessary.

Goblin was not home. Of course not. He was working his way through a long list of jobs bestowed upon him by me. Chuckle.

I found it hard to credit the possibility that one human being could make so huge a mess in a space so constricted. The inside of Goblin's tent was barely wider than either of us was tall and twice as deep. At its peak it was tall enough for me to stand up with two inches to spare. What looked like a milkmaid's stool, undoubtedly stolen, constituted the wizard's entire suite of furniture. A ragged burrow of blankets betrayed where he slept. The rest of the space was occupied by a random jumble, mostly stuff that looked like it had been discarded by a procession of previous owners. There was no obvious theme to the collection.

It had to be stuff he had acquired since his arrival here. Sahra would never have allowed him space on a barge for such junk.

The mist projector stood at the head of Goblin's smelly bedding, tilted precariously, leaking water. "If this is the safest place to keep that darned thing, then the whole Company is mad with delusions of adequacy."

A whisper came from the mist projector. I got down close to it, which offered me an opportunity to become intimately aware of the aroma permanently associated with Goblin's bedding, some pieces of which must have been with him since he was in diapers. "What?"

Murgen's strongest effort was barely audible. "More water. You need to add more water or there won't be any mist much longer."

I started to drag the evidence out of the tent.

Anger gave Murgen a little more voice. "No, dammit! Bring the water to me, don't take me to the water. If you suffer from a compulsion to drag me around, at least wait until after you water me. And don't waste time. I'm going to lose my anchor here in a few minutes."

Finding a gallon of water turned out to be a challenging experience.

"What took you so damned long?"

"Bit of an adventure coming up with the water. Seems it never occurred to any of these morons that we need to have some handy somewhere. Just in case the royal army decides to camp between us and the creek where we've been getting it, which is almost a mile away. I just unleashed several geniuses on the problem. How am I supposed to put this in here?"

"There's a cork in the rear. It might be of some use to you to start doing readings from the Annals. Like they do in temples. The way I used to do sometimes. Pick something situationally appropriate. 'In those days the Company was in service' and so on, so they have examples of why it might be useful to haul water up the hill before you have to use it, and such like. These are grown men. You can't just bully them into doing the right things. But if you start reading to them, they'll have heard tell of other times when the Annalist did that and they'll recall it was always right before the big shitstorm moved in. You'll get their attention."

"Tobo said you want to talk to me."

"I need to catch you up on what's going on elsewhere. And I want to make suggestions about your preparations for the plain, one of which is to listen to Willow Swan but the most critical of which is, you're going to have to upgrade discipline. The plain is deadly. Even worse than the Plain of Fear, which you don't remember. You can't ignore the rules and stay alive there. One idea would be for you not to burn or bury the man who was killed by the shadow last night. Make every survivor look at him and think about what *will* happen to all of you if even one of you screws up up there. Read them the passages chronicling our adventures. Have Swan bear witness."

"I could just bring a handful of reliables in to get you."

"You could. But the rest of the world wouldn't be very nice to the men you leave behind. Right now there's a shadow heading north to tell Soulcatcher where you are. She may know enough already to figure out what you're trying to do. She definitely doesn't want her sister and Croaker on the loose and nursing a grudge. She'll get here as fast as she can. And aside from Soulcatcher, there's Narayan Singh. He retains Kina's countenance, so he's extremely hard to trace but I do catch glimpses occasionally. He's on this side of the Dandha Presh and he's probably not far away. He wants to recapture the Daughter of Night and reunite her with the book you traded for the Key. Which, by the way, you should take away from Uncle Doj before he becomes overly tempted to try something on his own. And so Goblin can study it."

"Uhm?" He was a gush of information this morning, all of it carefully rehearsed.

"There's more to the Key than you see right away. I have a feeling the Deceiver overlooked something. Doj keeps picking at it, trying to find out what's inside the iron. We should find out more about it before we trust it. And we need to find out fast. It won't be all that long before that shadow gets to Taglios."

"River and Runmust are coming in. They're halfway responsible people. I'll turn some of the work over to them as soon as they're rested up. Then I can worry about—"

"Worry about it now. Let Swan sergeant for you. He's experienced and he's got no choice but to throw in with us now. Catcher will never believe that he didn't betray her."

"I hadn't thought of that."

"You don't have to do everything yourself, Sleepy. If you're going to take charge, you need to learn to tell people what needs doing, then get out of the way and let them do it. You keep hanging over their shoulders nagging like somebody's mother, you aren't going to get much cooperation. You seduced that fat boy yet?"

"What?"

"That local-yokel captain. The one who couldn't keep in step if you painted his feet different colors. You got him wrapped up yet?"

"You're zigging when I'm zagging. You lost me completely."

"Let me draw you a picture. You forget to tell him Catcher is going to stop by. You get him to make a deal. He keeps his job. He helps us out so he can get us out of his hair. When he isn't looking, you fix him up so when the shitstorm starts, he don't have no choice but to take his chances with us."

"I have him wrapped up, then. Seventy percent."

"Hey. Blow in his ear. Throw a liplock on his love muscle. Do whatever you have to. If Catcher loses him, she won't ever trust anybody else down here, either."

Goblin used almost the same language as Murgen had when I stopped to visit again. He found Murgen's advice fully excellent. "Grab fat boy by his prong and never let go. Give him a little squeeze once in a while to keep him smiling."

"I've probably said it before. You're one cynical mudsucker."

"It's all those years of watching out for One-Eye that done it to me. I was a sweet, innocent young thing when I joined this outfit. Not unlike yourself."

"You were born wicked and cynical."

Goblin chuckled. "How much stuff do you think you need to collect before we go up the hill? How long do you think it'll take?"

"It won't take forever if Suvrin cooperates."

"Never, ever, forget that you don't have long. I can't emphasize that enough. Soulcatcher is coming. You've never seen her when she's all worked up."

"The Kiaulune wars don't count?" He must have seen something extreme. He was determined to pound the point home.

"The Kiaulune wars don't count. She was just entertaining herself with those."

I forced myself to make the visit I had been avoiding.

The Daughter of Night wore ankle shackles. She resided inside an iron cage heavily impregnated with spells that caused ever-

increasing agony as their victim moved farther away. She could escape but that would hurt. If she pushed it hard enough, she would
die.

It appeared that every possible step had been taken to keep her
under control. Except the lethal step reason urged me to take. I had
no more motive for keeping her alive—except that I had given my
word.

The men all took turns being exposed to her, in pairs, at meal-
times and such. Sahra had not been lax. She appreciated the danger
the girl represented.

My first glimpse left me stricken with envy. Despite her disadvantages, she had kept herself beautiful, looking much like her
mother in a fresher body. But something infinitely older and darker
looked out through her pretty blue eyes. For a moment she struck me
not as the Daughter of Night, but as the darkness itself.

She did have plenty of time to commune with her spiritual
mother.

She smiled as though aware of the serpents of dark temptation
slithering the black corridors of my mind. I wanted to bed her. I
wanted to murder her. I wanted to run away, begging for mercy. It
took an exercise of will to remind myself that Kina and her children
were not evil in the sense that northerners or even my Vehdna co-
religionists understood evil.

Nevertheless . . . she was the darkness.

I stepped back, tossed the tent flap open so my ally, daylight,
could come inside. The girl lost her smile. She backed to the far side
of her cage. I could think of nothing to say. There was really nothing
we could say to one another. I had no inclination to gloat and little
news of the world outside to report, which might motivate her to do
something besides wait.

She had her spiritual mother's patience, that was sure.

A blow from behind rocked me. I clawed at my stubby little
sword.

White wings mussed my nattily arranged hair. Talons dug into
my shoulder. The Daughter of Night stared at the white crow and revealed real emotion for the first time in a long time. Her confidence
wavered. Fear leaked through. She pressed back against the bars behind her.

"Have you two met?" I asked.

The crow said something like, "Wawk! Wiranda!"

The girl began to shake. If possible, she became even paler. Her jaw seemed clenched so tight her teeth ought to be cracking. I made a mental note to discuss this with Murgen. He knew something about the crow.

What could rattle the girl so badly?

The crow laughed. It whispered, "Sister, sister," and launched itself back into the sunlight, where it startled some passing brother into a fit of curses.

I stared at the girl, watched the inner steel reassert itself. Her gaze met mine. I felt the fear within her evaporate. I was nothing to her, less than an insect, certainly less than a stubbed toe at the beginning of her long trek across the ages.

Shuddering, I broke eye contact.

That was a scary kid.

66

Our days began before sunrise. They ended after sunset. They included a great deal of training and exercise of the sort that had been let slide for too long. Tobo worked with almost fanatic devotion to improve his skills as an illusionist. I insisted upon daily readings from the Annals in an effort to reinforce the depth and continuity of brotherhood that were so much the foundation of what the Company was. There was resistance at first, of course, but the message sank in at a pace not unrelated to a growing realization that we were going to go up onto the glittering plain—really!—or were going to die here in front of the Shadowgate when Soulcatcher chose to write our final chapter.

The renewed training paid dividends quickly. Eight days after we reduced the fort below the Shadowgate, another mob like Suvrin's, but much larger, trudged in out of the country west of the New Town. Thanks to Murgen, we had plenty of warning. With Tobo and Goblin assisting, we sprang a classic Company ambush using illusions and nuisance spells that confused and disorganized a force that had

had almost no idea what it was doing already. We hit fast and hard and mercilessly and the threat evaporated in a matter of minutes. In fact, the relief force fell apart so fast we could not take as many prisoners as I wanted, though we did round up most of the officers. Suvrin generously identified those he recognized.

Suvrin was practically an apprentice Company man by now, so desperate was he to belong to something and to gain the approval of those around him. I felt halfway guilty exploiting him the way I did.

The prisoners we did take became involuntary laborers in our preparations for the future. Most jumped on the opportunity because I promised to release those who did work hard before we went up onto the plain. Those who failed to work hard would go along as porters. Somehow a rumor got started amongst the prisoners that human sacrifice might be involved in what we were going to be doing once we passed the Shadowgate.

I found Goblin in with One-Eye, whose recovery seemed to have been sped by Gota's presence. Possibly because he needed to be well enough to get away from her and her cooking. I do not know. They had the Key laid out on a small table between them. Doj, Tobo and Gota watched. Even Mother Gota kept her mouth shut.

Sahra was conspicuously absent.

She was carrying her snit over Tobo too far. I expect there was more to it than what she admitted, though. A big part would center on her fear of the near future.

"Right there," One-Eye said just as I leaned forward to see what Goblin was doing. The little bald man had a light hammer and a chisel. He tapped the chisel. A piece of iron flipped off the Key. This had been going on for a while, evidently, because about half the iron was gone, revealing something made of gold. I was so surprised at the wizard's lack of greed that I almost forgot to worry about what they were doing to the Key.

I opened my mouth. Without looking up, One-Eye told me, "Don't shit your knickers yet, Little Girl. We ain't hurting a thing. The Key is this thing inside. This golden hammer. You want to bend down a little closer? Maybe you can read what's inscribed on it."

I bent. I scanned the characters made visible by removal of the iron. "Looks like the same alphabet as the first book of the Annals." Not to mention the first Book of the Dead. Which I did not mention.

Goblin used the tip of his chisel to indicate a prominent symbol that appeared in several places. "Doj says he saw this sign at the temple in the Grove of Doom."

"It should be there." I knew that one. Master Santaraksita had taught me its meaning. "It's the personal sign of the goddess. Her personal chop, if you want." I did not name a name. I suggested, "Don't speak the name. Not in any of its forms. In the presence of this thing, that would be guaranteed to attract her attention." Everyone stared at me. I asked, "You didn't do that already, did you? No? Uncle, you don't know what this thing might really be, do you?" I had an intuition it was something Narayan Singh might never have surrendered had he been aware that it was in his possession. I thought it might exist solely so that the priest who carried it could obtain the attention of his goddess instantly. Even in my own religion, people had had a much more immediate and scary relationship with the godhead in ancient times. The scriptures told us so. But no such golden hammer played any part in the Kina mythology, insofar as I could recall. Curious. Maybe Master Santaraksita could tell me more.

Goblin continued chipping away. I continued watching. The process went faster as each fragment fell.

"That isn't any hammer," I said. "That's a kind of pickax. It's a Deceiver cult thing. And older than dirt. It has to be something of huge religious significance." I suggested, "Show it to the girl. See how she responds."

"You're as close to a Kina expert as we've got, Sleepy. What could it be?"

"There's actually a name for that kind of tool but I can't remember what it is. Every Deceiver band had a pickax like this. Not made out of gold, though. They used them in the burial ceremonies after their murders. To break the bones of their victims so they would fold up into a smaller wad. Sometimes they used to help dig graves. All with the appropriate ceremonies aimed at pleasing Kina, of course. I really do think somebody should show this to the Daughter of Night and see what she says."

It seemed like a thousand pairs of eyes were staring at me, waiting for me to volunteer. I told them, "I'm not doing it. I'm going to bed."

All those eyes kept right on staring. I had put myself in charge. This was something nobody but the guy in charge ought to handle.

"All right. Uncle. Tobo. Goblin. You back me up on this. That child has talents we can't guess at yet." I had been warned that she still tried to walk away from her flesh at night, despite all the constraints surrounding her. She was both her mothers' daughter and there was no telling what might happen when she had to suffer too much stress.

Tobo protested. "I don't like to be around her. She gives me the creeps."

Goblin beat me to it. "Kid, she gives everybody the creeps. She's the creepiest thing I've run into in a hundred fifty years. Get used to it. Deal with it. It's part of the job. Which they say you were born to do and which you did ask for."

Curious. Goblin the mentor and instructor seemed much more articulate than Goblin the want-to-be-layabout and slacker.

The little wizard suggested, "You carry the Key. You're young and strong."

The Daughter of Night did not look up when we entered the tent. Perhaps she was not aware of us. She seemed to be meditating. Possibly communing with the Dark Mother. Goblin kicked the bars of her cage, which rattled nicely and shed a shower of rust. "Well, look at her. Cute."

"What?" I asked.

"She's been working some kind of spell on the iron. It's rusting away a thousand times faster than it ought to. Clever girl. Only—"

The clever girl looked up. Our eyes meet. Something behind hers chilled me to the bone. "Only what?" I asked.

"Only every spell holding her and controlling her has that cage for an anchor. Anything that happens to it will happen to her. Look at her skin."

I saw what he meant. The Daughter of Night was not exactly rusty herself but did look spotty and frayed at the surface.

Her gaze shifted to Uncle, Goblin, Tobo . . . and she gasped, like she was seeing the boy for the first time. She rose slowly, drifted toward the bars, gaze locked with his. Then a little frown danced across her brow. Her gaze darted down to Tobo's burden.

Her mouth opened and, I swear, a sound like the angry bellow of an elephant rolled out. Her eyes grew huge. She lunged forward. Her shackles gave way. The bars of the cage creaked and let fall another shower of rust. They bent but did not give. She thrust an arm through in a desperate effort to reach the Key. Little bits of skin blackened and fell off her. And still she was beautiful.

I observed, "I guess we can safely say the thing does hold some significance for the Deceivers."

"You could say so," Goblin admitted. The girl's whole arm had begun to look like it had been badly burned.

"So let's take it away and see what else we can find out. And get the cage reinforced and her shackles replaced. Tobo!" The boy kept staring at the girl like he was seeing *her* for the first time. "Don't tell me he just fell in love. I couldn't handle it if we had to worry about that in addition to everything else."

"No," Uncle Doj reassured me. "Not love, I think. But the future, just maybe."

Although I tried to insist, he would not expand upon that remark. He was still Uncle Doj, the mystery priest of the Nyueng Bao.

67

Things came together nicely after the defeat of the relief column. Murgen said nobody else was likely to challenge us without help from beyond the mountains. Which help, unfortunately, was on the way already. Soulcatcher was airborne and lurching southward in small, erratic leaps that, nevertheless, were bringing her closer faster than any animal could do—even one of those magical stallions from the Tower at Charm—but still definitely very feebly for a flying carpet. Once upon a time the Howler could conquer the miles between Overlook and Taglios in a single night.

Soulcatcher had to rest several hours for every hour she spent aloft. Even so, she was on her way. And the impact of the news on the troops was electric. With only days left, or possibly only hours, everyone buckled down and put their back into it. I saw very little slacking, little wasted effort, and some very serious concentration when it came to honing military skills.

Suvrin was right in there with the troops, drilling his behind off. Literally. Though he had been with us only a short time, he had be-

gun to lose weight and show signs of shaping up. He approached me
soon after Murgen and Goblin began issuing regular reports about
Soulcatcher's progress. "I want to stay with you, ma'am," he told me.

"You what?" I was surprised.

"I'm not sure I want to be part of the Black Company but I do
know for sure that I don't want to be here when the Protector shows
up. She has a reputation for seldom letting herself be swayed by the
facts. The futility of me having resisted you won't impress her."

"You're right about that. If you shirked because you would've gotten killed doing what she expected, she'll arrange it so you get dead
anyway. In a less pleasant way, if possible. All right, Suvrin. You've
kept your word and you've been a good worker."

He winced. "You understand what 'Suvrin' actually means?"

"Junior, essentially. But you're stuck with it now. Most people in
the Company don't go by their birth names. Even most of the men
who go by regular names don't go by their real ones. They're all getting away from their past. And you will be, too."

He grimaced.

"Report to Master Santaraksita. Until I find something else for
you, your job will be to assist him. Old Baladitya is no use at all. He's
worse than Santaraksita, who keeps getting farther and farther
behind in his packing because he keeps getting distracted by his
books." Santaraksita had managed to acquire several antique volumes locally that had, miraculously, survived the countless disasters
that had beset the region these past several decades.

Suvrin bowed. "Thank you." There was a fresh bounce in his step
as he walked away.

I suspected he and Master Santaraksita might have a lot in common. Heck, Suvrin could even read.

Tobo materialized. "My father says to tell you that Soulcatcher
has reached Charandaprash. And that she's decided to rest there before she crosses the Dandha Presh."

"A few more hours' grace. Excellent. Means there's a good
chance there won't be anything left here for her to find but our
tracks. How are you getting along with your mother? Did you make
any effort at all?"

"Dad also says he wants you to post somebody with a warning
horn that can be sounded once the Protector gets dangerously close.
And he says you should pull in the pickets watching the pass now,

just in case Soulcatcher changes her mind about taking some time off."

That was a good idea.

Runmust and Riverwalker made the mistake of being close enough to be seen. I sent them to go bring the scouts home. "Tobo, you can't ignore your mother. You'll end up getting along with her worse than she gets along with your grandmother."

"Sleepy . . . why can't she just let me grow up?"

"Because you're her baby, you idiot! Don't you understand that? When you're twice as old as One-Eye you'll *still* be her baby. The only baby that cruel fate hasn't gobbled down. You do remember that your mother had other children and she lost them?"

"Uh . . . yeah."

"I've never had children. I never want to have children. In part because I can see how horrible it would be to see my own flesh and blood die and not be able to do anything to prevent it. Family is supposed to be extremely important to you Nyueng Bao. I want you to drop whatever you're doing. Right now. Go over and sit on that boulder. Spend two hours not thinking about anything but what it must have meant to your mother to see your brother and sister die. Think about how badly she must not want to go through that again. Think about what it must be like to be her after everything else she's had to go through. You're a smart kid. You can figure it out."

When you are around people long enough you get a feel for how they react. I could see his first petulant inclination was to remind me that I had been younger than he was now when I attached myself to Bucket and the Company, which had little to do with the argument at hand but which was the sort of tool you grab when you are that age.

"If you intend to say something, make sure it makes sense before you do. Because if you can't think logically and argue logically, then there isn't much hope that you'll have any success with the sorcery, no matter how talented you are. I know. I know. From everything you've seen, the bigger the wizards are, the crazier they are. But within the boundaries of their insanity, every one of them is rigorously, mathematically rational. The entire power of their minds serves their insanity. When they stumble it's because they let emotions or wishful thinking get in the way."

"All right. I surrender. I'll sit on the damned rock until it

hatches. Oh, Dad also said to tell you that Narayan Singh is somewhere close by. He can sense the Deceiver but he can't pinpoint him.
Kina is protecting him with her dreams. Dad says you should ask the
white crow to look for him. If you can find it and get it to sit still long
enough."

"Crowhunter. Maybe I'll call myself that. It sounds more glamorous than Sleepy."

"Tobo sounds more glamorous than Sleepy." Tobo headed for the
boulder and settled in an approved attitude. I hoped I had planted
seeds that would take root and sprout while he was trying to think of
everything else but.

"At least you get to change your name when you grow up. . . ."
Stupid. Anytime I feel like it I can tell everyone to call me whatever
strikes my fancy.

Crowhunter gave up her name. She was a failure. The white
monster was nowhere to be found. So I went and spent some time
with Sahra even though she did not welcome me right away. We recalled old days, hard times, her husband's lack of perfection, till I
thought she was relaxed enough to actually listen to what I had to
say about Tobo.

The villain himself scored a coup by showing up with an olive
branch at the perfect time. I elected to remove myself while things
were going well. I hoped the peace would last but did not count on
forever.

I would settle for one halcyon week. In a week we would know if
it was possible to resurrect the Captured. In a week we would either
be dead on the glittering plain or ready to return as a force of ultimate destruction. Or maybe . . .

68

The warning horn sounded deep in the night, when even those
who were stuck with guard duty were at their most sluggish. But
the man on horn duty was married to his job. He kept blowing and
blowing. In minutes our entire encampment was seething. And I was
out there with my heart in my throat, striding along, making sure the
chaos was only apparent, not real. Everyone remained calm and fo-

cused. There was no panic. I was pleased. Even a little training and discipline are better than none.

I ducked into Goblin's tent. Sahra and Tobo were there already and not at one another's throats. I must have gotten through to the kid. I should keep after them both. In my copious free time. I bent close to the mist projector. "What's the word?"

Murgen whispered, "Soulcatcher is airborne and moving south. She plans to arrive shortly after sunrise. She has a good idea where you are. During her rest time she sent a shadow down to scout your position. She didn't learn a lot more. The shadow didn't dare get close enough to eavesdrop. She plans to don one of her disguises and infiltrate your camp so she can find out what you're really up to. From the beginning, she's operated under the assumption that we're dead out here. Even though she didn't kill us directly when she trapped us. She flew out of there believing we'd be dead in just a few days. I expect learning that Croaker and Lady are still alive is going to be the kind of shock that ruins her whole century."

"How fast is she moving? Strike that. You said she'd get here just after sunrise. Is Mogaba with her?" That would make a big difference in how fresh she would be when when she arrived. Which would determine the shape of what I started doing now.

"No. If she manages to get in among you and unearths all the answers to the questions she has, she'll smash you, scatter you, grab the Key, then go back for the Great General." Murgen sneered when he used Mogaba's title. The fact that we never beat him once, heads up, during the Kiaulune wars, did nothing to ease our contempt for him as a deserter and traitor.

"Warn me if she does anything unexpected. Sahra, have you checked on your mother?"

"Briefly. Doj and JoJo are helping her and One-Eye. I think she was a little delirious. She kept muttering about a noose and a land of unknown shadows and calling the heaven and earth and the day and the night."

"All evil dies there an endless death."

"That, too. What is it?"

"I don't know. A phrase I picked up somewhere. It has to do with the plain but I don't know what. Doj might be able to tell you. He promised to be cooperative and forthcoming but since I passed on his offer to make me his apprentice, that hasn't materialized. My fault as much as his, probably. I haven't taken time to press him. I have work to do." I ducked out.

The excitement had become more rigorously organized. There were torches and lanterns to light the road to the Shadowgate. A band of our bravest were up near the gate already, arranging more lighting and fine-tuning the colored powders used as road marks. Loaded animals were beginning to line up. Likewise a train of carts. Babies cried, children whined, a dog barked without pause. Sounds of men slipping through the darkness beyond the light came from all around. Prisoners who had been sure we meant to drag them onto the plain to become human sacrifices were being chivied toward the New Town. Some of the harder men had wanted to use them as bearers instead of the animals, disposing of them as their usefulness ended. I had demurred. They would become obstinate and obstreperous after the first few died and we would not be able to eat them after we ate up the consumables they carried. Not that the majority of us would eat flesh anyway. But those who could would from the beginning.

I spied Willow Swan strolling through the mob. He spun off orders like a drill instructor. I approached him. "Gone nostalgic for the good old days when you were the boss Grey?"

"A true genius, whose name we won't bring up in present company, sent all the master sergeants to make preparations at the Shadowgate. She didn't detail anybody to keep things moving down here."

The unnamed genius had to admit that he was right. River, Runmust, Spiff, all the men I had known the longest and trusted the most, were up there or somewhere out in the darkness. I guess I just assumed Sahra and I could handle everything else. Forgetting that I would be sprinting around making decisions for everyone who could not make up their minds for themselves. "Thanks. If I don't get a better offer by my fortieth birthday, I'll marry you yet."

Swan made a halfhearted effort to click his heels. "So. How old are you today?"

"Seventeen."

"That's about what I guessed. With maybe another twenty years of experience, plus wear and tear."

"It's tough being a teenager today. Just ask Tobo. Nobody's *ever* had it as awful as he does."

He chuckled. "Speaking of kids, who's handling the Daughter of Night? Which I don't want to be me."

"Darn! I figured Goblin and Doj for that. But Goblin's tied up helping keep track of Soulcatcher, and Doj has Gota and One-Eye to worry about. Thanks for reminding me." I headed back toward Goblin's tent. "Hey, Short Wart! Leave it to Tobo and Sahra a while. We got to get the Daughter of Night loaded up."

Goblin came out muttering, surveyed the excitement, grumbled, "All right. Let's get at it. Only, how come the fuck we never gave her a name? So what if she don't want one. She don't want to live in no cage, either. Even Booboo would be easier than calling her Daughter of Night all the time. Whoa! What the fuck is that?" He stared past me, downhill.

I turned, saw a pair of red eyes bobbing in the darkness, coming closer fast. I grabbed for my sword. Then I frowned as I heard the hoofbeats. Then I said, "Hey, buddy! Is that you? What the heck are you doing here? I thought you had yourself a job working for the traitor."

The old black stallion stepped close, lowered its head to nuzzle the hair beside my right ear. I hugged it around the neck. We had been friends once upon a time but I had not thought we were so close that it would desert Mogaba and track me down over hundreds of miles once it discovered that I was still alive. The creatures had been created to serve the Lady of the Tower but were supposed to be used to passing from one secondary master to another. This one had been Murgen's before it had become mine, then I had lost it.

"You ought to get out of here," I told it. "Your timing's really lousy. Soulcatcher is going to be all over us in just a few hours. If we're not already up there on that plain."

The horse surveyed my companions and what it could see of the Company, shuddered. Then, turning its gaze on Swan, the stallion managed a very human snort.

I patted its neck. "I'm not sure I don't agree with you, but Willow does have his redeeming qualities. He just keeps them well hidden. Go ahead and tag along if you want. I'm not riding. Not without a saddle."

Swan chuckled. "So much for the conquering Vehdna horsemen whose pride disdained both saddles and stirrups."

"Admitting no shortcomings of my own, I still have to observe that most of those proud horsemen were over six feet tall."

"I'll find you a ladder. And promise never to say a word about how those proud conquerors fared as soon as they ran into cavalry who did favor saddles and stirrups."

"Bite him, buddy."

To my amazement, the stallion snorted and nipped at Willow's shoulder. Swan leaped back. "You always did have a temper and bad manners, half-ass."

"Might be the company."

"Far be it from me to interfere with your sparking, Crowhunter," Goblin said, "but I thought you had a notion to do something with Booboo."

"Sarcastic, eavesdropping mudsucker. I did, didn't I? And I overlooked our old pal Khusavir Pete, too. I haven't checked in on him lately, either. Is he still healthy?" The horse nuzzled me again. I patted its neck. Maybe it felt more nostalgic about our good old days than I did.

"I can check. You definitely overlooked him in your master plan."

"Oh, no, I didn't. Not a bit. I have a very special mission cooked up specially for Khusavir Pete. And if he pulls it off, not only will he get to stay alive, I'll forgive everything he did at Kushkhoshi."

Somebody shouted. A scarlet fireball blistered across the night. It missed its target. It did not miss a tent, however. Then another tent after that, then the crude wooden barracks the men had built while they were waiting for me to arrive. All three began to smolder.

"That was Narayan Singh," Willow Swan said, stating what two-score people had seen during the carmine instant. "And he had Booboo—"

"Can it, Swan." I started yelling at everyone nearby, trying to organize a pursuit.

Goblin told me, "Calm down, Sleepy. All we need to do is wait till she starts screaming, then go pick her up."

I had forgotten the incredible array of control spells attached to the Daughter of Night. Her pain would increase geometrically as she moved farther away from her cage. Then at some distance known only to Goblin and One-Eye, choke spells would kick in and tighten rapidly. Narayan could take her away from us but only at the cost of killing her. Unless . . .

I asked.

"The spells have to be taken off from outside. She could be her mother and sister, the Shadowmasters and the Ten Who Were Taken all rolled into one and she'd still have to have somebody else help her get loose."

"All right. Then we'll wait for the screams."

There were no screams. Not then or ever.

Murgen looked hard. He could find no sign. Kina was dreaming strongly, protecting her own. Goblin remained adamant that they had to be close by, that there was no way the Daughter of Night had shed her connection to her cage.

I told Swan, "Then you gather up some men and drag that cage up to the Shadowgate. We'll *make* her follow us."

The warning horn sounded again. Soulcatcher had crossed the summit. She was on our side of the Dandha Presh. There were hints of light in the east.

It was time to leave.

69

A brutal argument was under way aboard Soulcatcher's carpet as she approached her destination, skimming the rocks, the sun's blinding fires behind her. Part of her wanted to forget about assuming a disguise and infiltrating the enemy. That part wanted to arrive as a killing storm, destroying everything and everyone that was not Soulcatcher. But by doing that she would expose herself to the counterefforts of people who had shown themselves very resourceful in the past. Innovation was one of the more irksome traditions of the Black Company.

She grounded the carpet and stepped off, concealed it using a minor spell. Then she crept toward the Company encampment, a few yards at a time, until she found a good hiding place where she could undertake the illusion creations and modest shapechanges that would render her unrecognizable. That work required total concentration.

Back in the brush, not far from where she had set down, Uncle Doj crept forward and after having used his small wizard's skills to make sure there were no booby traps, demolished Soulcatcher's flying carpet in a straightforward, no-nonsense manner using a hatchet. He might be old and a step slower, but he was still very quick and very sneaky. He was almost all the way back to the Shadowgate when Soulcatcher appeared, looking the epitome of scruffy young manhood.

A white crow, balanced precariously in a bit of rain-hungry brush, observed her passage. When she could no longer glance back and see anything damning, the bird flapped into the place where she had changed and started going through the clothing and whatnot she had left behind. The bird kept making noises like it was talking to itself.

Soulcatcher entered the encampment where she had expected to find the remnants of the Black Company. It was empty. But up ahead she saw a long column already beyond the Shadowgate. One man with a sword across his back had not passed through the gate yet but he was moving swiftly, and a number of people were waiting for him just on the other side.

They did have the Key! And they had used the damned thing! She should have gotten here faster! She should have attacked! Dammit, everyone knew subtlety was no good with these people. Hey! They had to have known that she was coming. There was no other explanation for this. They had known she was coming and they knew where she was now and . . .

The first fireball was so accurately directed that it would have taken her head off if she had not been getting down already. In another moment the damned things were streaking in from several different sources. They set brush afire and shattered rocks. She got down on her stomach and crawled. Before she worried about her dignity, she had to get away from the focal point of the fire. Unfortunately, her efforts did not seem to matter. The assassins seemed to know exactly where she was and her disguise did not fool them for an instant.

As a swarm of fireballs closed in, she flung herself into a deep hole that had been a cesspit not that long ago. No matter. Right now shelter was priceless. Now the snipers could not get her without coming out of hiding and coming to her.

She took advantage of the respite to engineer, prepare and launch a counterattack. That involved a lot of color and fire and boiling, oily explosions, none of which did much harm because her surviving attackers had fled through the Shadowgate as soon as she went into the pit.

She climbed out. Nothing happened. She glared up the hill. So. Even the snipers were beyond the Shadowgate now. Nearly a dozen people were standing around there, waiting to see what she would do. She calmed herself. She could not let them goad her into doing something stupid. The Shadowgate was in extremely delicate shape. One angry, thoughtless move on her part might damage it beyond repair.

She conquered the rage that threatened to conquer her. She was ancient in her wickedness. Time was an intimate ally. She knew how to abide.

She limped uphill, urging her anger to bleed off in movement, with an ease no normal being could manage.

The slope immediately below the Shadowgate was covered with swaths and patches of colored chalk. A carefully marked safe path passed through. Soulcatcher did not yield to temptation and try to follow it. There was a chance that they had forgotten that she had gone this way before. Or perhaps they refused to believe she could recall that in those days the safe path had entered the Shadowgate eight feet farther west, just beyond that rusty, twisted iron cage lying on its side as though it was exhausted and dying. She waved a finger. "Naughty, naughty."

Willow Swan—damn his treacherous, should-be-dead bones!— and the Nyueng Bao family stared back impassively. The pale-faced little wizard Goblin smirked, obviously remembering whose fault it was that she could no longer walk normally. And the ugly little woman smiled evilly. She said, "I wasn't *trying* to suck you in, Sweet Stuff. I *did* suck you in." She lifted a hand and raised a middle finger in a sign obviously learned from a northerner. "Water sleeps, Protector."

What the hell did that mean?

70

No human being can jump as high as Soulcatcher did. Nevertheless, she managed to get her heels ten feet off the ground a gnat's breath before the fireball ripped through the air where she had stood. I should have kept my big darned mouth shut. Gloating will do you in every time. How many stories and sagas are there where the hero survives because his captor insists on wasting time bragging and gloating before the execution? Add another one to the roll, where Company Annalist Sleepy does the incredibly dumb deed and leaves the target not quite relaxed enough.

Of course, she was *fast*. Epically fast. Poor old Khusavir Pete only got off two more fireballs before Soulcatcher got to him where we had left him chained.

It did not play out the way I hoped, only the way I expected. Now Khusavir Pete would have a hard time repaying any debt he still owed us.

I caught a glimpse of motion, the white crow plunging like a striking hawk. It pulled out and glided away. I murmured to myself, "Sister, sister." I was beginning to read the messages.

"Come here, Tobo." He was carrying the Key. He was supposed to be up at the head of the column but had hung back so he could watch the fireworks. He was the only one of us who did not have the sense to be frightened. Because he was not up where he belonged, all progress had come to a halt above us. He wore a hangdog look as he approached. He expected to be chastised. And he would be, later. "Hold up the Key."

"But won't that—"

"The Company isn't a debating club, Tobo. Show her the Key. Today."

He hoisted the Key overhead angrily. The morning sunlight blazed off the golden pick.

Soulcatcher did not show much excitement. But I had not meant the demonstration for her benefit, really. I wanted Narayan Singh to know what he had let slip through his fingers.

It was the Key, of course, but it was also some ancient and holy relic of Kina's Strangler cult. In their glory days every Deceiver company priest had carried a replica. I muttered, "You win some, you lose some, Narayan. In the excitement you got the girl back. But I've got this. And I can carry it. You've got the Daughter of Night and you can take her anywhere you want to. If you can carry her and her cage." Goblin and One-Eye had crafted a masterpiece of wicked sorcery. She could not even escape by destroying the cage. Whatever happened to it would happen to her.

I was not pleased about having to leave the cage behind but the Shadowgate had been decidedly stubborn in resisting its passage. That could have been overcome by sheer muscle power but I had not been able to get enough men onto it fast enough to force it through before the fireballs started flying.

Good luck, Baby Darkness, dragging all that iron around whilst you pursue your wickedness.

I hoped Singh had left the Book of the Dead hidden on the other side of the Dandha Presh so it would be a long time before the girl and it embraced one another. Long enough for me to get where I wanted to go and accomplish what I wanted to accomplish.

"That's good, Tobo. Now get back up front and get this mob moving. Swan. Tell me about the camping circles. And give me your best guess about how soon we're likely to run into trouble because of breaks in the protection of the road."

"I don't remember them ever being more than a few hours apart. And although we used them as camping places, I think that they were actually crossroads. That's easier to tell at night." Ominously, he added, "You'll see. Everything is different at night."

I did not like the sound of that.

I was still in the rear guard and only halfway to the crest when Soulcatcher found out what had happened to her flying carpet. The sound of her anger reached us despite the dampening effect of whatever barrier stood between us and the rest of the world. The earth shivered at the same time.

Uncle Doj was not far away, standing at the edge of the road, watching for evidence of his success. I said, "She seems displeased with the prospect of having to walk home." My friend the horse stood behind me, looking over my shoulder. It made a sound that could have passed for a snicker if it had not been a horse making it.

Doj indulged in a rare smile. He was thoroughly pleased with himself.

Willow Swan asked me, "What did you do now?"

"Not me. Doj. He totally obliterated her means of transport. She's on her own two hooves, now. She's a hundred miles from her only friend. And Goblin's already fixed up one of her feet so she can't run or dance."

"What you're telling me, then, is that you've created another Limper."

He was old enough to remember that nemesis of the Company. I could not contradict him. I did lose my smile. I had read those Annals often because they had been recorded by the Captain himself when he was young. "Nah, I don't think so. Soulcatcher doesn't have the concentrated venom and nearly divine malice that possessed the Limper. She doesn't get obsessed the way he did. She's more chaos walking while he was malevolence incarnate."

I showed Swan my crossed fingers. "I'd better dash up front and pretend that I know what I'm doing. Tobo?"

"He went ahead without you," Doj said. "You upset him."

I noted that the column had resumed moving, which meant that Tobo was on the plain already, carrying the Key like a protective talisman.

I needed to give a lot of thought to the fact that that artifact, evidently considered a holy of holies by the Stranglers, may actually have been brought off the plain into my world by the ancestors of the Nyueng Bao. I had to spend some thought on what the Key might mean to the last informed priest of the Nyueng Bao.

71

S omething beside the road caught my attention just before I reached the crest and got my first close look at the glittering plain. It was a small frog, mostly black but with stripes and whorls of dark green upon its back. It had eyes the color of fresh blood. It clung to a slightly tilted slab of grey-black rock. It wanted to go somewhere, anywhere, but its right hind leg was injured and when it tried to jump, it just sort of spun around in place. "Where the heck did that come from? There isn't supposed to be anything alive up here." I had been looking forward to having the clouds of flies that followed the animals get thinned out when they buzzed out beyond the safe zones and encountered killer shadows.

Swan said, "It won't be alive for long. The white crow dropped it. I think it was bringing it along for a snack." He pointed.

At the white crow. Bolder than ever, the bird had made itself at home on the back of my friend the mystic stallion. The horse seemed content with the situation. Perhaps even a little smug when it looked at me.

"I just remembered," Swan said. "For what it's worth. Last time we came up here Croaker made everybody who belonged to the Company touch their badges and amulets to the black stripe that runs down the middle of the road. Right after he touched the stripe with the lancehead on the standard. Maybe none of that amounts to anything. But I'm a superstitious kind of guy and I'd be more comfortable—"

"You're right. So be quiet. I recently reread everything Murgen had to say about his trip and he thought it might be a good idea, too. Tobo! Hold up!" I did not believe the boy would actually hear me over the clatter generated by the column but did expect that people would pass the word. I looked at the hapless frog once more and marveled that the crow was smart enough to let it go. Then I hastened to overtake our fledgling wizard.

The column stopped. Tobo had gotten my message. He had chosen not to ignore it. Maybe he had caught something from the white crow.

His mother and grandmother both were right there with him where he waited, making sure he did sensible things. He was exasperated by the delay. He was already far ahead of everyone but Sahra and Gota. . . .

Ah! As I recalled, Murgen had had the same trouble with the Lance of Passion.

My first glimpse of the plain awed me. Its immensity was indescribable. It was as flat as a table forever. It was grey on grey on grey, with the road just barely darker. There was no doubt whatsoever that this was all one vast artifact.

"Hang on, Tobo. Don't go any farther," I called. "We almost forgot something. You need to take the Key and touch it to the black stripe that runs down the middle of the road."

"What black stripe?"

Swan said, "It doesn't show up nearly as well this time. But it's there if you look."

It was. I found it. "Come back this way. You can see it back here."

Tobo backtracked reluctantly. Maybe I should have Gota carry the Key. She could not move fast enough to outrun the rest of us.

I stared on, beyond Tobo, feeling a faint touch of that passion to hurry myself. I was getting close to my brothers now. . . . Dark-grey clouds were beginning to gather down there. Murgen had mentioned a nearly permanent overcast that, nevertheless, did not always seem to have been around during his nights. I could make out no hint of the ruined fortress that was supposed to be a few days ahead of us. I did see plenty of the standing stones that were one of the outstanding features of the plain.

"I see it!" Tobo shouted, pointing downward. The little idiot swung the pickax, burying the point in the road surface.

The earth shuddered.

This was no devastating quake like those some of us recalled from years ago, when half the Shadowlands had been laid waste. It was just strong enough to be sensed and set tongues wagging and animals protesting.

The morning sun must have touched the plain oddly, somehow, because all the standing stones began to sparkle. People ooh-ed and ah-ed. I said, "I guess this is why they call it glittering stone."

Swan demurred. "I don't think so. But I could be wrong. Don't forget what I said about the Company badges."

"I haven't forgotten."

Tobo pried the pick out of the road's surface. The earth shifted again, as gently as before. When I joined him he was staring downward, baffled. "It healed itself, Sleepy."

"What?"

"When I hit it the pick went in sort of like the road was soft. And when I yanked it back out, the hole healed itself."

Swan remarked, "The center stripe is getting easier to see."

He was right. Maybe that was because of the brightening sunlight.

The ground trembled again. Behind me, voices changed tone, becoming frightened as well as awed. I glanced back.

A huge mushroom of dark rouge dust with black filigree highlights running through it boiled up from whence we had come. Its topmost surface seemed almost solid but as it rose and moved, the pieces of junk riding on it fell off.

Goblin burst into laughter so wicked it must have carried for miles. "Somebody got into my treasure trove. I hope she learned a really painful lesson." I was close enough for him to add a whispered, "I wish it could be fatal but there's not much chance of that."

"Probably not."

"I'll settle for crippling her other leg."

I said, "Sahra, there's something I need you to do. You remember Murgen telling us how he kept getting ahead of everyone when he came up here? Tobo has been doing the same thing. Try to slow him down."

Sahra sighed wearily. She nodded. "I'll stop him." She seemed apathetic, though.

"I don't want him stopped, I just want him slowed down enough so everyone else can keep up. This could be important later." I decided the two of us needed to have a long talk in private, the way we used to do before everything got so busy. It was obvious that she needed to get some things out where they could be lined up and swatted down and pushed away from her long enough for her heart to heal.

She did need healing. And for that she had no one to blame but herself. She did not want to accept the world as it was. She seemed worn out from fighting it. And in those ways she had begun to look very much like her mother.

I told her, "Put a leash on him if that's what it takes."

Tobo glowered at me. I ignored him. I made a brief speech suggesting anyone who carried a Black Company badge should press it to the road's surface right where Tobo had wounded it. The public readings aloud I had been doing had included Murgen's adventures on the plain. Nobody questioned my suggestion or refused to accept it. The column began moving again, slowly, as we found ways to bless, if only secondarily, the animals and those who did not have Company badges. I stayed in place and said something positive to everyone who passed by. I was amazed at the number of women and children and noncombatants in general who had managed to attach themselves to the band without me really noticing. The Captain would be appalled.

Uncle Doj was last to go by. That troubled me vaguely. A Nyueng Bao to the rear, more Nyueng Bao to the front, with the foremost a half-breed . . . But the whole Company was a miscegenation. There were only two men in this whole crowd who had belonged to the Company when it had arrived from the north. Goblin and One-Eye.

One-Eye was almost spent and Goblin was doing his determined best, quietly, to pass on as many skills as he could to Tobo before the inevitable began to overhaul him as well.

I walked past the slow-moving file, intent on getting back up near the point so I could be among the first to see anything new. I did not see or feel any particular mission in anyone I passed. It seemed that a quiet despair informed everyone. These were not good signs. This meant the euphoria of our minor successes had collapsed. Most of these people realized that they had become refugees.

Swan told me, "We have an expression up north, 'going from the frying pan into the fire.' Seems like about what we've done here."

"Really?"

"We got away from Soulcatcher. But now what?"

"Now we march on until we find our buried brothers. Then we break them out."

"You're not really as simple as you pretend, are you?"

"No, I'm not. But I do like to let people know that things aren't always as difficult as they want to make them." I glanced around to see who might overhear. "I have the same doubts everyone else has, Swan. My feet are on this path as much because I don't know what else to do as they are out of high ideals. Sometimes I look at my life and it seems pretty pathetic. I've spent more than a decade conspiring and committing crimes so I can go dig up some old bones in order to find somebody who can tell me what to do."

"Surrender to the Will of the Night."

"What?"

"Sounds like something Narayan Singh would say, doesn't it? In my great-grandfather's time it was the slogan of the Lady's supporters. They believed that peace, prosperity and security would result inevitably if all power could be concentrated in the hands of the right strong-willed person. And it did turn out that way, more or less. In principalities that did 'Surrender to the Will of the Night,' particularly near the core of the empire, there were generations of peace and prosperity. Plague, pestilence and famine were uncommon. Warfare was a curiosity going on far, far away. Criminals were hunted down with a ferocity that overawed all but the completely crazy ones. But there was always bad trouble along the frontiers. The Lady's minions, the Ten Who Were Taken, all wanted to build subempires of their own, which never lacked for external enemies. And they all had their own ancient feuds with one another. Hell, even peace and prosperity create enemies. If you're doing all right, there's always somebody who wants to take it away from you."

"I never pictured you as a philosopher, Swan."

"Oh, I'm a wonder after you get to know me."

"I'm sure you are. What are you trying to tell me?"

"I don't know. Killing time jacking my jaw. Making the trip go faster. Or maybe just reminding you that you shouldn't get too distressed about the vagaries of human nature. I've been getting my roots ripped out and my life overturned and a boot in my butt propelling me into an unknown future, blindfolded, for so long now that I *am* getting philosophical about it. I enjoy the moment. In a different context I do Surrender to the Will of the Night."

Despite my religious upbringing, I have never cherished a fatalistic approach to life. Surrender to the Will of the Night? Put my life in the hands of God? God is Great, God is Good, God is Merciful, there is no God but God. This we are taught. But the Bhodi philosophers may be right when they tell us that homage to the gods is best served when seconded by human endeavor.

"Going to get dark after a while," Swan reminded me.

"That's one of those things I've been trying to avoid thinking about," I confessed. "But Narayan Singh was right. Darkness always comes."

And when it did, we would find out just how wonderful a talisman our Key was.

"Have you noticed how the pillars keep on glittering even though the sky has started to look like it's going to rain?"

"I have." Murgen never mentioned this one phenomenon. I wondered if we had not done something never done before. "Did this happen last time you were up here?"

"No. There was a lot of glitter when we had direct sunlight but none that seemed like it was self-generated."

"Uhm. And was it this cold?" It had been getting chillier all day.

"I recall a sort of highland chill. Nothing intolerable. Whoa. Sounds like party time."

A whoop and holler had broken out at the head of the column. I could not determine a cause visually, being of the short persuasion. "What is it?"

"The kid's stopped. Looks like he's found something."

72

What Tobo had found were the remains of the Nar, Sindawe, who had been one of our best officers in the old days and, possibly, the villain Mogaba's brother. Certainly those two had been as close as brothers until the siege of Jaicur, when Mogaba chose to usurp command of the Company. "Clear away from him, people," I growled. "Give the experts room to take a look." The experts being Goblin, who dropped to his knees and scooted around the corpse slowly, moving his head up and down, murmuring some sort of cantrips, touching absolutely nothing until he was certain there was no danger. I dropped to one knee myself.

"He got a lot farther than I would've expected," Goblin said.

"He was tougher than rawhide. Was it shadows?" The body had that look.

"Yes." Goblin pushed gently. The corpse rolled slightly. "Nothing left here. He's a dried-out mummy."

A voice from behind me said, "Search him, you retard. He might've been carrying a message."

I glanced back. One-Eye stood behind me, leaning on an ugly black cane. The effort had him shivering. Or maybe that was just the cold air. He had been riding one of the donkeys, tied into place so he would not fall if he dozed off, which he did a lot these days.

I suggested, "Move him over to the side of the road. We need to keep this crowd moving. We have about eight more miles to go before we stop for the night." I pulled that eight out of the air but it was a fact that we needed to keep moving. We were better prepared for this evolution than our predecessors had been but our resources remained limited. "Swan, when a mule with a tent comes along, cut it out of line."

"Uhm?"

"We need to make a travois. To bring the body."

Every face within earshot went blank.

"We're still the Black Company. We still don't leave our own behind." Which was never strictly true but you do have to serve an ideal the best you can, lest it become debased. A law as ancient as coinage itself says bad money will drive out good. The same is true of principles, ethics and rules of conduct. If you always do the easier thing, then you cannot possibly remain steadfast when it becomes necessary to take a difficult stand. You must do what you know to be right. And you do know. Ninety-nine times out of a hundred you do know and you are just making excuses because the right thing is so hard, or just inconvenient.

"Here's his badge," Goblin said, producing a beautifully crafted silver skull in which the one ruby eye seemed to glow with an inner life. Sindawe had made that himself. It was an exquisite piece from talented hands. "You want to take it?"

That was the custom, gradually developed since the adoption of the badges under Soulcatcher's suzerainty back when the Captain was just a young tagalong with a quill pen. The badges of the fallen were passed down to interested newcomers, who were expected to learn their lineage and thus keep the names alive.

It is immortality of a sort.

I jumped. Sahra made a startled noise. I recalled that something similar had happened to Murgen last time. Although in that case, only he had sensed it. I thought. Maybe I ought to consult him. An entire squad of soldiers had been assigned to tend and transport the mist projector as delicately as was humanly possible. Even Tobo was under orders to match his pace to that manageable by the crew moving our most valuable resource.

Tobo had not done a good job of conforming.

Carts creaked past. Pack animals shied away from Sindawe's remains but never so far they risked straying from the safety of the road. I had begun to suspect that they could sense the danger better than I could because I had to rely entirely upon intellect for my own salvation. Only the black stallion seemed unmoved by Sindawe's fate.

The white crow seemed very much interested in the corpse. I had the feeling Sindawe was someone it knew and mourned. Ridiculous, of course. Unless that was Murgen inside there, as someone had suggested, trapped outside his own time.

Master Santaraksita came along, leading a donkey. Baladitya the copyist bestrode the beast. He studied a book as he rode, completely out of touch with his surroundings. Perhaps that was because he could not see them. Or he did not believe in the world outside his books. He had the lead rope of another donkey tied to his wrist. That poor beast staggered under a load consisting mostly of books and the tools of the librarian's trade. Among the books were some of the Annals, on loan, including those that I had salvaged from the library.

Santaraksita pulled out of line. "This is so absolutely exciting, Dorabee. Having adventures at my age. Being pursued through ancient, eldritch, living artifacts by terrible sorcerers and unearthly powers. It's like stepping into the pages of the old *Vedas*."

"I'm glad you're enjoying it so much. This man used to be one of our brothers. His adventure caught up with him about fourteen years ago."

"And he's still in one piece?"

"Nothing lives on the plain unless it has the plain's countenance. Even including the flies and carrion eaters you'd expect to find around a corpse anywhere."

"But there are crows here." He indicated birds circling at a distance. I had not noticed them because they were making no sounds and there were only a few of them in the air. As many as a dozen more perched atop the stone columns. The nearest of those were now just a few hundred yards ahead.

"They're not here to feast," I said. "They're the Protector's eyes. They run to her and repeat whatever we do. If they touch down after dark, they'll end up just as dead as Sindawe did. Hey, Swan. Right now, up and down the column, pass the word. Nobody does anything to bother those crows. It might break holes in the protection the road gives against the shadows."

"You're determined to put me on Catcher's shit list, aren't you?"

"What?"

"She doesn't know I'm not dead, does she? Those crows are going to put the finger on me."

I laughed. "Soulcatcher's displeasure shouldn't worry you right now. She can't get to you."

"You never know." He went off to tell everybody I wanted those watchcrows treated like favored pets.

"A strange and intriguing man," Santaraksita observed.

"Strange, anyway. But he's a foreigner."

"We're all foreigners here, Dorabee."

That was true. Very true. I could close my eyes and still be overwhelmed by the strangeness of the plain. In fact, I felt that more strongly when I was not looking at it. When my eyes were closed it seemed as aware of me as I was aware of it.

Once we got Sindawe loaded I continued walking beside Master Santaraksita. The librarian was every bit as excited as he claimed. Everything was a wonder to him. Except the weather. "Is it always this cold here, Dorabee?"

"It's not even winter yet." He knew about snow only by repute. Ice he knew as something that fell from the sky during the ferocious storms of the rainy season. "It could get a lot colder. I don't know. Swan says he don't recall it being this chilly the last time he was up here but that was at a different time of year and the circumstances of the incursion were different." I was willing to bet that seldom in its history had the plain ever experienced the crying of a colicky baby or the barking of a dog. One of the children had sneaked the dog along and now it was too late to change anyone's mind.

"How long will we be up here?"

"Ah. The question nobody's had the nerve to ask. You're more familiar with the early Annals than I am anymore. You've had months and months to study them while I haven't had time to keep my own up to date. What did they tell you about the plain?"

"Nothing."

"Not who built it? Not why? By implication Kina is involved somehow. So are the Free Companies of Khatovar and the golem demon Shivetya. At least we think the thing in the fortress up ahead is the demon who's supposed to stand guard over Kina's resting place. Not very effectively, apparently, because the ancient king Rhaydreynak drove the Deceivers of his time into the same caverns where Soulcatcher trapped the Captured. And we know that the Books of the Dead are down there somewhere. We know that Uncle Doj says—without offering any convincing evidence—the Nyueng Bao are the descendants of another Free Company, but we also know that Uncle and Mother Gota sometimes mention things that aren't part of the usual lore."

"Dorabee?"

Santaraksita I found wore that expression he always put on when I surprised him. I grinned, told him, "I rehearse all this every day, twenty times a day. I just don't usually do it out loud. I believe I was hoping you would add something to the mix. Is there anything? By direct experience we know that it takes three days to get to the fortress. I assume that stronghold is located at the heart of the plain. We know there's a network of protected roads and circles where those roads intersect. Where roads exist there must be someplace to go. To me that says there must be at least one more Shadowgate somewhere." I looked up. "You think?"

"You bet our survival on the *possibility* that there's another way off the plain?"

"Yep. We didn't have anywhere left to run back there."

There was that look again.

Suvrin, plodding along and listening in silence, had that look, too.

I said, "Although I've been surrounded by Gunni all my life, I'm still unfamiliar with the more obscure legendry. And I know even less about that of the older, less well-known, non-proselytizing cults. What do you know about The Land of Unknown Shadows? It seems to be tied in with aphorisms like 'All Evil Dies There an Endless Death' and 'Calling the Heaven and the Earth and the Day and the Night.'"

"The last one is easy, Dorabee. That's an invocation of the Supreme Being. You might also hear it as the formula 'Calling the Earth and the Wind and the Sea and the Sky,' or even 'Calling Yesterday and Today and Tonight and Tomorrow.' You spout those off thoughtlessly because they're easy and you have to deliver a certain number of prayers every day. I'm sure Vehdna who actually keep up with their prayers take the same shortcuts."

Twinges of guilt. My duties of faith had suffered abominably the past six months. "Are you sure?"

"No. But it sure sounded good, didn't it? Easy! You asked about Gunni. I could be wrong in a different religious context."

"Of course. How about Bone Warrior, Stone Soldier, or Soldier of Darkness?"

"Excuse me? Dorabee?"

"Never mind. Unless something related occurs to you. I'd better trot up the line and get Tobo slowed down again."

As I passed the black stallion and white crow, the latter chuckled and whispered that "Sister, sister" phrase again. The bird had heard the entire conversation. Chances were that it was not Murgen, nor was it Soulcatcher's creature, but still, it was extremely interested in the doings of the Black Company, to the point of trying to give warnings. It seemed quite pleased that we were headed south and were unable to turn back.

Behind me, Master Santaraksita's group paused. He and Baladitya studied the face of the first stone column, where golden characters still sparked occasionally.

It is immortality of a sort.

73

The people of the former Shadowlands clung to the best cover
available while they watched Nemesis cross their country in a
slow and angry progression toward the pass through the Dandha
Presh. In more than one place Soulcatcher's appearance gave rise to
the rumor that Khadi had been reborne and was walking through the
world again.

She always did love a good practical joke.

What the witnesses saw seemed to be the goddess in her most terrible aspect. She was naked except for a girdle of dried penises and a
necklace of babies' skulls. Her skin was a polished-mahogany black.
She was hairless everywhere. She had vampire fangs and an extra
pair of arms. She seemed about ten feet tall. What she did not seem
was happy. People stayed out of her way.

She was not alone. In her wake came an equally naked woman as
white as Soulcatcher was dark. She was five and a half feet tall. Even
covered with cuts and bruises and dirt, she was attractive. Her face
was empty of all expression but her eyes burned with patient hatred.
She wore only one item of ornamentation, a shoulder harness to
which a cable ten feet long had been attached. That cable connected
her to the rusty iron cage floating in the air behind her. The cage enclosed a skinny old man who had suffered several severe injuries, including a broken leg and some bad burns. The girl was compelled to
tow the cage. She never spoke, even when the monster encouraged
her with a switch. Possibly she had lost the faculty.

Narayan Singh had been the unfortunate who triggered Goblin's
booby trap, not its beloved intended.

The Deceiver shared the cage with a large bound book. He was
too weak to keep it closed. Wind toyed with its pages. Once in a
while the breeze showed its vicious side and yanked a page away from
the book's tired binding.

Sometimes delirious, Narayan thought he was in the hands of his goddess, either being punished for some forgotten transgression or transported to Paradise. And perhaps he was right. It did not occur to Soulcatcher to wonder what use she had for him alive. Not that she was taking any special trouble to keep him that way. Nor did the Daughter of Night seem particularly concerned about his fate.

74

I managed to overtake Tobo before he sped through the crossroads' circle. "We're stopping here," I told him, hanging onto his shoulder.

He looked at me like he was trying to remember who I was.

"Back up to the circle."

"All right. You don't have to be so pushy."

"Good. The real you is back. Yes. I do. No one else seems to be able to restrain you." As we stepped into the circle, I told him, "There should be a . . . yes. Right here." There was a hole in the roadway surface, four inches deep and as big around as my wrist. "Put the handle of the pickax in that."

"Why?"

"If the shadows can get inside the protected areas, that's the direction they'll come from. Come on. Do it. We've got a ton of work to do if we're going to set up a safe camp." There were too many of us to get everyone inside the circle. That meant some would have to overnight on the road, not a practice encouraged by Murgen.

I wanted only the calmest personalities back there. Murgen guaranteed that every night on the plain would be some kind of adventure.

Suvrin found me trying to get Iqbal and his family moved toward the heart of the circle. The animals were hobbled there. And I had a feeling that the plain really did not like being trampled upon by things with such hard feet. "What is it, Suvrin?"

"Master Santaraksita would like to see you at your earliest convenience." He grinned like he was having a wonderful time.

"Suvrin, have you been getting into the ganja or something?"

"I'm just happy. I missed the Protector's state visit. Therefore I'm

all right until sometime that's still far off yet. I'm on the greatest adventure of my life, going places no one of my generation would have
thought possible even a few weeks ago. It won't last. It just plain
won't last. The way my luck runs. But I'm for damned sure having
fun now. Except my feet hurt."

"Welcome to the Black Company. Get used to it. Bunions should
be our seal, not a fire-breathing skull. Did anyone learn anything useful today?"

"My guess would be that Master Santaraksita might have come
up with something. Else why would he bother to send me to find
you?"

"You got bold and snarky fast once you got up here."

"I've always thought I'm more likable when I'm not afraid."

I glanced around. I wondered if stupid ought not to be in there
somewhere, too. "Show me where the old boy is."

Suvrin had the chatters. Bad, for him. "He's a wonder, isn't he?"

"Santaraksita? I don't know about that. He's something. Keep an
eye out that you don't accidentally find his hand fishing around in
your pants."

Suvrin had made camp for himself and the older men right at the
edge of the circle, on its eastern side. Santaraksita had to have
picked the spot. It was directly opposite the nearest standing stone.
The librarian was seated Gunni-style, cross-legged, as near the edge
as he dared get, staring at the pillar. "Is that you, Dorabee? Come sit
with me."

I overcame a burst of impatience, settled. I was out of shape for
that. The Company continued its northern habits—using chairs and
stools and whatnot—even though we now had only two Old Crew
souls left. Such is inertia. "What are we looking for, Master?" It was
obvious he was watching the standing stone.

"Let's see if you're as bright as I believe you are."

There was a challenge I could not ignore. I stared at the column
and waited for truth to declare itself.

A group of the characters on the pillar brightened momentarily.
That had nothing to do with the light of the setting sun, which had
begun creeping in under the edge of the clouds. That was painting
everything bloody. After a while I told Santaraksita, "It seems to be
illuminating groups of characters according to some pattern."

"Mainly in reading order, I think."

"Down? And to the left?"

"Reading downward in columns isn't uncommon in the temple literature of antiquity. Some inks dried quite slowly. If you wrote in horizontal lines, you sometimes smeared your earlier work. Writing downward in columns right to left suggests to me left-handedness. Possibly those who placed the stellae were mostly left-handed."

It struck me that writing whatever way was convenient for you personally could lead to a lot of confusion. I said so.

"Absolutely, Dorabee. Deciphering classical writing is always a challenge. Particularly if the ancient copyists had time on their hands and were inclined to play pranks. I've seen manuscripts put together so that they could be read both horizontally and vertically and each way tells a different story. Definitely the work of someone who had no worries about his next meal. Today's formal rules have been around for only a few generations. They were agreed upon simply so we could read one another's work. And they still haven't penetrated the lay population to any depth."

Most of that I knew already. But he needed his moments of pedantry to feel complete. They cost me nothing. "And what do we have here?"

"I'm not sure. My eyes aren't sharp enough to pick up everything. But the characters on the stone closely resemble those in your oldest book and I've been able to discern a few simple words." He showed me what he had written down. It was not enough to make sense of anything.

"Mostly I think we're looking at names. Possibly arranged in a holy scripture sort of way. Maybe a roll-call-of-the-ancestors kind of thing."

"It is immortality of a sort."

"Perhaps. Certainly you can find similarly conceived monuments in almost every older city. Iron was a popular material for those who considered themselves truly rich and historically significant. Generally, though, they were erected to celebrate individuals, notably kings and conquerers, who wanted following generations to know all about them."

"And every one of those I've ever seen was a complete puzzle to the people living around it now. Thus, a feeble immortality of a sort."

"And there's the point. We'll all achieve our immortality in the next world, however we may conceive that, but we all want to be re-membered in this one. I suppose so that when the newly dead arrive in heaven, they'll already know who we are. And, yes, even though I am a devout, practicing Gunni, I'm very cynical about what hu-manity brings to the religious experience."

"I'm always intrigued by your thinking, Master Santaraksita, but in today's circumstances I just don't have time to sit around musing on humanity's innumerable foibles. Nor even those of God. Or the gods, if you prefer."

Santaraksita chuckled. "Do you find it amusing to see our roles thus reversed?" A few months in the real world had done wonders for his attitude. He accepted his situation and tried to learn from it. I considered accusing him of being a Bhodi fellow traveler.

"I fear I'm much less of a thinker than you like to believe, Mas-ter. I've never had time for it. I'm probably really more of a parrot than anything."

"And I suspect that surviving in your trade eventually leaves everyone more philosophical than you want to admit, Dorabee."

"Or more brutal. None of these men were ever sterling subjects."

Santaraksita shrugged. "You remain a wonder, whether or not you wish to be one." He made a gesture to indicate the standing stone. "Well, there you have it. It may say something. Or it may just be remembering the otherwise unheralded whose ashes nourished weeds. Or it may even be trying to communicate, since some of the characters seem to have changed." His tone became one of intense interest as he completed his last sentence. "Dorabee, the inscription doesn't remain constant. I must have a closer look at one of those stellae."

"Don't even think about it. You'd probably be dead before you got to it. And would get the rest of us dead, too."

He pouted.

"This's the dangerous part of the adventure," I told him. "This's the part that leaves us no room for innovation or deviation or ex-pressing our personalities. You've seen Sindawe. No better or stronger man ever lived. That was nothing he deserved. Whenever you feel creative, you just go look on that travois. Then take another look. Gah! It smells like the inside of a stable here already. A little breeze wouldn't hurt." As long as it blew away from me.

The animals were all crowded together and surrounded so they could not do something stupid like wander out of the protective circle. And herbivores tend to generate vast quantities of by-product.

"All right. All right. I don't make a habit of doing what's stupid, Dorabee." He grinned.

"Really? What about how you got here?"

"Maybe it's a hobby." He could laugh at himself. "There's stupid and stupid. None of those boulders is going to make my pebble turn into a standing stone."

"I'm not sure if that's a compliment or an insult. Just keep an eye on the rock and let me know if it says anything interesting." It occurred to me to wonder if these pillars were related to the pillars the Company had found in the place called the Plain of Fear, long before my time. Those stones had even walked and talked—unless the Captain exaggerated even worse than I thought. "Whoa! Look there. Right along the edge of the road. That's a shadow, being sneaky. It's already dark enough for them to start moving around."

It was time I started moving around, making sure everyone remained calm. The shadows could not reach us if no one did anything stupid. But they might try to provoke a panic, the way hunters will try to scare up game.

75

Despite the numbers and the animals and my own pessimism, nothing went wrong. Goblin and I made repeated rounds of the circle and the tailback running north up the protected road. We found everyone in a mood to be cooperative. I suppose that had something to do with the shadows clinging to the surface of our invisible protection and oozing around like evil leeches. Nothing focuses the attention like the proximity of a bad death.

"There are other ways in and out of this circle besides the one we came in and the one we're going to use tomorrow," I told Goblin. "How come we can't see them?"

"I don't know. Maybe it's magic. Maybe you ought to ask One-Eye."

"Why him?"

"You've been around long enough that you should've discovered the truth. He knows everything. Just ask. He'll tell you." Evidently he was less worried about his friend. He was back to picking on One-Eye.

"You know, you're right. I haven't had much chance to talk to him but I did notice that he's going all-out to be a pain. Why don't we go wake him up, tell him he's in charge, and get ourselves some shut-eye?" Which is what we did, with slight modifications, after we made sure there was a watch rotation for every potential entry into the circle, whether it could be seen or not. With help from Gota and Uncle Doj, One-Eye was still capable of contributing a little something to his own protection. Not that he was willing to admit that.

I believe Goblin went off and whispered something to Tobo, too, after we went our respective ways.

I had just gotten comfortable on my nice rock bed when Sahra invited herself over for a chat. I really was tired and uncharitable. When I sensed her presence, I just wanted her to go away. And she did not stay long.

She said, "Murgen wanted to talk to you but I told him you were exhausted and needed to rest. He wanted me to warn you that your dreams may be particularly vivid and probably confusing. He said just don't go anywhere and don't panic. I have to go tell Goblin and One-Eye and Uncle and some others and have them spread the word to everyone else. Rest easy." She patted my hand, letting me know we were still friends. I grunted and closed my eyes.

Murgen was right. Night on the glittering plain was another adventure entirely. The landmarks were similar but seemed to be ghosts of their daytime selves. And the sky was not to be trusted.

The plain itself was still all shades of grey but now with some sort of implied illumination that left all the angles and edges clearly defined. Once when I glanced upward I saw a full moon and the sky crowded with stars, then only moments later, the overcast was back and there was nothing to be seen at all. The characters inscribed on the standing stones all seemed busy, which was not something Murgen had noted during his own visit. I watched for a moment, recognizing individual characters but no words. Nevertheless, I had an epiphany I would have to pass on to Master Santaraksita in the morning. The inscriptions on the pillars did begin at the upper right and read downward. For the first column. The second column read from the bottom upward. Then the third read back down. And so on.

I became more interested in the things moving amongst the pillars, though. There were some big shadows out there, things with a presence potent enough to terrify and scatter the little shadows radiating hunger as they crawled over the surface of our protection. The big ones would not come closer. They had about them an air of infinite, wicked patience that left me convinced they would be out there waiting if it took a thousand years for one of us to screw up and open a gap in our protection.

In dream, all roads leading into the circle were equally well-defined. Each was a glimmering ruler stroke running off to glowing domes in the distance. Of all those roads and domes, though, only those on our north-south trace seemed to be fully alive. Either the road knew what we wanted to do or it knew what it wanted us to do.

In an instant I was amazed, bewildered, terrified, exultant, having realized that in order to see what I was seeing, I would have to be at least a dozen feet above my normal height of eye. Which meant that I had to go outside my skin, the way Murgen did, and while I had wished for the ability a thousand times and the view was engrossing, the risks were none I cared to face when the opportunity was real. I sped a prayer heavenward. God needs to be reminded. I was totally, ecstatically, happy being Sleepy, without one shred of mystical talent. Really. If it was necessary that somebody in my gang do this sort of thing, Goblin or One-Eye or Uncle Doj or almost anyone else could have the magic, sparing only Tobo, despite him being the prophesied future of the Company. Tobo was still a little too short on self-discipline to be handed any more capabilities.

The presence of the small shadows was kind of like that of a flock of pigeons. They were not silent on that ghost-world level but they did not try to communicate unless with one another. It took me only moments to shut them out.

The skies above were more troublesome. Each time I lifted my gaze I saw that some dramatic change had occurred. Sometimes there was an impenetrable overcast, sometimes a wild starfield and a full moon. Once there were fewer stars and an extra moon. Once a distinct constellation hung right over the road south. It conformed exactly to Murgen's description of a constellation called the Noose.

Hitherto I had always suspected the Noose to have been a fabrication on Mother Gota's part.

Then, just beyond the golden pickax, I spied a strapping trio of the uglies Murgen had reported meeting in that very spot his first night on the glittering plain. Were they yakshas? Rakshasas? I tried to shoehorn them into Gunni or even Kina's mythology but just could not make them fit. There would be plenty of room, though, I did not doubt. The Gunni are more flexible in matters of doctrine than are we Vehdna. We are taught that intolerance is our gift of faith. Gunni flexibility is just one more reason they will all suffer the eternal fires. The idolators.

God is Great. God is Merciful. In Forgiveness He is Like the Earth. But He can become a tad mean-spirited with unbelievers.

I tried desperately to recall Murgen's report of his encounter with these dream creatures. Nothing came forward despite the fact that I had been the one who had written it all down. I could not for certain recall if his night visitors had been identical to these. These were humanoid and human-size but definitely lacking human features. Possibly they wore masks in the guise of beasts. Judging from their frenetic gestures, they wanted me to follow them somewhere. I seemed to recall something similar having happened during Murgen's episode. He had refused. So did I, although I did drift toward them and did attempt to engage them in conversation.

I did not, of course, have a knack for generating sound without a body or tools. And they did not speak any language I knew, so the whole business was an exercise in futility.

They became extremely frustrated. They seemed to think that I was playing games. They finally stamped away, obviously possessed by a big anger.

"Murgen, I don't know where you are. But you're going to have to spend some time clueing me in here."

The ugly people were gone. No skin off my nose. Now maybe I could get some sleep. Some real sleep, without all these too-real dreams and awful, improbable skies.

It started to rain, which told me which sky was the true sky and paramount above the me that lay twitching fitfully as the cold drops began to make themselves felt. There was no way to get in out of it. There was no way to erect tents or other shelters on the plain. In

fact, the matter of weather had not arisen during our planning ses-
sions. I do not know why, though it seems that there is always something big that you overlook, something to which every planner on
the team turns a blind eye. Then, when the breakdown or failure
comes, you cannot figure out how you overlooked the obvious.

Somehow we must have concluded that there was no weather on
the plain. Maybe because Murgen's Annals did not recall any. But
somebody should have noticed that the Captured made this journey
at a different time of year. Somebody should have realized that that
was sure to have some impact. Somebody probably named me.

It had been cool already when the rain began to fall. It grew
chillier fast. Crabbily, I got up and helped cover stuff to protect it,
helped get out means for recovering some of the water, then confis-
cated a piece of tenting and another blanket, rolled up and went
back to sleep, ignoring the rain. It was only a persistent drizzle and
when you are exhausted, nothing but sleep matters much.

76

I found Murgen waiting when I got home to dreamland. "You seem
surprised. I told you I'd see you on the plain."

"You did. But I don't need it to be right now. Right now I need
to sleep."

"You are. You'll wake up as refreshed as if you hadn't dreamed at
all."

"I don't want to be drifting around loose from my body, either."

"Then don't."

"I can control it?"

"You can. Just decide not to do it. It's pretty basic. Most people
manage it instinctively. Ask around tomorrow. See how many of
these people even recall being loose from their flesh."

"It's something everybody does?"

"Up here. It's something everybody can do. If they want. Most
don't want it so emphatically that they don't even recognize that the
opportunity is there. Which doesn't matter. It's not why I'm here."

"It matters a bunch to me. That stuff is scary. I'm just a simple
low-class city brat—"

"Cancel the old whine-and-toe shuffle, Sleepy. You're wasting time. I probably know as much about you as you know about yourself. There're things you need to know."

"I'm listening."

"Till now you've dealt with the plain well enough by letting the Annals guide you. Stick with the rules you've already made and you won't have any trouble. Don't dawdle. You didn't bring enough water—even if you slaughter your animals as you go, the way you planned. There's ice here that you can melt but if you waste time getting here, you'll end up having to kill more animals than you want. And take good care of them while they're still alive. Don't let them get so thirsty they start charging around looking for water and go busting through your protection. That'll heal itself but it does take time. The shadows won't give you time."

"Then we're safe from the break that killed Sindawe and some of the others?"

"Yes. You'll find Bucket tomorrow. I warn you now so you'll have time to prepare yourself."

I was prepared already. I had been prepared for a long time. Actually seeing Bucket dead would be difficult but I would get past it. "Tell me what I should do now that I'm here."

"You're doing it. Just don't do it slowly."

"Should I split the group? Send a strike force forward?"

"That wouldn't be wise. You wouldn't be able to manage whichever group you weren't with. And that'll be the one where somebody screws up and gets us all killed."

"You, too?"

"There's nobody else who can get me out if you fail. There isn't even anyone else out there who knows that we're alive."

"The Daughter of Night and Narayan Singh know. Probably." They had overheard enough to figure it out, certainly.

"Which means Soulcatcher does too, now. But you know, I don't really see those people developing an interest in raising the dead. Not to mention that now the Shadowgate can only be opened from this side. This is the last cast of the dice, Sleepy. And it's for everything."

I did not remind Murgen that Narayan Singh and his ward had a very strong interest in resurrecting someone who was practically his grave-mate. He was right about the Shadowgate, assuming there were no more Keys outside. "How did I know you were going to say something like that?"

He gave me the smile that probably won Sahra's heart.

I told him, "You should go see Sahra."

"I already have. That's why I was so late getting around to you."

"What can I say? Oh. I saw those creatures . . . the . . ." I did not know what they were called, so I tried to describe them.

"The Washane, the Washene and the Washone, collectively referred to as the Nef. They're dreamwalkers, too."

"Too?"

"I'm a dreamwalker. You can see me but only with your mind's eye. In some way that you remember me. The Nef are out here all the time. They may be trapped, or they may no longer have bodies to go back to. I've never been able to tell. They want to communicate so badly—because they want something badly—but don't seem capable of learning how. They're from one of the other worlds. If they no longer have bodies they may even be skinwalkers, so be very careful around them."

"The . . . duh . . . what are you blathering about?"

"Oh. We haven't talked about any of that yet, have we?"

"Any of what?"

"I really thought you'd figure most of it out by reading between the lines. The Companies had to come from somewhere and it would be hard to scratch out a living on a tabletop of bare stone. So they must have come from somewhere else. Somewhere very else, since the plain isn't so big you can't walk around it and discover that there's nowhere for armies to come from. The land just gets colder and more inhospitable."

"I'm real thick, boss. You should've drawn me some pictures."

"I wasn't keen on having anyone outside know. I didn't want anybody getting scared to come get me."

"You're my brother."

He ignored me. "I haven't slept here, so I have a lot of time on my hands. I've used some of it exploring. There are sixteen Shadowgates, Sleepy. And fifteen of them open onto places that aren't our world. Or did at one time. Most of them are dead now and in my state, I can't see what used to be on the other side without actually going out there. And I don't have the eggs to do that, because I like my own world just fine and I don't want to take a chance of getting trapped any farther away from it than I already am.

"Only four of the gates are still alive. And the one to our world is so badly hurt that it probably won't last many generations more."

I was lost. Completely. I was prepared for none of this. And yet he was right when he hinted that there were bells I should have heard ringing. "What does all that have to do with Kina? It isn't in her legend anywhere. In fact, what does it even have to do with us? It's not in *our* legend anywhere."

"Yes it is, Sleepy. The truth is just so old that time has totally distorted it. Examine Gunni mythology. There's a lot there about other planes, other realms of reality, different heavens and whatnot. Those stories go way back before the coming of the Free Companies, a thousand years or more. Near as I've been able to find out, when the first Free Company came off the plain, almost six hundred years ago, that event marked the first time our Shadowgate had been used in at least eight centuries. That's a lot of time for truth to mutate."

"Whoa. Whoa. You're starting to imply things I can't quite get my mind around."

"You'd better open it up and spread it out wide, Sleepy, because there's a whole lot more. And I doubt I've discovered even a tenth of it."

I have a dark, cynical, untrusting side that at times even doubts the motives of my closest friends. "Why is it that none of this ever got mentioned until now? This isn't fresh news to you, is it?"

"No. It isn't. But I told you, I want out of here. Badly. I chose not to pass on any information that might handicap you."

"Handicap me? What the heck are you talking about?"

"Kina and the Captured aren't the only things sleeping up here. There're also a lot of truths that would shake the foundations of our world. Truths I have no trouble imagining wholesale slaughters and holy wars arising to suppress. Truths I have no trouble seeing getting my family and the Company obliterated, they're so threatening."

"I'm trying to open my mind but I'm having trouble. I feel like I'm about to plunge into an abyss."

"Just hang on. I've been out here forever and I still have trouble with it. I think the way to start is, I should outline the history of the plain."

"Yes. Why don't you do that? That might be interesting."

"You still have that edge on your tongue, don't you? Maybe Swan is right and what you really need is a good . . . all right. All right. Listen closely. The plain was created so far back in antiquity that nobody on any of the worlds has any idea who built it, how, or why, though you have to believe that it was meant to be a pathway between the worlds."

"Why the shadows and standing stones and—"

"I can't tell you anything if I'm not the one doing the talking."

"Sorry."

"In the beginning there was the plain. Just the plain, with its network of roads that have to be walked a certain way to get to other worlds. For example, every traveler had to enter the great circle at the center of the plain before he can leave the plain again. Back then there were no shadows, no Shadowgates, no standing stones, no great fortress inside the great circle, no caverns beneath the stone, no sleeping gods, no Captured, no Books of the Dead. There was nothing but the plain. The crossroads of worlds. Or possibly of time. One rogue school of thought insists the gates all open into the same world but at times which are separated by tens of thousands of years.

"At some time still in unimaginable antiquity, human nature asserted itself and would-be conquerers began to charge back and forth across the plain. During a period of exhaustion the wise men of a dozen worlds combined to make the first modifications to the plain. They built a fortress in the great circle and garrisoned it with a race of created immortal guardians whose task it would be to prevent armies from passing from world to world.

"Then we pass to the edge of proto-history, the age now recalled poorly as it is distorted in Gunni myth.

"Those driven to conquer will try to do so, whatever the obstacles. Kina apparently started out as your run-of-the-mill, dark-lord type that arises every few centuries, as Lady's first husband was, only she was another in a line and association of many such, some of whom are now recalled as gods because of the impact they had on their times. The whole cabal decided to beef Kina up until she could overcome the 'demons' on the plain. In the process she did become what, for want of a better descriptive, we would have to call a god. And she behaved every bit as badly as her associates should have expected, with results more or less like those recalled in the mythology.

Once Kina was asleep, her associates opened the maze of caverns under the plain and buried her way down deep somewhere. Then they created Shivetya, the Steadfast Guardian, to keep watch. Or they conscripted a surviving demon of the same name and strengthened him and bound him to do the job, if you prefer a less common version of the story. Then, apparently too exhausted to recover their greatness, they faded away. So Kina came out on top even if she ended up imprisoned."

"Why didn't they just kill her? That's something I've never understood about these squabbles amongst the gods. There's only one version of the Kina myth where her enemies do anything but just tuck her in. And in that one, even after she's all chopped up and scattered around, they leave the pieces alive and trying to get back together."

"My guess would be she had some kind of deadman spell that entwined the fates of the other gods with her own. Those people wouldn't have trusted one another for a second. All of them would have had some protective mechanism like Longshadow used when he tied his fate into the well-being of the Shadowgate."

"But the Shadowgate doesn't depend on his health anymore. Not as long as he stays inside."

"I was just posing an example, Sleepy. Let's stick to the history of the plain. What followed Kina's downfall isn't documented at all, but more conquerers came and went and further efforts were made to dissuade them while keeping the plain open for commerce. The gates and Keys were created. One world gathered its sorcerers and had them steal the souls of millions of prisoners of war, creating the shadows and endowing them with a bitter hatred of everything living. They meant to close down the plain entirely. Which naturally led some other race to create the shields that protect the circles and roads. Nobody knows for sure how or when the standing stones began to appear but they're the most recent addition to the plain, probably put out by the precursors of the multiple-worlds' religious movement that produced the Free Companies. I understand that the stones aren't quarried, they're created things. They're immune to the shadows and indifferent to the protective shields but they're attuned to the various Keys carried away during the Free Companies' age."

"It's too much to grasp. It'll take a long time to digest. Kina is real, though?"

"Absolutely. Buried right down here under me somewhere. I've never been tempted to go look for her. I wouldn't want to accidentally cut her loose. I don't know how I could manage that but I definitely don't want to find out the hard way."

"What about Rhaydreynak and the Books of the Dead? Where do they fit?" Rhaydreynak's war on the cult of Kina antedated the appearance of the Free Companies by several centuries supposedly, yet there were scary similarities suggesting shared origins.

"The rise of the Free Companies is actually one of the least well known despite its being closest in time. There were many Companies over several hundred years. They came from several different worlds and went off into several more, representing almost as many different sects of Kina worshippers. Most seem to have been sent out to explore, not conquer or to serve as mercenaries or even to bring on the Year of the Skulls. What their true mission seems to have been was to determine which world should be awarded the honor of being sacrificed in order to bring on the Year of the Skulls."

"Then a bunch of worlds decided to gang up on ours?"

"Kina spanned many worlds. Her deviltry was almost universal, apparently."

"And we lost the toss and got to bury her in ours?"

"You're not in our world anymore, Sleepy. This's the in-between. Where you are depends on what gate you walk out. And these days you have only one choice. Its Shadowgate lies straight ahead, on the far side of the plain. It's as if the plain itself is closing down the alternate ways."

"I don't get it. Why would it do that? And how?"

"Sometimes its seems like the plain itself is alive, Sleepy. Or at least that it can think."

"Is it where we came from? Is it where the Captain spent most of his life trying to go?"

"No. The Company can't go back to Khatovar. Croaker will never reach the promised land. That Shadowgate is dead. The world where you're headed is very much like our own. To other worlds it's known by a name that translates into Taglian somewhat vaguely as The Land of Unknown Shadows."

Without thinking I responded, "All Evil Dies There an Endless Death."

"What?" Startled. "Yes. How did you know? They were the people who committed the murders that produced the shadows."

"I heard it somewhere. From a Nyueng Bao."

"Yes. Nyueng Bao De Duang. In current Nyueng Bao usage that means something like 'The Chosen Children' colloquially and nothing whatsoever that's sensible literally. In the days when their forebears were sent out from The Land of Unknown Shadows it meant, roughly, 'the Children of the Dead.'"

"You've been busy," I observed.

"Hardly, considering how long I've been trapped here. Try it for a decade, Sleepy. You won't have to put up with any of the distractions you complain about when you aren't getting everything you want to do done."

"No kidding? Seems to me I'm all of a sudden having to work even while I'm sleeping."

"Not for long. Whoever has control of that mist-making thing is trying to get me to answer him. Why don't you sneak around there and smash that sucker so I don't have to get dragged into it every time somebody wants my view on how to crack a walnut or whatever else the crisis of the moment happens to be."

"Not hardly, former boss. I'm carrying a whole bag of nuts myself."

"You would—" Murgen departed as though yanked away.

I could have sworn I heard the laughter of an eavesdropping white crow.

77

How come you're so crabby?" Willow Swan demanded when I snapped at him for no good reason. "Rag time again already?"

I blushed. Me, after twenty years among the crudest men on two hooves. "No, jerk. I didn't sleep very well last night."

"*What?*"

It exploded out of him like the shriek of a stomped rat.

"I didn't sleep well last night."

"Oh, yeah. Not our sweet little Sleepy. Guys, anybody, Ro, River, whoever, you want to step up and remind us about the Roar in the Rain last night?"

Riverwalker told me, "Boss, your snoring made more noise than a tiger in heat. We had people get up and move back up the road toward home to get away from the racket. There were people wanted to strangle you or at least put your head in a sack. I bet if anybody else knew what the hell we were doing and where we were going, you'd be on that travois with General Sindawe."

"But I'm such a sweet, delicate flower. I couldn't possibly snore." I had been accused of the crime before but only jokingly, never with such passion.

River snorted. "Swan decided not to marry you."

"I'm stricken. I'll see if One-Eye doesn't have a cure."

"A cure? The man can't even take care of himself."

I scrounged up something to eat. It was barely worth the effort and definitely not filling. We would be on short rations for a long time. Before I finished what morning preparations were possible for me, the forward elements were already moving. The general mood was more relaxed. We had survived the night. And yesterday we had shoved it to the Protector real good.

The relaxation ended when we found Bucket's remains.

Big Bucket, real name Cato Dahlia, once a thief, once an officer of the Black Company, was almost a father to me. He never said and I never asked but I suspect he knew I was female all along. He was very unpleasant to some of my male relatives, way back when.

You did not want to be the object when Bucket got angry.

I managed not to break down. I had had a long time to get used to the idea that he was gone, though there was always some small, irrational hope that Murgen was wrong, that death had overlooked him and he was buried with the Captured.

The men put Bucket on the travois with Sindawe without having to be told.

I tagged along and became entranced by one of those unaccountably irrelevant trains of thought that often take shape at such times.

We had left a truly nasty mess where we had spent the night, particularly in the line of animal waste. Likely the Captured had done the same during their passage along this same road. However, other than the odd corpse, there was no sign that they had passed through. There were no dung piles now, no gnawed, discarded bones, no vegetable waste, no ashes from charcoal braziers, nothing. Only human bodies lasted and they became thoroughly desiccated.

I would have to take it up with Murgen. Meantime, it was a mental exercise that would keep me from dwelling upon Bucket.

We trudged on southward. The rain came and went, never more than a drizzle, though sometimes the wind brought it stinging in from a sharp angle. I shivered a lot and worried about it getting cold enough to sleet or snow. No other evil found us. Eventually I spied the vague silhouette of our initial destination, that mysterious central fortress.

The wind began to blow steadily.

Some of the men complained about the cold. Some complained about the wet. Quite a few complained about the menu, and a handful insisted on complaining about all the complaining. I sensed few positive feelings concerning what we were doing.

I felt very much alone, almost abandoned, the whole day long despite well-meant efforts from Swan, Sahra and quite a few others. Only Uncle Doj did not bother because even at this late date he remained piqued because I would not enlist as his apprentice. He continued his emotional machinations. Several times I caught myself retreating into my away place and had to remind me that I did not need to go there now. None of those people could hurt me anymore. Not if I did not let them. I controlled their reality. They survived only in my memory. . . .

Even that is immortality of a sort.

We Vehdna believe in ghosts. And we believe in evil. I wondered if the Gunni might not be onto something after all. For them the pain inspired by the departure of loved ones is less personal and far more fatalistic and is accepted as a necessary stage of life that does not end with this one transformation.

If the Gunni, by some bizarre and remote practical joke of the divine, happen to be in possession of a more accurate theology, I must have been a bad, bad girl in a previous life. I sure hope I had fun. . . . Forgive me, O Lord of the Hours, Who Art Merciful and Compassionate. I have sinned in my heart. Thou Art God. There Can Be No Other.

78

There were flakes of snow in the air whenever the wind took to loafing. Then each time it found renewed ambition it hurled tiny flecks of ice that stung my face and hands. Though it sounded fearful, the level of grumbling never reached suggestions of mutiny. Willow Swan trotted up and down the column gossiping and dropping reminders that we had nowhere to go but straight ahead. The weather did not hamper him at all. He seemed to find it invigorating. He kept telling everyone how wonderful it would be once we got some real snow, say, four or five feet. The world would look better then, yes sir! He guaranteed it. He grew up in stuff like that and it made a real man out of you.

With equal frequency I overheard some advice—the fulfillment of which was physically impossible for anyone not some select variety of worm—as often the people cried out, offering up impassioned pleas to One-Eye, Goblin, even Tobo, to fill Swan's mouth with quick-setting mortar.

"Are you having fun?" I asked him.

"Oh, yeah. And they're not blaming you for anything, either."

His boyish grin told me he was not being some kind of unwanted hero. He was playing games with me, too.

All northerners seemed to have that capacity for play. Even the Captain and Lady, sometimes, had shown signs with one another. And One-Eye and Goblin . . . the little black wizard's stroke may have been a godsend. I could not imagine those two missing an opportunity for screwing up as grand as this one was if they were both in excellent health.

When I suggested something of the sort to Swan he failed to understand. Once I explained, he observed, "You're missing the point, Sleepy. Unless they're *extremely* drunk, those two won't do anything dangerous to anybody but themselves. I'm on the outside and I recognized that twenty years ago. How could you miss it?"

"You're right. And I do know that. I'm just looking for things to go wrong. I get gloomy when I try to prepare myself for the worst. How come you're so cheerful?"

"Right up ahead. Another day. Two, maximum. I get to say hi to my old buddies, Cordy and Blade."

I looked at him askance. Could he be the only one of us more excited than frightened by the possibilities inherent in releasing the Captured? Only one of those people had not spent the past fifteen years trapped inside his own mind. And I was not convinced that Murgen was not working overtime to maintain a false facade of sanity. The others . . . I did not doubt that quite a few would come forth stark, raving mad. Nor did the rest.

Nowhere was that fear more evident than in the Radisha.

"Tadjik," had remained almost invisible since she had rejoined us this side of the Dandha Presh. Though Riverwalker and Runmust stayed close, she needed no watching and made few demands. She stayed to herself, cloaked in brooding. The farther we moved from Taglios, the nearer we approached her brother, the more withdrawn she became. On the road, after the Grove of Doom, we had become almost sisterly. But the pendulum had been swinging the other way ever since Jaicur and we had not exchanged a hundred words a week this side of the mountains. That did not please me. I enjoyed her company, conversation and slashing wit.

Even Master Santaraksita had had no luck drawing her out lately, though she had developed an affection for his scholarly drollery. Between them, the pair could gut and flense a fool's argument faster than a master butcher ever cleaned a chicken.

I mentioned the problem to Willow Swan.

"I'll bet it's not her brother that's bothering her. He wouldn't be the biggest thing, anyway. I'd guess she's down about not being able to go back. Ever since she realized we're probably on a one-wayer here, she's been in a black depression."

"Uhm?"

"It's *Rajadharma*. That's not just a handy propaganda slogan for her, Sleepy. She takes being the ruler of Taglios seriously. You got her strolling on down here, month after month, seeing what the Protector did in her name. You have to understand that she's going to be upset about the way she let herself get used. And then she has to face the fact that she'll probably never get a chance to do anything about it. She's not that hard to understand."

But he had been close to her for thirty years. "We're going back."

"Oh, sure. And on the one chance in a zillion that we really do, who's going to have an army waiting? Can you say Soulcatcher?"

"Sure. And I can also say she'll forget us in six months. She'll find a more interesting game to play."

"And can you say 'Water sleeps?' So can Soulcatcher, Sleepy. You don't know her. Nobody does—except maybe Lady, a little. But I got closer than most for a while. Not exactly by choice, but there I was. I tried to pay attention, for what good it would do me. She isn't entirely inhuman and she isn't as vain and heedless as she might want the world to think. Bottom line, you need to keep one critical fact firmly in mind when you're thinking about Soulcatcher. And that is that she's still alive in a world where her deadliest enemy was the Lady of the Tower. Remembering that in her time Lady made the Shadowmasters look like unschooled bullies."

"You're really wound today, aren't you?"

"Just stating the facts."

"Here's one of your own right back. Water sleeps. The woman who used to be the Lady of the Tower will be back on her feet in an-other few days."

"You'd better ask Murgen if he thinks she'll want to bother get-ting up. I'll bet you it's not this cold where she's at." The breeze on the plain had begun to gnaw both deeply and relentlessly.

I did not disagree even though he knew the truth. He might not remember but he must have helped Soulcatcher move the Captured into the ice caverns where they lay imprisoned.

A murder of crows appeared from the north, fighting the wind. They had very little to say to one another. They circled a few times, then fought for altitude and rode the breeze toward Mama. They would not have much to report.

We began to find more bodies, sometimes in twos and threes. A fair number of the Captured had not been caught at all. I recalled Murgen's report that almost half the party made a break for the world after Soulcatcher got loose. Here they were. I did not remember most of them. They were Taglian or Jaicuri rather than Old Crew, mostly, which meant they had enlisted while I was up north on Murgen's be-half.

We came upon Suyen Dinh Duc, Bucket's Nyueng Bao body-guard. Duc's body had been prepared neatly for ceremonial farewells. That Bucket had paused in the midst of terror to honor one of the quietest and most unobtrusive of the Nyueng Bao companions spoke volumes about the character of my adopted father—and that of Duc. Bucket had refused to accept protection. He did not want a body-guard. And Suyen Dinh Duc had refused to go away. He had felt called by a power far superior to Bucket's will. I believe they became friends when nobody was looking.

I began to shed the tears that had not come when we had found Bucket himself.

Willow Swan and Suvrin tried to comfort me. Both were uneasy with the effort, not quite knowing if hugging would be acceptable. It sure would have been but I did not know how to let them know without saying it. That would have embarrassed me too much.

Sahra provided the comfort as the Nyueng Bao gathered to honor one of their own.

Swan woofed. The white crow had landed on his left shoulder and pecked at his ear. It studied the dead man with one eye and the rest of us with the other.

Uncle Doj observed, "Your friend was supremely confident that someone would come this way again, Annalist. He left Duc in the attitude called 'In Respect of Patient Repose,' which we do when a proper funeral has to be delayed. Neither gods nor devils disturb the dead while they lie so disposed."

I sniffled. "Water sleeps, Uncle. Bucket believed. He knew we'd come."

Bucket's belief had been stronger than mine. Mine barely survived the Kiaulune wars. Without Sahra's relentless desire to resurrect Murgen I would not have come through the times of despair. I would not have become strong enough to endure when Sahra's own time of doubt came upon her.

Now we were here, with nowhere to go but forward. I dried my eyes. "We don't have time to stand around talking. Our resources are painfully finite. Let's load him up—"

Doj interrupted. "We would prefer to leave him as he is, where he is, till we can send him off with the appropriate ceremonies."

"And those would be—"

"What?"

"I haven't seen many dead Nyueng Bao since the siege of Jaicur. You people do a good job of dancing around death. But I have seen a few of your tribe dead and there wasn't any obviously necessary funeral ritual. Some got burned on the ghats as though they were Gunni. I saw one man buried in the ground, as if he were Vehdna. I've even seen a corpse rubbed with bad-smelling unguents, then wrapped like a mummy and hung head-down from a high tree branch."

Doj said, "Each funeral would have been appropriate to the person and situation, I'm sure. What's done with the flesh isn't critical. The ceremonies are intended to ease the soul's transition to its new state. They're absolutely essential. If they're not observed, the dead man's spirit may be compelled to wander the earth indefinitely."

"As ghosts? Or dreamwalkers?"

Doj seemed startled. "Uh? Ghosts? A restless spirit that wants to finish tasks interrupted by death. They can't, so they just keep going."

Although Vehdna ghosts are wicked spirits cursed to wander by God Himself, I had no trouble following Doj's notion. "Then we'll leave him here. You want to stand beside him? To make sure he stays safe from traffic?" Bucket had placed Duc at the edge of the road so he would not be disturbed by the terrified fugitives back then.

"How did he die?" Swan asked. Then he squawked. The white crow had nipped his ear again.

Everybody turned to stare at Swan. "What do you mean?" I asked.

"Look, if a shadow got Duc and somebody tried to lay him out proper, that layer-outer would be here dead as a wedge, too. Right? So he must've died some other way, before—" A dim lamp seemed to come alive inside his head.

"Catcher did it!" the crow said. It was crow caw but the words were clear. "Haw! Haw! Catcher did it!"

The Nyueng Bao began to press in on Swan.

"Catcher did it," I reminded them. "Probably with a booby-trap spell. By the time Duc reached this point, she would've been ten miles ahead of anybody on foot. She was mounted, remember. From what I remember about Duc, he probably saw the trap as Bucket tripped it and jumped in the way."

Gota pointed out, "The Protector could not have left a booby trap to kill Duc if she had not been released." Her Taglian was the best I had ever heard it. The anger in her eyes said she wanted no mistake to be made.

Sahra whispered, "Suyen Dinh Duc was a second cousin to my father."

I said, "We've been through this before, people. We can't exonerate Willow Swan but we can forgive him if we recall the circumstances he faced. Do any of you really think you can get the best of the Protector, face-to-face? No hands? But some of you think so in your heart." Few Nyueng Bao lacked for arrogant self-confidence. "Here's your challenge. Run back and prove it. The Shadowgate will let you out. Soulcatcher is on foot. She's crippled. You can catch up fast. Can you ask for any more?" I paused. "What? No takers? Then lay off Swan."

The white crow cawed mockingly.

I saw a few thoughtful, sheepish faces but Gota's was not one of them. Gota had never been wrong in her life—except that one time when she had thought she might be wrong.

Swan let it roll off. As he had done for years. He had learned from the strictest instructress. He did suggest, "You said we need to keep rolling, Sleepy. Although I guess we meat-eaters can start on the vegetarians after their stories run out."

"Carry the Key, Tobo. Thank you, Sahra."

Sahra turned away. "Mother, stay with Tobo. Don't let him walk any faster than you do."

Ky Gota grumbled something under her breath and turned away from us. She followed Tobo. Her rolling waddle could be deceptive when she was in a hurry. She overhauled the boy, grabbed hold of his shirt. Off they went, the old woman's mouth going steadily. No gambler by nature, still I would have bet that she was fuming about what foul mortals the rest of us be.

I observed, "Ky Gota appears to have found herself."

Not one of the Nyueng Bao found any reason to celebrate that eventuation.

A mile later we came across the only animal remains that we would ever find from the earlier expedition. They were piled in a heap, bones and shredded dry flesh so intertangled there was no telling how many beasts there had been or why they had gathered together, in life or in death. The whole grim mess appeared to have been subsiding into the surface of the plain slowly. Given another decade, it would be gone.

79

The ugly dreamwalkers returned after dark. They were more energetic in their efforts tonight. The rain returned, too. It was more energetic and was accompanied by thunder and lightning that made sleeping difficult. As did the cold rainwater, all of which seemed determined to collect inside the circle where we were camped. The stone did not appear to slope but water sure behaved as though it did. The animals drank their fill. Likewise, the human members of the band. Runmust and Riverwalker directed everyone to fill waterbags and top off canteens. And as soon as someone raised his voice to bless our good fortune, the first snowflakes began to fall.

What sleep I did manage was not pleasant. A full-blown tumult was underway in the ghostworld and it spilled over into my dreams. Then Iqbal's daughter decided this would be a wonderful time to cry all night. Which got the dog started howling. Or maybe that happened the other way around.

Shadows swarmed over the face of our protection. They were more interested in us than they had been in the interlopers of Murgen's time. He told me so himself.

The shadows remembered ages past. I was able to eavesdrop on their dreams.

On their nightmares. All they remembered were horrors from a time when men resembling Nyueng Bao tortured them to death in wholesale lots while sorcerers great and small spanked the demented souls until, when they were released eventually, they were so filled with hatred of every living thing that even a creature as slight as a roach was subject to instant attack, with great ferocity. Some shadows, already evilly predatory by nature, became so wicked they even attacked and devoured other shadows.

There had been millions so victimized. And the only virtue in their creators was that they manufactured the horrors from invaders who arrived in countless waves from a world where an insane sorcerer-king had elevated himself to near-godhood, then had set out to take full mastery of all the sixteen worlds.

Uncounted tens of thousands of corpses littered the glittering plain before the shadows stemmed that tide. Scores of the monsters escaped into neighboring worlds. They spread terror and havoc until the gates could be modified to prevent their passage. For centuries no traffic crossed the plain. Then came another age of halfhearted commerce, once some genius devised the protection now shielding the roads and circles.

The shadows saw everything. They remembered everything. They saw and remembered the missionaries of Kina, who had fled my own world at the pinnacle of Rhaydreynak's fury. In every world they reached, the goddess's dark song fell upon a few eager ears, even amongst the children of those who had created the shadows.

Commerce on a plain so constrained and dangerous perforce remained light. It took determined people to hazard the crossing. Traffic peaked when the world we recalled as Khatovar launched a flurry of expeditions to other worlds to determine which would be best suited to host the cosmic ceremony called the Year of the Skulls.

Followers of Kina from other worlds joined that quest. Companies marched and countermarched. They argued and squabbled. They accomplished very little. Eventually a consensus took shape. The sacrifice ought to be the world that had treated the Children of Kina so abominably in the first place. Rhaydreynak's descendants should reap what he had sown.

The companies sent out were not swarms of fanatics. The plain was dangerous. Few men wanted to cross it. Most of the soldiers were conscripts, or minor criminals under the rule of a few dedicated priests. They were not expected to return. It became the custom for the conscripts' families to hold a wake for their Bone Warriors or Stone Soldiers before they departed—even though the priests always promised they would be back in a matter of months.

The few who did return usually came back so drained and changed, so bitter and hard, they came to be known as Soldiers of Darkness.

Kina's religion was never popular anywhere it took root. Always a minority cult, it lost what power it did have as generations passed and the early fervor faded into the inevitable, tedious rule of functionaries. One world after another abandoned Kina and turned away from the plain. Dark Ages took shape everywhere. One gate after another failed and was not restored. Those that did not fail fell into disuse. The worlds were old, worn, tired, desperately in need of renewal. The ancestors of the Nyueng Bao may have been the last large party to travel from one world to another. They seemed to have been Kina-worshippers fleeing persecution at a time when the rest of their people had become insanely xenophobic and determined to expunge all alien influences. The ancestors of the Nyueng Bao, the Children of the Dead, had vowed to return to their Land of Unknown Shadows in blazing triumph. But, of course, because they were safe on the far side of the plain, their descendants soon forgot who and what

they were. Only a handful of priests remembered, not entirely correctly.

A voice that did not speak aloud tickled my consciousness. *Sister, sister* it said. I saw nothing, felt only that featherweight touch.
But it was enough to spin my soul sideways and toss it into another
place where, when I caught my spiritual breath, the stench of decay
filled my nostrils. A sea of bones surrounded me. Unknown tides
stirred its surface.

There was something wrong with my eyes. My vision was warped
and doubled. I raised a hand to rub them . . . and saw white feathers.

No! Impossible! I could not be following Murgen's path. I could
not be losing my moorings in time. I would not stand for it! I willed
myself—

Caw! Not from my beak.

A black shape popped into sight in front of me, wings spread,
slowing. Talons reached toward me.

I spun, hurled myself off the dead branch where I had been
perched. And was sorry instantly.

I found myself just yards from a face five feet tall. It boasted more
fangs than a shark does teeth. It was darker than midnight. The odor
of its breath was the stench of decaying flesh.

The triumphant grin on those wicked ebony lips faded as I
evaded the swat of a gigantic, clawed hand. I, Sleepy, was in a
trousers-soiling panic but something else was inside the bird with
me. And it was having fun. *Sister, sister, that was close. The bitch is getting sneakier. But she will never surprise me. She cannot. Nor will she understand that she cannot.*

Who is "me?"

The exercise was over. I was in my body on the plain, in the rain,
shuddering while my mind's eye observed the capering dreamwalkers. I examined what I had experienced and concluded that I had
been given a message, which was that Kina knew we were coming.
The dreaming goddess had been pretending quiescence of recent
decades. She knew patience intimately, by all its secret names. And
I may have been given another message as well.

Kina still was the Mother of Deceit. Quite possibly nothing I had
learned recently was entirely or even partially true if Kina had found
a way to wander the shadowed reaches of my mind. I had no doubt
that she could. She had managed to inform entire generations and

regions with a hysterical fear of the Black Company before the advent of the Old Crew.

I swear I sensed her amusement over having quickened in me a deeper and more abiding distrust of everything around me.

80

Suvrin wakened me early. He sounded glum. I could not see his face in the darkness. "Trouble, Sleepy," he whispered. And I have to give him credit. He was first to realize the implications of the fact that it was snowing. But then, he had seen more of the white stuff than any of us but Swan. And Willow had been away from it long enough to turn into an old man.

I wanted to moan and groan but that would have done no good and we needed to get a handle on the situation right away. "Good thinking," I told him. "Thanks. Go around in that direction and wake up the sergeants. I'll circle around to the left." Despite my nightmares, I felt rested.

The snowfall in no way recognized the presence of the protection shielding our campsite. Which meant the boundaries were no longer obvious. I sensed a heightened killing lust amongst the shadows. They had seen this before. It would be snack time if anyone started running around nervously.

We had One-Eye and Goblin on our side. Tobo, too. They could winkle out the whereabouts of the boundaries.

But they needed a little light to do the job.

One by one I made sure everyone wakened and understood the gravity of the situation, especially the mothers. I made sure everyone understood that no one should move around until daylight.

Wonder of wonders, nobody did anything stupid. Once there was light enough, the wizards started drawing lines in the snow.

I arranged for teams to enforce the boundaries.

Everything went so well I was feeling smug before it turned time to go. Then I discovered that it was going to be a long day—which, of course, I should have known instinctively.

This next leg of the journey had taken the Captured only a few hours. It would take us far longer. The shattered fortress could not be discerned behind the falling snow. The old, old men would have to mark out every step before it could be taken, walking to either side of Tobo and the Key, keeping him centered on the road—but never getting ahead of him. Just in case.

A quarter mile along I was worrying about time already. We had too many mouths and too few supplies. Harsh rationing was in place. These people had to be gotten across the plain fast, excepting those of us who would bring out the Captured.

"This's getting out of hand!" Goblin yelled. "If it gets any heavier, we're up Shit Creek."

He was right. If this snowfall turned into a blizzard, we were going to have no other worries. If it worsened much, we were going to die out here and make Soulcatcher the happiest girl in the world.

She probably was anyway, now that she had had time to reflect on the fact that there was no one left able to dispute her in any whim she cared to indulge. Water sleeps? So what. Those days were over.

Not while I was still standing, they were not.

Swan joined me for breakfast. "How's my wife this morning?"

"Frigid." Darn! Open mouth, insert boot with manure veneer.

Swan grinned. "I've known that for years. Isn't this something? There's more than an inch already."

"It's something, all right. Unfortunately, I don't encourage myself to use the kind of language needed to describe it. Most of these people have never seen snow. Watch out for somebody to do something stupid. In fact, you might stick close to the Radisha. I don't want her getting hurt because somebody doesn't use his head."

"All right. Did you dream last night?"

"Of course I did. I got to meet Kina right up close, too."

"I saw lights on the road to the east of us."

That got my attention. "Really?"

"In my dream. They were just witchlights. Maybe the plain's own memories, or something. There wasn't anything there when I went to look."

"Getting bold in your old age, are you?"

"It just sort of happened. I wouldn't have done it if I'd thought about it."

"Did I snore again last night?"

"You solidified your grasp on the all-time women's championship. You're ready to compete at the next level."

"Must have something to do with the dreaming."

Sahra drifted up. She looked grim. She did not like what was happening even a little, the snow or the way we had to cope with it. But she bit her tongue. She understood that it was now too late to be a fussy mom. Like it or not, her boy was carrying us all right now.

One-Eye limped along using a staff somebody had made for him from one of the smaller bamboo weapons. I did not know if it was still armed. Very likely so, he being One-Eye. He told me, "I'm not going to last at this, Little Girl. But I'll go as long as I can."

"Show Tobo what to do and let him take over as soon as he's got it. Let Gota carry the pickax and you get up on the horse. Advise from there."

The old man just nodded instead of finding some reason to argue, betraying his true weakness. Goblin scowled at me, though, assuming he was going to get a large ration of unsolicited counsel. But he shrugged off the temptation to debate.

"Tobo. Hold up. You really understand what we have to do today?"

"I've got it, Sleepy."

"Then give your grandmother the Key. Where is that horse buddy of mine? Get up here, you. Carry One-Eye." I noted that the white crow had left the beast's back. In fact, the bird was nowhere to be seen. "Up you go, old man."

"Who you calling old, Little Girl?" One-Eye drew himself up as tall as he got.

"You, so old you've gotten shorter than me. Get your tail up there. I really want to get there today." I offered Goblin a hard look, just in case he got a notion to try poking sticks in the spokes. He just looked back blankly. Or maybe blandly.

Spoiled brat, me. I got my way. The ruined fortress loomed out of weakly falling snow around what felt like noon. Once Tobo got the hang of discovering the boundaries well enough to keep up with Goblin, the band began moving at a pace limited only by Mother Gota's capacities. And she seemed taken by a sudden urge to hasten toward whatever destiny awaited whoever arrived with the Key.

My natural pessimism went almost entirely unrewarded. Had Iqbal's boys not discovered the wonders of snowballs, I would have had nothing to complain about at all. Even then I would have been entertained had not a few wild volleys of missiles not strayed my way.

We arrived at the chasm Murgen had mentioned, a tear in the face of the plain rent by powers almost unimaginable. The earthquake responsible had been felt as far away as Taglios. It had flattened whole cities this side of the Dandha Presh. I wondered if it had wrought as much destruction in the other worlds connected to the plain.

I also wondered if the quake had been natural in origin. Had it been caused by some premature effort of Kina's to rise and shine?

"Swan! Willow Swan! Get up here."

Mother Gota had halted at the lip of the chasm simply because there was no way for her to go forward. The rest of the mob crowded up behind the leaders because, naturally, everyone wanted to see. I snapped, "Make a hole, people! Make a hole. Let the man get up here." I stared at the wrecked fortress. Shattered was too strong a description but its state of disrepair went way beyond neglect, too. I supposed if the original golem garrison were still around, it would be in perfect condition and right now the whole crew would be outside dusting off the snow patches attached to every little roughness of the stone.

Swan grumbled, "You need to make up your mind, darling. You want me to look out for the Radisha or—"

"Never mind. I don't have time. I'm cold and I'm cranky and I want to change that. Look at this crack. Is this the way it was before? Because even though it's pretty impressive, it's nowhere as huge as Murgen made me think it would be. Everybody but Iqbal's baby can skip across this."

Swan studied the gap in the plain.

Immediately evident to any eye was the fact that there were no sharp edges. The stone seemed to have softened and oozed like taffy.

"No. It wasn't like this at all. It looks like it's been healing, it's not a quarter as wide as it was. I bet in another generation there won't even be a scar."

"So the plain can heal itself. But not so things that were added later." I indicated the fortress. "Except for the spells protecting the roads."

"Apparently."

"Start moving across. Swan, stick with Tobo and Gota. Nobody else has any idea where to go from here. There you are," I answered an impatient *caw!* from above. If I kind of squinted and looked side-ways, I could make out the white crow perched on the battlements, looking down.

Still muttering to himself, though somewhat good-naturedly, Swan stepped across the crack, slipped, fell, skidded, got up exercising a string of out-of-shape northern expletives. Everyone else laughed.

I summoned Runmust and Riverwalker. "I want you two to figure out how to get the animals and carts across. Draft Suvrin if you want. He claims he's had some minor experience in practical engineering. And keep reminding everyone that if they remain calm and cooperative, we'll all get to sleep in a warm, dry place tonight." Well, maybe dry. Warm was probably too much to expect.

Uncle Doj and Tobo helped Mother Gota across. Sahra followed. Several other Nyueng Bao followed her. That made an awful lot of Nyueng Bao concentrated in one place suddenly. My paranoia began to quiver and narrow its eyes suspiciously.

I said, "Goblin. One-Eye. Come along. Slink? Where are you? Come with us." Slink I could count on to be quick and deadly and as morally reluctant as a spear when I pointed and said, "Kill!"

Uncle Doj did not fail to note the fact that even now I trusted him only incompletely. He seemed both irked and amused. He told me, "There isn't anything for our people here, Annalist. This is all for Tobo's benefit."

"That's good. That's good. I wouldn't want the future of the Company to be placed in the slightest risk."

Doj frowned, disappointed by my sarcasm. "I have not won your heart yet, Stone Soldier?"

"How could you? You keep calling me names and won't even explain."

"All will become clear. I fear."

"Of course. Once we reach the Land of Unknown Shadows. Right? You'd better hope there aren't any half-truths or outright cover-ups in your doctrine. 'All Evil Dies There an Endless Death.' It could still be true."

Doj responded with a baleful look but it seemed neither angry nor calculating.

I said, "Swan. Show us the way."

81

I think this's as far as I can take you," Swan told me. He spoke slowly, as though having trouble sorting out his thoughts. "I don't get it. Stuff keeps going away. I know I was farther inside than this. I know all the things we did. But when I try to remember anything specific, I lose everything between the time I got to this point until sometime during the gallop back. Stuff comes to me all the time when I'm not trying. I do remember that. Maybe Catcher messed up my brain somehow."

"There's an all-time understatement," Goblin muttered.

Swan ignored Goblin. He complained, "We were actually off the plain before I realized that we were the only ones who would be coming out."

I was not sure I believed that but it did not matter now. I grunted, suggested, "How about you make a guess? Maybe your soul will remember what your brain can't."

"First you need to get some light in here."

"What do I have wizards for?" I asked the gloom. "Certainly not anything useful or practical like providing a light. They wouldn't need one. They can see in the dark."

Goblin muttered something unflattering about the sort of woman who indulges in sarcasm. He told Swan, "Sit down and let me look at your head."

"Let me!" Tobo enthused at the same time. "Let me try to make a light. I can do this one." He did not wait for permission. Filaments of lemon and silver light crawled over his upraised hands, swift and eager. The darkness surrounding us retreated, I thought reluctantly.

"Wow!" I said. "Look at him."

"He has the strength and enthusiasm of youth," One-Eye conceded. I glanced back. He was still astride the black stallion, wearing a smug look but obviously exhausted. The white crow was perched in front of him. It studied Tobo with one eye while considering our surroundings with the other. It seemed amused. Then One-Eye began to chuckle.

Tobo squealed in surprise. "Wait! Stop! Goblin! What's happening?"

The worms of light were snaking up his arms. They would not respond to his insistence that they desist. He started slapping himself. One-Eye and Goblin began to laugh.

Meantime, the two of them had done something to Swan to clarify his mind. The man looked like he had just sucked down a tall, frosty mug of self-confident recollection.

Sahra saw nothing funny in Tobo's situation. She screamed at the wizards to do something. She was almost incoherent. Which betrayed how much stress she inflicted upon herself.

Doj told her, "He isn't in any danger, Sahra. He just let himself get distracted. It happens. It's part of learning," or words to that effect, several times, before Sahra calmed down and began to look defiant and sheepish at the same time.

Goblin told Tobo, "I'll take it till you get your concentration back." And in a moment there was light enough to see the walls of the huge chamber. Someone who is skilled at something always makes it look easy. The little bald wizard was no exception. He told One-Eye, "Help Swan keep his head clear."

I thought the place looked like a nice change from sleeping out in the weather. I wished there was fuel we could burn to heat it.

"Whither now?" I asked Swan. For some time I had been silently regretting not having caught Murgen while I was dreaming so I could have gotten reliable directions.

The white crow squawked and launched itself, leaving One-Eye cursing because it had swatted him in the face with its wings.

I was starting to understand the beast. "Somebody see where it goes. One of you sorcerer geniuses want to send a light with it?" Tobo had received control of his light again and had it working in good form but it took all his attention to manage it. I hoped he outgrew this more-confidence-than-sense stage before he took a really big bite of disaster.

Uncle Doj trailed the crow at a dignified pace. I supposed I ought to contribute something more than executive decisions, so I followed him. A ball of leprous green light from behind overtook me and made a nest in my tangled hair. My scalp began to itch. I had a suspicion One-Eye might be sneering at my personal hygiene, which, I confess, sometimes became the victim of a negligent attitude. Sort of. "This'll teach me to take my darn helmet off," I grumbled. I refused to allow him to flash me his smug, toothless grin by not looking back.

I had not been wearing an actual helmet. God save me, that would have been cold. I had been wearing a leather helmet liner, which had kept my ears from getting frostbitten. Barely. Winter. It was one of those things the planning team had not foreseen.

I hurried past Doj, who was startled when he saw my hair. Then he grinned as big as ever I had seen him do. I tossed him a blood-thirsty scowl. Unfortunately, to do so I had to turn around far enough to see One-Eye and Goblin suddenly stop exchanging handslaps and snickers. Even Sahra turned slightly sideways to conceal her amusement. All right. So suddenly I am the clown princess of the Company, eh? We would see. Those two would . . .

I realized that they had lured me into accepting their system of thought. Before long I would be setting traps so I could get even first.

The crow cawed. It was down on the cold stone floor. It danced back and forth, suddenly impatient. Its talons clicked softly. I dropped to my knees. It let me get almost within touching distance before it flopped farther into the darkness.

More light took life behind us as people and animals came inside, making the predictable racket. Every new arrival had to know what was going on.

The crow became a silhouette if I lowered my head and looked at it with my cheek against the floor.

I told Doj, "There's light coming from somewhere. This must be where the Captured got into the inner fortress." I got down on my belly. There was a definite gap in a wall of stone so dark it seemed unseeable even in the available light. I could not make out anything on the other side.

Doj got down and placed his own cheek on the floor. "Indeed."

I called, "We need some more light over here. And maybe some tools. River. Runmust. Have those people start setting up some kind of camp. And see what you can do about shutting out the cold." That would be difficult. There were several large gaps in the outside wall.

Goblin and One-Eye stopped grinning like fools and came forward dressed in their business faces. They kept Tobo right there with them, determined to teach him their trade quickly, hands-on.

With more light it was easier to see what the bird meant me to see, which had to be the crack Soulcatcher had sealed after working her wicked spells on the Captured. "There any spells or booby traps here?" I asked.

"The Little Girl's a genius," One-Eye grumbled. His speech had grown a little slurred. He needed rest badly. "The bird strutted through and didn't go up in smoke. Right? That suggest anything?"

"No spells," Goblin said. "Don't mind him. He's just cranky because him and Gota haven't had no privacy for a week."

"I'm gonna fit you out for all the privacy you'll need for a couple of eons, Runt Man. I'm gonna plant your wrinkled old ass—"

"Enough! Let's see if we can make the hole any bigger."

The crow made impatient noises on the other side. It had to have some connection with the Captured even if it was not Murgen operating from some lost corner of time. Certainly I hoped it was not Murgen from the future. That would imply a less than successful effort on our part now.

I grumbled and snarled. I stamped back and forth while half a dozen men expanded the hole, every one of them grousing about the shortage of light. I did not contribute much as a human candle, either. Maybe the thing in my hair was Goblin and One-Eye offering commentary on how bright I was. Though I doubted that after only two hundred years they could yet have developed that much cleverness and subtlety.

A larger and larger crowd piled up behind me. "River," I growled, "I said you should have these people do something useful. Tobo, get back from there. You want a boulder to fall on your head?"

A voice behind me suggested, "You ought to get more light on it so you can see if you need to do any shoring."

I turned. "Slink?"

"There were miners in my family."

"Then you're as near an expert as we've got."

One-Eye jabbed a thumb at Goblin. "The dwarf here has sapper experience. He helped undermine the walls at Tember." His face split in an ugly grin.

Goblin squeaked, a definite clue that "Tember" was an episode he did not recall fondly. I did not remember any mention of a Tember in the Annals. Reason suggested that the referenced event must have taken place long before Croaker became Annalist, which he had done at an early age.

Two of Croaker's more immediate predecessors, Miller Ladora and Kanwas Scar, had been so lax in their duties that little is known about their time—other than what their successors have reconstructed from oral tradition and the memories of survivors. It was during that era that Croaker, Otto and Hagop joined the band. Croaker says little about those days himself.

"Am I to take it, then, that I shouldn't invest unlimited faith in Goblin's engineering skills?"

One-Eye cawed like a crow. "As an engineer our bitty buddy makes a wonderful lumberjack. Things fall down wherever he goes."

Goblin growled like a mastiff issuing a warning.

"See, this here skinny little bald-egg genius sold the Old Man the notion of sneaking into this burg Tember by tunneling under its walls. Deep down. Because the earth was soft. It'd be easy." One-Eye snorted as he talked, his laughter barely under control. "And he was right. It *was* easy. When his tunnel caved in, the wall fell down. And the rest of us charged through the gap and sorted them Temberinos out."

Goblin grumbled, "And about five days later somebody remembered the miners."

"Somebody was just plain damned lucky he had a friend as good as me to dig him out. The Old Man just wanted to put up a gravestone."

Goblin growled some more. "Not so. And the real truth is, the tunnel never would've collapsed if this two-legged, overripe dog turd hadn't been playing one of his stupid games. You know, I almost forgot. I never did pay you back for that. You should've never brought it up, you human prune. Damn! You almost went and died on me before I got you paid off. I *knew* you were up to no good. You had that stroke on purpose, didn't you?"

"Of course I did, you nitwit. Every chance I get, I try to die just so's you can't backstab me no more. You want to be that way? I saved your ass and you want to be that way? Ain't no fool like an old fool. Bring it on, you hairless little toady frog. I maybe slowed down a step the last couple years but I'm still three steps faster and ten torches brighter than any lily-white—"

"Boys!" I snapped. "Children! We have work to do here." They must have driven the whole Company crazy when they were young and had the energy to keep it up all the time. "As of this moment, all the slates are clean of anything that happened before I was born. Just open me a hole so I can go see what we have to do next."

The two wizards did not stop growling and muttering and threatening and trying to sabotage one another in small ways but they did lend their claimed expertise to the effort to open the gap.

82

Once the opening had been expanded enough to use, there was a brief debate about who would use it first. The accord was universal: "Not me." But when I squatted down to duckwalk forward into the shadows, in hopes I could get a look at what might eat me a few seconds before its jaws snapped shut, several gentlemen turned all noble and chivalrous. I suspect it was significant that two of them, Swan and Suvrin, were not Company brothers.

Goblin grumbled, "All right. All right. Now you're making us look bad. All of you, get out of the way." He bustled forward.

He did not have to duck.

I did, just slightly, as I followed him through.

I did not *need* anyone to be noble or chivalrous or to go in before me.

"There is no God but God," I muttered. "His Works are Vast and Mysterious." I was five steps inside and had just bumped into Goblin, who had stopped to stare as well. "I presume that's the golem demon Shivetya."

"Or his ugly little brother."

Murgen had not kept me posted on the golem's state. At last report it had been just a single earth tremor short of plunging into a bottomless abyss, still nailed to a huge wooden throne by means of a number of silver daggers. I observed, "It appears the plain has been healing itself in here, too." I eased forward.

There was still a vertiginous abyss. I had to close my eyes momentarily while I regained my equilibrium. Shivetya remained poised over it but the gap clearly was narrower than Murgen had described. In closing, the surface had pushed the wooden throne upward somewhat. Shivetya was no longer in momentary peril of falling. It looked like a few decades would see him lying there with his nose pressed into healed stone, the overturned throne on top of him still.

Willow Swan invited himself to join me. He said, "That thing hasn't moved since last time."

I countered, "Thought you couldn't remember anything."

"Whatever the short farts did, it seems to be working. I recognize things when I see them."

Goblin told Swan, "Considering what could still happen if Shivetya starts jumping around, holding still seems like a pretty good idea. Don't you think?"

"Could you hold still for fifteen years?"

I said, "He's held still a lot longer than that, Swan. He's been nailed to that throne for hundreds of years. Or even thousands. He has to have been nailed down since before Deceivers fleeing Rhaydreynak came here on their way to other worlds and hid the Books of the Dead." That observation got me some looks, particularly from Master Santaraksita. I had not yet shared the tales I had gleaned from Murgen. "Else he would've stomped them good at the time. They would've looked like the kind of thing he was put here to guard against. I think."

"Who nailed him down?" Goblin asked.

"I don't know."

"Might be a handy piece of information. You'd want to keep an eye on a guy who could do that kind of thing."

"I would," Swan agreed. He grinned nervously.

"It's listening," I said. I moved along the edge of the abyss several steps, squatted. From there I could see the demon's eyes. They were open a crack. I could also see that there were three of them instead of two, the third being in the center of the forehead above and between the other two. This point had not come up before, though it was the sort of thing you would expect of a Gunni-style demon.

The oversight became self-explanatory as soon as the demon sensed my scrutiny. The third eye closed and vanished.

I asked Swan, "That throne look like it's solidly wedged?"

"Yeah. Why?"

"Just wondering if we could move it without losing it down that crack."

"I'm no engineer but it looks to me like you'd really have to work at it to dump it down there now. Obviously, it could go. One really stupid move . . . it's a hell of a deep hole. But . . ."

The curious kept piling up behind us. Their chatter was becoming annoying. Every single whisper turned into a gaggle of echoes that made the place seem more haunted than it was. "Everybody be quiet. I can't hear myself think." I must have sounded nastier than I intended. People shut up. And gawked. I asked, "Does anyone see a way to get that thing turned right side up and pushed back away from the gap?"

"How come you'd want to do that?" One-Eye asked. "Quit shoving, Junior."

Suvrin asked, "Using equipment we have on hand?"

"Yes. And it would have to get done today. I want the majority of these people back on the road south at first light tomorrow."

"That means using brute force. Right now. Some of us would have to get on the other side of the fissure and lift the top of the throne enough so people and animals on this side could get the leverage to pull it on up. Using ropes."

Swan said, "You try to stand it up the way it is there, the bottom end will just slide off the edge. Then it's a grand ride off to the entrails of the earth."

"How come you'd want to do that?" One-Eye demanded again. I ignored him again.

I concentrated on the argument spreading outward from Suvrin and Swan. I let it run for several minutes. Then I announced, "Suvrin seems to be the only one here with a positive view. So he's in charge. Suvrin, draft anybody you want. Help yourself to any resources you need. Sit Shivetya back up for me. You hear that, Steadfast Guardian? Gentlemen, if you have any ideas, feel free to share them with Mr. Suvrin."

Suvrin said, "I can't . . . I don't . . . I shouldn't . . . I guess the first thing we'd better do is get a solid idea of how much weight we're dealing with. And we'll have to rig up some way to get across the gap. Mr. Swan, you handle that. Young Mr. Tobo, I understand you're skilled at mathematics. Suppose you help me calculate how much mass we're dealing with here?"

Tobo grinned and headed for the throne, not at all intimidated by the demon.

"One adjustment," I said. "I need Swan with me. He's been here before. Runmust, you and Iqbal figure out how to get across. Willow. Come with me."

Out of earshot of the others, Swan asked, "What's going on?"

"I didn't want to remind anybody that the Company got this far once before. Somebody might recall a grudge against the man who made it impossible for our predecessors to go any farther."

"Oh. Thanks. I guess." He glanced at the clot of Nyueng Bao. Mother Gota continued to nurture her grudge. She had a son somewhere down under this stone.

"I may just have a strange perspective. I do believe all of us should accept responsibility for our actions but I'm not sure we ever understand why we do some things. Do you know why you cut Soulcatcher loose? I'd bet you've spent the odd minute here and there trying to figure that out."

"You'd win. Except it'd be more like the odd year here and there. And I still can't explain it. She did something to me, somehow. Just with her eyes. All the way across the plain. Probably manipulating my feelings about her sister. When the time came it seemed like the right thing to do. I never had a doubt until it was all over and we were on the run."

"And she kept her word."

He understood. "She gave me everything her eyes promised. Everything I could never have from the sister I really wanted. Whatever her failings, Soulcatcher keeps her word."

"Sometimes we get what we want and find out that it wasn't what we needed."

"No shit. Story of my life, Sleepy."

"Around fifty people came onto the plain. Two of you got away. Thirteen died on the road, trying. The rest are still out here somewhere. And you helped put them where they are. So I'm going to need you to show me. Are you still blind in the memory or have you started to remember?"

"Oh, those spells took. It's coming back. But not necessarily organized the same way that it happened. So bear with me when I seem a little confused."

"I understand." I kept an eye on the others as we talked. Sahra seemed to be putting herself under a lot of unnecessary stress. Doj looked ferociously ready to seize the day should an opportunity pop up. Gota was nagging One-Eye about something while keeping one grim eye aimed Swan's way. Goblin was trying to get the mist projector set up amidst a jostling crowd. I noted, "There seems to be more light than Murgen reported."

"Tons more. And it's warmer, too. If I was allowed a guess, mine would be that it has something to do with the healing that's going on."

I did feel overdressed for the indoor weather. It was not hot but it was warmer than the plain outside and there was no wind biting.

"Where are the Captured?"

"There was a stairway over there. We must have gone a mile down into the earth."

"You carried thirty-five unconscious people down there and got back in time to get away from the evening shadows? Without killing yourself?"

"Catcher did most of it. She has a spell that makes things float through the air. We roped the people together and pulled them along like a string of sausages. She did the pulling, actually. I stayed on the uphill end. More or less. At first. Because the stair has some twists and turns. We had trouble getting them around the corners. But a lot less trouble than if we'd carried them one at a time."

I nodded. I knew of other instances when Catcher had used the same sorcery. Seemed like a handy one to have. We could use it right here, right now, to hoist my future buddy Shivetya.

Curious. Once upon a time Murgen said that name meant "Deathless," although more recently I had been given the meaning "Steadfast Guardian." But I had been provided with whole new sets of creation myths and whatnot, too.

I fought off an urge to charge off and plunge down the stairway right then. I hustled back to talk it over with the others. Most of the crowd were preoccupied with an effort to get Shivetya's throne turned right side up by the power of talking about it. Suvrin told me, "It's a way to keep warm." And a way to work off some tension, no doubt. I heard plenty of traditional-style grumbling questioning the intelligence of any leader who wanted to play around with something like that great ugly thing over there on that throne.

I gathered everyone interested. "Swan knows the way down to the caverns. His memory is getting better all the time." Goblin and One-Eye preened. I gave them no chance to congratulate themselves publicly. "I'm going down there to scout. I want the rest of you to get camp set up. I want you to work out specifically how we'll divide up tomorrow so the majority can scoot on across the plain to safety." We had discussed this time and again—how we could break up the party, leaving the minimum number of people with the maximum stores to bring out the Captured while the rest moved on to, it was hoped, a more congenial clime.

Doj's position, so perfectly rational, was that we should ignore the Captured until we had crossed the plain, had gotten ourselves established in the Land of Unknown Shadows, and were capable of mounting a more thoroughly prepared and supplied expedition. But none of us knew what we would face at that end of this passage, and way too many of us were emotionally incapable of walking away from our brothers again now that we were this close.

I should have gotten more information out of Murgen while we still had some flexibility. Time was winnowing our options rapidly.

Sahra's response to Uncle's repeating his suggestion was blistering enough to melt lead. She might be reluctant to have her husband back but she was not going to delay any crisis.

Swan leaned over my shoulder and whispered, "If you hang around here waiting for all these people to agree on something, we're going to get very old and very hungry before anything happens."

The man had a point. A definite point.

83

I got my daily constitutional in before we reached the stairway. I began to appreciate just how vast the hall at the heart of that fortress was. My party dwindled into the distance. I observed, "This thing has got to be a mile across."

"Almost exactly. It's a few yards under, according to Soulcatcher. I don't know why. I wish we had a torch. I saw patterns in the flooring last time I was here, when there wasn't quite so much dust, but she wouldn't let me waste time looking at them."

There was a lot of dust. There had been none outside. The plain tolerated nothing alien except the corpses of invaders, evidently. Even here, we had yet to discover any sign of the animals or equipment that had accompanied the Captured south.

"How much farther?"

"Almost there. Watch for a drop-off."

"A drop-off?"

"A step down. It's only about eighteen inches but you could break a leg if it surprises you. I turned an ankle last time."

We found the drop-off. I stopped to look back once I stepped down. All sorts of genius was being invested in the assignments I had given. Closer, Sahra and the Radisha and several others to whom I had not given specific assignments had decided to follow me. I said, "You're right. It does look like there're some kind of inlays. If we have time, maybe we can take a closer look." I considered the edge of the stone. "This curves. And it's polished."

"That part of the floor is a circle. And it's almost exactly one-eightieth of the diameter of the plain. According to Soul-catcher. The raised part where the demon's throne used to sit is one-eightieth the size of this."

"That's probably got to mean something. It have anything to do with the Captured?"

"Not that I'm aware of."

"Then we'll worry about it later."

"The stairs start over here."

They did indeed, right next to the wall. The crack in the floor had extended clear through that. The wall's partial collapse had filled the gap there, then the material from the wall had been pushed back up as the fissure healed itself.

The stairs simply started. There was a rectangular hole in the floor. Steps went down, roughly paralleling the outer wall, away from the crack in the floor, which had healed almost completely. There was no handrail.

Twenty steps down we reached a landing eight feet by eight. The descending steps led off from our right. This flight appeared to go downward forever. Faint light crept up it, just strong enough so you could see where to put your feet.

Sahra and the Radisha had caught up close enough that I could hear them talking without being able to pick up specific words. Both women sounded frightened by the immediate future.

I could sympathize. I was nervous about achieving my life's ambition myself. Just a little.

"You want to go first?" Swan asked. He lacked considerable enthusiasm, I thought.

"Are there booby traps or something?"

"No. She probably wanted to, just in case somebody passed this

way someday, just for the sheer mean fun of it, but there wasn't
enough time. She piddled around so much, for so long, I didn't really
believe we'd ever get away. I'm sure we wouldn't have if she hadn't
been who she was. She spun spells that chased the shadows away.
She'd been in there before. And she'd practiced."

"There it is!"

"What?"

"Nothing. Just remembering something." Stupid me. All those
years I wondered how Swan and Soulcatcher had found time to bury
the Captured without getting gobbled up by shadows and I had overlooked the obvious, the fact that Soulcatcher was a major sorceress
and already had some experience manipulating shadows. You can be
screamingly blind to the obvious if you don't realize that you have
not opened up all the doors of your mind.

Forgive me, O Lord of the Hours. Be Merciful. Be Compassionate. I shall close the borders of my soul as soon as my brothers are
free.

At this point Swan had no incentive to steer me into danger. I
started downstairs.

The architects, engineers and stonemasons responsible had not
been determined to achieve geometric perfection. Though this portion of the stairwell continued downward in a specific general direction, it tended to meander from side to side of a straight line. Nor
were the steps of a uniform height. The builders had been thoughtful enough to provide landings every little way, though. I had a feeling those would seem to be miles apart once I started climbing up
again.

"If we have to bring One-Eye down here, we're going to have to
carry him back up. He won't survive the climb otherwise."

"You might want to organize what you're going to do before we
go down there, then."

"I can't decide what has to be done until I see what I'm dealing
with."

"You might call up your genie in a bottle. Get him to tell you."

"He's never said much about the place where he's at. Not
since he's been in there himself. It's like he's constrained against
that. I dreamed about it a few times but I don't know how accurate
my dreams were."

Swan groaned. "I really didn't want to make this trek."

"Will it be that bad?"

"Not going down. But heading the other way is likely to change your attitude."

"I don't know. I'm beginning to get a little winded just going in this direction."

"Then slow down. A few minutes isn't going to make a difference. Not after all these years."

He was right. And wrong. There was no rush for the Captured. But for us, with our limited resources, time was destined to become critical.

Swan continued, "You need to slow down, Sleepy. Really. It's going to get a little bit hairy in a minute."

He was absolutely right. But he understated the case dramatically.

The stairwell did a meander to the right. It caught up with the chasm caused by the earthquakes that had occurred during the reign of the Shadowmasters.

There was only half a stairway there. It hung in the face of a cliff. That left a whole lot of down on my right-hand side. And it was down that was entirely too well illuminated by a reddish-orange light that may have come from the stone itself, since there seemed to be no other obvious source. Though I did have trouble opening my eyes wide enough to look. Wraithlike wisps of vapor wobbled upward from somewhere down below. The air seemed warmer. I asked, "We're not heading into Hell itself, are we?" Some Vehdna believe *al-Shiel* is a place where wicked souls will burn for all eternity.

Swan understood. "Not your Hell. But I'd guess it's Hell enough for them that're trapped down there."

I stopped on the remains of a landing. The steps narrowed to two feet just below me. By leaning out slightly I could see clearly that the stairwell had been constructed inside a larger bore at least twenty feet in diameter. The shaft had been filled with a stone darker than that through which it had been cut. Maybe the bore had needed to be that big so Kina could be dragged down below. I asked, "Can you imagine what an engineering project this must have been?"

"People with plenty of slaves aren't daunted by big projects. What's the matter?"

"I have a problem with heights. This next part is going to take a lot of prayer and some outside encouragement. I want you to go first.

I want you to go slow. And I want you to stay where I can touch you. I believe in meeting my fears eyeball to eyeball but if it gets bad and I feel like I might freeze up, I want to be able to close my eyes and keep going." I was astounded by how calm and reasonable my voice sounded.

"I understand. The real problem then is, who's going to keep his eyes open for me? Whoa! Don't panic, Sleepy. I was joking! I can handle it. Really."

It was not the worst thing I ever dealt with. I never abandoned rational thought. But it was difficult. Even when Swan promised me that an unseen protective barrier existed on the abyssal side and demonstrated its presence, the animal inside me wanted to get the heck out of there and go someplace where the ground was flat and green, there was a sky overhead, and there might even be a few trees.

Swan assured me that I was missing one heck of a view, especially as we approached the lower end of the gap, where the light was brighter, revealing churning mists way below, mists that concealed the depths of the abyss. I kept my eyes closed until we were back into a closed cavern again.

I had started counting steps up top so I could get an idea of how deep we went but I lost count while I was pretending to be a fly crawling on a wall. I was too busy being terrified. But it did seem like we had traveled a long way horizontally as well as downward.

Almost immediately after I had that thought, the stair turned left, then left again. The orange-red light faded away. The stair made a couple more quick turns into a total darkness, which aroused whole new species of terrors. But nothing bit me and nothing came to steal my soul.

Then there was light again, growing so subtly I was never really aware of first noticing it. It had a golden cast to it but was extremely cold. And as soon as I was aware of it, I knew we were approaching our destination.

The stairwell passed right through a natural cavern. At one time that had been sealed off but the quakes had toppled the responsible masonry walls. I asked, "We here?"

"Almost. Careful climbing over the stones. They aren't very stable."

"What's that?"

"What?"

"That sound."

We listened. After a while, Swan said, "I think it's wind. Sometimes there was a breeze when we were down here before."

"Wind? A mile underground?"

"Don't ask me to explain it. It just is. You want to go first this time?"

"Yes."

"I thought you would."

84

Golden caverns where old men sat beside the way, frozen in time, immortal but unable to move an eyelid. Madmen they, some covered with fairy webs of ice as though a thousand winter spiders had spun threads of frozen water. Above, an enchanted forest of icicles grew downward from the cavern roof.

So Murgen described it once upon a time, decades ago. The description remained apt, though the light was not as golden as I expected and the delicate filigrees of ice were denser and more complex. The old men seated against the walls, caught up in the webs, were not the wide-eyed madmen of Murgen's visions, though. They were dead. Or asleep. I did not see one open eye. Nor did I see one face I recognized.

"Willow. Who are these people?" The bitter wind continued to rush through the cavern, which was a dozen feet high and nearly as wide, with a relatively flat floor, side to side. It sloped with the length of the cavern. It looked like ancient, frozen mud covered with a pelt of fine frost fur. Water had run through the cavern in some epoch before the coming of men.

"These ones? I don't know. They were here when we came down."

I leaned closer but was careful not to touch. "These caves are natural."

"They have that look."

"Then they've been down here all along. They were here before the plain was built."

"Possibly. Probably."

"And whoever buried Kina knew about them. So did the Deceivers chased here by Rhaydreynak. Hunh! This one is definitely deceased. Naturally mummified but definitely gone." The corpse was all dried out. Bare bone showed at a folded knee and tattered elbow. "These others? Who knows? Maybe the right sorcery could get them up and running around like Iqbal's kids."

"Why would we get them up? We're here to get the guys that me and Catcher buried. Right? They're on up there." He pointed upslope, where the light was even less golden, becoming almost an icy blue.

The light was not bright. Not nearly so much so as in the vision I had experienced. Maybe it was more a psychic witchlight than a physical one, more suited to the dreamwalker's eye. I mused, "They might be able to tell us something interesting."

"I'll tell you something interesting," Swan muttered to himself. In a normal voice, for my benefit, he said, "I don't think so. At least I don't think it would be anything any of us would want to hear. Catcher took extreme pains to avoid even touching them. Getting the captives past without disturbing them was the hardest work we did."

I bent to examine another of the old men. He did not look like he belonged to any race I knew. "They must be from one of the other worlds."

"Maybe. There's a saying where I grew up: 'Let sleeping dogs lie.' Sounds like exquisitely appropriate advice. We don't know why they were put down here."

"I have no intention of releasing any deviltry but our own. These men here aren't the same as those."

"There were several different groups last time. I doubt that that's changed. I got the feeling that they were dumped here at different times. See how much less ice there is around these guys? Makes me think it takes centuries to accumulate."

"Ow!"

"What?"

"I banged my head on this damned rock icicle thing."

"Hmm. I must've *over*looked it somehow."

"Get smart and I'll punch you in the kneecap, Lofty. Does it feel like it's colder in here than it ought to be?" It was not my imagination and not the icy wind, either.

"Always." His grin had gone away. "It's them. I think. Starting to realize somebody's here. It keeps building up. It can get on your nerves if you pay any attention to it."

I could feel the growth of whatever it was. Insanity becoming palpable, I suppose. That was the impression, anyway.

"How come we're able to move around in here?" I asked. "Why aren't *we* frozen?"

"We'd probably end up that way if we stayed long enough to fall asleep. These people all had to be unconscious when they were brought down here."

"Really?" We were up where there was less ice. The frost on the floor still betrayed the tracks left by Soulcatcher and Willow Swan years ago. The old men here were different. They resembled Nyueng Bao, except for one, who had been tall, thin and extremely pale. "But they don't stay asleep?" Several pairs of open eyes seemed to track me. I hoped it was my imagination, stimulated by the spookiness of the cave. I never actually saw any movement.

Footsteps.

I jumped hip-high to a short elephant before I realized that it had to be Sahra and the Radisha and whoever else had decided not to participate in all those exciting projects that were underway upstairs. "Go keep those people from stomping in here and messing everything up. I'll get an idea of the layout and try to figure out what we'll have to do."

Swan scowled and growled and grunted, then minced carefully back down the slight slope toward the stairwell. He talked to himself all the way. And I did not blame him. Even I thought nothing ever went right for him.

I took a step in the direction the old footprints led. My boots went out from under me. I hit hard, then slid downhill until I caught up with Swan, who did a convincing job of acting amused after he stopped me. "You all right?"

"Bruised my side. Hurt my wrist."

"I shoulda told you. That floor can be pretty slippery where there's a lot of frost."

"You're lucky I don't swear."

"Uhm?"

"You forgot on purpose. You're as bad as One-Eye or Goblin."

"Did I just hear my name taken in vain?" One-Eye's voice, punctuated by rasping panting more suitable to a lunger, came from the shadows down where the stair intercepted the cavern.

"God is Great, God is Good. God is the All-Knowing and All-Merciful. His Plan is Hidden but Just." And save me from the Mystery of His Plan because all I ever get is the Misery of His Plan. "What is *he* doing down here?" I asked Swan. "I know. I'll leave him behind. I know I'm definitely not going to carry him up out of here just so he doesn't suffer another stroke from the effort. Hit him over the head when he isn't looking." I began moving deeper into the cave again. "I'm going to try this one more time." Beneath my breath I continued my conversation with God. As usual, He did not trouble Himself to defend His Works to me. My fault for being a woman.

I nearly missed the transition from the ancient Nyueng Bao types to Company men because the first few modern bodies belonged to Nyueng Bao bodyguards. I halted only when I reached and recognized a Nyueng Bao bodyguard named Pham Quang. I studied him for a moment.

I backed up carefully.

When you looked for it, the boundary was evident. My brothers and their allies had several centuries' less frost accumulation upon them. They had only just begun to develop the delicate webbings that encased the older bodies. That seemed awfully fast, actually, considering how long some of the others must have been buried. Possibly Soulcatcher had indulged in a little artistry during her visit.

Interspersed with my brothers were several bodies so ancient that they had become completely cocooned. I intuited them as bodies only because the chrysalises slumped just like the Captured did.

A thought. It might be worthwhile having One-Eye along after all. Down here Soulcatcher might have taken time to set a trap or two, just for the devil of it.

The Nar generals Isi and Ochiba sat against the cave wall opposite Pham Quang. Ochiba's eyes were open. They did not move but did seem fixed on me. I hunkered down, got as close as I could without touching him.

Those brown pools were moist. There was no dust on their surfaces, nor any frost. They had opened quite recently.

A chill crawled down my spine. A very creepy feeling came over me. I felt like I was walking among the dead. In the far north, whence Swan came carrying travelers' tales, some religions supposedly pictured Hell as a cold place. My imagination, running with the terror that my brothers' situation sparked, had no trouble picturing this cave as a suburb of Hell.

I rose carefully and moved away from Ochiba. Now the cave floor was almost perfectly level. My brothers were not crowded together. The rest seemed to be scattered along the next several hundred feet, not all immediately visible because of a turn in the cave. A few old cocoon men were interspersed with them. "I see the Lance!" I announced. Which was wonderful. Now we could split into two parties and have both retain their capacity for accessing the plain.

My voice echoed like there was a chorus of me all talking at the same time. Hitherto, Swan and I had tried to speak softly. The echoes had been little more than ghostly whispers although extremely busy even at that level.

"Keep it down," One-Eye said. "What are you doing, Little Girl? You don't have any idea what you're dealing with here." He had gotten past Swan somehow and was headed my way. He was awfully damned spry for a two-hundred-year-old stroke victim. This business had him truly excited.

That left me suspicious. But I had no time to try reasoning out what angle the man might have.

I looked into another pair of eyes, these belonging to a long, bony, pallid man who had to be the sorcerer Longshadow. Longshadow was a prisoner of the Company. He had been brought along because neither Croaker nor Lady trusted anyone else to guard him and he could not be exterminated because the health of the Shadowgate, insofar as they had known, was dependent upon his continued well-being. And well that they had been so distrustful. It would be a much different and more terrible world if the Shadowmaster had been left behind to tinker at whatever wickedness took his fancy. Soulcatcher's evil was capricious and unfocused. Longshadow's malice and insanity were deep and abiding.

That insanity stared out of his eyes right then. On my mental checklist I made a tick that meant this one would stay right where he was. Others might have plans for him but they were not in charge. If we could work out how to strengthen our world's Shadowgate, maybe we could even execute him.

I continued moving, working my silent triage, constantly bemused because there were so many faces that I did not recognize. A lot of men who had enlisted while I was away from the center of the action. "Oh, darn!"

"What?" One-Eye was only a few steps behind me, gaining ground fast. His voice seemed to rattle as it echoed.

"It's Wheezer. The stasis didn't take for him."

One-Eye grunted, evidently indifferent. Old Wheezer came from the same tribe One-Eye did, although Wheezer was more than a century younger than the wizard. There had never been any affection between them. "He had a better run than he deserved." Wheezer had been old and dying of consumption when he joined the Company during its passage southward, decades ago. And he had continued to survive despite his infirmities and despite all the trials the Company had endured.

"Here're Candles and Cletus. They're gone, too. And a couple of Nyueng Bao and two Shadar I don't recognize. Something happened here. This makes seven dead men, all in a clump."

"Don't move, Little Girl. Don't touch anything before I have a chance to look it over."

I froze. It was time to acknowledge his expertise.

85

I haven't found them yet!" I snapped at Sahra and the Radisha. "I don't want to go any farther if One-Eye can't assure me that I'm not going to kill somebody just by being here." Against all advice, those two had pushed as far forward as I would let them go. I could understand that they wanted to see their husbands and brothers and boyfriends, but they ought to have sense enough to restrain themselves until we knew what we could and could not do without risking harm to those very husbands and brothers and boyfriends.

Sahra gave me a sharp, hurt look.

"Sorry," I said, insincerely. "Come on. Think. You can see that the stasis down here didn't work for everyone. Swan. How far up this tunnel do we have to go?" I could see a scatter of eight recumbent forms between myself and the curve, none of whom were immediately recognizable as the Captain, Lady, Murgen, Thai Dei, Cordy

Mather or Blade. "From where we stand now, roughly eleven people still aren't accounted for."

"I don't remember," Swan grumped. Bass echoes chased one another around the cavern. They were worse with my higher-pitched voice, though.

"Memory spell wearing off?"

"I don't think so. This feels more like something I never knew. I'm still a whole lot confused about what went on down here."

One big problem was that none of us really knew exactly how many Captured there were. Swan was the best witness because he had ridden with them, but he had not kept track, other than of key people. Murgen never had been any help because after he had become one of the Captured, he had apparently become unable to explore the immediate vicinity where he was confined.

"We need to get Murgen awake first thing. Nobody else will know all the names and faces." It seemed probable that some of the people I did not recognize just were not part of the Company. "One-Eye. Figure out how to wake these people up. As soon as I find Murgen, I want to get him into talking condition. Can I go ahead?" Squabbling echoes reminded me to keep my voice down.

Crabbily, One-Eye responded, "Yes. Just don't touch anybody. Or even anything that you don't recognize. And stop trying to rush me."

"*Can* you bring them out of stasis?"

"I don't know yet, do I? I've been too damned busy answering dumb questions. Leave me alone long enough and I might figure it out, though."

Tempers were getting short and manners were becoming frayed. I sighed, rubbed my forehead and temples because I had begun to develop a headache, listened to the sounds of more people descending the stair. "Willow, see if you can keep those fools out of here till One-Eye's ready." I looked ahead without eagerness. Not only did the cavern turn to the right, it steepened. The water-polished floor was covered with frost. The footing was going to be treacherous.

"Caw!"

The white crow was up there somewhere. It had been announcing itself repeatedly, sounding more impatient every time.

I moved forward carefully. When I reached the steeper floor, I knelt and brushed the frost away to improve the footing. I told Sahra and the Radisha, "If you *have* to follow me, you'd better be even more careful than I am."

They insisted. They were careful. Not one of us slipped and went flailing back down the slope. "Here's Longo and Sparkle," I said. "And that wad definitely looks like the Howler."

In fact, that wad definitely was that crippled little Master Sorcerer. He had been one of the Lady's henchmen in the far north, then our enemy down here. He had become a prisoner of war along with his ally Longshadow, and Lady must have foreseen some use for him or she would not have kept him alive. But he was not likely to get released while I was in charge. In his way, he was crazier than Soulcatcher.

The crow chided me for taking so long.

The Howler was awake. His will was such that he could move his eyes, though nothing more was within his capacity. One glimpse of the madness within those dark orbs and I knew that *this* man could not be permitted to make it back to the world. "Be very careful around this one," I said. "Or he'll nail you as surely as Soulcatcher nailed Swan. One-Eye. Howler is awake. He can move his eyes."

One-Eye repeated my warning, absentmindedly. "Don't get too close to him."

The crow began to nag. Its voice gave birth to a particularly annoying generation of echoes.

"Ah. Radisha. Here's your brother. And he seems to be in pretty good shape. No! Don't touch! That's probably what contaminated the stasis spells protecting the dead men. You'll just have to be patient, same as the rest of us."

She made a sound like a low growl.

The icy cave ceiling above us made creaking sounds that added to the volleys of echoes.

I continued, "It's hard. I know it's hard. But right now patience is the best tool we have for getting them out of here safely." Once I was sure she would restrain herself I resumed inching forward. The white crow cawed impatiently. Out loud I thought, "I do believe I'll wring that thing's neck."

The Radisha reminded me, "You'll build bad kharma. You might come back as a crow or parrot in your next life."

"One of the beauties of being Vehdna is that you don't have a next life to worry about. And God, the All-Powerful, the Merciful, has no love at all for crows. Except to use as plagues upon the un-righteous. Does anybody know if Master Santaraksita planned to come down here?" My organizational skills had vanished because of my own eagerness to reach the Captured. It occurred to me only now that the scholar's knowledge might prove especially useful here—if he could connect anything in this cave to known myth.

I got no answer. "I'll send for him if I have to. Ah. Sahra, here's your honey. *Don't touch!*" I said that a little too loudly. The echoes got very boisterous. Several small icicles broke loose from the ceiling. They shattered with an almost metallic tinkle when they struck the floor.

The crow spoke, very distinctly, "Come here!"

And I, having finally figured it out, told it, "If your manners don't improve dramatically, you might not get out of here at all."

The bird was strutting back and forth nervously in front of Croaker and Lady. Soulcatcher had left those two snuggled up to-gether, arranged so that the Captain had one arm around Lady's waist while she held his other hand with both of hers in her lap. Ad-ditional delicate touches suggested that Soulcatcher's wicked sense of play had peaked for this bit of still life.

If Catcher had left any booby traps at all, this was where they would be. "One-Eye. I need help." Any traps that existed were be-yond me.

Lady's eyes were open. There was no dust on them. She was an-gry. And the white crow wanted to tell me all about it.

"Patience," I counseled, close to becoming impatient myself. "Swan. One-Eye. Come on up here." Swan arrived first despite com-ing from farther away. I asked, "You recall anything special she did with these two? Any little bit of sneakiness?"

"No. I wouldn't worry about it. By the time she laid them out, she was worried about what might happen next. That's the way she is. When she's starting something, it's her whole world and she has no doubts about any part of it. But the closer she comes to getting fin-ished, the more trouble she has keeping her confidence up."

"Nice to know that she's human." I did not mean a word of that. "One-Eye. Look for booby traps around here. And make up your mind. Tell me if you can bring these people back, darn it!" My headache had not gotten any better. But, thank the God of Mercies, it had grown no worse.

Another icicle fell.

"I know. I know. I heard you the first time you asked." He grumbled something about wishing he knew a way to charm me up a better love life.

I stared past Croaker and Lady. The cavern went on. Pale light barely illuminated it. There was no gold in that at all now. A touch of silver, a touch of grey, a lot of blue ice. In fact, the sedimentary rock seemed to give way to actual ice now, ahead. "Willow. Did Catcher go up there when you were here?"

He checked where I was looking. "No. But she could have during an earlier visit."

Someone had traveled in that direction recently, in cavern scales of time. There were still clear tracks in the frost. And I suspected that I would not enjoy the journey once I began to follow them. But I would do so. I had no choice. I had failed elsewhere by letting Narayan and the Daughter of Night get away. That Kina undoubtedly supplied them with a subtle boost did not sufficiently signify. I should have been better prepared. "One-Eye. Talk to me. Can you resurrect these people or not?"

"If you'd stop barking for five minutes I could probably figure that out."

"Take your time, sweetness. It'll take us a while to starve." That ice up there must have been what Swan had meant when he mentioned ice on the plain.

"You've had all the fool-around time I'm willing to give you," I told One-Eye. "Can you do it? Yes or no. Right now."

"The shape I'm in, I need more rest." His speech was slow and slurred and had taken on an odd rhythm that made following him difficult. He was right, of course. *All* of us needed rest. But we also needed to finish our business and get off the plain. Hunger was a reality already. It was not going to go away. I feared it might become a companion as intimate and dreaded as it had been during the siege of Jaicur.

I had decided, already, that I would adopt Uncle Doj's suggested strategy. We would recover only a few people now. We would return for the others later. But that meant making cruel choices. Somebody would end up hating me no matter what I did. If I was really clever, I would find some good old-fashioned Goblinlike way of spreading the blame all around me. Those tagged to wait could not hate everybody.

And there went some good old-fashioned wishful thinking, Sleepy. We were talking about human beings. If there is any way to be contrary, unreasonable and obnoxious, human beings are sure to find and pursue it. With verve and enthusiasm at whatever might be the most inconvenient time.

86

Is anybody at all still up topside?" I demanded. I had settled down for a short nap when the timing had seemed appropriate and that had turned into a long nap that might have become a permanent nap had not so many people been around to keep me from drifting too far away. I dreamed while I was out, I knew that, but I remembered none of it. The smell of Kina remained strong in my nostrils, so I knew where I must have gone, though.

One-Eye was seated beside me, apparently assisting me with my snoring. A worried Goblin appeared, checking to make certain his best friend did not drift too far into sleep. Beyond me, Mother Gota had become engrossed in a protracted debate with the white crow. That must have been a classic dialog to disinterested listeners.

Goblin murmured, "From now on, don't make any sudden movements, Sleepy. Always look around you. Always make sure that you're not going to damage any of our friends."

I heard Tobo talking rapidly, softly, in a businesslike voice. I could not distinguish his words. Somewhere Uncle Doj rattled away, too. "What's happening?"

"We've started waking them up. It's not as complicated as we feared it might be but it takes time and care, and the people we bring out aren't going to be any use to us after they waken—if you had any plans along those lines. One-Eye worked it all out before he collapsed." The little wizard sounded grimmer suddenly.

"Collapsed? One-Eye collapsed? Was it just exhaustion?" I hoped.

"I don't know. I don't want to know. Yet. For now, I'm just going to let him rest. Right down on the edge of the stasis. Or even into it if I think that's necessary. Once his body regains its strength, I'll bring him out and see how bad it really was." He did not sound optimistic.

I said, "If we had to we could leave him here, in stasis, till we could give him proper treatment." Which reminded me. "You're not just getting everyone up, are you? There's no way we can nurse and feed the whole crowd." Surely the Captured would not be able to take care of themselves after fifteen years of just sitting around, stasis or not. They might even be as weak and unskilled as babies and have to learn everything all over again.

"No, Sleepy. We're going to do five people. That's all."

"Uhm. Good. Hey! Where the heck did the standard go? It was right over there. I'm the Standardbearer. I have to keep track—"

"I had it moved over by the gap to the stair. So somebody going that way can take it upstairs. Will you quit fussing? That's Sahra's specialty."

"Speaking of Sahra— Tobo! Where do you think you're going?" While I was talking with Goblin, the boy had slipped past and headed up the cave.

"I was just gonna go see what's up there."

"No. You're just gonna stay right here and help your uncle and Goblin take care of your father, the Captain and the Lieutenant."

He gave me a black look. Despite everything, he still had those moments when he was just a boy. He put on a pouty face that made me grin.

Willow Swan came up behind me. "I've got a problem, Sleepy."

"Which would be?"

"I can't find Cordy. Cordy Mather. Not anywhere."

From the corner of my eye I noted that the Radisha had overheard. She rose slowly from a squat in front of her brother, looked our way. She said nothing nor did anything otherwise that might betray an interest. It was not common knowledge that she and Mather had enjoyed an intimate relationship.

"You're sure?"

"I'm sure."

"You did bring him down here?"

"Absolutely."

I grunted. There was one other absentee whose nonpresence I had been willing to ignore until some rational excuse for her disappearance arose. The shapeshifter Lisa Bowalk, unable to shed the guise of a black panther, had gone up onto the plain as a prisoner but was not now to be found among the dead above or the Captured down below.

Lisa Bowalk had been possessed of a towering hatred for the Company, and particularly for One-Eye because it was One-Eye's fault that she had become trapped in the feline shape. I had to ask. "What about the panther, Willow? It's not around here anywhere, either."

"What panther? Oh. I remember. I don't know." He was looking around like he thought he might spot his old friend Mather hiding behind a stalagmite. "I remember we had to leave her upstairs because we couldn't get her cage around the first turn in the stair. I mean, it would have gone if Catcher and I didn't have anything else to mess with, but we couldn't manage it and the rest of the string both. So Catcher decided to leave the cage up there for later. I don't know what happened when later came. I don't remember much of anything that happened after we came down here. Maybe One-Eye should give me another dose of that memory spell." He tugged on and twisted the ends of his hair, girl-style, and stared down the slope. "I know I left Cordy right down there, just a little above Blade, where it seemed like the floor would be more comfortable."

"Right down there" was the downhill edge of the clot of seven dead men. There had to be a connection. "Goblin, what's the story? Are we going to wake these people up or not?" Me, ignoring everything he had said earlier.

Goblin responded with a sneer that turned into one of his big toad grins. "I've already got Murgen out."

"But I wanted him down here where I could ask questions."

"I mean I've got him out of stasis, bimbo-brain. He's right over there. I'm working on the Captain and Lady now. Tobo and Doj have been doing prelims on Thai Dei and the Prahbrindrah Drah."

Exactly according to my expectations. With the latter two men included entirely for political reasons. Neither was likely to contribute much to the Company's glory or survival.

I moved down to where Murgen lay snoring. The echoing racket and the melting ice webs were the only changes I saw. I squatted. "Anybody think to bring blankets down?" I had not. I am what you would have to call disorganized when it comes to present-tense operations. It had not occurred to me to bring spare clothing or blankets or gear. But I sure can plan bloodshed and general mayhem real well.

There were treasure chambers down here somewhere, though. I had glimpsed several in my dreams. There might be something useful there—if we could find them.

My stomach growled. I was getting hungry. The rumble reminded me that it would not be long before our situation became desperate.

Murgen's eyes opened. He tried to form an expression, a smile for Sahra, but the effort was too much for him. His gaze shifted to me. A whisper struggled through his lips. "The Books. Get . . . the Daughter . . ." His eyes closed again.

It was true. The Captured were not going to jump up and dance tarantellas when they were liberated.

Murgen's message was clear. The Books of the Dead were down here. Something had to be done before the Daughter of Night got another chance to begin copying them. And I had no doubt that she would manage that, despite Soulcatcher. She had Kina backing her up.

"I'll take care of it." I did not have a ghost of a notion how I would manage that, though.

87

The rescue was running smoothly, like a well-greased siege engine missing only a few minor parts. Goblin had Murgen and Croaker headed toward the surface aboard makeshift litters.

Croaker had not said a word, nor had he made any effort to do so, even though he had been awake and aware. He stared at me for a long time. I had no idea what was going on inside his head. I just hoped he was sane.

Before he departed, Murgen did give my hand a small squeeze. I hoped that was an expression of gratitude or encouragement.

I was not at all happy about his being unable to provide information or advice. I had not thought much about what role I would play after the Captured were wakened. I had operated on the unspoken assumption, more or less, that I would retire to my Annals—or even farther, to the Standardbearer job, if Murgen wanted to be Annalist again.

More and more people kept coming downstairs even though I had tried to send word up to warn everyone that they faced a horrible climb going in the other direction.

The white crow continued to curse and jabber semicoherently until it lost its voice. I was concerned about Lady. She had managed that feathery spy quite well for a long time, never giving herself away even when she did try to clue me in, but now she seemed to be losing control. Of herself. I assured her repeatedly that she would go upstairs as soon as I had bearers capable of getting her there. Doj, Sahra and Gota had Thai Dei ready to travel. I gave them the go-ahead. One-Eye would follow him, then Lady would go. The Prahbrindrah Drah would be the last, this time.

Tobo seemed fascinated by his father, apparently because he could not quite believe that the man was real in a fleshy sense. Circumstances had kept his parents separate almost since his conception.

The boy started to tag along after the rest of the family. I called out, "Tobo, stay down here. You have a job to do. See about your dad after we get Lady and the Prince moved out. Hello, Suvrin. Why're you down here?"

"Curiosity. Sri Santaraksita's curiosity. He insisted that he had to see the caverns. He drove me crazy reminding me how storied they are in religious legend. He couldn't be this close to something like that and not explore it personally."

"I see." I noticed the old librarian now. He was working his way up the line of old men, examining each and murmuring to himself. Occasionally he would bounce up and down in excitement. Swan had gone back to make him keep his hands to himself. He wanted to finger and sniff every bit of ancient metal and cloth. He seemed to have trouble understanding that those old men were still alive but very vulnerable.

"Swan. Bring him up here." I did want the benefit of expertise just a while ago. In a softer voice, I told Suvrin, "You're the one who's going to carry him back upstairs if he can't make it on his own. And I'll be right behind you, giving encouragement by poking you with a spear."

Suvrin seemed to have thought about the climb already. He was not looking forward to it, either. "The man has no concept—"

I interrupted. "What about Shivetya?"

"He's back right side up and safely away from the pit. I can't say he seemed particularly grateful, though."

"He say or do something?"

"No. It was his expression. And that was probably because we dropped him on his nose once. In think I'd have trouble being grateful for a pop in the snoot myself."

Santaraksita was puffing when he joined us. He was excited. "We're walking the actual roads of myth, Dorabee! I have begun begging the Lords of Light to let me live long enough to report my adventures to the bhadrhalok!"

"Who will call you a liar over and over again. Sri, you know the Right People don't become involved in actual adventures. All of you, follow me now. We're going to have another actual adventure traveling into mythology." I headed on up the steepening slope.

I soon discovered that someone had gone this way before me. At first I suspected Tobo had gotten farther than I had thought. Then I decided that the disturbances in the frost were too old for that, so concluded that Soulcatcher must have gone back this way, just to see what she could see.

Back there, small side caves entered the main cavern, few of them large enough to permit passage of an adult body. The main cave dwindled in diameter. We had to hunch down, then we had to crawl. Whoever had gone before us had done the same.

"Do you know what you're doing?" Swan asked. "Do you know where you're going?"

"Of course I do." Leadership tip: Sound confident even when you have no idea. Just do not make a habit of it. They will find you out.

I had been through here in my dreams. But only sort of evidently, because every few feet I ran into some detail I did not recall from those nightmares. And then we stumbled onto something that was far more than a mere detail.

The sole of a boot nearly smacked me in the face because I was concentrating on trying to decipher the story encrypted in the frost on the cave floor. That was the story of someone who had been moving wildly, maybe in a panic. Not only had the frost been rubbed away, in places the stone itself was bruised or chipped.

"I think I've found Mather, Willow." It was one of those odd moments when you discover the trivial. I noticed that Cordy Mather
really needed to have his boots resoled. I did not immediately wonder how a man's leg could stick out like that, with the toe pointing
halfway upward above horizontal while the man himself was lying on
his stomach. "We'd better stop right here and take a good look. I
don't see the man doing this to himself."

Swan said, "I'll get Goblin. Don't do anything till he gets here."

"Don't sweat it. I'm fond of my hide. If I lose it, I'll miss out
on our honeymoon." I drew my sword, for what good that might
do, then raised up slowly till the top of my head bumped the cavern
roof.

Cordy Mather had crawled over a hump in the floor. And something fatal had happened to him before he could get all of himself
onto the downward side.

Suvrin eased up beside me. Inexplicably, I found myself painfully
aware of him as a masculine presence. Luckily, he was even less in-
terpersonally adept than I was. He failed to notice my flustered and
uncomfortable reaction.

Odd. The urge was not something I would pursue, certainly. I just
wondered why I sometimes suffered these sudden, random impulses,
some of which were extremely difficult to resist. Ninety-nine percent
of the time I did not so much as *think* about the possibility of com-
bining myself, a man and a bed in a search for adventure.

Maybe I should not have been teasing Swan.

Suvrin said, "That sure doesn't look very appetizing. What do
you think happened?"

"I'm not even going to guess. I'm just going to sit here and wait
for the expert to show up."

"May I look?" Santaraksita asked.

Suvrin scooted back. He discovered that the older man was too
broad to pass by him there. So we all had to retreat twenty yards so
Santaraksita could get past us in turn. I admonished him repeatedly
not to go farther forward than I had. "I definitely don't want to have
to drag you out of here." Though I will grant that the man was a great
deal leaner now than when I had worked for him. "And because you
want to get home to tell the bhadrhalok all about this."

"You were right about them, Dorabee. They won't believe a word
I say. And not only because they're the Right People but because

Surendranath Santaraksita never had an adventure in his life. He never had the urge until this adventure had him."

"Rich men have dreams. Poor men die to make them come true."

"You persist in amazing me, Dorabee. Who are you quoting?"

"V.T.C. Ghosh. He was an acolyte of B.B. Mukerjee, one of the six Bhomparan disciples of Sondhel Ghose the Janaka."

Santaraksita's face lit right up. "Dorabee! You are a marvel indeed. A wonder of wonders. The pupil begins to exceed the master. What was your source? I don't recall ever having read of a Ghosh or a Mukerjee featured in the Janaka school."

I snickered like a prankster kid. "That's because I was pulling your leg. I made it up, Sri." And that seemed to leave him even more amazed.

Goblin broke it up. "Swan says you found a dead man."

"Yes. It looks like Cordy Mather from this end. I didn't see his face, though. I wasn't going to move anything anywhere until we had a good idea what happened to him. I'd rather it didn't happen to me."

Goblin grunted. "Pudgeman, you want to back down here so I can get past you? This tunnel gets pretty tight, don't it? Watch out you don't let your chubby butt plug it up. For how come do you want to go slithering around back here, anyway, Sleepy?"

"Because if I keep going this way far enough I'll get to the place where the Deceivers concealed the original Books of the Dead."

Goblin gave me a funny look but took my word for it. I talked to ghosts in mist machines. Birds talked to me. A talking bird was following me right now, at a distance. At the moment it did not have much to say because its throat was sore but it did manage to rip out a curse or two whenever it had to dodge somebody's flailing feet. "That's interesting."

"I thought so."

"Ah. Yeah. It's not sorcery, though. It's your basic mechanical booby trap. Spring-loaded. Stabs you with a poisoned pin. There're probably twenty more between here and where you want to go. What do you think Mather was trying to do?"

"If he woke up and found himself down here and didn't know where he was or what had happened to him, he might have panicked and taken off and just went in the wrong direction. I bet it's his fault all those guys back there are dead. He probably tried to wake them up."

Goblin grunted again. "There. That's disarmed. I'd better go ahead and see what else is waiting. But first we need to get Mather pulled back so you all can get past him."

"If you can weasel past him so can I."

"Yeah, you can. But what about your boyfriend and your sugar daddy? They've got a little more pork on them." He grunted and cursed softly as he fought Mather's remains back over the hump in the floor. I noticed, for the first time, that the echoes were different in this more confined space, jammed with bodies. They were almost nonexistent.

88

I do not believe it was miles to where the Deceivers of antiquity concealed their treasures and relics but my body believed that before we got there. Goblin disarmed another dozen traps and found several more that had fallen victim to time. The underground wind whimpered and whined as it rushed past us in the tight places. It sucked the warmth right out of me. But it did not dissuade me. I went where I wanted to go. And was hungry enough to eat a camel when I got there.

It had been a long, long time since breakfast. I had a dread feeling it could be longer still before supper.

"It feels like a temple, doesn't it?" Suvrin asked. He was less troubled than the rest of us. Though raised nearer this place than anyone else, he was less intimate with the legends of the Dark Mother. He stopped staring at the three lecterns and the huge books they bore long enough to turn to me and whisper, "Here." He offered me a bit of crumbling flax cake from the pouch he wore at the small of his back.

"You must have read my mind."

"You talk to yourself a lot. I don't think you realize you're doing it." I did not. It was a bad habit that needed breaking right now. "I heard you when we were crawling through the tunnel."

That had been a private discourse with my God. An internal dialog, I had thought. The subject of food had come up. And here was food. So maybe the All-Merciful was on the job after all.

"Thanks. Goblin. You feel any tricks or traps in here?" There were echoes again, though with a different timbre. We were inside a large chamber. The floor and walls were all ice that had been cut and polished by the flow of frigid water. I presumed the invisible ceiling was the same. The place did have a feel of the holy to it—even though that was the holiness of darkness.

"No traps that I can sense. I'd think they'd leave that sort of stuff outside, don't you?" He sounded like he wanted to convince himself.

"You're asking me to define the psychology of those who worship devils and rakshasas? Vehdna priests would guarantee you that there's nothing so foul or evil as to be beyond the capacity of those most accursed of unbelievers." I thought they would guarantee it. If they had heard of the Stranglers. I had not heard of them before I became attached to the Company.

Suvrin said, "Sri, I don't think you should—"

Master Santaraksita had recognized the ancient books as something remarkable and just could not resist going up for an up-close look. I agreed with Suvrin. "Master! Don't go charging—"

The noise sounded something like someone ripping tent canvas for half a second, then popped like the crack of a whip. Master Santaraksita left the floor of the unholy chapel, folded around his middle, and flew at the rest of us in an arc that admitted only slight acquaintance with gravity. Suvrin tried to catch him. Goblin tried to duck. Santaraksita bounced Suvrin sideways and ricocheted into me. The lot of us ended up in a breathless tangle of arms and legs.

The white crow had something uncomplimentary to say about that.

"You and me and a stew pot, critter," I gasped when I got my breath back. I snagged Goblin's leg. "No more traps, eh? They'd leave that sort of thing out in the caverns, eh? What the devil was *that*, then?"

"That was a magical booby trap, woman. And a damned fine example of its kind, too. It remained undetectable until Santaraksita tripped it."

"Sri? Are you injured?" I asked.

"Only my pride, Dorabee," he puffed. "Only my pride. It'll take me a week to get my wind back, though." He rolled off Suvrin, got onto his hands and knees. He had a definite green look to him.

"You've enjoyed a cheap lesson, then," I told him. "Don't rush into something when you don't know what you're rushing into."

"You'd think I'd know that after this last year, wouldn't you?"

"You might think, yes."

"Don't anybody ask how Junior is doing," Suvrin grumbled. "He couldn't possibly get hurt."

"We knew you'd be fine," Goblin told him. "As long as he landed on your head." The little wizard limped forward. As he neared the point where Santaraksita had gone airborne, he became very cautious. He extended a single finger forward one slow inch at a time.

A smaller piece of cloth ripped. Goblin spun around, his arm flung backward. He staggered a couple of steps before he fell to his knees not far from me.

"After all this time he finally recognizes the natural order of things."

Goblin shook his hand the way you do when you burn your fingers. "Damn, that smarts. That's a *good* spell. It's got real pop. Don't do that!"

Suvrin had decided to throw a chunk of ice.

On its way back, the missile parted Suvrin's hair. It then hit the cavern wall and showered the white crow with fragments of ice. The bird had a word to say about that. It followed up with a few more. I began to wonder if Lady had lost track of the fact that she was not, herself, the white crow, and in fact, was just a passenger making use of the albino's eyes.

Goblin stuck his injured finger in his mouth, squatted down and considered the chamber for a while. I squatted, too, after taking time out to keep Suvrin and Master Santaraksita from making even greater nuisances of themselves.

Swan slithered into the chamber, disturbing the crow. The bird said nothing, though. It just sidled away and looked put out about all existence. Swan settled beside me. "Wow. Kind of impressive even though it's simple."

"Those are the original Books of the Dead. Supposedly almost as old as Kina herself."

"So why is everybody just sitting here?"

"Goblin's trying to figure how to get to them." I told him what had happened.

"Damn. I always miss the best stuff. Hey, Junior! Run up there and show us your flying trick again."

"Master Santaraksita did the flying, Mr. Swan." Suvrin needed to work on his sense of humor. He did not own a proper Black Company attitude.

I asked, "Why not try it yourself, Willow? Take a run at the books."

"You promise to let me land on you?"

"No. But I'll blow you a kiss as you fly by."

"It'd probably help if you people would shut up," Goblin said. He rose. "But by being blindingly, blisteringly brilliant I've worked it out anyway, already, in spite of you all. We get to the lecterns by using the golden pickax as a passkey. *That* was why Narayan Singh was so upset when he saw what we had."

"Tobo still has the pick," I said. A minute later I said, "Don't everybody stumble all over each other offering to go get him."

"Let's just go together and all be equally miserable," Goblin suggested. "That's what the Black Company is all about. Sharing the good times along with the bad."

"You trying to con me into thinking that this is one of the good times?" I asked, crawling into the cave right behind him.

"Nobody wants to kill us today. Nobody's trying. That sounds like a good time to me."

He had a point. A definite point.

Maybe my Company attitude needed attention, too.

Behind me, Suvrin grumbled about starting to feel like a gopher. I glanced back. Swan had had an attack of good sense and decided to bring up the rear, thereby making sure that Master Santaraksita did not stay behind and tinker with things that might cause a change in Goblin's opinion about this being one of the good times.

"Where did he go?" I mused aloud. People were still working in the cave of the ancients, getting Lady and the Prahbrindrah Drah ready to go upstairs. But Tobo was not among them. "He wouldn't just run upstairs, would he?" He had the energy of youth but nobody was so energetic they would just charge into that climb on impulse.

While I tromped around muttering and looking for the kid, Goblin did the obvious and questioned witnesses. He got an answer before I finished building up a good mad. "Sleepy. He left."

"Surprise, surprise . . . what?" That was not all of it. The little wizard was upset.

"He turned right when he left, Sleepy."

"He . . . oh." Now I did have a good mad worked up. A booming, head-throbbing, want-to-make-somebody-pay, real bad mad. "That idiot! That moron! That darned fool! I'll cut his legs off! Let's see if we can catch him."

Right was downward. Right was deeper into the earth and time, deeper into despair and darkness. Right could only be the road to the resting place of the Mother of Night.

As I started out, with intent to turn right, I collected the standard. The white crow shrieked approval. Goblin sneered, "You're going to be sorry before you go down a hundred steps, Sleepy."

I was tempted to abandon the darned thing before we had gone that far. It was too long to be dragging around in a stairwell.

89

T his stair has no bottom," I told Goblin. We were puffing badly despite the direction we were headed. We had passed openings into other caves the stairwell had pierced. Each appeared to have been visited by human beings sometime in the past. We discovered both treasures and boneyards. I suspected Sri Santaraksita, Baladitya and I could not live long enough just to catalog all the mysteries buried beneath the plain. And every darned unknown ancient thing I glimpsed in passing called to me like the sirens of legend.

But Tobo was still ahead of us and seemed deaf to our calling. Perhaps just as we did not waste time and breath responding to Suvrin and Santaraksita, who kept calling down to us from ever farther behind. It was my devout hope they would be smitten by good sense and abandon the pursuit.

Goblin did not respond to my remarks. He had no breath left over.

I asked, "Can't you use some kind of spell to slow him down or knock him out? I'm worried. He really can't be so far ahead that he can't hear us. Darn!" I had gotten tangled with the standard. Again.

Goblin just shook his head and kept moving. "He can't hear." Puff-puff. "But he don't know that he can't hear."

Enough said. There *was* a bottom to the stair. And the Queen of Deceit was napping down there, with just a whisper of awareness left for manipulating a cocky, know-it-all boy who had a touch of talent and had taken possession of an instrument that could become a nasty weapon in the hands of those who would disarm her and have her slumber continue never-ending.

After a while we had to slow down. The unnatural light faded until it became too weak to provide a reliable forecast of our footing. The occasional breezes rising past us were no longer cold. And they had begun to bear traces of a familiar, repugnant odor.

When Goblin caught that smell he slowed way down, worked hard on regaining his breath before he had to suck that stench down in its full potency. "Been a while since I've come face-to-face with a god," he said. "I don't know if I've got what it takes to wrangle one anymore."

"And what would that be? I never realized that I was in the company of an experienced god-wrangler."

"It takes youth. It takes confidence. It takes brashness. Most of all, it takes a huge ration of stupidity and a lot of luck."

"Then why don't we just sit down here and let those sterling qualities carry Tobo through? Though I confess I'm a little nervous about his supply of luck."

"I'm tempted, Sleepy. Sorely and sincerely. He needs the lesson." Troubled, perhaps even a little frightened, he continued, "But he's got the pickax and the Company needs him. He's the future. Me and One-Eye are today and yesterday." He started picking up the pace again, which meant a rapid heightening of the intensity of my skirmish with the standard.

"What do you mean, he's the future?"

"Nobody lives forever, Sleepy."

The burst of speed did not last. We encountered a mist that complicated the hazards of darkness. The visibility turned nil and the footing became particularly treacherous for a short person trying to drag a long pole down a tight and unpredictable stairway. The moist air was heavier than anything I had experienced since the fogs above the corpse-choked flood that had surrounded Jaicur during the siege.

A chilling shriek came from far back up the stair. My mind flooded with images of horrors pouncing gleefully upon Suvrin and Master Santaraksita.

The shriek continued, approaching faster than any human being could possibly descend that stairway. "What the hell is that?" Goblin snapped.

"I don't—" The shrieking stopped. At the same time, I stepped down and there was no more down to step. I staggered, betrayed by the darkness. The Lance banged into overhead and wall. We had reached another landing, I assumed, until I felt around with my toes and the standard and could find no more edge. "What do you have over there?" I asked.

"Steps behind me. A wall to the right that goes forward about six feet, then ends. All level floor."

"I've got a wall on the left that just keeps going on and a level floor. Gah!" Something slammed into my back. I had only an instant of warning, the sound of wings violently flapping as a large bird tried to stop before it hit.

The white crow cursed as it landed on the floor. It flopped around for a moment, then started climbing me. That would have been a sight, I am sure, had there been any light to reveal it.

I fought down an impulse to bat the creature into the darkness. I hoped it was here to help. "Tobo!"

My voice rolled away into the distance, then came back in a series of echoes. The heavy air seemed to load those up with despair.

The boy did not answer but he did move. Or something moved. I heard a rustle from less than twenty feet away.

"Goblin. Talk to me about this."

"We've been blinded. By sorcery. There's light out there. I'm working on getting our sight back. Give me your hand. Let's stick together."

The crow murmured, "Sister, sister. Walk straight ahead. Look bold. You will pass through the darkness." Its diction had improved dramatically over the past year. Maybe that was because we were so much closer to the force manipulating the bird.

I felt around for Goblin, grabbed hold, pulled, dropped the standard, picked it up and pulled again. "All right. I'm ready."

That crow knew what it was talking about. After a half dozen steps we transited into a lighted ice cavern. Make that comparatively lighted. Dim, grey-blue light leaked in through translucent walls as though it was high noon just on the other side of a few feet of ice. Much more light radiated from the vicinity of the woman asleep on a bier at the center of the vast chamber, some seventy feet away. Tobo stood halfway between us and it, looking backward, completely surprised to see us there and equally baffled as to where there might be.

"Don't you move, boy," Goblin snapped. "Don't you even take a deep breath until I tell you it's safe to do so."

The form on the beir was a little fuzzy, as though surrounded by heat shimmer. And in spite of that, I *knew* the woman lying there was the most beautiful creature in the world. I knew that I loved her more than life itself, that I wanted to rush over there and drink deeply of those perfect lips.

The white crow sneezed in my ear.

That certainly took the edge off the mood.

"Where have we seen all this before?" Goblin asked, voice dripping sarcasm. "She must be awfully weak or she'd pluck something better from our minds than a replay of an old Sleeping Beauty fairy tale. There isn't a castle built like this anywhere south of the Sea of Torments."

"A castle? What? What castle?" The word for castle did not exist in Taglian or Jaicuri. I knew it meant a kind of fortress only because I had spent so much time exploring the Annals.

"We seem to be inside the keep of an abandoned castle. There're dormant rose creepers all over the place. There're tons of cobwebs. In the middle of everything is a beautiful blonde woman lying in an open casket. She just begs to be kissed and brought back to life. The part that always gets ignored, and that our ungracious hostess has overlooked here, is that the bitch in the story almost certainly was a vampire."

"That isn't what I see." Carefully, detail by detail, I described the ice cave and the absolutely not blonde woman I saw lying upon a bier at its center. While I spoke, Goblin finally worked some subtle spell on Tobo that kept him too confused to move.

Goblin asked, "Do you remember your mother, Sleepy?"

"I vaguely recall a woman who might have been. She died when

I was little. Nobody talked about her." We did not need to go into this. We had work to do right here, right now. I hoped he got that message from my tone and expression.

"What do you want to bet that what you're seeing is an idealized vision of your mother charged up with a whole lot of sexual come-hither."

I did not argue. That might be. He knew the artifices of darkness. I did keep moving forward slowly, closing in on Tobo.

"Which would mean that up close and quickly, she doesn't have a real good connection with what's outside her." Two decades ago it had become clear that Kina did not think or work well in real time, that she did best when she applied her influence over years rather than minutes. "I'm too old to be snared by temptations of the flesh and you're too unsexed and undefined." He grinned weakly. "The kid, on the other hand, is at that age. I'd give a toe or two to see what he sees. Ruff!" He gestured. Tobo collapsed like a wet sock. "Grab the hammer. Hang onto it hard. Don't get any closer to her than you absolutely have to. Drag Tobo back to the doorway." He sounded old and hollow and possessed by a despair that he did not want to share.

"What's going on, Goblin? Talk to me." This was a situation where we ought not to keep dangers to ourselves.

"We're face-to-face with the great manipulator who's been disfiguring our lives for twenty-five years. She's very slow but she's far more dangerous than anything we've faced before."

"I know that." But my reaction was elation. My spirits soared. All my hidden doubts, kept so carefully submerged for so long, now seemed trivial, even silly. This lovely creature was no god. Not like my God is God. Forgive me my weakness and my doubts, O Lord of Hosts. The Darkness is everywhere, and dwells within us all. Forgive me now, when the hour of my death stares me in the face.

In Forgiveness He is Like the Earth.

I grabbed hold of Tobo's arm and yanked him upright. I clutched him as tightly as I gripped the standard. He would not break away easily. Disoriented, he did not struggle when I pulled him back from the sleeping form.

I averted my eyes. She was beauty incarnate. To gaze upon her was to love her. To love her was to dedicate oneself to her will, to lose oneself within her. O Lord of the Hours, watch over and guard me in the presence of the spawn of *al-Shiel*.

"I need the pickax, Tobo." I tried not to think about why I wanted that unholy tool. At this distance Kina might be able to pluck that right out of my mind.

Moving slowly, Tobo removed the pick from under his shirt and handed it over. "Got it!" I told Goblin.

"Then get going!"

As I started to do that, Suvrin and Santaraksita, gasping violently, stumbled into the light. Both froze, staring at Kina. In soft awe, Suvrin declared, "Holy shit! She's gorgeous!"

Master Santaraksita seemed to be experiencing some confusion as he stared.

Suvrin started forward, drooling. I popped him in the funny bone with the dull end of the pick head. That not only got his attention, it relaxed his overwhelming interest in Kina. "Mother of Deceivers," I told him. "Mistress of Illusion. Turn around. Get the boy out of here. Take him back to his mother. Sri, don't make me hurt you, too."

Something like a bit of mist rose from and hovered over the sleeping woman's mouth. For an instant it seemed vaguely man-shaped, which reminded me of *afrits*, the unhappy ghosts of murdered men. Millions of such devils could be at Kina's beck.

"Run, goddamnit!" Goblin said.

"Run," the crow told me.

I did not run. I got hold of Santaraksita and started pulling.

Goblin was talking to himself, something about wishing he had had the good sense to steal One-Eye's spear if he was going to get himself into something like this.

"Goblin!" I heaved the standard. It was not my intent that it do so, but it stood straight up and bounced a couple of times on its butt before it tipped forward and fell into the little wizard's eager hands. He turned with it as the illusions surrounding Kina evaporated.

90

If Kina was ever human, if any of the countless forms of myth regarding her creation indeed resembled fact, a lot of work had gone into making her big and ugly.

She is the Mother of Deceivers, Sleepy. The Mother of Deceivers. That great hideous form covered with pustules from which infant skulls suppurated could no more be the true aspect of Kina than the sleeping beauties had been.

The stench of old death became powerful.

I stared at the body, now lying upon the icy floor. It was the dark purple-black of the death-dancer of my dreams but it dwarfed Shivetya. It was naked. Its perfect female proportions distracted from the ten thousand scars that marred its skin. It did not move, not even to breathe.

Another feather of vapor rose from one huge nostril.

"Get the fuck out of here!" Goblin shrieked. He jerked to the right suddenly, the Lance of Passion darting toward some target I could not see. The Lance's head burned like it was covered by flickering alcohol flames.

A huge, unheard scream tore at my mind. Suvrin and Master Santaraksita moaned. Tobo squealed. The white crow unleashed a random stream of obscenities. I am sure I contributed to the chorus. As I kicked and punched the others to get them going, I realized that my throat was raw.

Goblin whirled back to his left, thrusting at the wisp of mist that had left Kina's nostril a moment before.

Once again pale blue fire surrounded the head of the Lance. This time it ran a foot up the shaft before it faded. This time the Lance's head betrayed penstrokes of dark ruby glow along its edges.

Another wisp of the essence of Kina rose from her nose.

There was no darkness or mist hiding the entrance now. Kina's focus was elsewhere. Suvrin and Santaraksita were on the stair already, wasting breath babbling about what they had seen. I slugged Tobo up side the head with all the force I could muster. "Get out of here!"

When he opened his mouth to argue, I popped him again. I did not want to hear it. I did not want to hear anything. Not even a divine revelation. It could wait. "Goblin! Get your sorry butt in motion. We're out of the way."

The third wisp impaled itself upon the Lance's head. This time the fire crept two yards up the shaft, though it did not seem to affect the wood directly. However, this time the Lance's head became so hot that shaft wood in contact with it began to smolder.

Goblin started to back down but another wisp rose and drifted faster than he moved, getting between him and the stair. He thrust at it a few times but each time he did, it drifted out of reach. It continued to control his path of retreat.

I am no sorceress. Despite a life spent in the proximity of wizards and witch women and whatnot, I have no idea how their minds work when they are involved with their craft. So I will never be clear on what thought process led Goblin to make his decision. But from having known the man most of my life, I have to conclude that he did what he did because he believed it was the most effective thing that he could do.

Having failed to skewer the wisp, having noted that a second had appeared and had begun to circle him from the opposite direction, the frog-faced little man just whirled, lowered the head of the Lance and charged Kina. He let out a great mad bellow and drove the weapon through the flesh of an arm and into her ribs below her right breast. And just before the weapon struck home, one wisp flung itself in front, trying to block the thrust. The Lance's head was ablaze when it pierced demonic flesh.

The second wisp set Goblin aflame.

Even screaming, telling me to get out, Goblin continued to heave against the Lance, driving it deeper into Kina, possibly in some mad, wild hope of penetrating her black heart.

The blue flame feasted on Goblin's flesh. He let go of the Lance, threw himself to the icy floor, rolled around violently, slapping at himself. Nothing helped. He began to melt like an overheated candle.

He screamed and screamed.

On that psychic level where I had sensed her moments earlier, Kina also screamed and screamed and screamed. Suvrin and Santaraksita screamed. Tobo screamed. I screamed and staggered into the stairwell, retreating despite the urging of that mad part of me that wanted to go back and help Goblin. And there could have been no greater madness than that. The Destroyer ruled the cavern of her imprisonment.

Goblin had struck a fierce blow but in truth, its impact was no greater than the nip of a wolf cub at the ear of a dozing tiger. I knew that. And I knew that the cub, caught, was trying to buy time for the rest of its pack.

I gasped, "Tobo, go ahead as fast as you can. Tell the others." He was younger, he was faster, he could get there long before I could.

He was the future.

I would try to keep anything from coming up the stair behind him.

The screaming continued down below, from both sources. Goblin was being more stubborn than ever he had been with One-Eye.

We climbed as fast as Master Santaraksita could manage. I stayed behind the other two, already ready to turn and put the unholy pickax between us and any pursuit. I was convinced that the power of that talisman would shield us.

Darkness no longer inhabited the stair. Visibility was much better than it had been when we came down. So good, in fact, that had there been no landings to break up the line of sight, we would have been able to look up the stairs for a mile.

I was gasping for breath and fighting leg cramps before the screaming stopped. Suvrin had collapsed once already, losing what little his stomach contained. Master Santaraksita seemed the hardiest of us now, without a complaint to his name, though he was so pale I feared his heart would betray him before long.

As we fought for breath I stared downward, listening to the ominous silence. "God is Great." Gasp. "There is no God but God." Gasp. "In Mercy He is Like the Earth." Gasp. "He Walks with Us in All Our Hours." Gasp. "O Lord of Creation, I Acknowledge that I am Your Child."

Master Santaraksita had enough spare breath to chide, "He's going to get bored and find something else to do if you don't get to the point, Dorabee."

"How's this?" Gasp. "Help!"

"Better. Much better. Suvrin! Get up."

The white crow arrowed up the stairwell, nearly bowled me over landing on my shoulder. I did make the process more difficult by trying to duck the arriving bird. It lashed my face with flapping wings. "Climb," it said. "Slowly, without panic. Steadily. I will watch behind you."

We climbed for five or ten days. Hunger nagged me. Terror and lack of sleep made me see things that were not there. I did not look back for fear of seeing something terrible closing in. We moved slower and slower as the effort devoured our energies and will, and

our capacity for recovery. It became a major trek and an act of ultimate will to climb from one landing to the next. Then we began resting between landings, though neither Suvrin nor Santaraksita ever
suggested it.

The crow told me, "Stop and sleep."

No one argued. There are limits to how far and hard terror can
drive anyone. We found ours. I collapsed so fast I later claimed I
heard my first snore before I hit the stone of the landing. I was only
vaguely aware of the crow launching itself into the darkness, headed
downward again.

91

S leepy?"

My soul wanted to leap up and flail around in terror. My flesh
was incapable and quite possibly indifferent. I was so stiff and I hurt
so much that I just could not move.

My mind still worked fine. It ran as sparkling swift as a mountain
stream. "Huh?" I continued trying to get the muscles unlocked.

"Easy. It's Willow. Just open your eyes. You're safe."

"What're you doing way down here?"

"Way down where?"

"Uh—"

"You're one landing downstairs from the cave of the ancients."

I kept trying to get up. Muscle by muscle my body gradually
yielded to my will. I looked around, vision foggy. Suvrin and Master
Santaraksita were still asleep.

Swan said, "They were tired, guaranteed. I heard you snoring all
the way up in the cave."

Twinge of fear. "Where's Tobo?"

"He went on up top. Everyone went. I made them go. I stayed in
case. . . . The crow told me not to come down. But what's one landing? You think you can get moving again? I can't carry anybody. I can
barely keep going myself."

"I can manage one flight. Up to the cave. That's far enough for
now."

"The cave?"

"I still have something to do there."

"Are you sure you want to go out of your way?"

"I'm sure, Willow." I could tell it was a matter of life or death. For a whole world. Or maybe for multiple worlds. But why be melodramatic? "Can you get these two moving again? And headed toward the top?" I did not think Master Santaraksita could bear seeing what I intended to do next.

"I'll get them moving. But I'm sticking with you."

"That won't be necessary."

"Yes, it will. You can hardly stand up."

"I'll work it out."

"You go right ahead and talk. It'll get the kinks out of your jaw. But I'm staying."

I stared at him hard for some time. He did not back down. Neither did he betray any motive but concern for a brother he suspected of failing to be in her right mind. I closed my eyes for half a minute, then opened them to peer down the stairs. "God was listening."

Swan was working on Suvrin. The Shadowlander officer had his eyes open but seemed unable to move. He murmured, "I must be alive. Otherwise I wouldn't hurt so much." Panic flooded his eyes. "*Did* we get away?"

I said, "We're getting away. We've still got a long way to climb."

"Goblin's dead," Swan said. "The crow told me when it came up to get something to eat."

"Where is that thing?"

"Down there. Watching."

I felt a chill. Paranoia touched me. There had been a connection between Lady and Kina ever since Narayan Singh and Kina had used Lady as a vessel to produce the Daughter of Night. That had created a connection, a connection Lady had hammered into place cleverly, unbreakably, so that she could steal power from the goddess indefinitely. "Forgive me, O Lord. Drive these infidel thoughts from my heart."

Swan said, "Huh?"

"Nothing, part of the ongoing dialog between me and my God. Suvrin! Sweety. You ready to do some jumping jacks?"

Suvrin offered me an old-fashioned, storm-cloud glower. "Smack her, Swan. At a time like this, cheerful ought to be against the laws of heaven and earth."

"You'll be cheerful in a minute, too. As soon as you figure out that you're still alive."

"Humph!" He began to help Swan waken Master Santaraksita.

Upright now, I did a few small exercises to loosen up even more.

"Ah, Dorabee," Santaraksita said softly. "I have survived another adventure with you."

"I've got God on my side."

"Excellent. Do keep him there. I don't think I can survive another of your adventures without divine assistance."

"You'll outlive me, Sri."

"Perhaps. Probably, if I do get out of this and I don't tempt fate ever again. You, you'll probably graduate to snake-dancing with cobras."

"Sri?"

"I've decided. I don't want to be an adventurer anymore, Dorabee. I'm too old for it. It's time to wrap myself up in a cozy library again. This just hurts too much. Ow! Young man—"

Swan grinned. He was not that much younger than the librarian. "Let's get going, old-timer. You keep lying around here and whatever adventure you found down there is going to catch up and have you all over again."

A possibility that posed a fine motivation for us all.

When we finally got moving again, I brought up the rear. Swan wrangled my companions. I gripped the golden pickax so tightly my knuckles ached.

Goblin was dead.

That did not seem possible.

Goblin was a fixture. A permanent fixture. A cornerstone. Without its Goblin, there could be no Black Company. . . . You are mad, Sleepy. The family will not cease to exist simply because one member, unexpectedly, has been plucked out by evil fortune. Life would not end because of Goblin's absence. It would just get a lot harder. I seemed to hear Goblin whisper, "He is the future."

"Sleepy. Snap out of it."

"Huh?"

Swan said, "We're at the cave. You two. Keep climbing. We'll catch up with you."

Suvrin started to ask. I shook my head, pointed upward. "Go. Now. And don't look back." I waited until I saw Suvrin actually guide Master Santaraksita over the tumbled stones and onto the stairs. "We'll catch up."

"What's that?" Swan asked. He cupped an ear.

"I don't hear anything."

He shrugged. "It's gone now. Something from upstairs."

We entered the cavern of the ancients. The wonder had been polished off it by the trampling about of a horde of Company people. I was amazed that they had managed without damaging any more of the sleepers. As it was, almost all the wondrous ice webbing and co-cooning had broken up and collapsed. A few stalactites had fallen from the ceiling. "How did that happen?"

Swan frowned. "During the earthquake."

"Earthquake? What earthquake?"

"You didn't . . . there was one hell of a shake. I can't say exactly how long ago. Probably when you were all the way down. It's hard to tell time in here."

"No lie. Oh, yuck." I had discovered why the white crow had all that energy. It had been dining on one of my dead brothers.

Some evil part of me tossed up the thought that I could follow the bird's example. Another part wondered what would happen if Croaker found out. That man was obsessed with the holy state of Company brotherhood.

"You never know what you'll do until you're in the ring with the bull, do you?"

"What?"

"A proverb from back home. Means that actually facing the reality is never quite like preparing to face the reality. You never really know what you'll do until you get there."

I passed the rest of the Captured, not meeting any open eyes. I wondered if they could hear. I offered up some reassurances that sounded feeble even to me. The cavern shrank. When it came time to get down and crawl, I crawled. I told Swan, "Maybe it's good, you being here after all. I'm starting to have little dizzy spells."

"You hear anything?"

I listened. This time I did hear something. "Sounds like some-body singing. A marching song? Something full of 'yo-ho-ho's.'" What the devil?

"Down here? We have dwarfs, too?"

"Dwarfs?"

"Mythical creatures. Like short people with big beards and permanent bad tempers. They lived underground, like nagas, only supposedly big on mining and metalworking. If they ever did exist, they died out a long time ago."

The singing was getting louder. "Let's get this handled before somebody interrupts."

92

The pessimist in me was sure I would not be able to pull it off. If nothing else, the earthquake Swan mentioned would in some way have sealed the chamber of unholy books off from the rest of the world. If the chamber was not sealed off, then I would trip the only booby trap that Goblin had overlooked. If Goblin had not overlooked any booby traps, then the pickax would not be a protective key, it would be a trigger igniting the thousand secret sorceries protecting the books.

"Sleepy, do you know you talk to yourself when you're worried about stuff?"

"What?"

"You're crawling along there muttering about all the bad things that're going to happen. You keep on and you're going to convince me."

That was twice. I had to get that under control. I did not use to do that.

The place where the Books of the Dead were hidden had not changed visibly. The pessimist in me worked hard to find a dangerous difference, though.

Swan finally asked, "Are you going to study on it till we pass out from hunger? Or are you going to go ahead and do something?"

"I always was a better planner than a doer, Willow." I sucked in a peck of frigid air, took the pickax out of my waistband, intoned, "O Lord of Heaven and Earth, let there be no password that has to go with this."

"Right behind you, boss," Swan said, making a joke as he nudged me forward. "Don't be shy now."

Of course not. That would belittle Goblin's sacrifice and memory.

I realized that my breathing had turned to rapid, shallow panting as I reached the point where Master Santaraksita had achieved flight. I held the pick in front of me with both hands, muscles protesting its weight, squeezing it so tight I feared I would leave my fingerprints etched upon it permanently.

A tingling began in my hands. It crept up my arms as I eased forward. My skin crawled and I developed severe goose bumps. I said, "You'd better hold onto me, Willow." In case I needed yanking back. "In case you need the connection to the pick." The shield was not rejecting me. Not yet.

Swan rested his hands on my shoulders an instant before the tingling reached my body. I began to shiver. Suddenly I had the chills and shakes of an autumn sickness.

"Woo!" Swan said. "This feels weird."

"It gets weirder," I promised. "I've got one of those agues where the chill goes all the way to the marrow."

"Uh . . . yeah. I'm getting there, too. Toss in some joint aches, too. Come on. Let's get that fire started and warm ourselves."

Would fire be enough?

Once we moved forward another ten feet, the miseries stopped getting worse. The tingling on the outside faded. I told Swan, "I think it's safe to let go now."

"You should have seen your hair. It started dancing around when we were halfway through. It lasted only a couple of steps but it was a sight."

"I'll bet." My hair was a sight anyway, usually. I did not offer it nearly enough attention and I had not had it trimmed in months. "Got anything to start a fire with?"

"You don't? You didn't prepare for this? You knew it had to be done and you didn't bring—"

"All right, we'll use mine. I just don't have much tinder left. Didn't want to use mine up when I could use yours."

"Thanks a lot. You're getting as bad as those two nasty old men." Chagrined, he recalled that one of the nasty old men he meant had just completed his tenure with the Company.

"I learned from the best. Listen. I've been thinking about this. Even if we are past all the traps, the books themselves might be dangerous. Considering the way the brains of wizards work, it's probably not a smart thing to peek inside at the pages. One look at the writings and you're likely to spend the rest of your life standing there reading—even if you don't recognize a word—out loud. I recall reading about a spell that worked that way, once."

"So what do we do?"

"You notice that all three books are open? We'll have to come at them from underneath and tip the covers shut. So that they end up face-down. Even then we might want to handle them with our eyes shut when we go burn them. I've read about grimoires that had rakshasas bound into their covers." Although nothing as exciting as that ever turned up in the library where I had worked.

"A talking book that can read itself to me. That's what I need."

"I thought Soulcatcher made you learn how to read when you were the king of the Greys."

"She did. That don't mean I *want* to read. Reading is bloody hard work."

"I thought managing a brewery was hard work. You never shied away from that." Being shorter, I took the job of sneaking up on the three lecterns. I used extreme caution. They might have been great actors but I was soon convinced that they could not see me coming.

"I like making beer. I don't like reading."

He should have been the one getting ready to burn books, then. I was suffering a crisis of conscience as troublesome as any of my crises of faith. I loved books. I believed in books. As a rule I did not believe in destroying books because their contents were disagreeable. But these books contained the dark, secret patterns for bringing on the end of the world. The end of many worlds, actually, for if the Year of the Skulls successfully sacrificed my world, others connected to the glittering plain must follow.

This was not a crisis that needed immediate resolution. I had my answers worked out already, which was why I was on hands and knees under the lecterns while suffering verbal abuse from an infidel who had no use for my god *or* for the Deceivers' merciless Destroyer. I tipped the covers of the books shut while wondering if there was still some way the Children of Night could get to me.

"The covers appear to be blank," Swan said.

"You're looking at the backs of the books. I'm closing them so they're face-down. Remember?"

"Hold it." He held up a finger, cocked an ear.

"Echoes."

"Uhm. Somebody's out there."

I listened harder. "Singing again. I wish they wouldn't sing. Nobody in the band but Sahra can carry a tune in a bucket with a lid on it. You can come on up here now. I think it's safe."

"You *think?*"

"I'm still alive."

"I don't know if that's necessarily a recommendation. You're too sour and bitter for the monsters to eat. I, on the other hand—"

"You, on the other hand, are plain lucky that my god forbids me to reveal that the only thing interested in eating you would be the kind of beetle that flourishes on a diet of livestock by-product. Right there looks like a good place to start a fire."

Swan was up beside me now. "There" was some kind of large brazier-looking thing that still had a few charcoal remnants in it. It was made of hammered brass in a style common to most of the cultures of this end of the world.

"You want me to tear a few pages out for tinder?"

"No, I don't want you to tear pages out. Weren't you listening when I told you the books might make you want to read them?"

"I was listening. Sometimes I don't hear very well, though."

"Like most of the human race." I *was* prepared. In minutes I had a small fire burning. I lifted one of the books carefully, making sure it faced away from Swan and me. I fanned its pages out slightly and set it down in the flames, spine upward. I burned the last volume first. Just in case.

Something might interfere. I wanted the first volume destroyed to be one the Daughter of Night had not yet seen. The first book, which she had copied parts of several times and might have partially memorized, I would burn last.

The book caught fire eventually but did not burn well. It produced a nasty-smelling dark smoke that filled the cavern and forced Swan and me to get down on our stomachs on the icy floor.

The underground wind did carry some of the smoke away. The rest was no longer overwhelming when I consigned the second book to the flames.

While waiting to add the final book to the fire, I brooded about why Kina was doing nothing to resist this blow to her hopes for resurrection. I could only pray that Goblin's sacrifice had hurt her so badly she could not look outside herself yet. I could only pray that I was not a victim of some grand deceit. Maybe these books were decoys. Maybe I was doing exactly what Kina had planned for me to do.

There were doubts. Always.

"You're muttering to yourself again."

"Uhn." I possessed not so much as the faintest hope that Goblin's death had put Kina out of the misery of the world permanently.

"This feels so nice," I said. "I could go to sleep right here." And I did so, promptly.

Good old Willow's sense of duty, or self-preservation, or something, kept him going. He got the last Book of the Dead into the fire for me before he, too, settled down for a nap.

93

The singing soldiers proved to be Runmust, Iqbal and Riverwalker. They had come to rescue the rest of us when Tobo reached them with news of the disaster that had befallen us down below. They had found us by following the smoke. "At the risk of finding myself goaded into employing unseemly language, how is it that I find *anyone* singing? How is it that you haven't taken the road to The Land of the Unknown Shadows? I believe I was pretty insistent on the necessity for that."

Runmust and Iqbal giggled like they were younger than Tobo and knew a dirty joke. Riverwalker managed to maintain a more sober demeanor. Barely. "You're tired and hungry, so we don't blame you for being cranky, Sleepy. Let's do something about that. Settle down and have a snack." He could not restrain a big, goofy grin as he rummaged in his pack.

I exchanged glances with Swan. I asked, "You have any clue what's going on here?"

"Maybe there's a stage of starvation where you get lightheaded and silly."

"I suppose Jaicur could have been an exception."

Riverwalker produced something the shape and color of a puff-ball mushroom but a good eight inches in diameter. It looked heavier than a mushroom that size ought to be.

"What the hell is that?" Swan asked. River had several more in his pack. And his henchmen had brought packs, too.

Riverwalker produced a knife and began slicing. "A gift from our demon friend, Shivetya. Evidently after a day of reflection he decided we deserved a payoff for saving his big ugly ass. Eat." He offered me an end slice an inch thick. "You'll like it."

Swan started eating before I did. I had an ounce of paranoia left. He leaned my way. "Tastes like pork. Heh-heh-heh." Then he had no time for joking. He began wolfing the material, which looked exactly the same all the way through.

It had a heavy, almost cheesy texture. When I surrendered to the inevitable and bit into it, my salivary system responded with a flood. The experience of taste was so sharp it was almost painful. There was nothing comparable in my memory. A touch of ginger, a touch of cinnamon, lemons, sweetness, the scent of candied violets. . . . After the first shock a sense of well-being gradually spread outward from my mouth, and again from my stomach soon after the first mouthfuls hit bottom.

"More," Swan said.

Riverwalker surrendered another slice.

"More," I agreed, and bit into another slice myself. It might be poison but if it was, it was the sweetest poison God ever permitted. "Shivetya really gave you this?"

"About a ton. Almost literally. Fit for man and beast. Even the baby likes it."

Iqbal and Runmust found that news hilarious. Swan snickered, too, though he could not possibly have any idea what the joke might be. In fact, I found that assertion rather amusing myself. Heck, everything was amusing. I had begun to feel relaxed and confident. My aches and pains no longer formed the center of my consciousness. They had become mere annoyances way out of the edge of awareness.

"Continue."

Iqbal squealed, "He grew them. These nasty lumps developed all over him, like big-ass boils, only when they popped, out came these things."

Under more normal circumstances that idea and the images it engendered would have seemed repulsive. I grunted, took another wonderful mouthful, pictured the creation process, caught myself in the midst of a fit of giggles. I regained control, though that took an effort. "So it finally decided to communicate?"

"Sort of. When we left, it was trying to manage some kind of dialog with Doj. It didn't seem to be working all that well, though."

Swan sighed. "I haven't felt this relaxed and positive since Cordy and I used to go fishing when we were kids. This's the way we felt lying beside the creek in the shade, never really caring if we got a bite while we shared our daydreams or just watched clouds scoot overhead."

Even the recollection of his friend's fate did not break his mood entirely.

I understood what he was trying to communicate even though I had had no special friend with whom to share the rare, golden moments of childhood. I had had no childhood. I felt really good myself. I said, "This whatever-it-is is great stuff. River. You seen any side effects yet?"

"It's damned near impossible to stop yourself if you get the giggles."

"I'll try not to get started. Wow! I feel like I could whip twice my weight in wolves right now. Why don't we get going?"

Nobody took the opportunity to mention that me whipping twice my weight in wolves might entail me fighting only the back half of one of the monsters. Iqbal and Runmust continued to giggle over some shared joke of long ago.

"Boys," I said, pointing. "That way. Don't touch anything. Keep going. We're going to go back upstairs."

Dang me, I kept getting silly ideas. And every one of them made me want to start laughing. Riverwalker told me, "We found out that if we sing it helps us keep our minds on business." A big grin spread across his face. He began humming one of the filthier marching songs. It concerned the business that seems to be on the minds of most men most of the time.

I hummed along and got everybody started moving.

Foul-smelling smoke from roasted books filled the cavern. It seemed even stronger in the stairwell. Some of it drifted downward.

Kina was not yet aware, I was sure. She would have done *something* if she had known. But she would not remain ignorant forever.

I hoped we could get ourselves well on the road before she recovered enough to assimulate the truth. Her dreams were deadly enough.

94

I settled my behind onto the rise in the floor near the entrance to the stairwell. I sat there dully wondering why the excavation had been started way out here on the periphery. I did not concern myself about it much, though. I ate again. "This stuff could get addictive." And not because it made me feel happy and silly but because it took away aches and pains and every inclination to sleep. I could sit there knowing my body was at its physical limits without having to endure all the suffering associated with that state. And my mind remained particularly alert and useful because I was not preoccupied with the miseries plaguing my flesh.

Swan grunted his agreement. He did not seem to have been rendered as cheerful as the rest of us. Although, come to think of it, I was not doing much whistling or singing myself.

My mood improved after I had eaten again, though.

In one of his more lucid moments Riverwalker suggested, "We shouldn't waste any more time than we have to, Sleepy. The rest should all be gone by now but they went away hoping that you and the standard would catch up."

"If Tobo hasn't already told them, I've got some bad news about that."

"The boy said nothing about the standard. He may not have had a chance. Everybody was so shocked about Goblin and so worried about how to keep One-Eye from finding out. . . ."

"Goblin drove the Lance into Kina's body. It's still there. You know me. I'm completely hooked by the Company mystique. I believe that besides the Annals, the standard is the most important symbol we have. It goes all the way back to Khatovar. It ties the generations together. I'd understand if somebody wanted to go back after it. But that somebody isn't going to be me. Not in this decade."

That good feeling was moving through me again. I rose. Swan helped me step up to the higher floor level. "Hello!"

Riverwalker chuckled. "I wondered how long it would take you to notice."

The crack in the floor was almost gone.

I went and looked. It seemed to be as deep as ever but now was nowhere more than a foot wide. "How did it heal so fast?" I assumed our presence had been a catalyst. Glancing around the crack toward the demon's throne, I noticed Doj and Tobo hurrying our way. Shivetya's eyes were open. He was watching. "I thought you said everybody had left."

"The earthquake did it." River ignored the presence of Doj and Tobo.

Swan said, "It's the latest thing in home repairs. Go down there and stab that thing again, maybe the plain will heal up completely."

"Might get the clockwork running again," Doj said, having overheard our conversation as he arrived.

"Clockwork?"

Doj did a little hop. "This floor is a huge circle. It's a one-eightieth-scale representation of the plain as a whole, with a complete travel chart inlaid. It rides on stone rollers and was capable of turning before the Thousand Voices got curious and broke it."

"Interesting. I take it your chat with the demon proceeded informatively."

Doj grunted assent. "But slowly. That was the big problem. Just figuring out that communication has to be managed *very* slowly. I think that would carry over physically, too. That if he decided to stand up—if he could—it might take hours. But as the Steadfast Guardian, he never had to move fast. He controlled the whole plain from here, using the charts in the floors and the clockwork mechanisms."

Never had I seen Doj so straightforward and animated. The knowledge bug must have bitten him, along with its kissing cousin that makes the newly illuminated want to share with everyone. And that was not like Doj at all. Nor like any other Nyueng Bao of my experience. Only Mother Gota and Tobo ever chattered—and between them they revealed less than Uncle Doj on a particularly reticent day.

Doj continued, "He says his original reason for being created was to manage the machinery that saw that travelers got where they wanted to go. Over time there were battles upon the plain, wars between the worlds, this fortress was built around him, and at every stage he was saddled with additional duties. Sleepy, the creature is half as old as time itself. He actually witnessed the battle between Kina and the demons when the Lords of Light fought the Lords of Darkness. It was the first great war between the worlds, it did take place here on the plain, and none of the myths have got it close to right."

That was interesting and I said so. But I refused to allow the past's allure to seduce me right now.

"I must confess a grand temptation to create a permanent camp here," Doj enthused. "It will take lifetimes to recover and record everything. He's seen so much! He remembers the Children of the Dead, Sleepy. To him the passing of the Nyueng Bao De Duang happened just yesterday. We need only to keep him convinced that we should have his help."

I looked questions at each of my companions. Riverwalker finally volunteered, "He's got to have been stuffing himself with the demon food." Meaning he thought Doj was out of character a few leagues, too. "Several others also went through big changes when they overindulged."

"That much I understood already. Tobo. Have you undergone a complete character shift, too?" He had not said a word. That was remarkable. He had an opinion about everything.

"He scared the crap out of me, Sleepy."

"He? Who?"

"The demon. The monster. Shivetya. He looked inside my head. He talked to me there. I think he did it to my father, too. For years and years, maybe. In the Annals? When Dad thought Kina or the Protector were manipulating him? I'm betting that lots of times it was really Shivetya."

"That could be. That really could be."

The world is infested with superhuman *things* that toy with the destinies of individuals and nations. Gunni priests have been claiming that for a hundred generations. The gods were banging elbows with each other, stirring the cauldron. But none of those gods were my God, the True God, the Almighty, Who seemed to have elected to elevate Himself above the fray.

I needed the solace of my kind of priest. And there were none nearer than five hundred miles.

"How many stories are there about this place?" I asked Doj. "And how many of them are true?"

"I suspect we haven't yet heard one out of ten," the old sword-master replied. He grinned. He was enjoying himself. "And I wouldn't be surprised if most of them are true. Can you sense it? This fortress, this plain, they're many things at the same time. Until recently I believed it had to be the Land of Unknown Shadows. As your Captain believed that it had to be Khatovar. But it's only a pathway to other places. And Shivetya, the Steadfast Guardian, is many things, too. Including, I think, infinitely weary of being everything that he's had to be."

Tobo was so anxious to interject his own thoughts that he danced around like a little boy with a desperate need to pee. He announced, "Shivetya wants to die, Sleepy. But he can't. Not as long as Kina is still alive. And she's immortal."

"He's got a problem then, doesn't he?"

Swan had an idea. "He could divide up that life span and offer it to us. I'd take him up on it. I could use another couple thousand years. After I get away from this kind of life."

I moved us closer to the demon as we talked. My natural pessimism and sourness evidently reasserted itself, though I never stopped feeling younger and happier and more energetic than I had for ages. I just stopped giggling with the rest of them. I asked, "Where's your mother, Tobo?"

His good humor waned momentarily. "She went with Granny Gota."

A glance at Doj made me suspect that there had been a sharp encounter between Sahra the mother and men willing to accept her son as one of them. This was Nyueng Bao stubbornness again, from two directions. On this one the Troll must have sided with her grandson and Doj.

I changed the subject. "All right. You two claim you've been in Shivetya's mind. Or maybe he's been in yours. Whichever, tell me what he wants." I did not believe the demon was being helpful out of the goodness of his ancient heart. He could not be. He was a demon, accursed of God whether he was a creature of light or of shadow. To a demon we adventurers had to be as brief and transient as individual honeybees would be to us—though, like the bees, we might be able to make ourselves obnoxious for a short while.

Doj said, "He wants what anyone in his position would want. That seems obvious."

Tobo interjected, "He also wants loose, Sleepy. He's been pinned that way for a long time. The plain keeps changing because he can't get out to stop anybody."

"What's he going to do if we pluck the daggers out of his limbs? Will he go on being our pal? Or will he start busting heads?"

Doj and Tobo exchanged uncertain glances. So. They had not spent much time worrying about that.

I said, "I see. Well, he may be the sweetest guy on God's green earth but he stays right where he is for now. A few weeks or months more shouldn't make much difference to him. How the heck did he manage to get himself nailed to his chair?"

"Somebody tricked him," Tobo said.

Surprise, surprise. "You think so?"

It seemed there was a lot more light now than there had been when I was headed in the other direction with Swan. Or maybe my eyes had adapted to the interior of the fortress. I could make out the designs in the floor clearly. All the features of the plain could be found there except for the standing stones with their glittering gold characters. And those might have been represented by certain shadowy discolorations I was unable to examine more closely. There were even tiny points that seemed to be moving, which almost certainly meant something if one knew how to read them.

Shivetya's throne rested atop a circular elevation positioned at the heart of an intermediate raised circle just over twenty yards across. Doj assured me that that was roughly one-eightieth the diameter of the biggest circle and that that was an eightieth of the diameter of the entire plain. The smaller circle, I noted, also boasted its representation of the plain—in much less obvious detail. Presumably, Shivetya could sit his throne and, turning, could see the whole of his kingdom. If he needed more information, he could step down to the next level, where everything was portrayed in a scale eighty times finer.

The implications of the quality of the magical engineering involved in creating all this began to seep through. I was intimidated thoroughly. The builders must have been of godlike power. They had to have been as far beyond the greatest wizards known to me as those were beyond no-talents like me. I was sure that Lady and Longshadow, Soulcatcher and Howler, would have little more grasp of the forces and principles involved than I did.

I stepped in front of Shivetya. The demon's eyes remained open. I felt him touch me lightly, inside. For some reason my thoughts turned to mountainous highlands and places where the snow never melted. To old things, slow things. To silence and stone. My brain had no better way of interpreting the actuality of what Shivetya was.

I kept reminding myself that the demon antedated the oldest history of my world. And I sensed what Tobo had mentioned, Shivetya's quiet, calm desire not to grow any older. He had a very Gunni sort of desire to find his way into a nirvana as an antidote to the infinite tedium and pain of *being*.

I tried talking to the demon. I tried exchanging thoughts. That was a frightening experience even though I was filled with the confidence and good feeling that came from the gift food Shivetya had provided. I did not want to share my mind even with an immortal golem who could not possibly have any genuine comprehension of the things it contained or of why those troubled me so.

"Sleepy?"

"Huh?" I jumped up. I felt good enough to do that. I felt as good as I should have back in my teens, had I never had a need to feel sorry for myself. The healing properties of the demon's gift continued to work their magic.

Swan said, "We all fell asleep. I don't know for how long. I don't even know how."

I looked at the demon. It had not moved. No surprise there. But the white crow was perched on its shoulder. As soon as it recognized that I was alert, it launched itself toward me. I threw up an arm. The bird settled on my wrist as though I were a falconer. In a voice almost too slow to follow, it said, "This will be my voice. It is trained and its mind is not cluttered with thoughts and beliefs that will get in the way."

Marvelous. I wondered what Lady would think. If Shivetya took over, she would be deaf and blind until we brought her back from her enchanted sleep.

"This will be my voice now."

I understood the repetition to be a response to my flutter of unspoken curiosity.

"I understand."

"I will aid you in your quest. In return, you will destroy the Drin,
Kina. Then you will release me."

I understood that he meant for me to release him from life and
obligation, not just from that throne.

"I would if I had the power."

"You have the power. You have always had the power."

"What does that mean?" I recognized a cryptic, sorcerer-type pro-
nouncement when I heard one.

"You will understand when it is time to understand. Now it is
time for you to depart, Stone Soldier. Go. Become Deathwalker."

"What the devil does that mean?" I squeaked. So did several of
my companions, all of whom were awake now and most of whom
were gobbling demon food while eavesdropping.

The floor started moving, at first almost imperceptibly. Quickly I
noted that only the part immediately around the throne, that had
healed itself completely, was involved. I now knew that all the damage, including the earthquake so violent it had been felt as far away
as Taglios, had been initiated entirely by Soulcatcher during an ill-
conceived experiment. She had discovered the "machinery" and in
her willful, damn-the-consequences way, had begun tinkering just to
see what would happen. I knew that as fully as if I had been there as an
eyewitness, because an actual eyewitness had given me his memories.

I knew everything Soulcatcher had done during her several visits to the fortress, in a time when Longshadow believed he was the
total master of the Shadowgate and did not believe that others would
dare approach it even if they did possess a workable key.

I now knew many things as if I had lived them. Some were things
I was not eager to know. A few concerned questions I had had for
years, offering answers that I could share with Master Santaraksita.
But mostly it was just stuff I was likely to find useful if I was going to
become what Shivetya hoped I would.

A startled bluebottle of speculation buzzed through my mind. I
checked to see if I had an answer. But I had no memories of what
might have become of the Key that would have been necessary if, indeed, Longshadow, as Maricha Manthara Dhumraksha, with his stu-

dent Ashutosh Yaksha, had come to our world from the Land of Unknown Shadows.

And for sure, I did not get any relief from my fear of heights.

An instant after the floor stopped turning, the white crow
launched itself upward. And darned if I did not launch myself right
after it—though not through any wish of my own.

My comparisons rose behind me. In their surprise and fright several dripped weapons and possessions and, probably, body contents.
Only Tobo seemed to find unanticipated flight to be a positive experience.

Runmust and Iqbal sealed their eyes and belched rapid prayers to
their false vision of God. I spoke my mind to the God Who Is God,
reminding Him to be merciful. Riverwalker addressed impassioned
appeals to his heathen deities. Doj and Swan said nothing at all,
Swan because he had fainted.

Tobo babbled in delight, informing everyone how wonderful the
experience was, look here, look there, the vast expanse of the chamber stretches out below us like the plain itself. . . .

We passed through a hole in the ceiling and into the colder air
of the real plain. It was dusk out there, the sky still crimson over the
western horizon but already deep indigo directly ahead. The stars of
the Noose shone palely in front of us. As we descended toward the
surface, I found nerve enough to glance back. The fortress stood silhouetted against the northern sky, on its outside in worse shape now
than when we had arrived. All our clutter, everything dropped during our ascension or that we had had no time to grab, now flew along
right behind us.

For a while I watched eagerly for the standard to join the flock.
My hopes were disappointed. It did not appear.

In retrospect I cannot see why I should have hoped otherwise.

Now Tobo pretended he was a bird. By experimenting he discovered that he could use his arms to direct his flight, to rise and fall
somewhat, to speed up and slow down slightly. He never shut up for
a instant, loving every moment, continuously admonishing the rest
of us to enjoy the adventure, because none of us would ever have the
chance to experience anything like this again.

"Wisdom from the mouths of infants," Doj announced. Then he
threw up.

They were both right.

95

O ur flight ended where the rest of the band was camped at the last circle before the southwest road reached our destination shadowgate. Flying definitely offered the advantage of speed. We outflew the white crow, arriving less than two hours after our toes departed solid stone. That Shivetya fellow was a handy friend to have.

I tried to see what lay beyond the edge of the plain but it was just too dark. There might have been one or two small points of light out there. It was hard to tell.

We descended feetfirst, evidently immune to shadows. I had sensed several of those pacing us but they had shown no inclination to get too close. Which left me admiring Shivetya's power even more, for those things were little more than bundles of hatred and hunger to kill.

We passed through the top of the shielding protecting our brethren without compromising it. The whole band watched our arrival in disbelief. Tobo managed to direct himself toward his mother and accomplished a somersault before he touched down. I did not exactly get down and hug the stone surface but I was glad the ordeal was over. The Singh brothers rushed around looking for family. So did Doj, who ignored Sahra and went directly to Gota. Gota was not in good spirits and possibly was in ill health. I could not tell much more about anyone in the feeble light available from a changeable moon. Gota did not offer any complaint or criticism.

Swan stuck with me.

As soon as he convinced himself that it was safe to open his eyes, Riverwalker began bustling around being a busybody, devoutly determined to make sure everyone and everything conformed to whatever rules he happened to recall at the moment. I frowned, shook my head, but did not interfere. We all need our rituals to help us get by.

"Sahra," I asked, "how are they?" I meant those we had brought out of the caverns, because I had a suspicion that Gota's state meant nothing good and I did not want to hear what I feared it did mean.

Sahra could not feel friendly. She blamed me because she had discovered her baby strolling through the sky. Never mind that he had come down safely and could not stop raving about the experience.

What a fall from a great height might do to a body never oc-curred to him. But it certainly did to Sahra.

"No change in the Captured. One-Eye went into a funk when he heard about Goblin and hasn't spoken since. Mother isn't sure if it's emotional withdrawal or he had another stroke. What worries her is the possibility that he doesn't want to live anymore."

"Who would he fight with?" I did not mean to belittle, though it came out sounding that way.

Sahra showed me an instant of pique but did not reveal her thoughts. "Mother can be a handful."

"Probably what got them together in the first place." I made no mention of the fact that I feared Gota would not be with us much longer. The Troll had to be around eighty. "I'll go talk to him."

"He's asleep. It can wait."

"In the morning, then. Are we still in touch with Murgen?"

The light was good enough to reveal Sahra's anger. Perhaps she was right. I had not had my feet on the ground two minutes and al-ready I wanted to use her husband. But she managed the emotion. We had worked together for a long time now, early on with her usu-ally being the stronger one, only occasionally with me taking the lead role. We always managed without sharp words. We always man-aged because we knew we had somewhere to go and we had to col-laborate to get there. These days I took charge most of the time but she could do so when it was appropriate.

Only she was just about where she wanted to get to now, was she not? She had Murgen out of the ground. She would not need to go on with her role once he was up and around. Unless he was not the man she wanted him to be. In which case she would have to contrive a new Sahra all over again.

I am sure that had her on edge more than ever. Neither she nor Murgen were the people they had been. None of us were. There were going to be some difficulties adjusting, possibly some major difficul-ties.

I anticipated big problems with Lady and the Captain.

Sahra said, "I've done my best to keep the mist projector work-ing but I haven't been able to make contact since we left that fortress. He doesn't seem to be willing to leave his body anymore. And I can't get that to wake up more than it already is." So she was also afraid that the rescue might have been a mistake, that we might have hurt Murgen instead of saving him. Upbeat, hopefully, she said, "Maybe Tobo can help."

I wondered what had become of the tough, focused, dedicated Sahra who had been Minh Subredil. I tried to reassure this Sahra. "Murgen will be fine." Shivetya had given me the knowledge we needed to reanimate the Captured. "But we have to get him off the plain before we can wake him all the way up. Same for the others."

Riverwalker returned from his tour. "The demon food is going fast here, Sleepy. There's enough to get us off the plain and have a couple meals more but then we're on our own. We either eat the dog and the horses or we scrounge up something locally fast."

"Ah, well. We knew that going in. We're better off than we expected to be. Did anybody think to steal anything valuable while we were there?"

That comment got me blank looks. Then I realized that it was possible no one else had noticed the treasures I had discovered while chasing Tobo into the deeps of the earth. The boy would have said something if he had seen anything. He could not shut up.

Swan told me, "It'll be harvest time when we get there."

"What?"

He shrugged. "I just know."

So he might. "Everybody listen up. Get all the rest you can tonight. I want to get up and move out early tomorrow. And nobody knows what we'll run into at the end of the road."

Somebody grumbled something about if I wanted him to sleep, why did I not shut up and let him get to work?

I could not keep my eyes open myself, although it had not been that long since I had wakened by Shivetya's throne. In fact, my mind seemed to be shutting down. I said, "Forget everything else. I'm going to take my own advice. Where's a place I can wrap my blanket around me and lie down before I collapse?"

The only open space was back at the tail end of the Company. All my flying companions except Tobo had to migrate back there. I had planned to eat before I slept but exhaustion overwhelmed me before I swallowed my third bite of demon's food. My final reflection concerned whether God could overlook one of the Faithful accepting a gift from one of the Damned.

An interesting exercise. God knows all. Therefore, God knew what Shivetya was doing and allowed him to do it. Therefore, it must be God's will that we benefit from the demon's generosity. It would be a sin to defy God's will.

96

I dreamed strange dreams.
Of course I did. Was not Shivetya in my mind? Was I not in the haunted place of glittering stone?

Stone remembered. And stone wanted me to know.

I was in another place, then, in a time not my own. I was Shivetya as the demon experienced the world, everywhere at once, a pale imitation of God. I could be everywhere at once because by staring at the floor surrounding my throne, I connected with my realm as a whole. We became one knowledge, the singer and the song.

Men were moving across my face, a large band. I knew time differently from mortals but I understood that it had been ages since this had happened last. Mortals did not cross me anymore. Not often. Never in numbers like this.

There was enough Sleepy there for me to recognize Shivetya's memory of the coming of the Captured, before they stumbled into Soulcatcher's trap. Why would the demon want me to see this? I knew this story. Murgen had shared it with me several times, to make sure it got recorded in the Annals just the way he wanted.

There was no solid feeling of a personality surrounding me, yet I felt a mild pressure to abandon curiosity, to turn outward from questions, to cease being a viewpoint, to let the flower unfold. I should have paid more attention to Uncle Doj. The ability to abandon the self would have been a useful talent at a time like this.

Time was different for the demon, definitely. But he tried to accommodate the ephemeral mortal, to get to the point, to provide the information he thought I would find useful.

I watched the whole adventure, including the great and desperate escape that had devoured Bucket and had allowed Willow the chance to remain in the story as a pawn of wickedness. And I did not understand immediately because at first I observed only the finer details of a story already known in outline.

I was not completely stupid. I caught on. The question had occurred to me before but had not been critical. Now I just needed to reclaim enough self to recall that I had asked it.

The question was, what had become of the one member of that expedition for whom there was still no account? The incredibly dangerous apprentice shapeshifter Lisa Deale Bowalk, trapped in the form of a black leopard, had been carried onto the plain in a cage, as had the prisoners Longshadow and Howler. She had vanished during the excitement. Murgen never discovered what had become of her. That he mentioned.

I learned the truth. According to Shivetya.

Not every trivial detail became entirely clear. Shivetya had trouble focusing that tightly in time. But it seemed that Bowalk's cage had gotten damaged in the panicky rush to escape by brothers of the Company unfortunate enough not to be included amongst the Captured.

Panic mothers panic. The great, wicked cat caught the fever. Her violence was sufficient to complete the demolition of her cage. She ripped her way out, injuring herself in the process. She fled on three legs, carrying her left front paw elevated, allowing it to touch stone only when absolutely necessary. She whined horribly when she did. Nevertheless, she covered ground fast. She traveled nearly thirty miles before nightfall—but had chosen a direction at random and apparently did not recognize that she was not headed toward home until it was too late to change her mind.

She chose a road and ran. And in the night one small, clever shadow caught up, just short of the end of that road. It did what untamed shadows always do. It attacked. I found the result difficult to believe. The shadow hurt the panther but did not kill her. She fought it and won. And stumbled onward. And before a more powerful shadow could overtake and finish her, she staggered through a derelict shadowgate and became invisible to Shivetya. Which meant that she was last seen alive entering a world neither our own nor the Land of Unknown Shadows. I hoped that that crippled gate had finished her, or that it had injured her beyond recovery, because she was possessed of a hatred as dark as that which impelled the shadows, but hers was a hatred much more narrowly directed. And the Company was its object.

The fragment of Sleepy-self never entirely subsumed into the Shivetya overview wondered what the Captain would think when he learned that Bowalk had reached Khatovar by accident when it was supposed to be impossible for the Company to get there by intent.

The Sleepy-self did not see why this news was important enough for Shivetya to have hijacked my dreams, but significant it must be.

Significant, too, must be the Nef, the dreamwalkers, that Murgen had named the Washene, the Washane and the Washone.

I became more Shivetya, pulling away from the point experience of tracking the shapechanger. I became more one with the demon while the demon became more one with the plain, more purely a manifestation of the will of the great engine. I enjoyed flickers of memories of golden ages of peace, prosperity and enlightenment that had reached across silent stone to many worlds. I witnessed the passage of a hundred conquerers. I saw portions of the most ancient wars now recalled in the Gunni and Deceiver religions, and even in my own, for being Shivetya and embracing all times at the same time, I could not help but see that the war in Heaven, which was supposed to have occurred soon after God created the earth and the sky, and which ended with the Adversary being cast down into a pit, could be an echo of the same divine struggle other religions remembered according to their own predilections.

Before the war of the gods, there was the plain. And before the plain, there was the Nef. The plain, the great machine, eventually imagined Shivetya as its Steadfast Guardian and servant. In turn, the demon imagined the Washene, the Washane and the Washone in the likeness of the Nef. These dreamwalking ghosts of the builders were Shivetya's gods. They existed independently of his mind but not of his existence. They would perish if he perished. And they had had no desire to be called into being in the first instance.

Bizarre. I was caught amongst the personifications of aspects of religion in which I could not believe. Here were facts my faith forbid me to accept. Acceptance would damn me forever.

Cruel, cruel tricks of the Adversary. I had been gifted with a mind that wanted to explore, to find out, to know. And I had been gifted with faith. And now I had been gifted with information that put fact and faith into conflict. I had not been gifted with a priest's slippery dexterity when it came to reconciling the philosophically irreconcilable.

But perhaps that was not necessary. Truth and reality seemed to be protean on the plain. There were too many different stories about Kina, Shivetya, and the fortress in the middle. Maybe every story was true at least part of the time.

There was an intellectual exercise of a sacerdotal magnitude. What if my beliefs were completely valid—but only part of the time and only where I was located myself? What then? How could that be? What could that mean?

It meant unpleasant times in the afterlife if I persisted in relaxing my vigilance against heresies. It might be difficult for a woman to achieve Paradise but it would be no trouble at all for her to win a place in *al-Shiel*.

97

That must have been one kick-ass nightmare," Willow Swan told me, kneeling beside me, having just shaken my shoulder to waken me. "Not only were you snoring, you were grunting and squeaking and carrying on a conversation with yourself in three different languages."

"I'm a woman of many talents. Everybody says so." I shook my head groggily. "What time is it? It's still dark."

"Another talent emerges. I can't get anything past the old girl."

I grumbled, "The priests and the holy books tell us that God created man in His own image but I've read a lot of holy books—including those of the idolators—and not once have I found any other evidence that He had a sense of humor, let alone is the kind of person who would try to make jokes before the sun even came up. You're a sick man, Willow Swan. What's going on?"

"Last night you said we'd have to start early. So Sahra thought you meant we should be ready to go as soon as there's light enough to see. So we can get off the plain with plenty of daylight to spare."

"Sahra is a wise woman. Wake me up when she's ready to go."

"I think right now would be a good time to get up, then."

I raised my hands. It was just light enough to see them. "Gather 'round, people." Once a reasonable crowd had done so I explained that each of us who had stayed behind in the fortress had been given knowledge that would help us in times to come. "Shivetya seems very interested in our success. He tried to give us what he believed would be useful tools. But he's very slow and has his own demonic perspectives and doesn't know how to explain anything clearly. So it's extremely likely that there is a lot we know that we won't know we know until something makes us think of it. Be patient with us. We'll probably be a little strange for a while. I'm having trouble getting used to the reeducated me and I live here. New knowledge pops up every time I turn around. Right now, though, I just want to get off this plain. Our resources are *still* limited. We have to establish ourselves as fast as we can."

Those faces I could discern revealed fear of the future. Somewhere the dog whined. Iqbal's baby whimpered momentarily as Suruvhija shifted her from one nipple to the other. In my consideration, that child ought to have been weaned by now but I knew I had no justification for my opinion. None of my babies have been born yet. And it is getting a little late to bring them in.

People waited for me to tell them something informative. The more thoughtful now wondered what new troubles awaited us since we had actually made it this far. Swan could be right. It could be harvest season in the Land of Unknown Shadows. And it could also be the season for scalping foreigners.

I was troubled myself but had been faced with the unknown so often that I had calluses on that breed of fear. I knew perfectly well it would do me no good to fuss and worry when I had no idea what lay ahead. But worry I would, anyway. Even when knowledge contracted while I slept assured me that we would not encounter disasters once we shifted off the plain.

I had planned to offer a rousing speech but quickly discarded that notion. No one was interested. Not even me. "Is everybody ready? Then let's go."

Getting started took less time than I expected. Most of my brothers had not stopped to hear me say what they anticipated would be the same old same old. They had gone on getting ready to roll. I told Swan, "I guess 'In those days the Company . . .' works a lot better after supper and a hard day's work."

"Does for me. Works even better when I've had something to drink. And it's a kick-ass wowser after I've gone to bed."

I walked with Sahra for a while, renewing our acquaintance, easing the strain between us. She remained tense, though. It would not be that long before she had to deal with her husband in the flesh for the first time in a decade and a half. I did not know how to make that easier for her.

Then I walked with the Radisha for an hour. She, too, was in an unsettled mood. It had been even longer since she had had to deal with her brother in all but the most remote capacities. She was a realist, however. "There's nothing I can lose to him, is there? I've lost it all already. First to the Protector, through my own blindness. Then you stole me away from Taglios and robbed me of even the hope of reclaiming my place."

"Bet you something, Princess. Bet you that you're already being remembered as the mother of a golden age." That actually seemed a reasonable prediction. The past always seems better when the present consists of clabbered misery. "Even without the Protector back in the capital yet. Once we're established, the first mission I mean to launch will be to get word back to Taglios that you and your brother are both alive, you're really angry, and you're going to come back."

"We all must dream," the woman told me.

"You don't *want* to go back?"

"Do you recall the taunt you laid before me every day? *Rajadharma?*"

"Sure."

"What I may want is of no importance. What my brother might want does not signify, either. He's had his adventures. Now I've had mine. *Rajadharma* constrains us more surely than could the stoutest chain. *Rajadharma* will call us back across the uncounted leagues as long as we continue to breathe, through the impossible places, past all the deadly perils and improbable beings. You reminded me again and again of my obligation. Perhaps by doing so, you created a monster fit to battle the beast who displaced me. *Rajadharma* has become my vice, Sleepy. It has become my irrational compulsion. I continue to follow you only because reason insists that even though this path leads me farther from Taglios today, it is the shortest road to my destiny."

"I'll help where I can." I did not commit the Company, though. I still had the Captain and Lieutenant to waken and deal with. I started to move on. I wanted to visit with Master Santaraksita for a while and lose myself, perhaps, in an interplay of intellectual speculation. The librarian's horizons were much broader these days.

"Sleepy."

"Radisha?"

"Has the Black Company extracted sufficient revenge?"

We had taken away everything but the love of her people. And she was not a bad woman. "In my eyes you're just one small gesture short of redemption. I want you to apologize to the Captain once he recovers enough to understand what's happening."

Her lips tightened. She and her brother did not let themselves be slaves to considerations of station or caste, but still, apology to a foreign mercenary? "If I must, I must. My options are limited."

"Water sleeps, Radisha." I joined Suvrin and Master Santaraksita, taking a few minutes to visit with the black stallion on the way there. It carried One-Eye, who was breathing but otherwise did not look much better than a corpse. I hoped he was just sleeping an old man's sleep. The horse seemed bored. I suppose it was tired of adventures.

"Master. Suvrin. By some chance do you two suffer any memories you didn't have before we came to the plain?"

They did indeed, Santaraksita more so than Suvrin. Shivetya's gifts seemed shaped for each individual. Master Santaraksita proceeded to relate yet another version of the Kina myth and of Shivetya's relationship to the Queen of Death and Terror. This one assumed the point of view of the demon. It did not say much that was new, just shifted the relative importance of various characters and, laterally, blamed Kina for the passing of the last few builders.

Kina remained a black-hearted villain in this version, while Shivetya became one of the great unsung heroes, deserving of a much higher standing in myth. Which could be true. He had no standing at all. Nobody outside the plain had ever heard of him. I suggested, "When you get back to Taglios now, Master, you can establish a mighty reputation by explaining the myths in the words of a being who lived through their creation."

Santaraksita smiled sourly. "You know better, Dorabee. Mythol ogy is one area where nobody wants to know the absolute truth because time has forged great symbols from raw materials supplied by ancient events. Prosaic distortions of fact metamorphose into perceived truths of the soul."

He had a point. In religion, precise truth has almost no currency. True believers will kill and destroy to defend their inaccurate beliefs.

And *that* is a truth upon which you can rely.

98

I raised my head carefully to peer over the edge of the plain at the Land of Unknown Shadows. Willow Swan snaked up on my right. He did the same. Riverwalker copied him on my left. River said, "I'll be damned."

I agreed. "No doubt about it. Doj. Gota. Come and look. Will somebody bring One-Eye up?" The little man had started talking about an hour ago. He did appear to be in touch with the real world at least part of the time.

I beckoned the white crow. That darned thing was going to give us away if it kept circling.

"To who?" Swan asked. "I don't see anybody." Obviously, I was thinking out loud again. Swan weaseled sideways so Doj could crawl up beside me.

Doj rose up. He froze. After fifteen seconds he harrumphed.

Gota said it. "Is the same place we left. You got us turned around, you fool Stone Soldier."

At first glimpse it was identical. Only, "Look to the right. There isn't any Overlook. And never was. And Kiaulune isn't the New City." I never saw Kiaulune before it became Shadowcatch but doubted these ruins resembled that old city much, either. "Get Suvrin. He might know."

I continued to stare. The more I did so, the more differences stood out. Doj said it. "The hand of mankind rested more lightly here. And men went away a long time ago." It was only the shape of the land that was identical.

"Back about the time the earthquakes, you suppose?" What

would have been hardscrabble farmland in my world here looked like better soil that had been abandoned for twenty years. It was overgrown by brush and brambles and cedars but no truly sizable trees were yet evident except those that grew in orderly rows and those so distant they painted the foothills of the Dandha Presh a deep green that was almost black.

Suvrin arrived. I offered a few questions. He told me, "It does look like they say Kiaulune did before the Shadowmasters came. When my grandparents were children. The city didn't start growing until Longshadow decided to build Overlook. Only, I don't see anything down there now but ruins."

"Look at the shadowgate. It's in better shape than our own." But not in good repair by any standard. The quakes had taken their bites. "You can tell where it is." That was a weight off my shoulders. I had anticipated fighting starvation while we fussed with strings and colored powders in an effort to survey the only safe pathway through.

Several men carried One-Eye up and set him down amongst us. They silhouetted themselves above the skyline doing so. My grumbling did no good. On the other hand, no bloodthirsty hordes materialized below the shadowgate, so it was possible that we were not yet betrayed.

"One-Eye. Do you sense anything down there?"

I did not know if he would respond. He seemed to be asleep again. His chin rested on his chest. People gave him room because it was in these moments he began to ply his cane. After a few seconds, though, he lifted his chin, opened his eyes, murmured, "A place where I can rest." The wind that was always with us on the plain almost stole his words away. "A place where all evil dies an endless death. No wickedness stirs down there, Little Girl."

One-Eye's remarks excited everyone who had witnessed his most recent episode. Half a dozen more men exposed their silhouettes to anyone watching from below. Still others seemed to think we ought to trudge right on down there in a big, disorderly mob, right now.

"Kendo!" I called. "Slink! I want you each to take six men out through the gate. Fully armed, including bamboo. Slink, take the right side of the road. You take the left, Kendo. You'll be covering the rest of us as we come out. River, you're the reserve. Take ten men and wait just inside the shadowgate. You'll stay there and become the rear guard if nothing bothers them."

Training and discipline took over. A superior standard of both are among the Company's most potent tools. Properly employed, they become our deadliest tools. We try to inculcate discipline from a recruit's first day, right alongside a healthy distrust of everyone on the outside. We try to pound into his very bones what he needs to do in every situation.

The slope from the edge of the plain to the shadowgate seemed to stretch for miles. I felt bone-naked descending it without the standard. Tobo, carrying the golden pickax, had to take my place. I told him, "Don't get too fond of the job, kid. It may be all I have if we get the Captain and the Lieutenant back. And I won't even have that if your dad wants all of his old jobs back."

Experiment quickly proved no key but the pick was needed to leave the plain. The shadowgate did tickle and tingle, though.

The first thing I noticed outside was a powerful mixture of sagey and piney smells. There had been few odors on the plain. Then I noticed the incredible warmth. This world was much warmer than the plain was. It was early autumn here . . . as promised, Willow. As promised.

Kendo and Slink kept their squads moving, screening our advance. More and more people passed through the gate. I got myself hoisted onto the black stallion so I could see better. Which meant that somebody had to carry One-Eye. I told Sahra, "Let's head for those ruins." I was about to add something about shelter being easier to find there when Kendo Cutter shouted.

I looked where he pointed. It took a sharp eye to see them. The old men coming uphill slowly wore robes almost exactly the same color as the road and the earth behind them. There were five of them. They were bent and moved slowly.

"We did give ourselves away up there. And somebody was watching. Doj!"

Waste of breath. The Swordmaster was headed downhill already. Tobo and Gota were right behind him, which did nothing for Sahra's nerves. I rushed forward, caught the boy. "You stay back."

"But, Sleepy!"

"You want to debate it with Runmust and Iqbal?"

He did not want to argue with the large Shadar gentlemen.

I did not want to argue with the Troll. I let her go. She might be more intimidating than Doj, anyway. He was just one old man with a sword. She was a vicious old woman with a virulent tongue.

I checked my battered old shortsword. That was going to perform wonders if they climbed over Uncle Doj. Then I headed downhill myself. Sahra accompanied me.

The old men in brown looked at Doj and Gota. Doj and Gota looked at them. Those five men looked like they had been cast in the same mold, being nearly as wide as they were tall and very long in the tooth.

One of the natives said something rapid in a liquid tongue. The cadence was unusual but the words sounded vaguely familiar. I did catch the phrase "Children of the Dead." Doj replied at length in Nyueng Bao, which included the formulas "The Land of Unknown Shadows" and "All Evil Dies There an Endless Death." The old men seemed hugely puzzled by Doj's accent but recognized those phrases well enough to become visibly agitated. I could not tell if that was a positive sign or not.

Mother Gota began muttering the incantation that included "Calling the Heaven and the Earth and the Day and the Night," and that excited the old men even more.

Sahra told me, "Evidently the language has changed a great deal since the Children of the Dead ran away."

It took me a moment to understand that she was translating what Doj had said in an aside to Gota.

There was a stream of chatter from the old men, all apparently in the form of pointed questions that Doj could not answer.

Sahra said, "They seem to be extremely worried about someone they keep calling 'that devil-dog Merika Montera.' Also about a pupil of this monster, a supposed future Grandmaster. Apparently the two were driven into exile together."

"Merika Montera would be Longshadow. We know there was a time when he used the name Maricha Manthara Dhumraksha. He sent an agent named Ashutosh Yaksha to live among the Nyueng Bao in an effort to find and steal the Key that we've brought with us. The golden pickax."

Uncle Doj chided, "Sleepy, these old men don't speak Taglian or Dejagoran, but there's still a chance that they might recognize our version of names they fear and hate just a whole hell of a lot. Right now they're clamoring for answers about one Achoes Tosiak-shah. It sounds like Longshadow and Shadowspinner, before they were exiled, were the last of a race of outsider sorcerers who enslaved these people's forefathers—through their ability to manipulate killer shadows they summoned from the plain."

"Wouldn't you know? They brought their business with them. Tell these guys whatever they need to know. Tell them the truth. Tell them who we are and what we intend to do. And what we've already done to their buddies Longshadow and Shadowspinner."

"We might be wise to find out a little more about them before we become completely candid."

"I wouldn't expect you to break any lifetime habits."

Doj nodded slightly, betraying the slightest smile. He faced the old men and began talking. I found that my Nyueng Bao was improving. I had no trouble isolating "Stone Soldiers" and "Soldiers of Darkness" in his monologue. Native faces kept turning my way, always more surprised.

Sahra told me, "They're monks of some sort. They've been watching for a long time. Watching is what their order does. In case the Shadowmasters try to return. They did not expect anyone to come for real."

"They especially didn't expect women, eh?"

"That amazes them. And Swan worries them. Their ancestors' experiences with white devils were not positive."

Then, of course, the white crow swooped and landed on my shoulder. And the great black stallion, with its prune of a rider, came down to stick its nose in. And as the chatter picked up, still well-seasoned with "Stone Soldier" and "Soldier of Darkness" and "Steadfast Guardian," the rest of the band drifted forward, impelled by curiosity. First thing I knew, Tobo was right there beside me, along with Runmust, Iqbal and Suruvhija and all their offspring, the dog, and ever-increasing jabber about what should we do with the Captured, where were we going to set up camp. . . .

"You hearing these questions?" I asked Doj.

"I hear them. I think we're going to be granted this whole valley. For the time being. While they send messages to the Court of All Seasons and the File of Nine. We'll have more important visitors eventually. Until then—as I understand them—we can set down anywhere we want. The dialect is a little tricky, though, so be careful."

Dozens of veteran eyes scanned the valley for defensible positions. It took no effort to identify them. They were the same as those we recalled from the Kiaulune wars.

I wondered if all the connected worlds would be equally familiar physically.

I indicated my choice. No one demurred. Runmust and the Singhs hurried off to survey the site, accompanied by a dozen men armed for anything. The five old monks did not protest. Mostly they seemed bemused and amazed.

So it was that the Black Company reached the Land of Unknown Shadows instead of fabled Khatovar. There it was that the Company settled and rested and recovered. There it was that I filled book after book with words when I was not planning or leading expeditions to rescue the rest of my captured brothers, and even that devil-dog Merika Montera so he would be available for another, rather less pleasant encounter with justice than the one that had driven him into exile. The grandchildren of his former slaves feared him not at all.

I won him a stay, at Lady's request, so he could help with Tobo's schooling. The stay was good for as long as he did that job satisfactorily and not for a moment more. The old monks, as tight of lip as their cousin Doj, agreed that Tobo had to be trained but would not reveal their reasoning even to me.

At one time the Land of the Unknown Shadows had suffered many lean, pale bonesacks just like Longshadow. They were invaders from another world. They had brought no wives with them. Time did not love them.

And thus it was. And thus it was.

Soldiers live. And wonder why.

One-Eye survived another four years, suffering strokes, yet recovering slowly every time. Seldom did he leave the house we built for him and Gota. Mostly he tinkered with his black spear while Gota hovered around and fussed. He fussed right back and never stopped worrying about Tobo's education.

Once again Tobo was smothered in parents both real and surrogate.

He studied with One-Eye, he studied with Lady, he studied with Longshadow and Master Santaraksita, with the Radisha and the Prahbrindrah Drah, and with the masters of our adoptive world. He studied hard and well and much, much more than he wanted. He was very talented. He was what his great-grandmother Hong Tray had foreseen.

The Captured all returned to us, except for those who died beneath the plain, but even the best of them—Murgen, Lady, the Captain—were strange and deeply changed. Fey. But we were changed as well, by life, so that those of us they remembered at all were almost alien to them.

A new order came into being.

It had to be.

Someday we will cross the plain again.

Water sleeps.

For now, I just rest. And indulge myself in writing, in remembering the fallen, in considering the strange twists life takes, in considering what plan God must have if the good are condemned to die young while the wicked prosper, if righteous men can commit deep evil while bad men demonstrate unexpected streaks of humanity.

Soldiers live. And wonder why.

99

The Great General started south through the Dandha Presh moments after the Protector abandoned him so she could make more speed. Consequently he met Soulcatcher on the southern side of the summit just a week later. She talked to herself continuously in a committee of voices while she was awake and gibbering in tongues during her brief bouts of sleep. Mogaba thought the Daughter of Night seemed smugly pleased in the moment before she collapsed from exhaustion.

"Kill them," Mogaba urged the moment he had Soulcatcher's ear and a bit of privacy. "Those two can be nothing but trouble and there's no way you can profit from keeping them around."

"Possibly true." The Protector's voice was a sly one. "But if I'm clever enough I can use the girl to tap into Kina's power the way my sister did."

"If there's one thing I've learned from a life noteworthy for its regiments of disappointments, it's that you can't rely on cleverness. You're a powerful woman now. Kill them while you can. Kill them before they find a way to turn the tables. You don't need to become any stronger. There's no one in this world capable of challenging you."

"There's always someone, Mogaba."

"Kill them. They sure won't waste a second on you."

Soulcatcher approached the Daughter of Night, who had not moved since her collapse. "My dear sweet niece wouldn't harm me." The voice she chose could have been that of a naive fourteen-year-old responding to the charge that her twenty-five-year-old lover was interested in only one thing. Then she laughed cruelly, kicked the Daughter of Night viciously. "You even think about it, bitch, and I'll roast and eat you one limb at a time. And still make sure you live long enough to see your mother die first."

The Great General neither moved nor made any remark. His face betrayed nothing, not even to Soulcatcher's acute eye. But in his sinking heart he understood that yet again he had allied himself with complete and unpredictable insanity. And yet again he had no option but to ride the tiger. He observed, "Perhaps we should give thought to how to guard our minds against intrusion by the Queen of Terror and Darkness."

"I'm ahead of you, General. I'm the professional." This voice was that of a self-important little mouse of a functionary. It became that of a self-confident woman being conversational, the voice Mogaba suspected was Soulcatcher's own. It resembled closely the voice of her sister, Lady. "For the last week I've had nothing to do but nurture the blisters on my feet and think. I conceived marvelous new torments to practice upon the Black Company—too late to enjoy them. Isn't that the way it always goes? You always think of the perfect comeback about an hour too late for it to do any good? I suppose I'll find other enemies and my innovation won't be wasted. Most of the time, though, I considered how best to circumvent Kina's power." She did not fear naming the goddess directly. "We can do it."

The Daughter of Night stirred slightly. Her shoulders tightened.

She glanced up for an instant. She looked a little uncertain, a little troubled.

For the first time since her birth she was completely out of touch with her soul-mother. She had been out of touch for several days. Something was wrong. Something was terribly wrong.

Soulcatcher eyed Narayan Singh. That old man was not much use anymore. She could test her new torments on him once she had him back in Taglios, before a suitable audience.

"General, if I get caught up in one of those byways that distract me so often, I want you to nudge me back to the business at hand. Which will be empire building. And, in my spare time, the creation of a new flying carpet. I think I know enough of the Howler's secrets to manage. This past week has forced me to admit to myself that I have no innate fondness for exercise."

Soulcatcher prodded the Daughter of Night again, then settled on a rotten log and removed her boots. "Mogaba, don't ever tell anyone that you've seen the world's greatest sorceress stumped for a way to handle something as trivial as blisters."

Narayan Singh, who had been snoring fitfully, suddenly rose up and gripped the bars of his cage, his face contorted in terror, its butternut color all but gone. "Water sleeps!" he screamed. "Thi Kim! Thi Kim is coming!" Then he collapsed, unconscious again, though his body continued to spasm.

Soulcatcher growled softly. "Water sleeps? We'll see what the dead can do." They were all gone this time. It was her world now. "What else did he say?"

"Something that sounded like a Nyueng Bao name."

"Uhm. Yes. But not a name. Something about death. Or a murder. Thi Kim. Coming. Hmm. Maybe a nickname? Murder walker? I should learn the language better."

The Daughter of Night, she noted, was shaking more than Singh.

The wind whines and howls through fangs of ice. It races furiously around the nameless fortress but tonight neither the lightning nor the storm has any power to disturb. The creature on the wooden throne is relaxed. He will rest comfortably through a night of years for the first time in a long millennium. The silver daggers are no inconvenience at all.

Shivetya sleeps and dreams dreams of immorality's end.

Fury crackles between the standing stones. Shadows flee. Shadows hide. Shadows huddle in terror.

Immortality is threatened.